Praise for
KRISTINE KATHRYN RUSCH'S DIVING UNIVERSE

"The Diving Universe, conceived by Hugo-Award winning author Kristine [Kathryn] Rusch is a refreshingly new and fleshed out realm of sci-fi action and adventure."

—*Astroguyz*

"Kristine Kathryn Rusch is best known for her Retrieval Artist series, so maybe you've missed her Diving Universe series. If so, it's high time to remedy that oversight."

—*Analog*

"This is classic sci-fi, a well-told tale of dangerous exploration. The first-person narration makes the reader an eye witness to the vast, silent realms of deep space, where even the smallest error will bring disaster. Compellingly human and technically absorbing, the suspense builds to fevered intensity, culminating in an explosive yet plausible conclusion."

—*RT Book Reviews* (Top Pick) on *Diving into the Wreck*

"Rusch delivers a page-turning space adventure while contemplating the ethics of scientists and governments working together on future tech."

—*Publishers Weekly* on *Diving into the Wreck*

"Rusch's handling of the mystery and adventure is stellar, and the whole tale proves quite entertaining."

—*Booklist Online* on *Diving into the Wreck*

"The technicalities in Boss' story are beautifully played…. She's real, flawed, and interesting…. Read the book. It is very good."

—*SFFWorld* on *Diving into the Wreck*

"Kristine Kathryn Rusch's *Diving into the Wreck* is exactly what the sf genre needs to get more readers...and to keep the readers the genre already has."
—*Elitist Book Reviews* on *Diving into the Wreck*

"Rusch keeps the science accessible, the cultures intriguing, and the characters engaging. For anyone needing to add to their science fiction library, keep an eye out for this."
—*Speculative Fiction Examiner* on *City of Ruins*

"Rusch's latest addition to her Diving series features a strong, capable female heroine and a vividly imagined far-future universe. Blending fast-paced action with an exploration of the nature of friendship and the ethics of scientific discoveries, this tale should appeal to Rusch's readers and fans of space opera."
—*Library Journal* on *Boneyards*

"Rusch follows *Diving into the Wreck* and *City of Ruins* with another fast-paced novel of the far future... [Rusch's] sensibilities will endear this book to readers looking for a light, quick space adventure with strong female protagonists."
—*Publishers Weekly* on *Boneyards*

"Filled with well-defined characters who confront a variety of ethical and moral dilemmas, Rusch's third Diving novel is classic space opera, with richly detailed worldbuilding and lots of drama."
—*RT Book Reviews* on *Boneyards*

"...a fabulous outer space thriller that rotates perspective between the divers, the Alliance and to a lesser degree the Empire. Action-packed and filled with twists yet allowing the reader to understand the motives of the key players, *Skirmishes* is another intelligent exciting voyage into the Rusch Diving universe."
—*The Midwest Book Review* on *Skirmishes*

The Diving Universe
(Reading Order)

THIEVES

A DIVING NOVEL

KRISTINE KATHRYN RUSCH

*wmg*PUBLISHING

Thieves

Published 2021 by WMG Publishing
www.wmgpublishing.com
Cover and layout copyright © 2021 by WMG Publishing
Cover design by Allyson Longueira/WMG Publishing
Cover art copyright © Philcold
ISBN-13: 978-1-56146-371-8
ISBN-10: 1-56146-371-X

THIEVES

A DIVING NOVEL

THE BONEYARD

NOW

1

I FLOAT OUTSIDE THE *SOVE*, staring at the winking lights ahead of me. They look like a starfield, even though they are not. I am deep inside the Boneyard, a graveyard of old Fleet ships.

Three large ships float nearby, with smaller ships beside them. The ships appear to have been placed haphazardly with no real sense of order. They point in different directions, and some are what I would consider upside down, even though "up" and "down" have no real meaning in space.

I am out here alone, at my own insistence, so I can have time to contemplate what's before me. My environmental suit—a new version that Yash Zarlengo has redesigned for the umpteenth time—feels a little too tight. The new compression fabric that she used adheres to my skin, making me uncomfortable, even though I've been wearing this suit, or one of its cousins, for weeks now.

Unlike my older (and less effective, according to Yash) suit, this one aggressively reminds me that it exists. It monitors every part of my body, searching for the smallest physical change. The suit also monitors its own exterior, and—until I figured out how to shut it off—it would also notify me of each and every change.

I nearly died in this Boneyard several weeks ago. My diving companion, Elaine Seager, was badly injured. She's getting better, but the doctors back at the Lost Souls Corporation—and the consultants they've brought in—believe she will never recover completely.

That scared Yash who, as an engineer, believes that tech can and will save us from everything.

Elaine's injuries don't scare me as much. They just make me aware of the fact that my time in the universe is limited, and I need to work both harder and smarter to accomplish all that I want to do.

Such as figure out this silly Boneyard.

We have spent months here, diving vessels, testing them, and removing the viable ones. We take those vessels back to Lost Souls—or rather, someone on my team does.

I have found a haven in the Boneyard. I'm much more suited to diving vessels than I am to running a large corporation filled with diverse and interesting personalities. I prefer to be alone. I used to dive with a small team only after I had found the derelict vessels on my own. My single ship and I traveled everywhere, and I miss that solitude almost daily.

Which is probably why I'm out here by myself. The *Sove* is a Dignity Vessel or, rather, a DV-Class vessel, as my Fleet friends call these ships. The *Sove* is built for 500 crew along with their family members.

While we have a team of fifty to sixty depending on how many have gone back to Lost Souls and whether or not I've requested help in a certain area, we barely fill the *Sove's* tech requirements. We're always behind on personnel and training at Lost Souls, and it shows on missions like this.

The *Sove* is behind me. I'm aggressively tethered to it—at least three lines are hooked to my suit, two in the usual places that Yash had designed for tethers, and one attached to my old diving belt, along with some of my old equipment. The fact that I insist on that old belt bothers some on my team, but that doesn't stop me.

I do what I want because, no matter how hard I fight it, I am the one in charge.

The crew thinks I don't know that a bunch of them—maybe as many as half—are watching me out of the portals and on screens. Everyone worries about me, particularly after my near-death, but I feel curiously liberated.

I survived that traumatic experience. I'll survive others.

What I'm doing right now is only mildly dangerous. I'm not diving anything alone. I'm wearing the tethers because Mikk, who has been beside me for years, insisted upon it. I knew better than to argue; I would have insisted on it for him if our roles were reversed.

The suit's monitors are attached to all kinds of equipment inside. Every little detail is getting sent back to the *Sove*, including my physical readings, and the readings from the suit's exterior. The suit has four cameras which record the visuals around me from the front and back of my hood, as well as from the places where my right and left shoulders meet my arms. I can turn on cameras on the bottom of my boots and some underneath my wrists if I want to. Should something go seriously awry, the data stream will give my team clues as to why.

The suit picks up everything, except the one thing that sent me out here: The music.

In this part of the Boneyard, I hear choral music in twenty-four-part harmony. It rises and falls in half-tones, crescendoing and decrescendoing in irregular, almost unpredictable intervals. I also hear other songs, farther away. Some sound like bells, ringing on a distant hillside. Others sound like old-fashioned piano music. And still others sound like human voices, melding in an atonal pattern.

The music doesn't really exist. It's simply the way that my senses perceive the *anacapa* energy levels mingling inside the Boneyard itself. If the music becomes too loud or too piercing, I know I'm in an energy field that's too strong for me, a field that might hurt or crush me.

Yash designed this suit to minimize the amount of energy that I can feel in my bones. That internal vibration is what causes these sounds. Not everyone feels these vibrations or "hears" them, as the case may be.

If the suit is actually working as designed, then my sensitivity is much higher than it has ever been. In my old suit, this level of sound would have been almost unbearable.

I haven't told Yash this, not since the incident. Yash is back at Lost Souls, working on finding the Fleet, based on information we have brought back from this Boneyard. I haven't spoken to her in a long time.

I've spoken to Coop a lot, but I rarely tell him anything of substance. Jonathan "Coop" Cooper is the captain of the *Ivoire*, a DV-Class ship that found itself 5,000 years in its own future. He and I have a relationship that some would call casual, but which is pretty intimate, given who we both are. Or maybe given who I am.

Anyway, Coop isn't here either. He is currently helping Yash find the Fleet that they believe still exists.

I think it a fool's errand: even if they find the Fleet, it will be 5,000 years different. But this errand has focused them for years now, and it seems to give their lives meaning.

I cannot argue with that, any more than I can argue with the joy that I feel every time I enter an abandoned ship for the very first time.

Right now, though, it's not the abandoned ships around me that have caught my attention. It's that starfield which really isn't a starfield. It's something else entirely, and—most interestingly to me—it dims the sound of the music, especially when I get close.

I was close a few days ago, as I came out the rear hatch of an ancient orbiter. The sound was almost muted, which startled me. I have been in the Boneyard every single day for months, and the sound—while different, depending on where I am—has always been overwhelming.

So I've sent out the remaining five members of the Six, those who have the genetic marker that can enable them to survive in this kind of malfunctioning *anacapa* energy field and who are also familiar with the music. (Fleet members, who also have the gene, don't seem to hear the malfunction as music, which I find odd.)

The five all said that the music sounded different, but only one, Orlando Rea, described the difference as muted. I never prompted any of them by describing the sound, only asked them to get close to the starfield and see what they experienced.

That is what they reported.

We're doing more investigation—necessary investigation—but I wanted to see this for myself, out here, away from the constant barrage of questions from the others on the *Sove*. I also wanted to be as far as I could from the protection of the DV-class vessel.

I like floating in space, even though I probably shouldn't. I like having only the thin layer of an environmental suit between me and something so vast that I really have few words for it.

It doesn't quite feel like I'm in space, not when I'm floating here. The Boneyard is huge, larger than some planets I've visited. We'll never be able to dive all of the ships, which deeply disappoints me—not because I'm a completist, but because I feel like the history of the Fleet is here or at least part of it, and I adore history.

I want to learn everything I can.

It's as if I'm in an all-you-can-eat buffet, filled with foods I love, and I've been told I must eat my way out. I will never get to everything, and I'm overwhelmed half the time, and I'm still excited, each and every moment of each and every day.

We have worked deep into the Boneyard. We're following a trail that I've devised. I have a wish list of ships from Lost Souls. A variety of people compiled the list. Coop and Yash want certain kinds of Fleet vessels, mostly DV-Class, although Yash has started asking for others that I'd never heard of.

Ilona Blake, who runs Lost Souls because she can handle people oh so much better than I can, and because she actually cares about getting things done, has a completely different wish list. She wants defensive vessels as well as vessels we haven't seen before, because she wants to mine the technology for money.

She's monetized many of our discoveries already, turning them into tech that Lost Souls can develop and resell to various organizations within the Nine Planets Alliance.

I have been told to use my judgement, which apparently everyone still trusts, and I do use it. But I have a wish list of my own. I want to dive ships that have left their history intact, ships that still have information on their computers, ships that tell us as much about the past as they will help us with the future.

I find it ironic that I'm the one obsessed with the past, even as Yash and Coop search for information about what happened to the culture they left behind.

Or, Coop would say, that maybe it's not ironic. It's my love of history that led me to him and the *Ivoire*, the ship that brought them on that perilous journey from 5,000 years ago to now. They arrived over five years ago, and are still getting their footing.

I'm not sure I ever would.

Mikk pings me.

"What are you seeing?" he asks, and I smile. He knows what I'm seeing. He can see it too.

I've just been silent too long for his tastes. I'm not even sure I've moved.

"I'll tell you when I get back," I say.

This excursion of mine—which isn't a dive, really, although that's what we called it back on the ship—isn't timed. Usually we time any exploration a crew member makes outside the ship. I usually insist on that.

The missions have a duration, one that we adhere to, and we have goals that we have to meet on our journey, whatever it is.

But this isn't a journey. It's just an observation, and I never placed a timeline on it.

I hit the team with this trip so fast that no one thought to suggest a timeline either.

Which is probably making Mikk nervous.

It would have made me nervous, if he had been out here by himself.

I glance at the timer which I have running in the clear part of my hood, beneath my left eye. Running the timer is a force of habit. I start it when I emerge from the airlock, and shut down the timer the moment I return.

I've been here for less than fifteen minutes. But I haven't done anything dramatic, which is probably bothering him.

I have moved to the very edge of the tethers, which places me as close to the starfield as I can get.

There is no atmosphere in the Boneyard, even though there are some energy cross currents. Something—we don't know what, exactly—holds the ships and the ship parts scattered throughout this gigantic place in exact position. Even when we board the smaller ships, our movement makes no difference in that placement.

Which led me to believe, initially anyway, that the starfield was something else entirely—a bit of energy, tiny bits of ships that reflect some of the ambient light in this place. To be honest, I didn't pay much attention to the starfield when I first saw it, because we have seen so many strange things since we started working the Boneyard.

In addition to intact ships that have been stored here, the Fleet also stored ship parts and destroyed bits of ships. Sometimes the parts are scattered around the ships, and sometimes they aren't. Sometimes parts of a certain type congregate together as if someone designed that section of the Boneyard that way.

Perhaps someone had.

But the deeper we've gotten into the Boneyard, the more I think that we're seeing different intelligences at play in the way everything is organized.

The placement of ships along the edge, where we first entered the Boneyard, is haphazard at best. They seem tossed in, left wherever they were placed with no thought of leaving pathways for other ships to get past them. The extra ship parts and remains of damaged ships are tossed in as well, sometimes so close to nearby ships that we can't get between them.

Farther in, ship parts have been placed with similar parts. Smaller ships are lined up in rows, their noses pointing in the same direction. Larger ships are equidistant from each other, and all facing the same direction as well.

Still farther in, undamaged ships rest next to each other, while damaged ships squeeze into a smaller space. In that section of the Boneyard, there are no ship parts at all.

Here, where we're currently working, the ships form necklaces around the starfield. The pattern seems different. Large ship, small ship,

ship part, almost like multi-sized beads. The necklaces (as we've started to call them) run up, down, around, and diagonally. They form an actual curtain around this area, one that made the starfield impossible to see as a field when we were not as deep into the Boneyard.

Only in the last week did I even see the field. At that point, I thought it *was* a starfield, viewed through some kind of barrier. I didn't think much about it. We were focused on the ships we were diving, not on what was ahead of us.

If someone had asked me (and no one had), I would have said that the starfield was a gap in the Boneyard, or we had reached one of the edges earlier than we expected.

But assumptions always bother me. I learned early in my diving career that assumptions lead to mistakes. So I double-checked myself, first with my own scans and then with the help of others on the crew.

Our scans showed we were deep in the Boneyard and had a long way to go in all directions if we wanted to travel out of it on regular power. We weren't even in the center of the Boneyard. In fact, we were so far away from the center that it would take us years at the pace we are currently working to get to the center.

We are moving forward (or what we consider to be forward) into the Boneyard, using the *Sove's* regular drive. We let ourselves through the security field on the outside of the Boneyard, using ancient codes that still worked.

But for the rest of our work—getting the ships back to Lost Souls, for example—we use the ships' *anacapa* drives, after one of our engineers ensures that the drives are actually working. The drives travel across a fold in space—at least, that's how Yash explains it—covering a tremendous amount of distance in minutes instead of years.

We have to be very careful when we use *anacapa* drives inside the Boneyard. Yash worries (and she has gotten me to worry) that the wrong type of *anacapa* energy might cause some kind of chain reaction in here, something that might send a bunch of ships into foldspace, or worse (or maybe not worse) make the ships explode.

It's the *anacapa* energy that has me bothered. We can measure it. There is all kinds of what I call rogue *anacapa* energy throughout the Boneyard, leaking from the ships with working drives. Some of the energy is exactly as we would expect from a dormant drive—just a low-level reading, when we get close enough to the ship to experience it.

But a lot of the energy is spiky and random—filled with power sometimes, and without much at other times. Sometimes the energy seems corrupted, and other times it gives off readings that our sensors make no sense of.

I record all of it—the *Sove* records all of it—but I don't send much of it back to Lost Souls. Technically, Ilona can't cancel this mission, but she can make it almost impossible for me to run the mission. She can take away supplies or not authorize personnel.

And Yash, in particular, would monitor what happens in the Boneyard and have an opinion about it, one Ilona would listen to.

I'm not giving them the ability to have an opinion.

Not yet, anyway.

But I might, if I can't figure out this starfield.

Because the energy readings around it here, near these carefully placed ships, is different. Not in the types of readings, which vary from day to day and hour to hour in every section of the Boneyard we've traveled through.

But in the *level* of the readings.

There's less energy here around these carefully placed ships. They seem to have working *anacapa* drives. Even the small ships have *anacapa* drives, and that's unusual. The Fleet stopped outfitting small ships with *anacapa* drives sometime before Yash and Coop were born.

The random *anacapa* energy, the kind that indicates a deteriorating or damaged drive, is almost nonexistent, at least the closer we get to that starfield.

Then Mikk and I turned our attention to the starfield, and what was behind it. According to our scans, more ships lie behind that starfield curtain, all of them in the same neat rows that are in front of it.

Our scans didn't get the right level of energy readings, though, for that number of ships, at least, depending on what we had seen before in the Boneyard. (And, I know, I can't really depend on that, because each section of the Boneyard has been different so far.)

Still, the differences afforded me the time to study the field. And what I learned shook me. I discovered that I can take the images of those ships *outside* the starfield, and place them on top of the images of the ships *inside* the starfield, and they match exactly.

Either the Fleet or its minders got *really* precise, or they created some kind of ghost scan.

No matter which scanner I use, no matter how I calibrate our instruments on the *Sove*, I get that ghost scan reading.

And I've started to suspect that the scan will show up on any Fleet equipment.

I want to use a different vessel to scan that starfield, some vessel not made by the Fleet. Unfortunately, we don't have any with us.

And we did that deliberately. This Boneyard has fired on non-Fleet ships in the past.

Even my environmental suit, with its limited scanning capability, was built with Fleet tech. But I brought some non-Fleet tech with me on my old diving belt. Besides my ancient diving knife, which I recovered from one of my old diving partners, Karl, after his tragic death, I carry a few tiny probes and three small scanners of different vintages.

I pluck the one of those old scanners off my belt. This scanner is the "newest" of the three, although I wouldn't exactly call it new. It's also the least sophisticated.

The scanner fits nicely in my hand. I had forgotten how malleable my old tech was. It feels like an old friend, one I haven't given enough thought to over the decades, one I forgot that I loved.

I hold the scanner in front of my belly, out of the view of any of the cameras on my suit. As long as I only move my eyes to look at the scanner, not my entire head.

I don't want someone to yank me back to the *Sove* in a great panic before I have a chance to use the scanner.

Using the scanner is my biggest risk. If the Boneyard hates *all* non-Fleet tech, then there is a very good chance the Boneyard will fire on me.

And that will be the end of me.

But I'm gambling that there's lots of small, random, non-Fleet tech in this Boneyard. Some of that non-Fleet tech might be in the cargo holds of the old ships around me; other parts might be grafted onto ships after some emergency on some distant planet.

I'm gambling that the Boneyard only objects to active, working, non-Fleet ships, the kind that might want to steal ships from the Boneyard itself.

Like we are.

A fact I do my best to ignore.

Someone left these ships in the Boneyard. They're protected by a forcefield that we are able to get through because we know the codes and we have a Fleet vessel, apparently of the right vintage.

But that someone might return for these ships.

Coop believes that the Fleet has stored the ships in the Boneyard because it didn't know what else to do with them. Yash agrees with a slight difference; she thinks the ships were stored here so that they could be used by traveling Fleet vessels like Security Class ships that sometimes have to go backwards.

I've even heard a few members of the *Ivoire* crew say that they believed the ships were here in case some Fleet vessel got stuck in foldspace and needed them, but I think that's more of a reflection on the problems the *Ivoire* had than it is anything that the Fleet tried to create with this Boneyard.

The Boneyard is a mystery to me, and as I do with all mysteries that I find in space, I'm exploring it.

The fact that I'm removing ships from it at the same time makes me a lot more nervous than I want to admit.

Until this last year, I was never the kind of wreck diver who plundered the abandoned ships that I found. I had some of my divers report the ancient abandoned ships. A few even claimed them, so that they would get the wealth found on the ships. And one tried to get me in trouble with the Enterran Empire (back when I lived there), by claiming that I was trying to co-opt stealth tech (which turns out to be *anacapa* technology).

But now I have found a literal planet-sized graveyard of abandoned ships, and I am taking some back to my own corporation, for personal use, and I feel guilty about it.

Guilty, and worried, and afraid we'll get caught.

By whom, I have no idea, since everything we've found in this Boneyard so far points to the fact that no one—not outside ships, not the Fleet itself—has been inside this Boneyard in at least a thousand years, maybe more.

We can't be certain, because we can't cover the entire area of the Boneyard. But we've found even more information on the ships we've sent back. Many of the ships had a baseline program running, even though the ships were powered down. That program monitored every contact the ships had, every unusual thing that happened around them while they were powered down. Some even had systems that edited the information into highlights, marked with the year something occurred.

We have real-time video and information about when other ships were added to the Boneyard, and I'm sure that Yash is pulling information from that in her quest to find the Fleet.

What I watched seemed straightforward. I hadn't seen anything that seemed out of the ordinary. The ships arrived, the skeleton team that brought them would leave, usually on a small ship, and then the larger ship would remain powered down. Occasionally it would wake up when other ships or ship parts were placed near it.

And then it would sleep again.

Maybe we just hadn't hit the exciting part of the Boneyard yet.

And every time I have had that thought of late, I find my mind drifting to that starfield. Maybe what's behind it is the exciting part of the Boneyard.

Maybe that's why I'm out here.

I'm ready to find out.

I raise the scanner so it's directly in my line of sight. Images of the scanner have just gone back to the *Sove*. Right now, a handful of people, staring out those portals or looking at the feed, have gasped, stunned that I'm holding something they don't recognize.

I'm sure a few of them are panicked, worried that I've gone off some kind of deep end.

Where did she get that? Why is she holding it? What the hell is she doing?

I smile at the imagined words, and brace myself for Mikk's voice, but he doesn't say anything.

He doesn't have the right to. He's the one who attached my tethers. He saw the belt. He commented on the knife.

Are you sure you should take Karl's knife? Mikk asked. He's an old spacer like me, and we're both just a bit more superstitious than we probably should be.

The sentence that went unsaid was *He died wearing it, you know.*

Technically, he didn't, though. Technically, he had unhooked his belt with all of his safety equipment, backup breathers, and his knife—or maybe it had all come undone in the strange time field he had found himself in back at the place the Enterran Empire and the Nine Planets call The Room of Lost Souls, and the *Ivoire* crew calls Starbase Kappa.

But Mikk is correct about one thing: Karl had the knife with him on the mission that killed him.

I know that. After Karl died, I started carrying the knife on some dangerous missions to honor him, and to help myself remember the risks that we take.

I had stopped doing that over the years.

But I've wanted the knife beside me on my dives since I got injured. I don't have lingering effects—at least I don't have noticeable ones—from that near-death incident, and I don't want to forget it.

The knife is a reminder to me to be careful as much as it is a talisman.

Only I didn't explain that to Mikk. Instead I said, *I'm taking it.*

He glanced down at my belt and shook his head slightly. There is absolutely no way that he missed the fact that I was carrying other equipment too.

He didn't say anything about it, though. He knows me very well. He knows that I am unorthodox still, despite the corporation, the large operations, the various businesses I run.

He knows I like to take risks.

And, I like to believe, that he understands them.

I take a deep breath of the filtered air, conscious of the fact that my heart rate has increased. I'm sure someone inside the *Sove* has noted that as well. I'm sure they're having serious conversations about what to do with me right now.

And the moment I have that thought, I shut it down.

I need to concentrate, and I don't need anyone else in the middle of my work.

I squeeze the scanner. Red rays of light reflect off a nearby ship. The scanner is so old that it actually uses light to show which side is the functioning side, just in case someone can't figure it out from the grip.

I move the scanner from the right side of my body to the left. Then I move the scanner up and down.

I'm sending information back to the *Sove*, but not in the usual way. The information goes to me, to my quarters, to some equipment I set up there.

If he's smart, if he planned for this, then Mikk will be able to piggyback off the signal and get the same information.

But I hadn't instructed him to do that, so I'm not going to expect it of him. Mikk is good, but he can't always read my mind.

I try not to expect him to.

I scan as much of the area before me as I can without letting go of the scanner. I had initially thought of sending some of the old non-Fleet probes to the starfield, and then ruled that out. They were mobile and active; something inside that field or whatever generated that field might consider the probe some type of weapon.

Or might recognize it as non-Fleet tech and therefore consider it hostile.

It might be another way of getting me shot.

I'm not worried about the Boneyard attacking the scanner. My gloved hand covers most of it. Only the front of the scanner is pointed at the starfield, and I am quite far away from it. At least three DV-Class ship lengths away, maybe more.

The scanner vibrates in my hand, a signal that the scanner has gathered all the information it can from the area I pointed it at. I learned a long time ago, with this scanner, that it doesn't handle small differences well. So it really doesn't matter if I hold the scanner up for ten minutes or fifty. If it scans an area at one time, scanning that same area later won't give me any different information.

So, I squeeze the scanner, shutting down the scan function. Then I shut the scanner off, and tuck it back into its place on my belt. Then I grab another scanner, one that's a bit fussier, and turn it on.

I had set the controls back on the *Sove*, so that I wouldn't have to do any programming out here, and I'm grateful for that now. Because my internal clock tells me I've been out here too long.

If I were running a dive from inside the *Sove*, I would tell my diver it was time to come back to the ship.

Mikk hasn't said that yet, but that's probably due to the fact that I'm the one on this dive, not some member of our crew.

I have to press my gloved thumb against the side of the scanner to start the scan. I hold the scanner up, like I did with the last one, and press the scanner's side. There's no old-fashioned red light, nothing except a quiet beep inside my hood to tell me that the scanner is working.

And then, in a small square on the lower right of my faceplate, an image shows up. The image is blurry at first, and not at all what I expect.

I had thought I would see reflected light, or the ships that had shown up in the *Sove's* scans, bizarrely lined up like the ships outside the field.

But I hadn't expected the blur.

I had set this scanner to send me the actual visuals. The telemetry, the readings in every different form, are being sent, as with the last scanner, back to Mikk and to my quarters.

It takes me a moment to remember how this scanner works in the wild. I press my thumb against it again, which sets the scan at maximum. I won't run it at maximum for long, because this scanner has a weird battery glitch that has always irritated me about it. But I want to see that visual one more time.

As the scanner recalibrates, I catch the sound of my own breathing. It's ragged. My heart rate has probably gone up again, and I'm sure Mikk won't like that. Nor will anyone else.

I force myself to breath slower. The filtered air tastes dry, almost flat. I'm pushing this dive to its edges, and I know that.

The visual winks out for a second and then returns, stronger and clearer. What I had taken to be a blur isn't. It's an actual barrier that I can't see past. As I watch it, lights rotate through it.

What I had thought was the winking of a light through atmosphere, the way that starlight seems to wink to someone on a planet below, is actually faint lights appearing at intervals on that barrier. It's some way of letting someone—something—us, maybe—know that the barrier is both there and working.

The visual part of the scanner doesn't show any ships at all. It shows nothing past that barrier.

"That's enough, Boss." Mikk's voice is so loud that it startles me. I jump. I wish I could take back the startle reaction: it means I'm not paying enough attention to everything around me. Only to that scan.

Then he says the words I have been expecting for at least twenty minutes. "I'm calling an end to this dive. Right now."

I open my mouth to protest, then close it. I know he's right. I also know that I set an example for the crew with everything that I do.

And I'm always the one who insists on procedure. I'm the one who tells each diver they have to listen to their monitor. I'm the one who stresses over and over again that failing to follow these rules could lead to death.

But oh, do I understand the temptation to ignore them. Especially right now.

Especially as my eye catches a glimpse of something on that visual. It's a white trail, almost as if some ship were traveling by, venting chemicals against the blackness of space.

That white trail leads into the barrier.

I raise my gaze just enough to look at what still seems like a starfield to me. The white trail looks like the edges of a galaxy, or maybe an asteroid belt, at least from this distance.

I glance at the visual again, and realize that what the scanner shows is something more akin to a comet tail.

A mystery. An enigma. Mysteries and enigmas hook me every time.

"Boss." Mikk sounds fierce.

I haven't answered him, which is probably scaring the heck out of him, even though he can see from my suit readings that I'm still alive.

"Yeah," I say curtly. Then I add, because I can't stop myself, "This is fascinating."

"I don't care," he says. "You're coming back to the ship."

I sigh, probably audibly enough that anyone monitoring this dive can hear me.

"Yeah," I say again. Then I move the scanner right to left, as I did with the previous scanner, only faster than I probably should have. "I'm coming."

I feel like a recalcitrant child. I'm probably acting a bit like one too. I shut off the scanner. That small square image vanishes, and I actually miss it.

I'm learning something, and whenever I do that, I feel alive.

I replace the scanner on my belt, then turn to my left, careful not to get entangled in my tethers.

I grab one of them, and use it to pull myself back to the *Sove*.

I resist the urge to look over my shoulder. I almost feel as though if I do, I will be tempting fate, preventing myself from traveling back to the ship.

We've found—I've found—yet another mystery inside this Boneyard— and it has me intrigued.

2

ONCE I RETURN TO THE *SOVE,* I make myself follow all of my post-dive rules, even though I don't want to. I shower, I eat something, I drink three full glasses of water. I also let the ship's systems evaluate me as I shower, after I dump my suit into one of the repair-and-refresh units. Those units make sure that the suit hasn't sustained any damage in the dive or that the material isn't cracking from wear or some kind of strange use.

I put on a loose-weave tunic and a pair of matching wide pants. The overly tight compression feature of that new environmental suit made my skin sensitive to the touch. I'm going to have to tell Yash about that and see if she can change it.

But not right now. Right now, I have more important things to do.

I leave my quarters without drying my close-cropped hair. I'm carrying a spotted apple, aware that I should probably get dinner in an hour or two, and self-aware enough to know that I probably won't.

I head down the corridor to one of the small meeting rooms near the officer's mess. There aren't enough people on this ship to have separate eating areas, so the officer's mess is dormant.

I doubt most people on the ship even know the mess is there. And I know most of them aren't aware of all of the meeting rooms that dot various corridors throughout the *Sove.*

Mikk and I established this meeting room as ours early in the missions to the Boneyards. He and I have been through a lot together, and we have a shorthand. Even though I'm not military, and I don't run my teams the way that the Fleet officers like Coop and Yash do, I have to follow some kind of hierarchy. It gives the Fleet members of my crew some kind of comfort, and it also makes things easier for the rest of the crew.

I have placed the old-timers in positions of power, without giving them any real rank. Still, the crew knows who they should consult with on various issues.

If I were to give folks a rank, though, I would make Mikk my first officer. He's the person on this ship whom I trust the most.

He's waiting for me in the small meeting room. It's not much bigger than the living room in my quarters—a square box with walls set to the default brown color that's predominant on this deck. We could have used my quarters for this meeting, since I've commandeered the captain's suite, but I don't feel the need for that level of privacy.

This meeting room will do just fine.

The furniture is all adjustable. It's recessed into the floor until it's needed. Whoever enters the room first calls up one of the preset furniture programs and the room fills almost immediately.

Mikk chose a small square table and only two chairs. Around him are floating gray balls of various sizes. Those balls are clearly waiting for visuals or telemetry or some other kind of information to get programmed into them.

He's sitting across from the door, hands folded together. He's a large man, larger than most spacers, larger than most divers. We've always made special suits for Mikk because he doesn't fit into anything regulation. He has developed a few lines around his mouth over the years that I've known him. I'm not sure if the bags under his eyes are permanent or there because he's been worrying about my solo dive.

It makes me realize how little I have focused on him recently—and how much of a toll these missions are taking out of him.

On the tabletop are some cut vegetables, sliced fruit, two different kinds of bread, and various protein pastes. Two large, covered glasses have bluish-gold liquid inside, which I recognize. That's the only kind of vitamin and energy replacement drink that I can tolerate.

He doesn't think I'm operating on all cylinders, or he wouldn't have brought this stuff. He thinks I'm off my game.

I'm not. He's been overly worried about me since I got injured, and I no longer protest that fact. I'm actually a bit touched by it. It's nice to have someone worry about me, even if they're worrying unnecessarily.

Still, I toss the spotted apple in the air, and catch it with my right hand, before setting it on the table as I sit down.

Mikk grins at me. He knows that I have just reminded him that I'm doing Just Fine. If I said anything aloud, he might not agree. Not that it's anything we need to discuss.

"You brought a lot of strange information back," he says as I settle into my chair.

"No kidding," I say. "How much have you examined?"

"Not as much as I would like. We have some thinking to do." He taps one of the holographic balls, and the ball changes from round to flat. It shows the starfield as the field looks to Fleet scanners.

Then he taps another ball, and it turns from round to flat. It shows that blurred image I saw from the second scan.

Finally, he taps a third ball. It also turns from round to flat and shows the actual barrier with that weird whiteness that looks like a comet tail.

Then, moving his hands like a man conducting music, he puts all three together. The combination looks like a grayish black muddled mess, with the occasional gleaming light.

Except for the right-hand corner, where the white comet trail exists. There, the white leads into a blackness that seems deeper than any other blackness on the makeshift screen.

I stare at it.

"What do you make of that?" I ask.

"I've been examining it since you got back," he says. "The telemetry from the two old scanners that you used shows energy waves, like the ones we've been seeing in the Boneyard."

"And on the scans done by the *Sove?*" I ask.

"Nothing," he says.

"Nothing?" I repeat. There can't be nothing in space. Something should show up, even in the Boneyard. Some kind of reading or energy field or something—just to keep the ships from moving out of their stationary positions.

"It's a gap in the record," he says.

The word *gap* catches me. "The rest of that barrier shows up in the telemetry."

"Yeah," he says. "As a starfield."

"But that isn't?" I ask.

"It's a blankness, as if the telemetry isn't reading anything."

I stand up. I can't sit with that information. If whatever created that barrier was programmed to look like a starfield, then a blankness meant that the programming was flawed or had decayed or has been damaged.

"And on my scans?" I ask, then catch myself. Apparently, I think of the old scanning equipment as mine and the *Sove's* scanning equipment as the Fleet's.

Mikk shoots me a bemused glance. He caught my slip-up, but he doesn't correct me. Maybe he agrees with it. He's never said much about the Fleet's takeover of our lives, but he has been very willing to go along with my non-Fleet tech adventures over the years.

"On the old scanning equipment," he says, "that area shows up as a hole in the barrier."

"A hole," I repeat. An opening. A way in. "And the white stuff?"

"I don't know," he says. "It shows up visually, but not on anything else. You might not have been close enough to get the right kind of reading."

"Or it might be another ghost image," I say.

He shrugs. "Or it might be something that our old equipment can't measure."

I nod, trying to contain my growing excitement. More mysteries. The unexpected kind.

I'm a bit surprised at myself for growing so jaded about diving ancient and abandoned ships, but I probably shouldn't be. I don't like to have other people impose structures on me. Or to be accountable to others.

So, yes, I'm diving the Boneyard and have been for months. But it's beginning to feel like work now. Yes, there's mystery in it, but *expected* mystery of a kind that says, *What will this ship bring?* not *What is this ship?* or *What exactly are we dealing with here?*

The barrier—the starfield—the thing that we're facing now, the thing I spent hours staring at today—that brings up the kind of mysteries I like. I don't know what I'm looking at, who established it, or why it's there.

Although I can guess on the who part. That's the Fleet. They put a barrier inside a barrier, for a reason I don't exactly understand. And what's even more confusing is that they modified Fleet equipment to get an inaccurate reading of what that barrier is.

"A hole," I say again.

Mikk looks at me.

"We don't have any non-Fleet ships," I say.

He nods, as if he expected me to say that.

"No, we don't," he says. His tone isn't questioning. He knows exactly what I'm thinking. "We might be able to get someone to rig the *Sove's* sensors to match the equipment on those scanners."

"I don't want to use the *Sove*," I said. "A smaller ship would be better."

He grins. "We shouldn't go in there without knowing what we're facing."

"You're right," I say. "We shouldn't."

But we both know that we're going to. One way or another. We're going to see what's behind that curtain, the thing someone in the Fleet didn't want anyone else in the Fleet to know about.

"We need to gather as much information as we can before we go in," he says.

"But we need to do so without closing that hole," I say.

"If, indeed, it is a hole," he says.

We stare at each other for a moment. We have a mission. One that interests both of us. One that might be both risky and impossible.

I grab the spotted apple and toss it in the air, catching it with my right hand. I need to burn off some energy, because otherwise I'll just bounce my way around the room.

I'm probably more excited than I should be. Which tells me how much I've been keeping myself contained.

"Let's plan our next steps," I say.

And so we do.

THE FLEET
TEN MONTHS AGO

3

VICE ADMIRAL IRENA MBUYI'S YOUNGEST DAUGHTER was throwing a tantrum to end all tantrums. Klara might have only been two, but she was a forceful two, with the lung capacity of an opera singer. Which was probably no accident, since Irena's wife, Noemi, had given up just such a career on Sector Base K-2 when she decided to throw in her lot with a senior officer in the Fleet.

Not that Mbuyi felt very senior at the moment. She was on her hands and knees, trying to get Klara untangled from the stem of the kitchen table. The table was retractable, although the family had never retracted it, so it only had one base.

Klara couldn't really wrap her chubby arms all the way around it, but somehow she managed to hold on.

And every time Irena touched her, Klara screamed as if Irena was trying to kill her.

Klara was the second youngest. Noemi had the youngest, Joel, with her on the *Santé 15*. He was barely six months old, and in that time had succumbed to a variety of ailments. His lungs hadn't developed fully, and the doctors on this ship, the *Kutelekezwa*, had decided he needed to see the specialists on the *Santé 15* to determine what, if anything, they could do.

Noemi had taken him there earlier that morning, leaving Irena with the children. She managed to get the four school-age children off to class without much of a hitch, although she could have used the help of her teenagers. But they were residing on the *Brazza* now, and were only home during breaks. She hadn't realized how much she would miss having the presence of three almost-adult children in the quarters, but she did.

Particularly on mornings like this. Klara was supposed to go to her hour-long music class, but she was refusing to leave. Her tantrum had started when Noemi left with Joel. Klara had been clingy since her sister Qadira qualified for the honors classes on the *Brazza*, forcing her to board with the oldest two.

But *clingy* didn't describe this tantrum. Klara leaned against the table stem, her little face red, her eyes squinched up, and her mouth open in the loudest wail Irena had ever heard coming out of a child that size. And that was saying something, since she had helped Noemi raise the other seven.

Nine children seemed like a lot—and it was, for ship life—but the family had developed a rhythm. Usually. The *Kutelekezwa* was Irena's ship. Even before she was transferred here, she was able to give instructions about living quarters. The size of her family, along with the fact that she and Noemi had adopted three of the children, gave her access to three regular-size officers' quarters, which Irena had redesigned to be one big family unit.

There were bedrooms on both sides of the living spaces. The private kitchens of two of the quarters were recessed, making another bedroom (in one), and a play area (in the other). That left the central kitchen, which was just galley sized, and three different seating areas if the family wanted to eat together.

Neither Irena nor Noemi were cooks, however, so mostly, they took the children to the family mess for nightly dinner, and that taught all of the kids to behave well in a group situation.

If Irena had taken Klara to the mess, Klara wouldn't have screamed like this. She would have shoved her little fist in her mouth and snuffled, holding the tears in until one of her parents took her out into the corridor.

But this tantrum—it was sincere. Klara was off-balance without her baby brother and her other mother and the loss (in her mind) of her favorite sister. However, Klara was also not above adding some screams for the sake of theatrics.

Irena had never had a child who calculated her reactions like Klara did. She knew how to get the maximum response for the right kind of (very dramatic) effort.

And Irena—Vice Admiral in charge of so many things, so many lives, so many decisions—didn't feel in charge at the moment. She was being bested by a screaming two-year-old in a stained pink romper, with one bare foot.

"Baby," Irena said in her calmest voice, "come to Mami."

She almost added *and we'll talk about this,* but there was going to be no talking to this child. Not at the moment. And if things continued to escalate, Klara would scream herself hoarse. Then Noemi would know just how bad it had gotten.

At that thought, the door trilled as someone entered. Irena cringed. No one who had the access codes should see the vice admiral like this, her own bare feet sticking out of her black trousers, her white blouse unbuttoned, and her black-and-red jacket tossed on the kitchen counter in a crumpled heap.

She wasn't even sure what the worst case was—Noemi seeing the depths of Irena's incompetence with their demanding two-year-old or one of Irena's two assistants witnessing Irena's inadequate response to a toddler's meltdown.

"Vice Admiral." The female voice was calm and cool and belonged to Lieutenant Commander Cynthia Reyes. "I can come back."

Irena could only see Reyes's shoes, which were black and crisply polished. The hems of her trousers hit the top of the shoes at the perfect angle, draping ever so slightly over the edge of the shoes, hiding Reyes's socks.

Irena had the sense that Reyes would never crawl on the floor after an errant child, even one who had stopped screaming for one moment. Klara looked surprised at the new voice, raised a fist to her mouth, and then—apparently—remembered what she had been doing, because she snuffled.

The snuffles were the precursor to the continuation of the tantrum.

Irena reached for Klara, but not fast enough. Klara saw her, and latched onto the table stem again, and screamed.

"Hey, Klarita!" Another voice joined the mix. Lieutenant Zavi Gundersen crouched down on the other side of the table. Her upbeat tone caught Klara's attention, and Klara turned toward her.

Gundersen was thin and angular. She looked like a stick bent uncomfortably in three places—ankles, knees, and hips. The wide smile on her face was real because her black eyes shone with pleasure.

"Remember me?" she asked Klara.

Apparently, Klara did, because she snuffled again. Then she sobbed, head down.

Irena reached for her, but Gundersen waved a long hand ever so slightly, stopping Irena.

"Really, baby?" Gundersen said. "You're being silly."

Irena looked at her in surprise. Gundersen was still smiling, and Klara was still sobbing. Reyes's feet shifted ever so slightly.

"We should leave," Reyes said, presumably to Gundersen. "Let the Vice Admiral deal with the family situation. We can wait."

"But Klarita can't, can you, baby?" Gundersen's voice had gone up ever so slightly. Not quite baby talk, but close enough. The way that Noemi talked to the youngest children, almost like they were little adults, but with just a hint of that high voice the experts said that children needed to hear.

Klara put a hand on the floor, and twisted herself so that she could see Gundersen more clearly. The sobbing continued, with just a little less conviction now.

"You want a hug, baby girl?" Gundersen asked.

Irena was moving ever so slightly, ready to grab her daughter the moment she let go of the table stem. But Gundersen flicked her gaze at Irena, and shook her head so slightly that the movement was barely visible.

Gundersen extended her arms, just enough to keep from looking too eager. She kept that soft smile on her face.

"Well," she said calmly, "I need a hug."

Irena winced. Klara was the only one of her children who did not respond with great empathy. Klara didn't usually care what someone else needed; Klara cared about what Klara needed.

And apparently, Klara needed a hug, because she put both hands on the floor and crawled to Gundersen. Gundersen swept Klara up in her arms, then rocked backwards, as Klara snuffled again.

Irena opened her mouth to warn her, but Gundersen shook her head one more time. She rocked from side to side, one hand cradling the back of Klara's head, the other wrapped around Klara's middle.

Klara buried her face in Gundersen's neck and let out a soggy sigh.

Irena half-smiled in surprise. She had never seen Klara do anything like that.

Irena backed out from under the table, then sat on her knees for a moment before levering herself up. Gundersen remained seated, still hugging Klara, who was emitting small, sad sounds.

Reyes stood stiffly beside the table, clutching a tablet, her mouth in a thin line. Her dark brown hair was pulled back in a bun, with no strands loose on either side the way that most officers with long hair wore theirs. Her dark eyebrows had been plucked into submission and her narrow chin was set, probably because she was clenching her teeth.

Her pale gray eyes—her best and most expressive feature, really—met Irena's with something bordering on contempt. Reyes had made it clear early on that she would have nothing to do with Irena's family, even if they visited Irena's offices on the other side of the ship.

The fact that Reyes was here, in Irena's quarters, at this time of the morning, alongside Gundersen, meant that something was up. Particularly since Irena had let them both know she would be covering for Noemi until Klara joined a little friend and that friend's parent in music class.

Gundersen stood, using only her legs, maintaining her balance while still holding a now-quiet Klara. Klara peered at Irena. Irena's temperamental daughter had the same judgemental look in her eyes that Reyes had.

But Gundersen didn't. She was smiling softly, her eyes tilted up with more amusement than the rest of her face indicated.

"You want me to take her?" Irena asked Gundersen. Irena really didn't want to take Klara. Irena didn't want the crying to start up again.

Gundersen shook her head with that ever-so-slight movement again.

"Really," Reyes said, just a bit of annoyance in her tone. "We can discuss this later."

"I would think," Irena said, "that something important was happening, since you came all the way to my quarters."

"Something surprising," Gundersen said, using that half-baby-talk voice. Klara shifted ever so slightly in Gundersen's arms, a warning to all of them that the temper tantrum could start up again at any moment.

"What is it?" Irena had donned as much of her professional persona as she could, given the knees of her trousers were covered with lint from the floor, and her blouse had just a bit of breakfast on the sleeve.

Normally, she liked to look as crisp as Reyes did, but that wasn't possible, not on this morning.

"We got a notification from a Scrapheap we didn't even have in our records." Reyes set the tablet she'd been holding on the tabletop.

"Another one?" Irena said. She had teams digging through records, trying to find the Scrapheaps that the Fleet had abandoned over the millennia.

Irena was in charge of lost, abandoned, and decommissioned ships, and that included dealing with Scrapheaps old and new. Policies on Scrapheaps had been haphazard at best, just like the record-keeping, and when Irena got this assignment—nearly a decade ago now—she had been determined to enforce all of the rules concerning Scrapheaps.

But she had to find all the Scrapheaps first, and that had proven more daunting than she expected. They had found half a dozen lost Scrapheaps over the years, but she knew, just based on the number of decommissioned ships in the records, that there had to be a lot more.

She didn't even want to think about the lost ships or the ships whose records had been somehow deleted or the destroyed ships whose pieces ended up in one Scrapheap or another. She had come to the conclusion, just like so many other admirals before her, that Scrapheaps were more trouble than they were worth.

Yet, the Fleet kept building them. It was impossible for Command to destroy perfectly good ships in real time. Just getting permission to destroy old Scrapheaps still caused difficulty, although various vice admirals who had once held Irena's job had streamlined the process.

Now, she only had to go to Command if the Scrapheap in question held something unusually valuable. And, she had realized, as she settled into the job, that *she*, not Command, got to determine what *unusually valuable* meant.

"This one's old," Gundersen said, looking at Klara. Klara tilted her head, clearly thinking that Gundersen was discussing her. No one had ever used the word "old" to describe Klara before.

Gundersen was keeping Klara's attention while managing to forward the conversation. Noemi had that skill as well. Irena would have once said—before she became a parent—that it was just a normal parenting skill that someone with a lot of children had, but Gundersen was childless, and Irena had a lot of children. Irena had never managed that skill.

Come to think of it, Reyes had four children and should have been equally comfortable dealing with Klara. Irena had never seen Reyes's children, but she had a mental image that all of those kids lined up in regimental order whenever Reyes clapped her hands. Reyes's children probably never dared have a temper tantrum, particularly in front of guests.

Irena forced her attention back to the new—well, old—Scrapheap. "How old?" she asked.

"The closest sector bases are W and Y." Reyes tapped the tablet, and a hologram rose from it. Apparently, Reyes hadn't yet put the new Scrapheap into the system, or they could have accessed everything from Irena's backup bridge built in a secure room next to the kitchen.

The hologram was square. It looked like someone had carved a chunk out of that particular sector of space and hung it over the table. Space was not square, and it looked wrong to Irena. If she was dealing with a square surface, she preferred 2-D.

She squinted ever so slightly, forcing herself to concentrate on what Reyes had said.

"W and Y?" Irena asked. The oldest Scrapheap she had dealt with had been in an abandoned sector between Sector Bases G-2 and H-2. "I thought Scrapheaps built before Sector Base B-2 had been destroyed."

"Apparently not," Reyes said drily.

Images slowly populated the hologram, showing the star systems and an old sector base map. Something about the map seemed wrong. Irena squinted at it, trying to see what, exactly, bothered her.

Part of the problem was that the hologram was see-through, and directly beyond it stood Gundersen and Klara. Klara was squirming in Gundersen's arms, trying to wrestle herself free. Once she did that, all hell would break loose again.

Gundersen, maybe sensing Irena's distraction, turned and moved to the left, so that Klara wasn't directly in Irena's line of vision.

Irena smiled ever so slightly as a kind of acknowledgement, then squinted at that hologram.

Sector Base W—or what had been Sector Base W—glowed redly near what was, for Irena, the upper left-hand corner. Other planets and an asteroid belt filtered through the middle of the square, and along the edge of the right-hand side, Sector Base Y—or what had been Sector Base Y—glowed redly, as well.

Klara kicked and moaned, but this time Irena barely noticed. Something was off about the sector bases.

"Show me this in two-d," she said to Reyes.

Reyes tapped the tablet, and the hologram flattened itself into a 2-D surface. That surface squished all the images together, so that they looked like one mass.

"Show me the trajectory from W to Y," Irena said. "Map it in red."

Reyes tapped something, and a squiggly red line appeared, winding its way around some planets and something that Irena couldn't make out.

But the line told her enough to solidify her hunch.

"Show it to me in three dimensions again," she said.

The map eased out. The shape appeared first, then all three red parts—W, Y, and the line. The line vanished on the face of the plane near Irena, though. So she clasped her hands behind her back and started to walk to her left, stopping suddenly because to travel left meant that she would approach Klara.

Klara had a finger in her mouth. She was staring at the hologram as if she had never seen anything like it—and maybe she hadn't.

Gundersen swayed, keeping one hand on Klara's back, but turning just enough so that Klara could stare at the hologram.

Irena walked in the opposite direction, still staring at the hologram. The red line looked more like dots and a line from this angle. The red twisted downward, awkwardly.

"Can you show me other planets that would sustain human life?" she asked Reyes.

"From that period?" Reyes asked. "I have no idea if I can do that."

"Current information would be fine," Irena said.

"You're acting like we have current information from those sectors of space." That disapproving tone again.

However, it took all of Irena's strength not to smile. This time, Reyes was directing the tone at herself. She probably saw what Irena saw.

That was the best part about Reyes. She could absorb a lot of information quickly, and her mind—as fussy as it was—often worked along the same lines that Irena's did.

Suddenly bits of yellow dotted the hologram. The bits of yellow were all over those sectors of space. Some of those bits were on a typical Fleet trajectory.

That was what bothered Irena. The trajectory that went from Sector Base W to Sector Base Y was abnormal.

"I don't suppose you know the history of that area," she said to Reyes.

Reyes made a dismissive sound. "I have never contemplated Sector Bases without a 2 behind their letter in my life."

"Something went awry." This from Gundersen in that sing-song voice. She held Klara's right hand at the wrist—the soggy hand that still had drool on it—and was waving it back and forth.

With Gundersen's swaying and the way she held Klara's tiny hand, it looked like the two of them were dancing.

"Clearly," Irena said. "And on this side of the square, I have no data at all. It drops out for a large part of the hologram."

"That's the problem." Reyes raised her head. "Our systems show that as a black area in space."

"What?" Irena asked.

"Like a big, black nothingness," Reyes said. "Only inside that nothingness is one of the biggest Scrapheaps we've found yet."

Nothingness. Irena frowned, then remembered something from her days in school. For a period in the Fleet's history, it used data holes and other masking techniques as information shields. The entire area would show up as a darkness on a star map, provided the ships used similar tech to the Fleet's tech.

For less sophisticated tech, the darkness would show up with a warning. Or as something impenetrable—a tight asteroid belt or some kind of black hole.

Gundersen was watching her closely, still "dancing" with Klara. Reyes was frowning at the hologram.

Irena had no idea if either of them had learned about that particular defense in their schooling, and she wasn't going to educate them right now.

"If our sensors aren't showing the Scrapheap," she said, "how did you find it?"

"It contacted us," Reyes said.

Irena straightened. "It what?"

"It sent us a message," Reyes said. "Complete with coordinates and imagery."

"Of what?" Irena said.

Gundersen had stopped swaying. She was watching Irena closely. Klara was the only one who wasn't watching her. Klara was still staring at the hologram as if she could understand it.

"The Scrapheap notified us of a breach," Reyes said. "And by the time we were able to actually view the contact, it had sent several more."

"What was it trying to tell us?" Irena said.

"It wanted us to know that a ship had been stolen out of the Scrapheap," Reyes said.

Irena let out a breath. Gundersen was still staring at her. So was Reyes. They seemed disturbed. Irena didn't understand why.

"Ships get stolen from Scrapheaps all the time." Irena felt odd telling her two assistants that. They knew it. They had studied it. "It's an unfortunate side of decaying and underdeveloped shielding technology."

Reyes lifted her head, her gaze flat—the look Reyes got when she wasn't going to correct a superior officer.

"This ship was targeted," Reyes said. "The team that took it activated its *anacapa* drive."

"They knew what they were doing," Gundersen said. She wasn't using that sing-song voice anymore. "There were no false steps, no time spent on study."

Klara looked up at her in wonder, as if she hadn't heard Gundersen's real voice before.

Irena frowned. "This team, as you call it. They knew how to work *anacapa* drives?"

"They tried to break into the Scrapheap using one," Reyes said. "They were rebuffed. So they used some old codes and managed to create an opening in the forcefield around the Scrapheap."

"Old codes...of ours?" Irena asked.

Now Klara shifted again, and looked at Irena with a worried frown. Irena knew that frown. It was a precursor to worried crying.

"Yes," Reyes said. "From thousands of years ago."

"Thousands...?" Now it was Irena's turn to frown. "When did this breach happen?"

"As near as we can tell," Reyes said, "nine, maybe ten months ago. It took the information a bit of time to find us."

Nine or ten months ago? That wasn't what Irena had expected. She had expected something older. That was how they had found so many Scrapheaps in the past. Something would activate, travel across ancient nodes, and arrive years, maybe centuries, later.

"You're certain of the timing?" Irena asked.

"Positive," Reyes said.

"Using ancient codes?" Irena said.

Reyes nodded.

"And they knew how to use an *anacapa* drive. You're certain of that too?"

"They had one on the outside," Reyes said. "They were using a DV-Class ship. An extremely old one, although not as old as those codes."

Irena looked at the hologram again. Sector Bases W and Y were closed down thousands of years ago, if the systems had followed the usual Fleet formula for opening and closing bases.

Ancient ships, ancient codes, *anacapa* drives.

"Where did they take this ship they stole?" Irena asked.

"The information we got wasn't sophisticated enough for us to figure that out," Reyes said.

"There's a lot of distortion inside that Scrapheap," Gundersen added. "We're not sure if the distortion is from the area where the ship was taken or if it is all over that Scrapheap."

Irena nodded. This was a new problem, one she hadn't faced before. Which was probably why she was being looped in early.

"What do we know about this Scrapheap?" she asked.

"Nothing," Reyes said. "We had lost track of it."

Her voice was flat. The fact that the Fleet lost track of things was the bane of her existence. When Reyes got promoted to vice admiral, she would probably set up an overhaul of the entire Fleet record-keeping system—if someone let her.

"So," Irena said, "we don't know if this Scrapheap has Ready Vessels."

"I think we have to assume it does," Gundersen said. She hadn't moved at all, and neither, surprisingly, had Klara.

Gundersen's gaze met Irena's and Irena finally understood the reason for the meeting.

Someone was taking ships out of a Scrapheap. Someone who had knowledge of, or had figured out how, to work an *anacapa* drive.

The codes suggested that someone was or had been part of the Fleet or had found information about the Fleet.

But the Fleet left too much tech behind. Finding out information about the Fleet wasn't impossible, even though it would take effort.

And there was one other consideration that her assistants probably didn't know: the Fleet didn't invent the *anacapa* technology. The Fleet had stolen it.

The culture that developed the *anacapa* drive would know how to use it.

"All right," Irena said. "See what else you can find out about this Scrapheap. I'll meet with you both this afternoon, and we'll set up a plan of action."

"Yes, Vice Admiral," Reyes said.

Gundersen nodded once, then bent slightly to set Klara down. Klara clung and started to whine.

"Come to me, baby," Irena said with a little too much command in her voice. Noemi hated it when she talked to the children as if they were recruits.

But Klara didn't seem to mind. She extended her chubby arms and leaned so far toward Irena that Gundersen nearly dropped her.

Irena scooped her daughter in her arms. Klara smelled of soap and sour milk. She was warm and damp, and her face was still lined with tears. Irena used her thumb to wipe the tears away, and her daughter gave her a watery smile.

Reyes collapsed the hologram of the sector, and picked the tablet up off the table. Irena almost told her to leave it, then changed her mind.

She had some overall investigation to do before that afternoon meeting. She wouldn't have time to delve into the details of this new old Scrapheap.

"When we meet this afternoon," she said as she adjusted Klara in her arms, "let me know where the closest Scrapheap to this one is, according to our records. And if any Scrapheaps created around Sector Base U or V have been destroyed."

"Records don't go back very far," Reyes said, as she always did. Those sentences served as both a reminder that the information wasn't always collected, and a warning that Reyes wouldn't be able to do this task because of the lack of information.

Gundersen lowered her gaze, as she often did when she was trying not to roll her eyes.

"We haven't destroyed Scrapheaps for very long, in the scheme of things," Irena said. The destruction of Scrapheaps had been a controversial maneuver, one that kept being taken off the Fleet's agenda, and put back on whenever there was some kind of incident around Scrapheaps.

The command that Irena had taken over had only had the mandate to completely destroy Scrapheaps for the past 500 years or so. Before that, the Fleet had mandated the removal of Ready Vessels from Scrapheaps, which had proven more difficult than it sounded. The destruction of Scrapheaps had been easier, which was why an entire subclass of ships were developed for just those missions.

Current Scrapheaps—and yes, the Fleet still corralled ships into Scrapheaps, despite the opposition from many in command—did not contain Ready Vessels.

Klara caught a few strands of Irena's hair and tugged. The pain was minimal, but it caught her attention, just like the thought of Ready Vessels did.

Irena captured Klara's hand in her own, but kept her gaze on her assistants.

"One thing," she said. "That ship, stolen from the Scrapheap. Where was it?"

"What do you mean?" Reyes asked. "Inside the Scrapheap."

There was an implied "of course" after Scrapheap. Sometimes, Reyes didn't think before she spoke. If she had, she would have realized that Irena was asking a different question.

"We don't have an internal map," Gundersen said, trying to clarify. "We don't even know how big it is or when it was assembled or any other real detail about the Scrapheap."

Apparently, Irena's question hadn't been as clear as she thought it was.

"I mean," Irena said, "did these thieves have to go through a second forcefield to get to the ship?"

"You want to know if it was a Ready Vessel," Gundersen said. "Without the map, we can't know that."

"If they went through two forcefields," Irena said, tilting her head to ease the pressure on her hair. Klara was still tugging, hard, "then they took a Ready Vessel."

"You taught us not to make assumptions," Reyes said. "Particularly about Scrapheaps. Every Scrapheap is different—"

"Except when it comes to internal forcefields," Irena said. "Only the control towers and the Ready Vessels have forcefields inside the Scrapheap itself."

"Let me take this," Gundersen said, looking at Reyes. Reyes opened her mouth and then closed it again.

As Irena watched the interaction between her assistants, she used her thumb to slowly open Klara's fist, closed around those strands of hair.

Gundersen glanced at Reyes rather pointedly, then said, "I've gone through the information that the Scrapheap sent us. Not as thoroughly as Lieutenant Commander Reyes, but enough to tell you that the ship taken from the Scrapheap was not too far from the external forcefield, and the thieves who took that ship did not go through a secondary forcefield."

"I wouldn't commit to that," Reyes said. "There's a lot we don't know—"

"The placement of the ship alone guarantees that it's not a Ready Vessel." Gundersen kept her gaze firmly on Irena now. Gundersen's words were crisp and certain, which Irena appreciated.

"Do we know if the thieves have returned?" Irena asked.

"Not at this moment," Gundersen said. "I'm going to ping the Scrapheap so that it knows this message, at least, got through. I have no idea if we'll get more messages before that or not. But, eventually, we will resume normal communications with the Scrapheap, and then I'll be able to answer your question."

Normal communications. Usually there was a direct route of communication between the Scrapheaps and the Fleet. But that direct route became a problem for some of the older Scrapheaps, particularly when the Fleet updated its tech, but didn't send an update to the older parts of the Fleet left behind.

Sending such an update was not without its controversies. The Fleet was always paranoid about sending modern tech to sectors it would never see again.

"I want to know this afternoon if we've had more contacts," Irena said. She was still moving her thumb, trying to get Klara's fist open. The hair was stuck to Klara's sweaty skin.

Reyes frowned. "The system is—"

"I understand that it's convoluted," Irena said. "We're going to need to figure this out."

"Ten months ago is a long time," Reyes said, looking at Gundersen, confirming Irena's suspicion. Gundersen was the one who brought this here, not Reyes.

"Not if someone is stealing *anacapa* drives," Irena said. "That gives them access to us. And, depending on what they're taking, comparable technology."

Klara put her hand down, pulling out several strands of hair, and let go. The pain was sharp and sudden, but Irena didn't wince. Instead, she cradled her daughter close.

Reyes glanced over at Gundersen. Gundersen bit her lower lip. Irena couldn't tell if they were distressed because of the ship theft or the possibility it could be a Ready Vessel or both.

"Forgive me, Admiral," Reyes said, after another quick glance at Gundersen. "But don't you think that's a stretch? I mean, if the thieves found Ready Vessels, why come after us? I know the Fleet has policies that try to prevent things like that from happening, but as far as I know, it never has happened. So why should we assume that these thieves are interested in us?"

Irena felt a flash of irritation. Reyes was competent when given a task, but difficult otherwise. Maybe it was time to move her laterally and find a new assistant.

"Think it through, Lieutenant," Irena said. Klara snapped to attention, her little body suddenly rigid. Apparently Irena's tone was sharper than she usually used around her daughter. "These thieves already know how to use an *anacapa* drive. They already have codes, albeit ancient ones. They know how to operate a Dignity Vessel."

Reyes raised her chin slightly, which Irena recognized as Reyes trying not to challenge her.

"We have to assume," Irena continued, "given all of that, that these thieves know about the Fleet."

"So why come and challenge us, sir? Why not steal the tech and use it for whatever reason? Why would they come for us?"

"They might not," Irena said. "But we never approach a new culture assuming they're benign. We go in cautiously. We hope they're benign, but we're prepared in case they are not. That's what we're doing here."

Reyes lowered her chin ever so slightly. Clearly, she hadn't thought of it that way.

"No matter what," Irena said, "this is why our division exists. We do not want our tech in the hands of anyone else. The fact that these thieves got in, and recently, is a serious problem for the Fleet."

"I know that, sir," Reyes said.

"Do you?" Irena asked, adding even more sharpness to her tone.

Klara put her hand on Irena's shoulder, as if she were bracing herself. At least she wasn't crying anymore.

"We brought this to you," Reyes said, and this time, she let her defensiveness into her tone.

"Actually, bringing this to me was Gundersen's idea," Irena said.

Reyes started, confirming Irena's guess.

"And she was right," Irena said. "This cannot wait. We need to figure out what, exactly, is going on, and how measured our response should be."

"Measured?" Reyes asked.

"Yes," Irena said, not wanting to go any deeper into the minutiae, not at this moment, anyway. "Get me the information I asked for by this afternoon, and we will proceed from there."

"Yes, sir," Reyes said.

Gundersen nodded. She picked up the tablet, as if she didn't want Reyes to have custody of it any longer. Perhaps Gundersen understood what Irena had been thinking. After all, Gundersen had survived the loss of two other assistants. They had been moved laterally as well. Maybe Irena's behavior toward her assistants was more predictable than she thought.

"Treat this like a real-time emergency," Irena said to Gundersen. "Because it is."

"Yes, Admiral," Gundersen said, in a tone that meant *I know.*

Irena didn't find that tone annoying at all. It was as if they were having a different conversation than the one she'd been having with Reyes.

Irena dismissed them both. She was glad her daughter was calm now, because underneath, Irena wasn't.

Her division rarely had real-time emergencies, but when it did, they took a lot of time, resources, and political capital. She'd never had something big like that on her watch, but she'd assisted her predecessor on a crisis that hadn't been as severe as this one might be.

And that crisis had been difficult enough.

But Irena couldn't think about that, not right now. She had Klara to deal with, and research of her own to do.

And then there was Joel to think of, or not think of, at least at this moment. Because his medical problems made Irena feel helpless, and she couldn't feel helpless, not when she needed to be strong for work itself.

She sighed and rocked Klara.

"How about a little lunch, baby girl," she said, adjusting her daughter in her arms again. A domestic task would focus them both, before everything got crazy.

Just like Irena knew it would.

THE BONEYARD
NOW

4

WE TAKE A BATTLEFIELD SCOUT SHIP on our mission to the starfield. I have brought seven people with me, and only one of them is Fleet trained. I would like to tell myself that I wasn't excluding Fleet-trained personnel, but maybe I am.

I want to return to my old diving roots, and this is one way to do so.

The battlefield scout ship is nothing like my old ship, *Nobody's Business*, however. The Fleet has a variety of scout ships, most designed to travel easily from space into a planet's atmosphere and back again. Those scout ships operate well in atmosphere.

This one doesn't. It's a battlefield scout ship because it's designed to explore starbases and shipping lanes with crews that vary in size from twenty to forty. The battlefield scout ship has long-range sensors which are better than the sensors on most small ships, and those sensors are designed to pick up everything from human life signs to anything that might be used as weaponry.

The battlefield scout ship also has its own weaponry and defense systems. I checked both before we boarded, then had Mikk double-check me. I don't know what we're going into, and I want to be prepared.

The *Sove* has several battlefield scout ships, as well as more fighters than I would like. But Coop insisted that we need all the defensive capability we can get, and Ilona agreed. Our DV-Class ships are armed as well or better than the DV-Class ships of Coop's day.

As a result, this battlefield scout ship has a designation: S-BSS-19. I'm calling it BS19, partly because I feel a little BS-y, and having a snide nickname for the ship takes some of the seriousness out of our mission.

Mikk couldn't modify the sensors on the BS19 to act like the sensors on my scanner, so he did the next best thing: he took one of the old scanners and hooked it into the BS19's sensor array. We'll get the benefit of Fleet scans, and the benefit of non-Fleet scans, or so he tells me.

I probably should have had Zaria Diaz and her team of engineers modify the BS19, but I didn't want to wait for them to do the work "properly," whatever that would mean to them. Besides, part of me doesn't want Fleet involvement on this mission at all.

It's not that I distrust my Fleet counterparts, but I'm acutely aware that our goals inside the Boneyard are very different. The Fleet members can easily ignore what's going on behind that starfield, and continue finding DV-class vessels to bring back to Lost Souls, not just for the tech, but also for the history buried in those ships' files.

Me, I'm so ready to go on this adventure that I'm having trouble maintaining a sense of calm. I'm bouncing—at least internally—and I am being extra cautious on everything that I do. I know myself when I'm like this: I want to push forward, no matter what the risks, and I don't dare.

We're in a situation I've never really been in before. We're operating inside a gigantic storage area, filled with damaged ships and surrounded by a forcefield. The defensive capabilities of the Boneyard are strong, and escape from the Boneyard itself isn't easy.

The BS19 doesn't have an *anacapa* drive. Mikk and I discussed whether or not we wanted a battlefield scout ship with an *anacapa* drive. We've added a few to the *Sove*, or rather, Ilona did, by executive order. She wanted us to be able to explore something and escape quickly.

I'm worried that activating an *anacapa* drive behind that barrier posing as a starfield might be dangerous or even deadly.

I don't know what's there. As each day passes, I have come up with different scenarios. The latest is that whatever is behind that barrier is even more deadly than the damaged ships outside of it. Maybe there are loose *anacapa* drives behind that barrier or experimental tech that the Fleet couldn't bring itself to destroy.

Part of me is deep-down terrified that we're going into a part of the Boneyard that is so dangerous we might not be able to survive it. And another part of me hopes that supposition is true. It gives me something to fight against, which I feel like I've lacked for a long, long time now.

Not that we're going behind that starfield at the moment. We're just going to send in probes.

We've decided on four batches of probes. We're sending in Fleet probes first, because we don't want to trigger anything inside the Boneyard that might attack non-Fleet tech. Then we're sending in a single non-Fleet probe, one of my old favorite models from years ago. We'll repeat if necessary. If not, we might follow one of the probes inside.

I haven't told anyone on the *Sove* what, exactly, we're doing. Nor have I let anyone at Lost Souls know. The *Sove* crew will continue their mission to finish prepping that next ship that will go back to Lost Souls. I figured if anyone asked what we were doing—and so far, no one has—that I would tell them we're looking for another ship to dive.

No one would think twice about that.

The entire eight-person team is crowded into the command and control area of BS19, the area that the designers labeled a "bridge." It's too small to be a bridge, really. It's set up for about five people to have individual workstations if the captain of the ship wants such things.

But it's too large to be a cockpit. It fits the eight of us easily, even if we have the command chairs raised out of the floor, which we do not.

The reason I think this area is labeled a bridge is only because BS19 has weapons capability, and it's better to have a separate command area for weapons control.

Of course, as acting captain of this mission, I can access all of the ship's functions on my command board, which I made holographic. I also have it tethered to me, at least for the time being, so that the holographic board follows me around the bridge.

We have three large holographic screens running so that the entire team sees the same things in real time. I don't want team members monitoring different things unless I ask them to. Since the information is so different from Fleet scanners to my old scanners, I want to make sure we're working off the same data streams when we take action.

At the back of the bridge, we also have a roundish holographic ball that represents the Boneyard itself. As we get information we trust, we're going to program it into that ball.

Right now, the bottom right of that ball is populated with the ships, ship parts, gaps in the field, and the pathway that the *Sove* has taken to this point. The starfield itself is represented by a jagged white line. Aside from that, the holographic ball is a monotonous gray.

Mikk stands to my left. He's half a head taller than me, which I always forget when he's sitting down. Those gravity-formed muscles of his make him seem shorter, at least to me.

On his other side stands Roderick, who has dived for me off and on for years. He was with me when the *Ivoire* arrived in the caverns beneath Vaycehn, and he was there when Karl died. He's done a lot of side work for Lost Souls, but he only tried being a full-time employee once. He lasted about a year before he went back on his own.

We contract with him—or rather, I do—when we have missions that require a lot of wreck diving. He's one of the best I know.

Like Mikk, Roderick has gravity-formed muscles, but he's not as tall as Mikk. Roderick is quieter too. He hasn't said much—to me anyway— during our months in the Boneyard. He doesn't seem to be talking with anyone, somehow keeping his opinions to himself.

He's not even talking to the other member of my old diving team— Tamaz. Tamaz is also gravity-strong, but has let himself thin down in the years that I've known him. He never worked directly for Lost Souls, although he's often worked for me. He ran his own company for a while, then gave it up to hire out.

Like Roderick and Mikk, he lacks the gene that allows him to work in failing *anacapa* energy fields. All three of them can work in standard *anacapa* fields.

So they can't dive any of the ships here until someone re-establishes the environmental controls and either disables the *anacapa* drive or makes certain that it's running properly.

Which relegates all three men into piloting and supervising positions. None of them like that; to them, it's almost like being demoted. But we need them. *I* need them, particularly since I'm constantly surrounded by Fleet personnel, who have no trouble at all working in dying or decaying *anacapa* energy fields.

The presence of all three men probably means I've been planning some kind of break from the Fleet-focused dive work for some time. I just hadn't realized it until now.

I have also brought three members of the Six. The Enterran Empire searched for people who had the gene that protects them from decaying *anacapa* energy. Only back when the Six were discovered, the Empire didn't know (and probably still doesn't) that *anacapa* energy is unique to the Fleet. The Empire thought the *anacapa* energy was some kind of stealth drive that had been lost over the years.

The Six didn't want to work for the Empire and ended up working for me.

Because of what happened to me and Elaine on that dive that went wrong, I made sure that Nyssa Quinte is on this—and all of my dives now. After some of our earlier dives, Quinte got medical training. She's now a dive medic, and a damn good one.

If she had been with us in the Boneyard on the mission where Elaine and I got injured, we probably wouldn't have been in that part of the Boneyard at all. Unlike most ship's medics and all Fleet personnel, Quinte can hear malfunctioning *anacapa* fields, just like I can.

In fact, every member of the Six can. Two others work the entire Boneyard mission right now, and they are with me on this trip. Fahd Al-Nasir has become an employee of Lost Souls. He prefers working on ground crews, searching for things like lost sector bases (such as the one we were exploring when the *Ivoire* arrived), but I managed to cajole him to join us in the Boneyard.

Again, after Elaine got injured.

Orlando Rea was the only other member of the Six on that particular team, and he thinks I brought in the others too late. I'm only alive because of his quick thinking on a dive Yash and I had to take before I was completely healed from my injuries. I keep saying I'm not superstitious, but maybe I am deep down, because I don't want to dive anymore without Orlando somewhere nearby.

The final member of our eight-person team is Gustav Denby. He is Fleet trained. He had just started his service on the *Ivoire* when it got stuck in foldspace and ultimately ended up here. He's been part of Lost Souls longer than he served on a Fleet ship.

I'm the one who taught him how to dive. He still has a bit of the Fleet rigidity about methods and practices inside ships, but when it comes to a dive, he's all mine.

I'm piloting the BS19 for the moment, although I'll probably hand off to Roderick soon. He's a good pilot, especially of small ships. I didn't warn him I'd be handing off, though. I didn't warn anyone, although they have to suspect, since everyone on board is a diver.

What I did tell them is that I want to run this mission as if it were one of my old dives of unknown vessels off the *Nobody's Business*. Only Mikk, Roderick, and Tamaz know fully what that means.

It means be ready for anything, and at a moment's notice.

Everyone has been assigned and told to bring their kit, because I'm not sure when we'll return to the *Sove*. I want to use the BS19 as our main ship until we know exactly what's happening with that starfield.

Mikk and I mapped out the course toward that hole in the starfield—or that barrier or whatever is before us. The course takes us past five DV-Class ships, all of which have gaping holes in their hulls.

Gaping holes usually don't remain so on most Fleet vessels. The nanobits that comprise much of the Fleet's tech rebuild any damage, often within a matter of minutes.

Either the holes in those DV-Class vessels are the result of some kind of catastrophic failure or the nanobits themselves were unable to continue repairing the ships after some kind of crisis.

That really doesn't matter to us, because we would never dive those ships. We rule out all of the obviously damaged ships that we see around us, and only dive the ones that are intact.

Normally, we wouldn't even pass through a grouping of damaged ships like this.

But Mikk and I decided to keep this trip as separate from the *Sove* as possible. We even circled around behind the *Sove* as we started on this trip. We went as far away from the starfield as we could at the beginning of our mission, and then traveled through some damaged ships before we got to this point.

We don't want this trip to seem like a mission from the *Sove* to anyone who is looking at the trip from the outside. If anyone does. Or will.

We've stopped at the edge of the damaged DV-Class vessels, right at the start of the necklaces of ships. For quite a distance past those ships, there is nothing at all. If the controlling intelligence of the Boneyard wanted to, it could place another half dozen ships between us and the starfield.

But it has placed nothing.

I bring BS19 to a full stop right here, just past the grouping of damaged DV-Class vessels and slightly in front of the necklaces of intact ships.

Those intact ships in their careful pattern bother me, but I can't quite figure out why. Mikk says he doesn't like them either, because they look like a guard unit around the starfield.

Before we left, I asked a number of the Fleet personnel if they'd seen any guard formation like that one anywhere else.

They hadn't. And that makes me even more nervous.

As we stop, Mikk, Roderick, and Tamaz start running scans of that empty area between the necklace of ships and the start of the starfield. I open the portals, so that we can actually see what's ahead of us, and I float the holographic screens behind us all, next to the gigantic holographic Ball of Knowledge, as Fahd has started to call it.

From here, through the open portals, the vastness between us and the starfield looks like any other kind of space without much in it. It's dark blue with bluer areas of light, and up ahead, white, gold, and red pinpoints of light wink.

Just like they did when I was tethered outside of the *Sove*.

I feel an ever-so-slight disappointment. Part of me hoped that we would see something different up close.

But the logical part of me, the part that understands how the equipment works, knows that every aspect of this ship was designed by the Fleet, so whatever is showing us the "Fleet vision" of this starfield works on the portals as well.

I bring one of the holographic screens forward. This one is getting its information from the non-Fleet scanning equipment that Mikk jury-rigged to the console.

I raise that holographic screen so that it sits between the two portals—at least as far as my vision is concerned. Everyone crowds around me and stares.

"It's blurry," Fahd says in irritation. "What the hell would cause it to be blurry?"

The question is rhetorical, because what we're seeing is exactly what the scans picked up earlier.

"Looks like a smudge to me," Nyssa says.

To me as well, now that she says so. As if someone has taken their thumb across the image of the starfield and rubbed all of the colors together in a fit of pique.

I'm not looking at the smudge or the blurriness so much as the space between the necklace of ships and the starfield. On this screen, that space is darker, denser, as if it isn't getting as much ambient light as the other scans would suggest.

I call up the energy readings for that area, and am somewhat surprised. There is no errant *anacapa* energy at all, which I probably should have expected. After all, there are no damaged ships in that area.

There are no ships, period.

The readings coming off the ships in the necklace are precisely what I would expect to see from any dormant ship that has an *anacapa* drive. Faint energy signatures. They don't leak into that area, because these ships have been in place for a very long time.

The starfield isn't giving off any energy either, and I would expect it to. If it's creating this grand illusion, then it should give off some kind of energy, right?

A shudder runs down my back. Maybe I'm reading this information all wrong. Maybe the starfield isn't an illusion. Maybe we're seeing a hole in the Boneyard, and the Fleet equipment is picking it up properly.

Or maybe, we're seeing an opening that leads directly into foldspace.

Maybe that starfield is a starfield—just in some other galaxy, very far from this one.

Mikk is watching me, not the screens before us.

"What are you thinking?" he asks.

I don't answer. Instead, I modify one of the sensors on the holographic panel before me, looking for the reading that we get from *anacapa* drives as ships head into foldspace. I'm feeling shivery and slightly giddy.

Wouldn't the Fleet engineers who looked over our readings and all of those scans have seen this as a foldspace opening if, indeed, it is one? Wouldn't they have said something?

Of course they would have said something, I admonish myself silently. They have no reason to hide the information. But I can't shake the doubts, suddenly.

"Boss?" Mikk asks.

Orlando looks at me from the edge of the portals. He's studying everything, hands behind his back, as if it's already a life-and-death situation.

He doesn't say anything to me, although he mouths, *You okay?*

That phrase is like a blast of cold air. Am I okay?

No, not really. I'm about to take us into the unknown—the *real* unknown—for the first time since that dive with Yash after I got injured. Those two dives—the one that injured me, and the one afterward—made me question myself, my judgement, and my willingness to take risks.

I've been through that kind of mental questioning before, after the deaths of some of my divers the first time I encountered what we were then calling "stealth tech." I almost abandoned diving at that point.

And then I faced my fears head on, and somehow, found myself here in this future, which is as strange to me as it is to the *Ivoire* crew.

I need to trust myself, and my people. The Fleet crew on these various dives using the *Sove*, they are my people as well. I didn't train them, but I employ them. And they're smart, loyal, and more capable than I have a right to expect.

"Boss?" This time, the query comes from Tamaz. I'm scaring my crew, and that's not a good thing.

"I want to add a probe," I say, surprising even myself.

Mikk's mouth thins. Tamaz raises his eyebrows. Fahd glances at Orlando, as if they have had some conversations about me.

And there I am, being paranoid.

Some of that comes from working with too many people. I used to second-guess myself when I worked alone, but I didn't worry about what my team thought of me.

"When?" Mikk asks, and it takes me a moment to understand his question. He's asking when I want to add the probe, to what part of the mission exactly.

"Right now," I say. "Right up front. I don't trust this buffer space between the necklace of ships and that starfield-barrier."

Nyssa lets out an audible breath. "I'm glad you said that. I've been worried about it too."

"But you didn't say anything." Denby sounds almost accusatory. He hasn't been on many dives with Nyssa. He doesn't understand that she still thinks of herself as less capable than the other divers.

She's not as creative, but she's a lot more cautious. And sometimes we have to listen to caution.

I have to listen to caution.

"I…um…figured you guys had already ruled that out," Nyssa says.

"Always best to check," Mikk says, with a sideways glance at me, as if he's worried about speaking for me.

He shouldn't be. He's right.

But, for the first time in a while, I don't care what the team thinks. I'm still contemplating that extra probe.

I scroll through the data around me, looking at the telemetry. The telemetry seems to match on both the Fleet and non-Fleet scans. That should make me feel better, but it doesn't. If anything, it makes me trust the readings less.

I move the images before me on the non-Fleet screen so that I can see that opening in the starfield-barrier. The opening looks the same here, except for a slightly ragged glow near what I would call the top edge. That glow is whitish. It takes me a moment to realize that the comet trail we had seen earlier is either gone or not visible from this angle.

"That opening looks different on the non-Fleet scans," I say to Roderick. "I want you and Tamaz to see if there's a real difference or if the comet trail—whatever we're calling it—has vanished because we're approaching it from a different angle."

"Do you want me to check the Fleet scans?" Denby asks.

I almost say no, because his question feels more like a rebuke of Nyssa than it does a desire to get something done. But maybe it's both— an example to Nyssa to ask questions at the right time, *and* a desire to do something right now.

"Sure," I tell him. "Check those scans as well."

I'm not going to mention that I'm wondering if the starfield is an actual starfield, viewed through a portal into foldspace. If that's the case, I want my team to stumble on it through data.

I don't want to assume anything.

And with that thought, I let out a small breath. That's the old Boss. Me, the woman I thought I had lost. The woman who made no assumptions, but discovered whatever she discovered in the course of a dive or a day or an adventure, using what she learned in each moment to build on the next.

Preconceptions ruined conclusions.

I hadn't forgotten that, but I had ceased making it my usual practice.

"Mikk," I say, "I want to use one of the BS19's standard probes first."

He moves his head back ever so slightly. I recognize the movement for what it is—a quiet way of suppressing the surprise he felt at the order I just gave.

We had discussed the BS19's probes as we set up our plan, and we had ruled those probes out. The *Sove* had better probes, smaller and more sophisticated, and we decided to use those in the Fleet part of the probing.

Mikk moves his jaw a little, his eyes narrowing. I can almost see the debate he's having with himself.

He and I planned this mission, and now I'm messing with it. In the old days, before the Fleet, before Lost Souls, he would have followed my instruction, no questions asked. He knew—back then—that no matter what *we* had decided, what *I* chose was what mattered.

But now, after years of working the Fleet way, after years of cooperating with Lost Souls, I haven't taken control like I used to. If I planned a mission with the help of someone else, I gave them equal power in the relationship.

I had made this trip different, just with the team I had chosen. And doing so, without firmly stating that I was in charge, is what's causing Mikk issues at the moment.

"I know we decided against using these probes," I say to him, making it easier, even though in doing so, I'm not settling the control issue—in his mind or mine. "But now that I see what's ahead of us, I'm thinking that maybe the probes for a battlefield scout ship are exactly what we need to send out first."

He lets out a small breath, and then nods. He understands.

"What do you mean?" Nyssa blurts. I guess she's decided that our admonition to speak up applies to all aspects of the mission.

I don't have to explain myself to the entire team, but in this instance, it doesn't hurt.

"Ultimately," I say to her—and the others, by default— "this little ship is a warship, designed to scout areas in a wartime situation. So the probes are designed to pick up weapons or things that can be used as weapons, as well as hidden ships or energy signatures or defensive screens that aren't visible on standard telemetry."

"Why wouldn't you use those in the first place?" Nyssa asks, then glances at the others, as if she feels like she's doing something wrong.

"We should have." Mikk shakes his head slightly. "Neither of us were thinking about battles and battlefields. We were worried about what we might find and the different readings."

My gaze meets his. He nods just a little.

"This emptiness…" he says.

"If you can call it that," I put in as he pauses slightly.

"…that's how some cultures set up a defensive perimeter around military bases or areas that they want to protect that are far from their usual base of operations," Mikk says.

"Land-based cultures?" Denby asks. Everyone who got their start with the Fleet has trouble thinking of cultures as anything other than traveling nations. Even though most of the cultures the Fleet encountered have been land-based.

"Maybe that's what tripped us up," Mikk says, and I can't tell if he's being polite to Denby or if Mikk actually believes he and I have ventured into Fleet-think.

Denby turns and looks at one of the screens behind us. He folds his hands behind his back and walks toward it.

"The question is, then," Denby says so softly that I have to strain to hear him, "would the Fleet do something like that, and why."

Good question, but not relevant at the moment. We still haven't entirely figured out these Boneyards yet, since it looks like the Fleet constantly abandons them. Does the Fleet build them to keep ships out of the hands of miscreants like us? And if so, why?

Because it would be easier to destroy old ships than it would be to store them like this.

That shuddery half-realization feeling fills me again, but the connections that my brain is making aren't quite visible to me yet. I'm getting a hunch, but I haven't *gotten* the hunch yet. It's right there, on the tip of my brain, and it has something to do with Fleet culture.

"One BS19 probe," I say to Mikk. "The smallest that we have."

He nods at me. "Following the trajectory that we're going to take?"

We have a route mapped out to that opening, although I'm not entirely sure we're going to take it.

I think about his question for a moment. If we send the probe that way, we alert the controlling intelligence of the Boneyard as to our plan.

If there is a controlling intelligence.

If anyone is monitoring us at all.

And, honestly, there doesn't seem to be. If something—someone—were monitoring the Boneyard, they would have stopped us from stealing the ships by now.

Unless we've fooled them. Unless they think we belong to a branch of the Fleet and we're taking these older ships for Fleet use.

I let out a sigh of exasperation—at myself. I've become guilty of overthinking everything, which leads to second-guessing, which is more crippling than the injuries I suffered not long ago.

"Yes," I say to Mikk. "Send it along our planned trajectory. Have its scans set wide, though, taking in as much area as possible."

"Got it," he says. "Let me set up for release. I'll let you know when I'm ready."

And then he leaves the bridge.

I feel his absence acutely. But he needed to leave. We decided not to launch the probes remotely when we set up this plan. Probe releases can look like we're launching physical weapons, actual torpedoes or bombs.

We had decided, before we left, that we didn't want to confuse the Boneyard. Or the controlling intelligence. Or the sensors.

We're being as cautious as we can.

I only hope we're being cautious enough.

5

IT TAKES TIME FOR MIKK TO PREPARE the BS19 probe. He needs to program the route, set up the type of scans, and make sure that the information will flow to us, even if the probe never returns to BS19.

Then he has to physically place the probe in one of the airlocks on the side of the ship. The two other probes that we were going to send first are already in airlocks.

What we planned to do—what we will do, even with this probe—is open the airlock doors, let the probe tumble out, and then engage its tiny engine.

To any kind of automated eye, the probe won't look *launched*. It'll look like it was lost or abandoned. We even calculated the time that we would let the probes float on their own before engaging the engines. We figured a good minute or two would be more than enough to fool any automated sensors.

The problem with our plan is, of course, if anything is monitored by humans. They might see the ruse for what it is.

Mikk returns to the bridge in less than twenty minutes. I had expected it to take longer, but the BS19 is a much smaller ship than the *Sove*. I guess I've gotten used to the distances inside DV-Class vessels.

"Ready?" I ask.

He's breathing hard. He must have hurried from the airlock to here. We had chosen one of the airlocks at the back of the ship, so he did cross some distance. The scout ship is smaller than a DV-Class vessel, yes, but still a large enough ship to take some time to cross it.

"I used a bigger probe than you asked for," he says. "I wanted to make sure it had all of the functionality we were looking for."

"That's fine." I wasn't wedded to the probe's size. I just didn't want to use a huge probe, because those often look like mines or small bombs, but a medium-sized one will work just as well as a small one in this instance.

Mikk wipes a hand over his bald head, then takes one last deep breath as he settles in.

Everyone else is in place. We've spent the past twenty minutes double-checking the readings we're getting, making sure nothing is different.

And, except for the loss of that comet trail thingie, nothing is.

"All right," I say. "Here goes."

First, I open yet another screen before us, showing the visuals from the airlock side of the ship. The ship's side is a gleaming black, and the exit in front of that airlock looks like a simple line on the ship's side. The visual we're getting comes from a composite of three cameras, each placed equidistant from the exit. All of the exits on this ship have at least three cameras focused on them.

They also have two cameras above and below the exit. I have programmed those cameras to engage when the exit door opens.

I glance at the team. Nyssa and Tamaz are watching me. Roderick studies his own holographic console as does Mikk. They almost look like brothers as they work right now.

Fahd has folded his hands together as he watches the screen I just raised. Denby is turned slightly, so that he can see the new screen, me, and the screens behind us. Orlando has moved beside me and is watching me work, which I don't mind at all. He's a silent backup, one I don't really need but am glad is there.

Once the screen is in place, and I'm certain all of the cameras are working, I slide open the exit door.

For a minute, nothing happens. And then the probe—shaped like a giant pear covered with silver dots—tumbles out.

It spins as it falls away from the BS19, and as it falls, it does look like a bit of space debris, something that just randomly fell off the side of this vessel.

Our designated two minutes last forever. I keep checking the clock I have running on my control panel, stunned at how five seconds can feel like fifty.

Finally, it's time to engage the probe, which Mikk does with the flick of a wrist.

The probe ceases tumbling. It rights itself, the wide roundness facing away from the BS19 and the pointed top facing toward us. Then it rotates so that its designated front moves away from BS19 and toward that starfield.

"We're getting telemetry," Roderick says.

Fahd stops watching the screen and looks at his own control panel. Orlando calls up a screen for himself.

Nyssa continues to stare at the screen in front of us, which still shows the images from the cameras attached to this ship.

The probe is moving with purpose now, heading toward the starfield at a good clip. I don't call up the visuals the probe is sending back, because I would rather watch the probe itself. I can analyze the data it is sending after its little trip is done.

It zigs once, veering quickly left and down.

"I didn't program that," Mikk says, even though he doesn't have to. The fact that he didn't program that little maneuver is obvious. But he seems nervous about it.

I'm not. These battle scout probes are designed to avoid any problems that they detect. The non-Fleet probes that we're going to use from my *Nobody's Business* era won't veer off their programmed course, even if it takes them into some kind of debris.

The BS19 probe circles wide, then zooms upward again, getting back on the mapped route. It zips along as if it has an intelligence behind it that is eager to get to its destination.

Its destination is the edge of the starfield-barrier. I don't want that probe to go inside of the starfield-barrier, just in case the Fleet does actively use the area. Someone or some ship would recognize that probe for what it is.

I squeeze my left hand into a fist, then make myself loosen the grip one finger at a time. The involuntary gesture irritates me. It means I'm more nervous than I thought I was.

Roderick makes a small sound. I glance at him. He's watching the data that the probe is transmitting back to us. He doesn't even seem to realize that I've looked at him.

He's frowning, hard. I don't ask him what he sees, because we'll have plenty of time to assess all of this later.

It doesn't surprise me—or rather, it shouldn't surprise me—that he's seeing something right now. The information from that zig should have just returned to us.

Mikk has his hands clasped behind his back. He's watching the probe maneuver forward as if it's his own child.

As the probe gets closer to that opening in the starfield-barrier, Tamaz bends over his flat holographic screen as well. He's monitoring the information, just like Roderick is.

I smile. It feels good to have the old team together. I hadn't realized how much I missed them.

Nyssa glances over at me. She's biting her lower lip. Then she turns back to the main screen, the one that Mikk and I are watching. Denby keeps swiveling his head between that screen, his own holographic screen, and the Ball of Knowledge.

My heart rate has increased. I don't know what I'm expecting, but I'm expecting something. And then I make myself breathe out, trying to calm myself. Because expecting something is the same as making assumptions. Sometimes, someone who expects something will create drama where there is none.

The probe heads at a downward angle from our ship. I glance at my own screen. The probe has nearly reached that area where our projections placed the ragged edge.

If I were a bit more ambitious than I am, I would match the probe's path to the images we have of that comet trail thingie. But I don't. I do make a small note to check the readings that come back from this area.

The tension on the bridge has increased. I can hear it in sharp intakes of breath, see it in the way that everyone focuses just a bit more on what, exactly, they're doing.

Orlando takes one step forward so that he's beside me. He doesn't say anything when he gets nervous. He goes deeper into himself. And he's doing that here.

The probe finally reaches that ragged edge, then disappears off our screens. We have no way to see inside that edge—not yet anyway—and so I expected to lose the probe as it went behind the barrier, but I still find it a bit disconcerting as the probe vanishes.

Roderick mutters something, which sounds vaguely like "What the…"

I'm about to ask him what he sees when the probe spirals out of that opening, and back into the seemingly empty area of space where it had been a moment ago. The probe is whirling top over bottom, out of control, but heading back in our direction with some speed.

"What's going on?" I ask Roderick, since he's the only one monitoring the telemetry as far as I can tell.

"I don't know, exactly," he says, "but it reacted like it hit something."

"Hit something?" Orlando asks, turning slightly. "As in a ship?"

"As in a barrier," Roderick says.

Mikk is bent over his screen as well, fingers dancing across the holographic surface. Denby has turned around completely. He's looking at the screens behind us.

The probe is still spinning. It can't seem to right itself. I can't even tell if it's trying to do so.

"Whatever it hit damaged it," Nyssa says.

"No," Roderick says. "Whatever it hit shut it off."

"We're not getting any more telemetry?" I ask.

"No," Roderick says.

"I can't reboot it," Mikk says. "It's as if I can't even communicate with it."

The probe spirals away from our ship, off the initial course we had set. Soon it will reach part of the necklace of ships. Maybe it will get through them or maybe not. It might actually hit one of them. I'm not sure what'll happen then.

"Is it too far away for us to try to snare it?" I ask. The BS19 has a minimal tractor function, but I don't like it. It's a broad function, using some kind of combination of magnetic energy and something particular to the Fleet, something I've never really learned well.

What I do know about that function is that it can scoop up more than the thing it's aimed at.

I almost regret asking the question in the first place.

"I don't know." Tamaz is the one who answered me.

Mikk is still trying to contact the probe, so that he can reboot its tiny engine.

"It's risky," Orlando says to me about snaring the probe.

I nod. I'm about to belay that order when the probe spins into the necklace of ships below us. It slams into the side of a DV-Class vessel, which changes the probe's trajectory. It spirals beneath the vessel, and out of our visual range.

Fahd changes some of the scans we're running off BS19, so we can barely see the probe, spinning away from us in two directions—it's behind us now, and going lower (or maybe I should call that deeper) into the Boneyard.

"Let it go," I say, even though saying that isn't necessary—at least for the snare.

Mikk still huddles over his screen though, fingers moving. He's still trying to reboot the probe.

"Mikk," I say. "Let it go."

"It'll have information in its buffers," he says. "Things it didn't manage to send to us."

"Yeah," I say. "I know. But we'll be sending more probes soon."

Or not, depending on what we see from the information we got off this probe.

"It shouldn't have shut down," Mikk says. "It's not built to shut off like that. As long as I could get a signal to it, I should have been able to access any of its systems."

I know that and so does everyone else on the bridge. Mikk is speaking out of frustration, yes, but also out of concern. As long as we are close to that probe, even if we can't see it, we should be able to control it.

And we can't.

I look up at the visuals in front of me. The starfield-barrier looks no different than it had an hour ago. But the way I feel about it is different.

I hadn't expected it to repel a probe like that. Nor had I expected the starfield-barrier to be able to shut the probe down.

Sending probes usually gives us more answers than questions.

Not this time.

Or rather, not yet.

THE FLEET
TEN MONTHS AGO

6

IRENA GOT TO HER OFFICE SUITE an hour later than planned. She felt frazzled and tired, and for her, the workday hadn't really started yet. She had to take Klara to her music class, because Klara wouldn't go willingly with the friends she'd been so excited to see when they initially arrived at the Mbuyi family quarters.

When Klara realized her friends were going to take her from her Mami, she started screaming, launching into yet another full-fledged temper tantrum. Rather than try to placate her or have someone else deal with the drama, Irena had taken her to class herself.

The teacher had taken one look at Klara's chubby, tear-lined face, and immediately distracted her so that Irena could escape. Early on in her motherhood, Irena felt guilty about such tactics, but after nine children, guilt had become a luxury.

She had hurried home, changed clothes again (because hers were tear-stained and, as she discovered after removing them, lunch-stained), and contacted Noemi about their youngest, since Irena hadn't heard anything.

Apparently, she hadn't heard because Noemi had decided to wait until she had news before contacting Irena. The doctors wanted to do two more sets of tests which would take the rest of the afternoon. Noemi had already arranged for childcare from mid-afternoon onward, so

Irena was covered (and was grateful), but childcare didn't ameliorate the actual worry she felt about Joel.

Even with his various illnesses, Joel was a cheerful child, the opposite, in many ways, of Klara, and his little smiles in the face of adversity had captured Irena's heart. She didn't want to think about what he was going through this afternoon, even though her mind kept wandering back to it.

The superstitious part of her, a part that had not existed before she had become a parent, worried that Klara's tantrums and tears were in anticipation of a crisis to come, as if Irena's temperamental daughter was somehow psychic.

Irena believed that was all nonsense, but the depth of Klara's discomfort had left Irena unsettled.

That, and the brand-new but ancient Scrapheap that Irena's assistants had brought to her.

Throughout lunch and as she had little breaks in the Klara drama, Irena's mind kept returning to that Scrapheap. Several things bothered her about it.

The first thing was the biggest: the Fleet had somehow lost track of the Scrapheaps. Irena knew the history. The Fleet had lost track of Scrapheaps from several millennia ago. Thousands of years ago, when one finally contacted the Fleet about—ironically—theft, the Fleet had sent a ship back to investigate that Scrapheap.

The mission had been a disaster, leading to court martials and disgrace for families that had lasted generations. But the one thing that had come out of the mission was the idea that Scrapheaps, particularly ancient ones, might not be necessary.

That nugget—that idea—was the beginning of Irena's division. There had always been a division for ancient and abandoned ships—and that division had developed the Scrapheaps in the first place. At least, that was what the historians hypothesized. Because there was no real record of those early centuries of the Fleet. Just some information cobbled together by historians, usually because some admiral needed the information to do her job.

Irena half smiled as she had that thought. Now she was that admiral, and she needed information to do her job. She had assigned her assistants to find out some of it, but some of it she wanted to review herself.

She finally made it to her office suite about a half hour later than she had planned. She had already contacted Gundersen and Reyes, and put off the afternoon meeting by another hour. That would give Irena enough time to check certain facts.

Her office suite took up an entire deck of the *Kutelekezwa*. Almost everyone who served on the *Kutelekezwa* worked in her division in one way or another, except those who actually maintained the ship. But the people who worked in this office suite were the ones who were actually tasked with the decision-making. They knew almost as much about the things the division did as she did.

Unlike many vice-admirals who ended up heading entire divisions of the Fleet, Irena had worked in this division from the start of her career. She had started on Foldspace Search Vessels and moved up the chain of command, even designing and building a Scrapheap as the Fleet moved into a new sector.

She liked to think that her Scrapheap was organized well, that the ships stored there were not only safe, but tamper-proof. She had them stored in their own bubbles, with ship numbers and names kept in files pertaining to the Scrapheap, and each ship in good enough shape that it would be automatically activated and returned to the Fleet at any point.

She had made harsher decisions than her predecessors. Most of the vessels in the Scrapheap she had set up were in good condition, needing little maintenance. Those vessels were simply retired and outdated, but their tech was still good—at least by modern standards.

They weren't Ready Vessels, though, set up to go to war. They were just old ships that the Fleet couldn't bring itself to destroy.

At some point, the *Kutelekezwa* would join one of the Scrapheaps. She thought it ironic that her division was located in one of the older Administration Vessels in the Fleet. The ship had been designed long before she was born. Its tech was as up-to-date as it could be, but the

Admiralty had decided, in its wisdom, that Irena's division didn't need the latest, greatest technology or ship design.

Anything looking backwards in the Fleet—or sideways, as she told her staff—was relegated to the lower levels of power within the Fleet itself. That was one reason why it was taking so long to make complete decisions about Scrapheaps. Farther up the chain of command, no one really cared what happened to older, decommissioned ships, unless something called attention to them.

A theft of this nature in a Scrapheap of this nature—by someone with old codes and a working knowledge of *anacapa* drives—might be just the thing to call attention to Scrapheaps.

And maybe more issues. As far as Irena knew, there had never been a Scrapheap break-in by an organization with knowledge of *anacapa* drives and old codes. She would have to check that, of course. She didn't know the entire history of Scrapheaps.

But she had a good working knowledge, probably better than anyone else, and she couldn't recall anything like this ever.

She had her focus entirely back on her job by the time she got to her deck, although she did a quick double-check of her appearance as she stepped off the elevator. She had simply exchanged one pair of black pants for another, and wore a gray shirt instead of white, because she might have to hurry to her quarters when Noemi and Joel got home.

Irena wore the same black jacket with red piping that she had placed on her counter when Klara started her serial tantrums. The jacket was the only thing that hadn't gotten stained during the crisis.

Irena straightened her back as she walked into the open area of the office suite. She had redesigned the entire thing when she took command. The previous vice admiral had gone for small areas with desks, like a series of captain's ready rooms.

Irena believed that design isolated the staff and made them less productive. She set up work areas and sitting areas out in the open, along with conference rooms, research suites, and one gigantic map area in the very back that—as best as she could recreate it—showed all of the sectors the Fleet had ever traveled through.

The early sectors were woefully incomplete. In fact, the beginning of the map was deliberately fuzzed, because no one knew the origins of the Fleet. There was a history of the Fleet, but it wasn't official. The origins changed depending on how they were told, and where they were told.

Sometimes, Irena liked to think, that the Fleet was forever—that it had no beginning and it would have no end.

The middle sectors on her gigantic holographic map seemed finished enough, but of course, the only ones that were completely up-to-date were the ones she designed, starting as a cadet.

She kept the map up always, and had it fill the back of the room. The imagery was small, since it covered such a vast distance. The map was darker than she usually made her holograms, because it didn't show the back wall at all.

Instead, space itself seemed solid, black and gray and bluish near some sectors, filled with whitish swatches in other places, winking stars, and points of lights that varied from actual white to a deep and majestic maroon.

Sometimes she stopped in front of the map and stared at it, marveling at the distances the Fleet had traveled in its lifetime. Sometimes, she stood in front of the map and stared at it, marveling at not just the vastness of space, but at the variation within it. No section was the same as any other, although some of them had similar features.

And some sectors, she knew, had elements no one understood. Or rather, no one in the Fleet understood. When Fleet members wanted to do a lot of research into an anomaly, they were allowed to. But if their research was not completed when the Fleet was leaving the sector, then they had to make a choice—remain with the Fleet or do the research.

Many people left the Fleet at that point, and, as far as she knew, never reported their findings to the Fleet.

It was one of the aspects of the Fleet that she found annoying: the lost information or, rather, the disinterest in places and things of the past. Very few people here seemed to realize that some things within the universe repeated, and understanding something they found in the past might actually help in the future.

But she knew how all this information could get lost. She had an example of it in a secondary map room. That room also had a large hologram, using the Fleet's official maps. But, for example, those official maps didn't have the location of every known Scrapheap. The official maps also removed decommissioned starbases and smaller Fleet outposts in the interest of reducing the size of the map.

Old information was never restored to the official map. The only information added to an official map was the current information, the kind that was just being discovered.

She let that map update itself, knowing that it would both delete and add as the Fleet deleted and added.

As she strode into the office suite now, nodding at her staff, scattered along the various pieces of furniture or standing to one side, working on a holographic screen in front of them, she headed directly for her large map.

It glimmered and glowed against the wall, looking—as it always did to her—like a living thing with its own mind and will. The universe remained mysterious, its origins as murky as the Fleet's, but its beauty caught her every single time she looked at it.

Or, rather, looked at this sliver of it. Vast, and only partially knowable. Not even the Fleet, which had (as far as she and the Fleet itself knew) seen more of the universe than any other organization still in existence, had only experienced a small fraction of it.

She rather liked that there were still mysteries in the universe, that there would always be, at least in her lifetime, mysteries in the universe. It reminded her that she was not all-powerful, nor was the Fleet.

No one was. And no one knew everything.

Which she was being forcibly reminded of today.

For a moment, she toyed with blocking off the map so that her staff couldn't see what she was researching. Then she realized that raising the opaque wall that separated this map area from the rest of the room would draw attention to her work, unlike standing quietly in front of it.

During her workday, she often stood in front of the map, gaining inspiration from it. No one would think twice about what she was doing right now.

She had no idea why she felt the urge to keep this Scrapheap and its problems secret from most of her staff. Maybe because she wanted to be alone with the news or maybe, as she had thought earlier, once this became known, everything would change.

She wasn't sure she was ready for that kind of change.

Nor was she ready for all of the questions that would come her way once she told her team what her assistants had discovered. She needed time alone with the information, the opportunity to think about it, and a sense of just how far away this incursion was.

She opened the simple control panel on a holographic screen before her. The simple control panel only allowed her to view parts of the map, not change any of it.

She made two requests of the system. She wanted distance calculations as she worked, and she wanted historical time calculations. She wanted to know how long it had been since the Fleet worked the sectors of space she was now viewing.

She wouldn't be able to get the full answer to the time question because the map and its simple functions didn't have all of that information. She should only be able to discover when the Fleet left the area and, perhaps, when it established the Scrapheap.

Other pieces of information, such as the last time the Fleet had sent a ship into the Scrapheap, or if the Fleet had returned to the sector to deal with a crisis, would be stored in a different system—if the Fleet had that information at all.

The Scrapheap itself would have the information as to the last time the Fleet placed a ship inside it, but she doubted her staff could access that information from this distance. Reyes had said that it had taken months for the Scrapheap to send information on the thefts to the Fleet.

Irena knew based on past experience that the only way to interact with a lost Scrapheap, at least initially, was to use the channel that the Scrapheap had used. Which meant that it would be difficult, if not impossible, to find out when the Scrapheap had last been touched by the Fleet.

She let part of the map work on the information she had requested. Now, she wanted to see how that Scrapheap had been rendered on this map.

She tapped the screen before her, and entered the coordinates that her assistants had given her for the Scrapheap. The map roused itself, a movement like a wave, flowing through the entire holographic image.

She loved that movement. Every time she urged the gigantic map to make that movement, she smiled. The request would ripple its way through the map, making the map seem like some kind of living creature, with some kind of mind of its own.

The ripple worked its way through the map, and it slowly reoriented itself. She watched, hands clasped together, as the map moved swiftly, twisting the images she saw from the sector the Fleet was in now to a sector so old that it was no longer discussed as part of Fleet history. No one alive had memory of anyone who had visited or served in that sector. She doubted any Fleet family even had stories about ancient family members who had lived in that sector.

If she were quizzed, she wouldn't be able to name anyone who had served in the Fleet during that time nor would she know exactly what kind of ship design was dominant when the Fleet roamed that part of space.

The map kept turning, and moving, taking longer than she had ever seen it do before.

This, apparently, was the farthest location she had ever asked the map to show her.

The map shuffled and rolled, like gelatin in a closed glass circle: solar systems, asteroid belts, stars, all shifting by her so quickly that she couldn't quite absorb where and what they were.

Finally, the map settled on the coordinates she had entered.

What faced her was blackness. Not a black emptiness of a lack of information. She had seen that on the map before (and probably some of it had rolled by her in that rapid transition), and that blackness looked like holes in a blanket. Usually, when the hologram didn't have the necessary information, it left that section blank.

She had designed it that way, so that she knew where the gaps in the Fleet's knowledge were. In the Fleet's official map, the program rendered what it thought would or should be in the missing area. So the representation was often false or based on faulty information.

Here, the information was there—planets existed on the edges of the blackness—but there was nothing before her.

She wasn't surprised. She had seen that kind of blackness before. It was a shielding design used by the Fleet in one of its paranoid periods. The Fleet would either create an emptiness in the star maps or it would create a fake star map.

The emptiness existed in maps used by standard Fleet tech as well as most other known tech that scanned the area.

The shield prevented anyone from inadvertently going to or near a Scrapheap. The old thinking was that a black emptiness in a star map would seem threatening.

Over the centuries, the Fleet learned that the opposite was true: a black emptiness in a star map inspired others (not just the Fleet) to go directly to that emptiness to see what was there.

The Fleet had stopped using the masking tech as a shield a long time ago. Irena couldn't remember the timeline exactly, but she knew that the Fleet had stopped using the masking tech by the time Sector Base G-2 had opened.

She entered her own access code and made the map reconfigure, so that it showed all of the high-security areas. In the past, she had learned that was the only way to get through that black emptiness.

The map reconfigured. It didn't ripple this time. It simply winked out for a half second and then reappeared.

And this time, right before her, was the outline of a vast Scrapheap, one of the largest she had ever seen. It spanned the entire distance of the black emptiness, which she had not expected. When she had seen the black emptiness in the past, it had expanded to include the area around whatever the Fleet had been hiding.

This time, the black emptiness had not expanded into the area. The black emptiness only covered the outline of the existing Scrapheap.

Or, at least, the Scrapheap as it had existed when the information that the map relied upon had been entered into the Fleet's systems.

And she was not certain how long ago that was.

She was a bit surprised that the Scrapheap even showed up, given that the Fleet had lost it.

Irena pivoted and looked behind her. Just as she suspected, no one seemed to notice what she was doing. She was feeling vaguely unsettled, and no one seemed to notice that either.

Standing here, looking at the map before her—the map she had designed—she realized she had never asked how the Scrapheaps she had been working with had been located. Had someone done a simple search in the Fleet's database or on the official map, looking for Scrapheaps? If that someone (or the someones) had used a simple search in the official map, the search would have left out this Scrapheap, because the black emptiness would have shielded the Scrapheap's existence even from a Fleet researcher.

It would have taken someone of Irena's status to locate this Scrapheap.

That realization rocked her back on her heels. If her assumption was correct, then the Fleet had lost an entire group of Scrapheaps, all of which had been protected by unusual (and outdated) shielding tech.

She let out a small, almost inaudible sigh, then turned back toward the map. The newly discovered Scrapheap spread before her like a stain.

She tapped the holoscreen before her, entering in a command to bring up all nearby Scrapheaps, including those the Fleet had either destroyed or decommissioned.

The map faded for a moment, then flared, before it settled. Two other Scrapheaps appeared. One was closer to what had been Sector Base U, and another was between Sector Bases Y and Z. Those Scrapheaps had all been decommissioned long ago, the ships mined for parts before the rest of the Scrapheap had been destroyed.

Technically, there should have been no Scrapheaps in that region of space at all. Not any longer.

She started to search for shielded Scrapheaps, then stopped herself. Right now, she had three tasks: she had to continue her usual work; she had to deal with this new discovery; and she had to monitor her youngest child.

She glanced at the time, in the upper left-hand corner of the holo-screen. No word from Noemi yet. And maybe there wouldn't be until this evening.

Irena kept hoping that the silence meant solutions. Part of her wished she had gone along on the appointments, and the rest of her knew that she would be just as nervous waiting for news there.

She took another deep breath, and studied the newly discovered Scrapheap. It wasn't in between the two other Scrapheaps. It was along the trajectory the Fleet *should have* followed, but didn't.

Which raised her suspicions. But something else did as well: that shielding tech.

If her assumptions were correct, and the Fleet had lost track of Scrapheaps using the masking tech, then the other two Scrapheaps in that region of space hadn't had the same kind of shielding.

But this newly discovered Scrapheap had. The Fleet might lose track of its history but, in real time, the Fleet rarely made arbitrary decisions. If the Fleet had decided that this Scrapheap needed extra shielding, they had a solid reason to make that decision.

Standing here, using this rudimentary system, she didn't have access to more secure information. But she would guess, based on the shielding alone, that this Scrapheap had Ready Vessels.

But most of the Scrapheaps, if not all, from that period contained Ready Vessels. So there had to be more to this Scrapheap than she could surmise with what she knew.

She made a mental note to have her researchers start looking for Scrapheaps with this kind of shielding. She knew she would be doubling her staff's workload, but the search needed to be done, if she was going to fulfill her unit's mission.

She tapped the screen in front of her again, returning it to the normal settings. The map rippled, as if it were waving at her, before it jauntily executed her command.

Normally, she would have smiled at it, but she didn't feel like smiling right now.

Instead, she needed to go into one of the research rooms and see what she could discover before her meeting. If she was lucky, she would learn the history of that Scrapheap.

But she'd never been that kind of lucky in the past, and she doubted it would start now.

The map settled, showing her exactly where the Fleet was in real time. No nearby Scrapheaps (of course), just the familiar star map of this sector, with some vague outlines of the sectors beyond.

She shut down the holographic commands, and turned once again. No one on her staff was studying her. No one was frowning this way. For her, so much had changed, and they simply continued doing their jobs, as if nothing was different.

She let out one last sigh. She would end up making a lot of decisions this week, here about the Scrapheap, and in her personal life, about Joel.

And at this moment, she had no idea what those decisions would be, which added to that unsettled feeling.

But something about this Scrapheap, about the notification, and the existence of the Scrapheap itself, made the feeling worse. The discovery of the Scrapheap felt monumental—even though, at the moment, she had no idea why.

THE BONEYARD

NOW

7

WE MEET IN THE CONFERENCE AREA just off the bridge. The conference area on a BSS-Class ship is tiny, more like a captain's ready room than the kind of conference area found on a DV-Class vessel.

But the conference area on all of the scout ships made in this era by the Fleet have triple encryption protocols, so any data we display here is as protected as it can be. No one can hack into our systems while we're sharing this information. No one else—not even anyone on the BS19—can see exactly what we're doing in this room.

Unless we leave the walls around the conference area clear.

If we do that, we can see into the bridge, and they can see us as well.

But I really want someone to monitor what's going on in and around BS19. I need my bridge crew, however tiny, to pay attention to the ship and the surrounding area, rather than help us plan the next step.

The two team members who have the least to contribute to this discussion are Nyssa and Denby. I need everyone else. I sent them all to research the information we received from the probe before it stopped communicating with us. I gave the team two hours to see what they could find.

I nod at Nyssa and Denby as I pass through the bridge to the conference area. They're both standing as they monitor various screens. It doesn't even look like Denby has moved since I left. He's still watching screens in the back of the bridge as well as the ones I'd left running up front.

The Ball of Knowledge floats in the back of the bridge, looking no different than it had earlier. There's no new data to add onto the ball—not yet, anyway.

When I arrive at the small conference room, I find Mikk already inside. He has the walls on clear, but he has called up the table and enough chairs for the entire team. However, he's not sitting in any of the chairs. He's pacing back and forth as if this little adventure with the probe bothers him more than most things we've done.

I opaque the walls as I close the door.

"I'm not going to bring in the whole team," I say.

He stops, and frowns at me. That's not how I did things in the old days. In the old days, we would have all gathered on the bridge or in the cockpit or in some central area, and then we would have discussed as a group what was going on.

I guess, no matter how much this trip feels like an old pre-Fleet dive trip, it really isn't.

It takes him a moment to process what I said, which tells me just how preoccupied he is. Then he says, "Okay," without inflection, as if keeping a few team members in the dark doesn't bother him at all.

He puts his hands on the back of one of the chairs, and looks down, as if he's trying to steady himself. If he thought that I was making a bad decision by leaving out Nyssa and Denby, he would have said so.

"What's on your mind?" I ask him.

He's more likely to tell me before the others get here. Otherwise, he might keep the information to himself, particularly if it isn't pertinent to the mission.

"The probe has been reprogrammed," he says.

So he got through. Finally. I feel a thread of relief. It worried me more than I thought that we had lost control of that probe.

He's frowning at me, and that's when I realize that getting through upset him. Maybe he found something that we hadn't anticipated.

"Great," I say. "When will it come back here?"

"It won't." His voice is flat. If anything, his frown has grown deeper.

"Mikk, we're better off with the data—"

"I didn't reprogram it, Boss," he says.

That catches me. I swallow the admonition I was about to give him, overexplaining as I'm sometimes wont to do.

I blink hard, trying to figure out exactly what he's telling me.

"You didn't," I repeat.

"Yeah." He stares at me.

"Then who did?" I ask.

He shakes his head once. "I have a theory—"

The door opens and Roderick enters. He's carrying an old tablet, one of the ones I brought from *The Business*.

Both Mikk and I look at him guiltily.

"Am I interrupting?" Roderick asks.

I shake my head.

"Tamaz is right behind me," Roderick says. "If we need to—"

"It's fine," I say, even though it's not. Not entirely. I turn my attention back to Mikk. "What's your theory?"

He shakes his head slightly. "Let's just wait for everyone."

I frown, wondering if I should pull Mikk aside, just as Tamaz enters. He is also carrying one of the old tablets.

He holds the door, and Orlando enters, followed closely by Fahd. Fahd looks at the opaqued walls, then at me, as if questioning that decision.

I no longer am. If someone other than Mikk reprogrammed that probe, then we might be in trouble.

I had thought we were alone in the Boneyard. I am now worried that we are not.

"Give me one second," I say. I slip through the door, back onto the bridge, surprising both Nyssa and Denby.

They turn toward me. Nyssa puts her hand on the floating console in front of her, as if she's going to bring it with her.

"I still want you two to stay here for the moment," I say. "We'll catch you up after the meeting. Something's changed, and we don't know what it is yet. I need you to monitor everything closely. If something goes wrong or it looks like we're under threat, warn the *Sove*, and then get us back there as fast as you can."

"You think someone might come after us?" Nyssa asks.

"It's a possibility," I say. "More so now than it was a few hours ago."

"Is someone behind that starfield?" Denby asks.

"We don't know yet," I say. "Let me gather the information and then I'll make sure you're briefed. Right now, though, I need your full attention on keeping us safe. Can you do that?"

I have no idea what I'll do if they tell me that they can't.

Denby glances at Nyssa, as if seeing how she's going to respond. She doesn't give him a second glance. She nods.

I would have thought she would defer to him. But I keep forgetting how strong she can be, especially when she knows she's the only one we're relying on.

"We'll do the very best we can," Nyssa says.

Denby lets out a small breath, as if he's going to add something, but I don't let him. I return to the conference room, pulling the door closed behind me.

I have to trust the two of them, and I do. They'll be hypervigilant now, and if they need to, they'll get us out of here quickly.

No one is sitting down in the conference area, probably because Mikk hasn't sat down. He's still holding the back of that chair.

"Either we need the chairs or we don't," I say. Fahd smiles nervously at me, as if I've said exactly what was on his mind.

Tamaz and Roderick sit down, as if they're relieved by my curtness. Orlando hesitates, glances at Mikk, then at me, and finally sits. I sit too, followed by Fahd.

Mikk still doesn't sit down. He probably won't, until we get past his news.

"Catch them up," I say to Mikk.

He does. He tells the rest of the team exactly what he told me, without adding anything new. He carefully expresses only the facts.

"Mikk was just about to tell me his theory when the rest of you arrived," I say. "So, Mikk...?"

His lips thin. His fingers tighten on the back of that chair, and for a half second, I feel as if he's going to push it away from himself. Instead, he pulls it out and sits down heavily, almost as if his legs can no longer support him.

"My theory is this," he says, "and realize that at the moment, it's just a theory, based on bits and pieces of information."

He's trying to avoid making an assumption, which he knows I hate.

"I think that probe hit some kind of energy barrier. It not only shut down the probe, but it injected something into the probe. When the probe finally rebooted, it had a completely different operating system with different orders."

"You're basing that on what, exactly?" Orlando asks. There's no challenge in his tone. He's clearly curious.

"The probe's current trajectory." Mikk taps the tabletop, and two screens rise up. One floats in front of Mikk's side of the table, the other floats up in front of Orlando and Fahd, who sit at the other end.

The screen, which is in two dimensions, shows as much of the Boneyard as we've already mapped. A red line that ends in a pulsing red dot moves beneath our position, heading what I would call—looking at that map—straight down.

"The red dot is the probe," Mikk says. "It started on this trajectory when it finally rebooted. It also sped up. It's still speeding up, in fact. If it stays on the current course, it will reach the end of the Boneyard in a little over two hours."

A pinkish line appears ahead of the red dot, like a ghost line. Mikk is using that to make the path very clear.

"What happens when it reaches the end of the Boneyard?" Tamaz asks. "It can't go through the forcefield."

"I suspect it can," Mikk says. "If it has the right codes—and I'll wager it does now—a small opening will appear in that forcefield, and the probe will go right through it."

"To where?" Roderick asks.

I'm not asking a single question. Because Mikk is just guessing, and the farther out he gets, the more he's speculating.

"I don't know," Mikk says. "But the probe is going really fast. We'll have an answer shortly."

It would take the *Sove* days to get out of the Boneyard. Of course, the *Sove* is huge, and the probe is very small, and it doesn't have to negotiate its way around much larger ships.

"How could they reprogram something that quickly?" Fahd asks.

"Fleet technology," Mikk says. "I'm guessing that whatever the probe hit could manipulate its systems because that something was *designed* to manipulate the systems."

"Well, we can test that," I say.

Mikk is nodding, and so is Orlando. We have non-Fleet technology with us. Even if the Fleet engineers were good enough to reprogram Fleet tech on the fly, no one can plan for all kinds of tech they would encounter.

"We have to change our plans, though, with the probes." I fold my hands in front of me. "I'm not willing to do that yet. Let's see what kind of information the probe sent us before it got damaged."

I use the word "damaged" on purpose. Whatever happened to that probe changed it—damaged it.

I shift in my seat so that I face Fahd. He's watching Mikk, mouth in a thin line, as if Fahd's trying to figure out what Mikk is thinking.

"Let's layer the information," I say. "Fahd, we'll start with your timeline as a base."

He glances at me nervously, as if he doesn't quite trust what he has. Then he taps on the tabletop, opening a large holographic screen.

"I was planning to do this in three parts," he said. "The overall file which shows everything, including the timing, and the timing itself, and then only the big events."

I have startled him, then.

"Let's use the overall file as our base," I say. "Unless there's something we need to see in the other files…?"

"Um—ah." He shakes his head. "I'd rather hear what the others say before I comment."

Well, that's odd and a bit mysterious, but I don't comment on it. Fahd might simply be overly careful.

His screen widens.

"Two dimensions, right?" he asks.

"For the moment," I say.

He sends the information to his screen, which shows the probe in white against the darkness of that empty space between us and the starfield-barrier. Each little movement has a time stamp. So in addition to the probe's movement, time stamps appear.

Nothing looks different than what we already saw earlier.

"Anyone examine the energy readings?" Mikk asks.

"I did," Fahd says. "Boss wanted to know about that comet trail area, and I figured I'd look at energy to see it."

Roderick leans back in his chair. His gaze meets mine, and I understand what he's thinking. They had also examined the energy.

"What did you find?" I ask Fahd.

"Nothing," Fahd says. "I marked where that comet trail thing was in our previous scans, and there's no change in the readings from the probe around there. The energy levels seem consistent."

I like that he uses the word *seem*. Because I suspect that's really what we're getting from the probe. Information that *seems* correct, but isn't.

"They aren't consistent, though," Roderick says.

He waves the tablet he brought with him, then looks at me.

"May I?" he asks.

He's interrupting Fahd's presentation, such as it is, but that doesn't matter—not if we're doing things the old way.

"Yeah," I say, and that single word comes out a bit more curtly than I wanted it to. "Go ahead."

Roderick sets the tablet on his lap, apparently unwilling to put it on the table—which is, after all, a source of Fleet tech.

He taps the tabletop and produces his own screen, sending it next to Fahd's. Positioning it the way that he does makes it seem like the information flows from one screen to the other.

The images look the same, except for the time stamps, which glow faintly across the screen.

Fahd leans forward, his lips pursed. "I thought you said the energy levels aren't consistent."

Roderick lifts the tablet again, manipulating its screen with his fingertips. A hologram appears over the tablet. He glances at me apologetically.

I had forgotten that the tablets made it hard to display something in two dimensions. Unless that display was filtered through other tech, which is not something we're about to do at the moment.

"We labeled each kind of energy we could identify with a different color," Roderick says.

The small three-dimensional image shifts as he adds the colors. There are so many that my eye can't track them at first. Then I see the pattern.

There's placid greens near us and the other stationary ships. There's a whitish energy pattern near the starfield-barrier.

In between, however, the image is nearly black with all of the colors overlaid on each other.

Except in one place.

Midway across, a ball glows white and orange, almost like a flame encased in a lighting unit.

"What the hell's that?" Mikk asks.

But I can see it with the time stamp ever so faintly, and the trajectory of the probe filtering through from Fahd's screen.

"That's where the probe zigged, isn't it?" I ask.

"Yeah," Roderick says.

"I understand that," Mikk says with irritation. "But what is it?"

I resist the urge to open my own screen on the tabletop to run the telemetry I have. I want to hear what my team says first.

"I think it's some kind of weapon," Roderick says.

Tamaz nods slowly.

"A mine?" Fahd asks.

"Maybe," Roderick says. "We have the energy readings, which are intense and different, and something we don't entirely understand."

"But they're clearly Fleet readings," Tamaz says.

"Meaning what?" Mikk asks.

"Meaning that the energy signatures have a familiar component," Tamaz says. "Something we've only seen in Fleet tech."

I want to look at this myself. None of us are the kinds of experts that we need to examine Fleet tech.

I rest my hands on my thighs, so that I'm not tempted to open any screens before me. I could get lost in all of this data very quickly.

"Are you telling me," I say slowly, "that the probe we sent—the Fleet-made probe—recognized whatever that was, and zig-zagged around it."

"Yes," Roderick says.

Mikk stands up, as if that news is too much for him.

"Then why doesn't it show up on any readings?" he asks. "It should be in the probe's data."

"Fascinating, isn't it?" Tamaz says calmly.

Mikk walks over to the screen showing the probe itself. It has moved even faster than I thought it would. It is close to that forcefield at the edge of the Boneyard.

I half expect Mikk to ask if they have some kind of theory, but he doesn't. He stares at the probe as if it's some kind of enemy of ours.

It bothers him deeply.

"Did you figure out why the probe zigged when the data it's sending back doesn't show that weapon at all?" I ask.

"We have three guesses," Roderick says. "The first is that the probe is built to recognize those weapons, and to avoid them."

That makes sense to me. Battlefield scout ships would recognize Fleet weaponry. Probes are usually designed to look for new information, to send back readings from an unfamiliar area. This probe might have the weaponry programmed into it.

"Our second guess," he continues, "is that this probe, maybe even this ship, has some kind of rudimentary map of this Boneyard programmed into it."

"Why would it?" Mikk snaps. He's still standing with his back to us. "None of the ships we've found here have a map."

"That we know of," I say. "We haven't specifically looked."

We've taken ships and the data from them. We looked at the histories of how they got into the Boneyard and generally did not find that. We have not looked to see what kinds of star maps exist in the ship's records.

Or at least, our dive teams that have been working the Boneyard haven't. I have no idea if the team back at Lost Souls has. I doubt it. Yash and Coop, who are the most likely two to dig through the star maps, are looking for evidence of the Fleet. They might try to find how and when the Boneyard was established, but not a map of its internal layout.

I shake my head slightly. I'm a bit stunned that I never thought to look closely for some internal map. I'm so used to diving things that have old, shutdown, and irrelevant systems, that I always assume the old systems either have no information at all or useless information.

I let out a small breath, then stand. Everyone looks at me.

"One second," I say.

I let myself out of the conference room. Nyssa raises her head, startled.

"We're not getting any unusual readings," she says. "Everything looks normal."

"Let's hope it stays that way," I say.

Denby nods once, curtly, as if I'm expressing something he's been thinking.

"Nyssa," I say, "while you're monitoring, can you search through the system archives here, and see if inside the star maps there is a map of the Boneyard?"

"What?" she asks, as if she doesn't understand the question.

"In the BS19?" Denby asks.

"Yes," I say. "This ship should have the same maps in its systems as the *Sove*."

"Does the *Sove* have one?" Nyssa asks.

I shake my head slightly, still a bit stunned at myself. "We haven't looked."

Denby opens his mouth as if he's going to say something, and then he half-smiles. None of us have looked, and that's on all of us. One of us should have come up with this by now.

"I can search," Nyssa says. "It shouldn't distract me from monitoring."

"You'd think that a map like that would change with each new ship," Denby says.

"If it even exists," I say. "After all, we found the *Sove* here. It might have maps of other Boneyards, but not this one."

The ship was in bad shape when we found it, just like the other ships we've found in this Boneyard. Usually something stored in a junkyard doesn't have the map of the junkyard.

At least in the universe I grew up in. But the Fleet has always had different operating systems from the kind I expect in ships. So it's worth a look.

"Thanks," I say to them, and return to the conference room.

Mikk is still standing by the screen showing the probe. The probe has slowed again, or maybe I just thought that it was moving a bit faster earlier when it really wasn't.

As I sit back down, I say to Roderick, "You were going to tell us the final of your three guesses about the probe."

He nods, then looks at Tamaz, who nods as well.

"The third one," Roderick says, "is the one we think is most likely. We're dealing with an informational disconnect here, and that's what has brought us so close to that thing which looks like a starfield."

I'm already ahead of what he's going to say, but I let him finish.

"We think that the scanning system is set up to provide a false image here to Fleet ships," he says, "even when other parts of the ship's systems can register what's really going on."

"Why would the Fleet deceive itself?" Fahd asks.

"They have a lot of need-to-know protocols," Tamaz says. "At least, that's what it seems like to me, when I've talked to folks who served on the *Ivoire*."

They do. I've noticed that in the past as well.

"It's the chain of command," I say. "If you don't have a high enough rank, you don't know things."

"Like where a mine is?" Mikk says. He turns slightly. "That doesn't make sense."

"It does if the ship or probe or whatever can recognize the mine and steer around it," Roderick says. "The Fleet doesn't want to blow up its own stuff."

Why they've done this doesn't really matter, at least not right now. How they've done it is much more relevant to us.

"Well, we do know, now," I say, "that the probe has information that's not showing up in the data stream that we got from it."

"At least, not showing up in a recognizable way," Roderick says.

And I didn't bring anyone with the kind of skill set to find that information on this little trip. I'm sure Diaz, back on the *Sove*, can figure this out.

The question is whether or not we go back now, or continue on the mission, sending a non-Fleet probe into that starfield.

I'm not even putting that part up for a vote. We're going to send the non-Fleet probe into the starfield. I want to see the readings it sends back. I also want to see if it can be reprogrammed.

"Boss," Mikk says.

I look over at him. His voice sounded strange, constricted almost.

"Look." He moves away from the screen he was monitoring. The probe has reached the forcefield and, as expected, a small opening has appeared in the field.

We all watch as the probe heads toward the opening. My heart is pounding hard, and I'm not sure why. The unusual maneuver? The fact that the probe is out of our control? Or the idea that it will leave the forcefield and enter a well-patrolled area of space.

A lot of ships travel around this Boneyard. And some of those ships have shady crews, as we learned when we discovered the Boneyard. Any one of those ships might pick up the probe.

They wouldn't find out much information about us, but they would be able to reverse engineer some of the Fleet's tech. I don't think that's any kind of threat, but it is something that seems odd, especially given the protections built into the Boneyard.

When we first discovered it, we saw it as a blankness on a star map. An empty area that was huge and impenetrable.

Which is—come to think of it—another sensor miscue.

That consistency makes me believe in Roderick's third guess more than the other two. The Fleet has designed this area to be difficult to read for anyone who doesn't have clearance.

But why?

"Here it goes," Mikk says, nodding toward the probe.

It zips through that opening as if it had made the opening itself. Then the probe visibly speeds up as it heads outside of the Boneyard.

Roderick leans back in his chair, watching closely. Tamaz curls his fingers over the tablet he's holding.

Orlando stands, just like Mikk.

They're as tense as I am, and for no real reason.

The opening in the forcefield closes, flaring white for a moment before fading altogether—at least on that two-dimensional screen.

Fahd turns away, almost in disgust.

I'm not disgusted. I want to see what happened in three dimensions. I want as much data on this as possible, and I want it right now.

I open my mouth to give the order, when the probe expands. Then that throbbing red dot winks out altogether.

"What happened?" I ask.

Mikk whirls, taps the tabletop, and gives us an actual visual from— what, exactly? The probe?

All we get is the glitter of the forcefield, and nothing more. He goes back to the two-dimensional screen, then fights with the data stream on the tabletop.

Orlando steps beside him and helps.

I open my data stream, but as I do, Mikk lets out a small, almost despairing sound.

"What?" I ask.

"It's gone," he says quietly.

"Yeah," I say. "We watched it leave the Boneyard."

"No, Boss," he says. "That not what I mean."

His gaze meets mine.

"It's gone," he says. "It doesn't exist anymore."

"Are you sure?" I ask. "We're having sensor problems—"

"I'm sure," he says. "The probe exploded."

8

"DID THE PROBE SELF-DESTRUCT?" I ASK.

Mikk shakes his head. "I have no idea. I can't raise it. My systems tell me that it doesn't exist."

We don't need more than that. Roderick and Tamaz work on their non-Fleet tablets to see what kind of readings they get. I use the tabletop, as do Orlando, Fahd, and Mikk. We are working quickly, trying to find something—anything—about that probe, when there's a hesitant knock on the conference room door.

Without stopping my other work, I use the tabletop commands to swipe the door open.

"Um…" The voice belongs to Nyssa. "You should probably see this."

I turn. She looks pale.

"Are we under attack?" I ask, because that's the next step, considering all that's happened.

"Um, what?" she says. "Um, no. No. We're okay."

I let out a small breath.

"I thought maybe, well, you'll see. Unless you have it."

I hate dithering, and I hate it when Nyssa lets herself feel insecure. Apparently she didn't believe she should bother us, so she's feeling really uncomfortable.

"Can you show it in here?" I ask.

She looks at all of the screens, floating at different angles, and at Mikk's face, which is still unbelievably grim.

"I—um—it's already set up on the bridge," she says.

I nod, then stand, beckoning the others as I do so. They swivel their chairs, moving away from the table or coming around it. I don't watch.

Instead, I follow Nyssa out of the door.

Denby is standing near the captain's station, his hands threaded before him, rubbing his thumbs together as if they ache. Maybe they do. He looks even more tense than he had earlier in the day.

We crowd around him. He's watching Nyssa, seeming even more uncertain than she is. Or nervous. Or slightly terrified.

I can't read him as well as I can read the others.

Nyssa stops near Denby, and puts a hand over his. He is nervous, then, more nervous than she is. She nods at one of the floating screens.

I stop beside her, and the rest of the team crowds around me. The bridge feels even smaller than it is because we are all standing so close.

The screen stops floating. It widens and then spreads into three dimensions. It fills the front of the area on the bridge itself. And an image resolves itself around the front. It takes a moment before I understand what I'm seeing.

It's the Boneyard, from the outside. We placed free-floating scanning equipment outside the Boneyard months ago, like little beacons, just far enough away that we hoped the equipment wouldn't be detected.

My team would routinely check the equipment, view the feeds, try to see if anything changes while we're inside the Boneyard. We don't want to be surprised by another vessel—or a group of vessels—that somehow gets inside.

As I recognize the area out there and that edge of the Boneyard, I suck in a breath. I've been worried that entering the starfield-barrier would get us noticed, and now I'm afraid it has.

Although Nyssa says we are not under attack.

"This was just a few minutes ago," Denby says.

He separates his hands, then starts up the image before us. For a moment, nothing changes. The forcefield around the Boneyard barely shows itself, only as tiny glimmers that occasionally appear to someone who knows where to look.

Then an opening in the Boneyard forcefield appears in the upper right-hand corner of the image. The opening is round, and about the size of a human being. The edges are crisp and dark, outlining the opening clearly. Through it, parts of several ships, including one DV-Class vessel become apparent.

Mikk takes a step forward, until he's right beside me. He's vibrating with agitation.

He knows—I know—that the next thing we're going to see is the probe. And we're right.

The probe zooms through that opening as if on special assignment—special *rapid* assignment. The probe seems to be heading toward something, but what I can't tell.

I wish we had two more screens running, one showing all the telemetry outside of the Boneyard and the other showing the energy readings. I expect to see another reading like that of the weapon we were just looking at.

Instead, the probe zooms past the beacons we set. A few swivel to track it—I can tell that from the way their imagery shifts—and then they continue to follow the probe. It zooms, as if it knows exactly where it's going.

Then, blackish lines reach toward it, envelope it, and cover it. It freezes for a moment, literally stopping, before it turns black, then blue, then orange. It expands, just like we saw in the conference room, getting wider and wider and wider.

And then—it explodes.

Only the explosion doesn't send pieces of the probe careening into the area around it, the way I would have expected.

Instead, the black lines surround the probe, preventing the pieces from scattering out into space. The lines seem to absorb the pieces, and then they recede.

"What the hell are those things?" Fahd asks.

"We didn't analyze them," Nyssa says. "I got you all instead."

Roderick has already moved to the station he'd been working at before. He brings up another screen—two dimensional—and floats it in front of us. It shows the Boneyard, near that opening.

After the probe vaults through the opening, a couple of our scanners remain on the Boneyard, even as the probe hurries past them.

Those scanners record the images we're seeing now.

As the opening closes, small circles appear around it. Those circles are black. They glisten slightly.

Then, shortly after they're created, black goo wobbles out of them, moving quickly, heading right past our equipment, so close that we can see the edges of the material. It's something solid, something concrete, but gelatinous. Maybe even made of nanobits.

It went by the scanners so close that I'll wager we can get some very good readings off it.

"That's what attacked the probe," Roderick says, ever so softly.

"The Boneyard." Mikk's voice is flat, almost like he's surprised by what he sees.

I am surprised, and yet I'm not. The Boneyard attacked us once, and we worked very hard to make sure it never happened again.

"We have to analyze all of this," I say. "Thank you, Nyssa."

There's no point in returning to the conference room. We're going to finish our discussion out here.

"What the hell happened?" Denby asks.

He's not asking for an explanation of what we've just seen; he wants to know what it means, what caused it, and—most likely—whether or not we're in some kind of danger.

"The Boneyard protected itself," Roderick says before I can speak.

"Technically," I say, "the Boneyard protected whatever is behind that starfield-barrier thing we're trying to explore."

Roderick looks sideways at me. I can feel everyone else's attention, even the people behind me. They shuffle slightly, adjust their positions, so that they can see me while I'm talking.

"Think about it," I say. "That probe got behind that barrier, and then something happened to it."

"It also dodged some kind of weapon as it went into the barrier," Mikk says. He knows where I'm going with this, but I'm not sure everyone else does.

"Whatever happened behind that barrier changed the probe," I continue. "Mikk couldn't contact it anymore."

"It didn't even register as one of our probes," he says.

I nod. "He couldn't reboot it, but something did, giving it a trajectory out of the Boneyard. Then the Boneyard destroyed it—and made sure that no bit of that probe would get into anyone else's hands."

Fahd curses quietly. Or maybe it's not a curse, but some kind of exclamation of surprise.

"You'd think that reprogramming it would be enough," Tamaz says.

"You'd think that reprogramming it and sending it out of the Boneyard would be enough," Roderick says.

I shake my head. "By sending it out of the Boneyard, the risk is that the probe could be rebooted again and the information pulled off of it."

"You can't pull information off exploded small pieces of that probe," Mikk says. "That's not how the information is stored on it."

"But this system probably wasn't just designed for that type of probe," I say.

"Heck," Denby says. "That could've been us, if we went in there."

In a Fleet vessel. He had a point. For a moment, I saw us, struggling with a failing ship that had been reprogrammed, trying to get the systems back online before we were tossed out of the Boneyard for good.

Before we were attacked by those black gooey things.

I shake off the image.

"We don't know that," I say. "For all we know, the system was designed to deflect probes."

"Or to warn Fleet ships that they're too close," Mikk says.

"We didn't get a message from behind that barrier, did we?" Fahd asks. "Some kind of warning that didn't make it into this bridge?"

Denby leans forward, his fingers moving. Roderick is also working his board.

"No," Denby says.

"Not even a whisper of anything," Roderick says.

"But we didn't get as close as that probe did," Tamaz says. "We're just floating here, among the abandoned ships. We're not a threat."

Not yet. But we might have become one if we just powered forward.

Denby lets out a small breath. "We turn around now, right, Boss? Look at the information we got, see if it's enough?"

Mikk lets out a bleat of a laugh. It's involuntary, and actually has a bit of mirth in it.

Roderick is grinning, and so is Tamaz. Even Fahd is smiling.

Nyssa isn't smiling, but she's shaking her head, as if she can't believe that Denby asked that question.

"Be nice to him," I say. "He's never gone on a real dive with me."

Denby looks at the rest of the team in confusion. "It's the only logical thing to do. Whatever is behind that barrier could kill us."

"I know," I say. "And that makes it ever so much more interesting."

"We're not going back to the *Sove?*" Denby looks at me as if I'm insane.

The rest of the team looks down. Or looks away. Or doesn't move at all. The bridge has become silent, although I suspect that if one of my team lets a guffaw loose, the bridge will erupt into laughter.

Denby doesn't seem to notice. His eyes are wide, and he might even be a bit frightened. Maybe he really does think I'm crazy.

Maybe I am, but I'm the same kind of crazy that I've always been. I like challenges. I like dangerous challenges. I like learning about things.

I especially like going to places that no one else would go to, at least not anyone sensible.

My team knows that—my *old* team. We've hidden our agenda time and time again, including on the trip to Vaycehn, where we first met Denby and the *Ivoire.*

Until this trip to the Boneyard—heck, until this *moment* in the Boneyard—I would have argued that I haven't done anything as dangerous as my old historical dives were. Not the tourist dives, but the dives where I actually explored old wrecks.

Denby has never been on any of those dives, but everyone else on the bridge has.

Orlando has his head down, his lips twitching in the corners. Mikk has moved so that he can't see Denby or me. Roderick's gaze meets mine, his eyes twinkling.

I'm the one who has to look away, or I'll laugh as well, which is probably not what Denby expected when he blurted the question.

I make myself take a deep breath, and focus on the concern he has. It's a legitimate concern. Standard operating procedure for any sensible leader—Fleet or not—would be to leave that area behind the starfield-barrier alone.

I rarely use standard operating procedure—which always drove Coop and Yash crazy—and I'm not always sensible, at least in the obvious ways.

"We might go back to the *Sove*," I tell Gustav. "I'm not certain yet. We have a lot of data to go through."

"But we're not going into that barrier, right? Into that starfield?" Denby has actually folded his arms in front of himself and he's rubbing his hands on his biceps.

Mikk will probably express surprise at Denby's behavior later—after all, Denby is a trained officer of the Fleet. He should be able to handle surprises from the person in charge, and he shouldn't seem nervous about them. But the Fleet never really asks its officers to make difficult choices like the one I'm making. The Fleet usually follows a logical path, and if the captain veers off of logic, the entire crew can support each other.

There are risks, yes, but not the kind of risks that could obliterate a ship's systems, reprogram it, and then send it out into space to be destroyed.

Well, except in here. In a system clearly designed by the Fleet.

"Let's comb through the records," I say, "and make sure we don't have a map of the Boneyard."

"You don't think the Fleet would put information about this area on a map of the Boneyard, do you?" Tamaz asks. Apparently, it's his turn to sound incredulous.

I shrug. "If the Fleet is supposed to avoid this area inside the Boneyard, and there is a map of the ships here, then there might be some kind of warning built into the area."

"Yeah," Roderick mutters. "Like there was around the Room of Lost Souls."

It's not a fair comparison. The Room of Lost Souls, where my mother died, was an old, improperly shut down starbase. There were warnings around the Room, but they came from other ships, and myths, and legends.

I named my corporation after that room, to remind myself of the dangers of unknown parts of space.

Maybe I should pay attention.

But I feel like I am. Even if I haven't completely done my due diligence here.

We haven't found out if there are myths and legends in the communities that surround this Boneyard. We didn't investigate that in our hurry to explore this place.

And to raid it.

I let myself get pushed by the crew of the *Ivoire*, who are vainly searching for the Fleet, even though they're now 5,000 years in their future. They might not like what they find.

I might not like what they find.

"If there is a map in any of these ships," I say, "then there might be information about this area, and Diaz might know how to access it."

"What are you scheming, Boss?" Mikk asks. He seems a lot more alive than he had just a few minutes ago.

He's finally paying attention to what we're doing here. It's as if the explosion of the probe brought him out of whatever funk losing the probe had sent him into.

"Think about it," I say. "The Fleet designed this system to destroy *Fleet* equipment that finds this material. Why would any organization do that?"

"Are we certain that the Fleet did it?" Denby asks.

"We are not," I say. "But the evidence suggests it. Our non-Fleet tech, so far, has a different reaction to these systems."

"Besides," Roderick says, "we learned the hard way that it's almost impossible for non-Fleet vessels to get into the Boneyard."

I like the *almost*. We have yet to find a non-Fleet vessel in here, but we're all assuming there are some.

"If our guess is correct," I say, "the Fleet doesn't want other parts of the Fleet to know about whatever's behind that starfield-barrier. And that has me intrigued."

"The Fleet protects its people from dangerous things," Denby says primly, almost judgmentally. I suppose he has a right to be that judgmental, considering what I'm planning. I want to take my team into an area that has just wiped a probe, reprogrammed it to leave the Boneyard, and then made it explode.

Nyssa lets out a small laugh, which startles me. She's shaking her head at Denby.

"The Fleet does *not* protect its people from dangerous things," she says, almost as if he has offended her. "They don't know exactly how their main drive works. That's scary. The *anacapa* drive sends us all into foldspace, which no one understands—and you all were trapped in, before somehow, we pulled you out of it."

Denby's face pales. Tamaz glances at me, as if he expects me to stop this. I'm not going to.

"Every time I hear about some of the Fleet's practices, I cringe," Nyssa says. "We're different, that's all."

"Okay," I say. "That's enough for now. I don't know how we're going to proceed here. We're going to get more information, and we might end up going to that starfield-barrier. I don't know yet. It will be all right, Gustav, if you don't want to be on the team if we do go."

He straightens ever so slightly. "I'll do whatever you need," he says in that same prim tone.

We've offended him, then. Which I shouldn't care about, but I do. He's a good man. After all these years, though, he's just not used to the way I do things on what I consider to be a real dive.

I give him a small smile.

"Well," I say, "right now I don't have a decision about what we're doing with that starfield-barrier. I do know that we need to go back to the *Sove*—"

"What?" Mikk says. "No. Let's send one of the non-Fleet probes through that opening first. Then we can go back."

Denby shifts from foot to foot. He still isn't happy, after all these years, when someone contradicts me. Fleet officers believe that challenges should be made in private, unless there's an emergency reason not to do so.

Mikk's interruption doesn't bother me, though, any more than Denby's question had.

"I thought about sending in the other probe," I say, "but there are a number of reasons to wait."

Mikk places his hands on his hips. He doesn't say, *Name one*, but he doesn't have to. I can feel the challenge.

"We don't know what happened to that probe," I say. "We're assuming at the moment that whatever happened was automated and as dumb as machines often are."

Mikk raises his chin. Denby stops fidgeting. I have his full attention again.

"But it might not be," I say. "Whatever is behind that starfield-barrier might be watching us, might even know that we launched the probe on purpose rather than dropped it accidentally."

Roderick nods. Tamaz folds his tablet against his hip.

"If there's a doubt, though," I say, "we'll erase that doubt when we release a second probe, even if we do it the same way."

"That's not the only reason you're going back to the *Sove*," Mikk says. "Because you could drop another probe from a different location."

"I could," I say, "but there's a lot we need at the *Sove*. We have some engineering and technical expertise there that none of us have here."

"True enough," Orlando mutters.

"We can find out more faster if we go back," I say.

"We can just contact them to get that information," Denby says.

"And have our communications intercepted?" Nyssa asks.

"We don't know if that will happen," I say. "But I'd rather not risk it."

Denby nods. He seems to understand that.

"However," I say, "I'm most worried about the ship. *This* ship. It's a battlefield scout ship."

"Which benefits us," Mikk says.

"Which benefit*ted* us," I say, correcting him. "But we're announcing a warlike intention if we send it into that starfield-barrier."

"Since that starfield-barrier just attacked us, I'm thinking that's not a real problem," Tamaz says.

"Oh, but it is," I say. "If whatever is behind that starfield-barrier can reprogram a probe from one of these vessels, then what can it do to the entire vessel?"

Orlando lets out a small breath, as if realization has just dawned on him.

Denby grins, then nods. "You're thinking these ships are designed to be reprogrammed?"

I wasn't thinking that until right now, but to deny that I had that thought is to make me seem as dumb as I really am.

"It's possible," I say.

"Is that something the Fleet would do?" Nyssa asks.

"I don't know," Denby says. "I don't understand the Fleet as well as I want to. I'd like to think that they wouldn't build ships that are so easily compromised, but I'd like to think that they wouldn't destroy their own equipment either."

"There's a lot of evidence for that view." Fahd speaks up for the first time. "After all, we're filled with a Boneyard of evidence. These ships are here, waiting for something, most of them damaged, a lot of them unusable, maybe ever. The idea that the Fleet would rather destroy something than keep it around is counterintuitive."

"Unless that something has dangerous information," Mikk says.

I nod.

"Would we get a different small ship from the *Sove?*" Roderick asks me.

"I'm thinking about it," I say. "Or from the Boneyard itself. Maybe something newer."

I wish, for the first time in a long time, that I had brought my single ship or *Nobody's Business*, not separately, but in the *Sove's* ship bay. When I planned this mission, I had discussed bringing one of my old ships along inside the *Sove*, but we had had so much trouble with the old tech and the Boneyard, all of us had determined that bringing the old tech was a bad idea.

Although I hadn't entirely been able to let that idea go, which was why we have tablets and scanners and some diving equipment that I am unwilling to leave Lost Souls without.

"You want a ship that the starfield-barrier can't recognize?" Nyssa asks.

"Or one that it does," Denby says, "because that ship has been here forever."

"I doubt that will make a difference," Mikk says. "This anomaly seems to be targeting Fleet *tech*, not Fleet ships or familiar ships."

"I'm aware of that," I say. "But the key word you're using here is *seems*. I want a better eye on all of this than mine before we take the next step."

"And what is that next step?" Orlando asks.

I almost feel like he's testing me, as if he already has an answer in his head.

"Sending in the non-Fleet probe," I say.

"And then if they reprogram it?" Denby asks.

The very idea sends a little thrill of excitement through me. Another challenge.

"We're taking this one step at a time, Gustav," I say. "Each step will lead us to the next. We might not end up moving in a straight line, but we'll get there."

He frowns at me. "What, exactly, is 'there'?" he asks.

"Figuring out what's behind that starfield-barrier," I say.

"And what if it's nothing?" he asks.

I grin. "At least we'll know," I say. "At least we'll know."

THE FLEET
TEN MONTHS AGO

9

"WITH A CURSORY SEARCH," Reyes said, "this is what we know."

She was standing in the middle of the research room closest to Irena's gigantic map, hands clasped behind her back. Reyes still had her tablet, but she had placed it on one of the side tables.

She was working entirely without notes.

Irena admired that. As irritating as Reyes was—and she was supremely irritating—she was one of the best researchers Irena had ever had on her team.

"We have no modern record of this Scrapheap," Reyes said. "I did a rapid search of our entire database, mostly using coordinates, and found nothing at all. I don't know when we last put a ship into this Scrapheap or removed one."

Irena was sitting in the chair kitty-corner from the door. She had both sides of the door slightly opaqued, so she could just barely see through it.

Mostly, she saw furniture and little else. Occasionally, though, one of her staff would walk by on the way to something else, sometimes carrying a tablet, but more often than not, moving with purpose on a mission she knew nothing about.

Gundersen sprawled in one of the softer chairs near the wall. Her head rested on her right hand, her other hand on the arm rest. Every now and then, she had to stop her fingers from tapping impatiently against the top of the arm rest.

Reyes didn't seem to notice.

Irena had made the mistake of making Reyes go first—or, rather, listening to Reyes's enthusiasm when she volunteered to present her information.

Reyes had started with a recap of everything they had discussed this morning, as if this morning hadn't happened at all. Perhaps Reyes believed that Irena hadn't heard anything they had discussed because of Klara's disruptions. Or maybe Reyes was trying to embed all of that information firmly in her brain so that she had all of the details under her command.

Irena hadn't hurried her up, because Irena knew that interrupting Reyes sometimes meant that Reyes would start all over again.

"There were two other Scrapheaps near this one," Reyes said. "One was between Sector Base U and Sector Base V. The other was between Y and Z. There should have been one between V and W, somewhere, but I found no record of it. And this one isn't in the right spot for that Scrapheap. If we want more information, we'll need to get some of the researchers on this."

Irena nodded. Gundersen gave her a sideways look. Perhaps Gundersen could tell Irena had already ferreted out some of this information.

"My records tell me those Scrapheaps were destroyed," Irena said, to forestall any more discussion, even though she had asked for the information initially. "Is that what you found?"

"After Ready Vessels and working ships were removed," Reyes said. "But removed where, I can't tell you."

"They were moved to the Scrapheap we're dealing with now," Gundersen said. She sat upright, as if she wanted to be prepared for a battery of questions. "Not all of the ships and not the Ready Vessels. But the bulk of the working ships were moved to this Scrapheap."

"You know that for a fact?" Reyes asked. It sounded like a challenge. Maybe it was. It wasn't unusual for assistants to argue and jockey for position.

Irena had just never noticed it between these two before.

Gundersen tilted her head to one side, as if acknowledging that maybe her information wasn't as accurate as she wanted it to be.

"I know that the ships were moved to a nearby Scrapheap, and that the information I found said that it was the same nearby Scrapheap. This is the only Scrapheap nearby," Gundersen said.

"That we've found so far," Reyes said.

Irena wasn't in the mood for squabbling. "What about the Ready Vessels? You said they weren't taken to the Scrapheap. Where were they taken?"

"I couldn't find that in the time that we had," Gundersen said. "I'm not sure that information is even available. But as Lieutenant Reyes said, we'll probably need some real researchers on this. Because what we're getting is either old or contradictory."

Reyes remained standing, as if she were the one in charge of the meeting. She had her hands clasped behind her back.

Even though she was standing tall, she seemed uncertain, which was unusual for her. Maybe she was as unsettled by this Scrapheap as Irena was.

"We did get some more information from the Scrapheap this afternoon," Gundersen said.

Reyes looked sharply, almost accusatorily at her. Irena resisted the urge to raise her eyebrows and smile slightly, like she would do at her children when they got into one of these sorts of power struggles.

"We have images of the ships that attempted to enter the Scrapheap, as well as some information on the vessels taken," Gundersen said.

"Any idea who was in those ships?" Irena asked.

"The ones that finally entered the Scrapheap?" Gundersen said. "No. Except this: the backup codes used were over five thousand years old."

"Five...thousand?" Reyes sounded surprised. Which was good, because Irena was. "Codes that old actually worked?"

"Obviously," Gundersen said drily.

Irena had to step in now. The squabbling was getting a bit too pointed. She said, "I'm surprised at that as well. I knew we had backdoor access codes. I didn't expect codes to be that old."

"I'm not sure those are the usual backdoor codes," Reyes said. "I'm wondering if some of the tech, copied from Scrapheap to Scrapheap, hadn't been properly scrubbed."

"Or properly updated," Gundersen said. "Maybe that means we can use those same codes to get into other Fleet security systems."

"There's one way to find out," Irena said. "We test it on existing systems."

"Wow." Reyes sat down in one of the nearby chairs. "If that's the case, we've just discovered a weakness in all of the Fleet's security."

"Let's not get ahead of ourselves," Gundersen said. "That Scrapheap is old too. I'm sure someone discovered this problem centuries ago."

"I'm not." Irena shifted, feeling restless. "We'll need to investigate the codes before we come to a conclusion."

Although she already had part of one. It wouldn't surprise her to find bits of old programming in newer systems. The Fleet thought itself invulnerable, and it didn't care about the older sectors. That combination would make it possible—maybe even likely—that the same bits of code were used as a backup.

She shook off the thought, though. She had more pressing concerns.

She told her assistants about the blackout shield, and the fact that the other two Scrapheaps hadn't had that level of protection.

"It might be as simple as a redesign," she said. "Especially if the Fleet decided to use this Scrapheap we just discovered as a bigger storage area for ships it deemed more important."

"But you don't think it is," Gundersen said, placing her elbows on her knees and dangling her hands inward. So seemingly relaxed, unlike Reyes, who looked like she might bolt at any moment.

"No, I don't," Irena said. "I think there's something important in that Scrapheap."

"More important than Ready Vessels?" Reyes asked.

"It would seem that the Fleet of the time thought so," Irena said. Her restlessness got the better of her. She stood as well. "We don't know if this was the only break-in or just the first. Nor do we know if these thieves ended up taking Ready Vessels. All we know is that the thieves took a

DV-Class ship, somewhat easily, I might add. We don't know what they did subsequently."

Reyes, frowning slightly, turned toward Irena. Gundersen remained motionless, sitting in a relaxed position, but her body was suddenly tense.

"What we have to decide," Irena said, "is how we're going to respond to this. Do we research the Scrapheap, figure out what it's hiding—if we even can—or do we take action now? And if we take action, what type of action should we take? Do we try to track down the thieves? Do we reinforce the Scrapheap? Or do we destroy it, like we've done with so many others?"

Gundersen let out a small breath, as if the very choices made her uncomfortable. Reyes nodded. It would seem she had already thought of the choices.

"Research is both the safest and most dangerous option," Reyes said. "Safest in that we know what we're facing. Most dangerous in that we would be wasting time that might lead to a wasted opportunity."

Irena nodded.

"But if we go back, then we let whoever is stealing from the Scrapheap know that we're guarding it, and we might even give them a handle on our position," Gundersen said, with appropriate Fleet paranoia.

Irena had no idea if the paranoia was warranted. In all her years working with Scrapheaps, she had never encountered other cultures nearby. The Scrapheaps seemed to exist out of time, remnants of life that the Fleet had abandoned and mostly forgotten.

Even though the Fleet was paranoid about other cultures and about being located, that paranoia, like everything else about the Fleet, occurred in real time.

The Fleet never liked fighting other cultures or invading the wrong territory. But those were concerns about going forward, or establishing sector bases, not concerns about some military force finding them from the past.

Gundersen gave her a small smile, and in that smile was a bit of concern.

"I didn't mean to stop the conversation," Gundersen said.

Reyes looked at her as if Reyes had just realized that the conversation had ceased.

In reality, the silence hadn't been very long.

"The factor that Sector Base Y moved along a different trajectory has me concerned," Irena said. "Generally, we do something like that when we find a region of space inhospitable. And usually it's because there aren't any planets that will sustain us easily, not without breathing masks or some kind of extreme protection against a hostile environment."

She ran a hand along her jacket, smoothing it. An ever-so-faint clean scent of the lotion that she and Noemi used on the babies rose from the jacket itself, and she almost rolled her eyes at herself. She must have set the jacket on top of some lotion that had been smeared on the kitchen counter.

"But you don't think that's what it was," Reyes said.

"I know it's not," Irena said. "We saw the habitable planets in that region this morning."

"Now," Reyes said.

"Probably then," Irena said. "We don't update our databases about the places we've visited."

"Just because there are habitable planets," Reyes said in her dry tone, "doesn't mean we found the right spot to set up a sector base."

"I know." Irena wasn't even annoyed that Reyes explained something she already knew. "That's what concerns me. Sometimes the problem is as simple as being unable to find land that suits us, and sometimes it's as simple as the planet we're looking at is overpopulated."

"But sometimes, the cultures in that region are space-faring and hostile." Reyes wasn't using the dry tone anymore. She actually sounded like she was having a revelation.

Maybe she overexplained things because she needed to remind herself, not Irena or the people she worked with.

"Or just plain hostile," Gundersen said.

"Space-faring is what concerns me," Irena said. "And would be the most likely if the Fleet decided to leave a sector of space because of a hostile culture. We could always move to a different planet if the culture we encountered wasn't space-faring. But if it was, we would not want to engage. And so we would find a completely different sector, and move forward by going just a bit sideways, as we did here."

"I didn't find anything in the research," Gundersen said, "not that I had a lot of time to research."

That last was not a rebuke. It was just a statement of fact.

Irena nodded. She hadn't encountered anything either, but then, she had never encountered anything, not in all of her years working Scrapheaps and abandoned ships.

If the Fleet moved away from a sector because of an aggressive culture, the Fleet hadn't kept records of that. Perhaps because the Fleet ceased thinking about that sector.

She sighed, then paced. Both Reyes and Gundersen watched her.

Irena wasn't usually one to pace, but she needed to move. The day had thrown a lot of things at her, and she had to work at maintaining her focus.

"We leave a lot of people behind," Irena said, as much to herself as to her assistants. "Entire families, entire cities sometimes. People who are committed to the sector base or life on the planet that we're moving away from."

Gundersen nodded. Reyes walked slightly to the left, nearer to Gundersen, so that Irena had more room to pace.

"They would all know old codes," Irena said.

"You think that whoever broke into that Scrapheap is descended from the Fleet?" Gundersen asked.

Irena shrugged. "That's as logical as thinking that another culture discovered our systems. Maybe more logical."

"What would they need ships for?" Reyes asked.

"What do people usually need ships for?" Irena asked.

"They took a DV-Class vessel," Gundersen said softly.

"Which as close to a warship as we get if we're not talking about Ready Vessels," Irena said.

"People who work in sector bases don't know about Ready Vessels," Reyes said.

"Not true," Gundersen said. "Ready Vessels are built in the most secure wings of sector bases. There's always a subset of engineers and others who know Ready Vessels exist."

"And how to work *anacapa* drives," Irena said. "There's a lot of non-traveling personnel who use and repair *anacapa* drives inside of sector bases."

"I thought we pulled *anacapa* drives from sector bases," Gundersen said.

"I thought we shut down and decommissioned those bases entirely," Reyes said.

"Just because we close the doors to a base," Irena said, "doesn't mean we destroy the knowledge of that staff that had worked inside the base. It takes decades, sometimes a century, to shut down a sector base. There's a lot of time to prepare if someone wants to keep their hands on the technology."

"I thought we didn't allow that," Reyes said.

"And who is going to go back and prosecute?" Irena stopped pacing.

It was all speculation, the entire conversation, which was something she could do all day. Speculation was fun and it felt like she was taking her team somewhere when she really wasn't.

"May I ask a heretical question?" Gundersen asked.

Reyes, mouth thin, looked down at her. Gundersen didn't even seem to notice.

"Why do we need to do anything regarding that Scrapheap?" Gundersen asked.

Reyes raised her eyebrows.

Irena started to answer, but she didn't get a word out before Reyes said, "Why do we need to do our jobs?"

Gundersen's jaw set. Irena lifted one hand, ever so slightly, trying to keep the tensions in the room down.

"Admiral, I'm not being frivolous. We had no idea the Scrapheap existed until yesterday. The theft occurred ten months ago, in a sector we haven't visited in maybe a thousand years, maybe more. So, in all seriousness, why should we respond to this?"

"Are you suggesting we just ignore it?" Reyes asked.

Irena lowered her hand. She was going to let this play out.

"No matter what we do, we'll use resources," Gundersen said. "We'll use up time for research or maybe a ship to return to the site of the theft or maybe more than one ship. I understand the theft, but if the Scrapheap hadn't found us, we would be blissfully unaware of it. We *were* blissfully unaware of the Scrapheap and that theft for a long time. We don't go backwards, so why do we care about what happens behind us?"

"This from the woman who said they might be able to track us?" Reyes said.

Irena didn't interject. She thought about it for a moment. Gundersen had a compelling argument.

Irena's job required her to respond to a breach in a Scrapheap. Active responses were her choice. She could send a ship to investigate. She could send several ships to figure out the politics and cultures of the sector. She could send the Abandoned Ship Detail to discover what was in that Scrapheap and see if any of it was worth salvaging.

She could send the Scrapheap Removal Team to destroy that Scrapheap. She could even send a fighter unit to track down the thieves and destroy them.

But she couldn't ignore this. Not easily, and not without violating orders. She would have to convince both of her assistants to toss the information they had received from the Scrapheap, and while Gundersen might think that a good idea, Reyes clearly didn't.

If Irena decided to do nothing, then she would have to report to her superiors. Ship loss and ship theft were things that the Fleet took very seriously, even if the theft was of a ship that had been out of commission—literally—for thousands of years.

The reports, the arguments, the discussions—she would be in rooms like this for at least a week, presenting and defending a case for ignoring the Scrapheap.

And if she decided to ignore this, as Gundersen was saying, if Irena asked Gundersen and Reyes to pretend they had never seen this, things might be easy. Things might go their way.

Or the Scrapheap would continue to send messages and the Fleet would want to know—her *superiors* would want to know—why Irena had ignored the first contact.

It was actually easier to take action. The entire system was *designed* to force her to take action.

So she would.

The question was: What kind of action did she want to take?

"You're not taking this suggestion seriously?" Reyes asked.

Gundersen looked over at her, then sighed and leaned back in the chair.

"She said they might be able to *track* us, and now she's suggesting it's no big deal." Reyes was finally raising her voice.

"Both things might be true," Irena said. "And yes, I was seriously considering the lieutenant's suggestion. Although I would have had to go to my superiors to request permission to ignore this summons."

Reyes's cheeks were flushed. Gundersen's flushed as Irena said that she would go to her superiors.

"It's a worthy suggestion," Irena said, "for the very points that the lieutenant raised. We don't know what we're going to find. Nor do we know if it even matters to us. And we will be wasting resources."

"Then we do research," Reyes said.

"With what, exactly?" Irena asked. "We can research what we know of our own history, but it will tell us little about the situation *now* in a sector that far behind us."

She half-smiled at herself. She hadn't expected to make a decision, but it seemed that she had.

"The logical thing," she said, "the *sensible* thing, is to send a small group of ships back, maybe three. I'd say that we should send one, but that might put them in danger if something truly nefarious is going on back there."

"Nefarious?" Reyes repeated softly. Irena wondered if Reyes had even realized she had spoken aloud.

"Yes," Irena said. "If we have thieves who are systematically work-ing the Scrapheap, they might not look kindly on being interrupted. We know that they have two DV-Class ships, and they know how to use *anacapa* drives. We can only surmise that they know how to use the weaponry as well. So, I'm leaning toward three ships."

"All DV-Class?" Gundersen asked.

"No," Irena said. "We need an SC-class as well. Maybe two Dignity Vessels and a foldspace rescue vehicle. I'd like suggestions from both of you on how to do this, and who you think would be a good fit for the mission."

Irena sank into a nearby chair. She no longer felt restless. Apparently reaching a decision had calmed her.

"I also want as much information as we can gather on the region," she said. "What happened so that we had to move Sector Base Y? Were there hostiles in the area? Do we have any current information about what's going on there?"

Reyes was still frowning. Gundersen hadn't moved.

"I'll make a final decision on what we're going to do in a few days," Irena said. "I need as much information as you can give me."

"All right." Gundersen placed her hands on the arm of the chair and levered herself out of it. "We'll get the researchers organized and see what we can find."

"Admiral," Reyes said slowly, as if she wasn't quite sure if she should say anything at all.

"Lieutenant?" Irena asked.

"Since we're dealing in hypotheticals…" Reyes glanced at Gundersen. Gundersen looked at her like she had never seen her before.

And Gundersen was right: Reyes almost never dealt in hypotheticals.

"Yes, Lieutenant?" Irena said.

"Maybe that extra level of security, sir, that shield you saw, the one that blocked Fleet scans?" Reyes asked. "Do you think it was designed because the Fleet faced a big threat? A hostile culture like you said or, maybe, um, I feel odd saying this, but you know, maybe, a faction of the Fleet itself?"

Gundersen looked at Reyes as if she had lost her mind. Irena stared at her as well.

The question made sense. It made a lot of sense.

And Irena didn't like the implications.

"I hadn't thought of that, Lieutenant, but it is logical," Irena said.

Now, Gundersen looked at her as if she were the one who had lost her mind.

"The Fleet doesn't have that kind of an internal struggle," Gundersen said. "We—"

"We have lost more history than we have," Irena said. "We know our culture now, not the culture from then."

Then she stood as well.

"But the time for speculation is over. I've made a decision. Now we need as much information as we can get while we assemble the proper team."

While *she* assembled the proper team. And that would take some time, and a bit of work with her superiors. Just not as much as abandoning the Scrapheap would have.

Her assistants glanced at her. She dismissed them, and they filed out of the room. She pushed the door closed and leaned on it for a moment.

This certainly wasn't the day she had expected when she had gotten up. It wasn't the day she expected last week, either.

She was going to have to set aside the other projects she was working on to find the right ships to take a long foldspace journey to a sector that the Fleet had abandoned long ago, to defend a Scrapheap that the Fleet no longer cared about.

Although she had a hunch they wouldn't be defending the Scrapheap at all. Once they found what was going on, she suspected her team would destroy that Scrapheap.

She just hoped they could do so while the thieves were nowhere near the Scrapheap.

Then all that had to happen was that the thieves would return to nothing except bits and pieces of a completely ruined Scrapheap. Ships gone, *anacapa* drives gone, and Ready Ships gone.

But she knew better than to plan that much right now.

She knew how she wanted the mission to go. Whether or not it would was another matter entirely.

THE BONEYARD

NOW

10

WE RETURNED TO THE *SOVE* TWO DAYS AGO, and I gave all of our accumulated data to Zaria Diaz and her engineering team to see what they could figure out. I let Mikk, Roderick, and Tamaz continue their examination of all that data as well, partly because Mikk is still angry at the reprogramming of that probe.

I'm working the data a different way. I've scoured the *Sove* to find all the non-Fleet tech, so that we have backups of various systems if we need them.

I also have a team monitoring that opening in the starfield-barrier, on both Fleet tech and non-Fleet tech. In addition, another team is monitoring the outside of the Boneyard.

I doubt that explosion caught some other group's attention, but in case it did, I want to know.

I also want to know if the Boneyard or the barrier itself contacted anyone. I'm worried that something or someone is on the way.

I don't tell the crew about that fear. They're unnerved enough about the reprogramming of the probe. None of us likes the idea that something behind that starfield-barrier can wipe out an entire operating system and replace it with a different set of command instructions.

I've been working mostly in my quarters, examining the data myself, and sketching out various ideas. I'm tempted to send more BSS probes into that area between the ships and the starfield-barrier itself, just to see if there are more weapons salting that part of space.

So far, no one—including me—has turned up a map of the Boneyard. Denby wanted to contact Lost Souls and ask for one, and normally, I would agree, but I'm feeling paranoid. I don't want to send out any kind of communication that could tip our hand with any kind of intelligence behind that starfield-barrier if there is such an intelligence.

I'm feeling restless. Half the *Sove's* crew is still working on a nearby DV-Class vessel, getting it ready to return to Lost Souls. We've pulled some of the most technically minded people off that job and put them on this starfield-barrier.

I want to pull everyone off the other vessel, have all of my crew working on the starfield-barrier, but I know better. If something goes really wrong because of our exploration of the starfield-barrier, then that DV vessel may be the last large ship we remove from the Boneyard.

I actually woke out of a sound sleep (from the four hours I had allowed myself) worrying about losing the wealth of ships in the Boneyard. I thought—briefly—that we should stop exploring the starfield-barrier.

And then I woke up enough to realize that whatever happened to that probe could easily happen to us if we venture in the wrong area. We're working on borrowed time here in the Boneyard, and we have to remember it.

We've been lucky so far. I have no idea if that luck will continue.

Zaria Diaz contacted me about an hour ago. She's finished her preliminary look at all of the data we brought back and has something to report.

She wants to report immediately, but I'm the one who decided on the hour-long wait. I want Mikk, Roderick, Orlando, and Tamaz to join us. I thought about bringing in the rest of my old team, but decided against it. They're curious, I'm sure, but if I decide to dive with them into that area behind the starfield-barrier, I will do so after I have all of the information I need.

We're meeting on the bridge of the BS19. The ship herself is ensconced in the ship bay. Diaz is the one who suggested the location, so I assume she has something to show us.

I arrive early. The ship bay is filled with small ships, some of which we've used and many that we haven't. I don't spend a lot of time here, because I usually know what ship I want to use before I venture into the bay.

This time, I hurry toward the BS19. The air in the bay is cooler than I expected and smells faintly of burning rubber. The scents are always different here, and I'm not sure why. I think some of the ships have an odor all their own, and that odor can permeate the entire bay.

BS19 looks smaller than I expect. Some of that is the effect of being in the bay, which is large and can accommodate dozens of small ships. When I'm inside BS19, it seems like the entire world, but out here, it's just one ship of many.

One of BS19's exterior doors is open, and someone has lowered a ramp, which means I'm not the first person to have arrived. That's unusual. I generally am the first person onsite anywhere.

I climb up the ramp and walk through the door and the open airlock into BS19 itself. I always find it strange to do work in a vessel that's not actually in space. The BS19 feels different than it did two days ago, almost as if part of the life has been sucked out of it.

I make my way to the bridge. Diaz is already inside. She's a small woman, almost child-sized, which makes her perfect for the job she had on the *Ivoire*. She was second engineer there, and usually handled a lot of the hands-on work, which meant crawling into tiny areas, and doing a lot of behind-the-systems repair.

Her small size has come in handy on our work here in the Boneyard as well. She's able to maneuver into crevices and wedge into broken areas on some of the ships we consider viable.

She often discovers problems with them simply by scooching herself into those tiny spaces.

She isn't in a tiny space here. She's in the center of the bridge, surrounded by a gigantic three-dimensional image of the starfield-barrier, the dark area around it, and the ships where we had stashed the BS19. In her right hand, she holds an old tablet. Another tablet sits on top of one of the consoles, but that tablet is Fleet-made.

I'm making my way to her side when Mikk enters the bridge. He doesn't look as agitated as he did two days ago. The bags under his eyes have vanished. Clearly he's gotten some sleep. He's also carrying a tablet.

Apparently, I'm the only one who has come without props or support.

"You found something," Mikk says when he sees how Diaz arranged the bridge.

Diaz smiles. The look lights up her small face and makes her dark eyes flash. She seems younger when she smiles, almost too young to have finished training, let alone have served on the Fleet for years before finding herself here.

"Yeah," she says. "And I wouldn't have found it if you hadn't sent that probe."

Mikk reaches my side. We stand somewhat awkwardly in the middle of the aisle between the consoles, far enough back that we can see the entire 3-D projection as one large image.

At that moment, Orlando, Roderick, and Tamaz arrive. They spread out slightly behind me and Mikk, so that they can all see Diaz's 3-D projection as well.

Orlando frowns at me, apparently thinking that we've started without him. We almost did.

I give him and Tamaz a slight smile, then turn my attention back to Diaz. She has seen the interchange between all of us. She waits just a moment before continuing.

Just as I'm about to encourage her to go on, she sweeps a hand toward the projection.

"Watch." Diaz taps the console to her left, nearly knocking the Fleet tablet over.

The 3-D projection starts moving, just a little. The ships shift, and occasionally the starfield-barrier winks, like it had when we first saw it.

"Now look," she says as she taps the console again.

Suddenly, that dark area between the ships and the starfield-barrier fills with glowing lights. They're ivory and burnt orange, and most of them have some kind of halo around them.

They're placed at seemingly random intervals. My eyes can't find a pattern to them at all.

"Holy crap," Mikk says. "What are they?"

"Mines," Diaz says calmly, as if she expected to find mines in the middle of the Boneyard.

I'm not calm. My heart rate has spiked. We had considered going into that area—or rather I did—without returning here first. I have no idea if the BS19 would have managed to weave around those mines like the probe had.

Simply by eyeballing those mines, it looks to me as if the BS19 couldn't have fit between some of them.

"A minefield makes no sense," Mikk says. "There's so much random energy in the Boneyard that any type of explosion might set off a chain reaction and destroy the whole thing."

"You'd think." Diaz still sounds calm, almost bemused. "But these aren't standard mines."

Mikk frowns. I do too. I didn't know there were such things as "standard" mines. Maybe there is for the Fleet, however.

"What are they then?" he asks, before I can figure out how to ask my questions.

"These mines," Diaz says, "are very weak. They're designed to damage whatever hits them, but not to destroy it—unless that something is small, like our probe."

Mikk shakes his head. "That still makes no sense. The mine would explode, no matter what it did, and that energy would interact with the other energy in the Boneyard."

"Unless it was designed to work in the Boneyard," Orlando says.

Diaz nods at Orlando, as if he was some kind of prize pupil.

Mikk's agitation is back. He's clearly not accepting Diaz's theory. "So," he says, "you're saying the probe hit one of those mines on the other side of that starfield-barrier?"

"No," Diaz says. "I'm not saying that."

I put a hand on Mikk's arm just to calm him. I want Diaz to finish without interruption. He glares at me, then takes a deep breath.

"As far as I can tell," Diaz says, addressing me more than anyone else, "these mines exist as warnings, not as something that will destroy anything that comes in contact with it."

I slide my hand off Mikk's arm. I don't entirely understand what she means, but I'm willing to listen.

"To put it in human terms, these mines are like a hand to the chest to stop someone from coming into a room, not a blast from a laser pistol or even a shove backwards," she says.

"Like a warning siren?" Roderick asks.

"Yeah," Diaz says, but her tone is a bit doubtful.

"If they wanted to do that, why not signage?" Orlando asks. "Signs that pop up or—"

"Or a forcefield," Mikk says, "preventing anyone from going through."

"Well," Diaz says, "that's exactly what that starfield-barrier thing is. It's a forcefield. Most non-Fleet vessels wouldn't be able to get through it. But Fleet vessels, with the right authorization, would be able to—if they knew it was there."

I'm confused. I walk over to the image floating in front of us.

"But you know what it is now," I say.

"Yes." Diaz shrugs a little. "And it was the probe that got me there. Let me just present this, okay? It'll make more sense in order."

I hope it will make more sense, because right now it makes none. Why would there be a protected space inside the Boneyard—protected from the Fleet itself?

Diaz shuts off the image of those mines.

"This is what our sensors 'see,'" she says. "And as far as I can tell, that's uniform across all of our Fleet equipment."

Roderick nods. He's clearly impatient. Orlando doesn't move, but Mikk shifts from foot to foot. He hates organized explanations. He wants the nugget, not what leads to it.

"But that probe went around the mine, so it clearly could sense the mine," Diaz says. "That's what I started with. And it brought me to this."

She brought the mines back up. They add a splotch of color around that gray area.

"What we're seeing as a starfield is as fake an image as that emptiness around the mines, and it's designed so that we ignore it. A kind of nothing-to-see-here," she says.

Which is like a huge *notice-this!* sign to me. Tamaz gives me a sideways glance, with a grin. He has worked with me long enough to know that.

"The starfield is actually a forcefield," Diaz says. "From my preliminary analysis, it's a much stronger forcefield than the one surrounding the Boneyard."

Mikk raises a finger. "Why would the forcefield be stronger here—"

"I don't know whys," Diaz says. "Again, let me present this. I have some information at the moment, and a lot of questions."

"Be patient, Mikk," Orlando says, with just a touch of exasperation.

Mikk bites his lower lip, then takes another deep breath, as if that will calm him down.

"The opening that the probe went through," Diaz says, "is actually a hole in the forcefield. From what I can tell with my preliminary analysis, the whitish material that we've seen is the forcefield trying to repair itself."

It's my turn to bite back a question. Wouldn't a forcefield use nanobits for repair? And aren't those usually black?

Then I think it through. Nanobits create something solid, like parts to a ship. I'm not exactly sure what the Fleet's forcefields are made of, except that they're related to *anacapa* energy.

"I'm going to deal with what happened to the probe behind that forcefield in a minute." Diaz addresses that sentence to Mikk. "But first, here's how I found some of the information."

She shuts down the imagery altogether. The bridge seems much smaller than it did a moment ago. A moment ago, it seemed to contain this part of the Boneyard. Now it has darkened screens and a bit of floor space.

"It was really clear to me from the probe's behavior," she says, "that it has two operating systems. One that sent false information back to us—that preprogrammed information we saw—and another that could read the area just fine."

I nod. Now it's my turn to be as impatient as Mikk. We know this.

"I needed to isolate those systems," she says. "And it took me a while to even find the correct one. I've been away from the Fleet for a long time now."

That last sentence seems like a non sequitur to me. I almost say so when she smiles.

"I forget about rank sometimes. If we had an admiral on board this ship, we—or at least, the admiral's staff—would see what's actually here. The rest of us, including Coop, do not have authorization."

"What the hell?" Mikk asks. "Why do that?"

"They're storing something valuable in this Boneyard," Diaz says. "I'm not sure what it is, but they don't want the entire Fleet to know."

My heart rate has crept up. Something valuable, like a hidden treasure. What better way to hide it than with a bunch of garbage?

That suddenly explains why the ships haven't been repaired, and why there's so many bits and pieces of ships, yet no record of anyone trying to get those bits and pieces or any clear reason for a forward-traveling Fleet to have storage for damaged ships *behind* them.

I never did like Yash's guess, which was that the Fleet didn't want other cultures to get their ships and reverse engineer them. Why would the Fleet care if it's constantly moving forward?

"I have to ask," Tamaz says, "if we don't have the authorization to see the correct scans, how did you find this one?"

"I didn't find all of it," Diaz says. "Not yet, anyway. But I isolated the readings we got from the probe when it went around that mine, and I followed the anomalous ones. I was able to access some encrypted information that the probe sent along with the fake information. It's complicated. I can show you if you want."

Tamaz shakes his head.

"Were you able to figure out what's behind that forcefield?" I can't keep the question inside anymore.

"Not exactly," Diaz says. "But I was able to figure out what happened to the probe."

Mikk exhales. "Finally."

Diaz shoots him an irritated glance.

"When the probe went through the forcefield," she says, "it stopped sending us information almost immediately."

"So you don't know what's back there," Orlando says, almost to himself.

She shakes her head a little. We're all irritating her, which is probably fair, since her insistence on going slowly is beginning to irritate all of us.

"The probe got caught in yet another defensive system," she says. "At first, I thought it was part of the forcefield, almost a secondary one. Like a web or something that would catch something, wipe its systems, and fling it back."

"That makes sense with the altered trajectory," Mikk says.

"It does," Diaz says, "but that's not what happened. The probe was inside that forcefield, when something realized it didn't belong, and hit it with an energy beam. I'm not going to call it a weapon, because it wasn't built to destroy."

"You're sure about that?" I ask. "Because the probe did explode."

"Outside of the Boneyard. And yes, I checked all of that information. The explosion was triggered by the Boneyard's standard defensive weapons. On the outside."

Diaz picks up the Fleet tablet, hits something on it, and a new image appears. The area closest to us glows, except in the far-right corner, where everything is dark. In that darkness, the probe floats. It seems incredibly large, given everything around it, which tells me what kind of scale we're dealing with.

"Half of this is a simulation that I've built," Diaz says. "We have telemetry on this and some really esoteric data, but no clear visuals. I will show you the visuals we have from the probe in a minute. But let me show you this first."

She taps the tablet again, and the probe moves forward. As it does, beams of blue light hit it. The probe shudders, glows blue, and then changes direction, heading out of the forcefield and back into the Boneyard proper.

She shuts down the imagery. "That's a defense built for Fleet tech," she says. "Whatever is in that light, and I only got a bit of it, alters the systems inside a probe—at least—and maybe inside a ship."

"All of the systems?" Orlando asks.

"I don't think so," she says. "I think it shuts down communications, turns off scans, and alters navigation. Since those three things are pretty much what a probe's systems are made of, those beams changed the probe entirely. But a ship is more complicated."

Roderick lets out a sigh.

"It would be a heck of a gamble to figure that out," Mikk says, probably to me.

"Maybe," Diaz says. "But I'm still analyzing that beam. I'm not exactly sure what it is, but I suspect I'll know soon enough."

"That reprogramming got the probe out of the Boneyard," I say. "And then those weapons out there made it explode. Which I wouldn't have thought the Boneyard would do to any kind of Fleet tech."

"That," Diaz says, "was one forcefield communicating with another. The trajectory was reprogrammed into the probe, and then the exterior forcefield was notified that this—thing—was inside the Boneyard. The thing—as the Boneyard saw it—was ejected and destroyed once it was a safe distance from the Boneyard itself."

"So," Mikk says, "when it caught all the bits and pieces in the explosion, it did so to protect the forcefield."

"Maybe," Diaz says. "For all we know, that's how the destructive weapons work around the Boneyard. If there was a lot of debris floating in this area, it would be a warning to other ships that there's something here, defending the Boneyard itself."

"They already know that," I say.

"The regional ships, sure," Diaz says. "But everyone else sees the Boneyard as a blank spot on their star map, something to be avoided. Bits of broken-down ships would be too much of a hint as to what's inside, don't you think?"

I nod, not so much because of what she says but because of that blank area. The Fleet is hiding everything about the Boneyard in plain sight.

"This is a really well-thought-out system," Diaz says, "and it's designed to keep the Fleet away from this center area."

"Unless you have a high rank," Orlando says.

"Yeah," Diaz says.

"Which makes Boss want to go in there all the more," Tamaz says.

I let out an involuntary laugh, and the others join me. He defused the tension. I suspect that was his intent.

"True enough," I say. "I always want to know what others want to keep hidden from me."

"Well then," Diaz says, "you can have a glimpse of it."

She taps the tablet, and the image of the blue-glowing probe disappears. What appears in its place is grainy and incomplete, and two dimensional—I think.

"This is the visual that the probe managed to get before the lights hit it."

"I thought it didn't send anything back to us," Mikk says.

"Just this," Diaz says. "And it arrived in a nanosecond. I almost missed it."

"It looks like a blur to me," Orlando says.

I squint at it. I can barely make out shapes. I'm not sure if what's bothering my eyes is the two-dimensional imagery, the black, white, and gray resolution, or the complete lack of clarity in the data.

"Is this as clear as it gets?" I ask.

"Well." Diaz gives me a sideways look. The look might even have a bit of nerves in it. "I worry about cleaning it up, because I don't want to add information. Let me show you the three-dimensional image first, and then the cleaned up one."

She moves a finger across her tablet, and the image vanishes. Another appears in its place. Most of our holoimages are round. But this one isn't. It is half a circle, probably because that's all the information the probe could get in that nanosecond. The back of that half circle is completely flat, and the information toward the back half is spotty, resulting in gaps in the image.

Normally, a computer program would fill in those gaps, but Diaz obviously did not allow that.

I appreciate it, and it frustrates me at the same time.

Because what's in the front of that circle looks decidedly shiplike, as if several ships were lined up in rows, up, down, sideways.

I frown, and squint some more. Because I might be interpreting the information that my eyes are seeing incorrectly. If I am looking at ships, I'm not looking at a familiar ship. The shape is different from any I've seen. They're blocky, almost square, with edges and angles, instead of smooth curves like DV-Class ships.

All of the Fleet's bigger ships—at least the ones we've seen—are smooth with curves. The smaller ships have angles and edges, mostly so that they can tuck into a ship bay next to another ship, without some computer program making a map of where each ship should go (and revamping that map every time a new ship gets added).

Everyone else in the room is squinting at the image too, as if narrowing our eyes will make the unclear data clearer. Everyone except Diaz, who is watching us instead of looking at the image she has called up.

"Okay," I say to her. "Besides the visuals, what kind of data was that probe able to scoop up?"

Her mouth thins, and she shakes her head. "Not much. I tried to see if there was information on what those things are, what they're made of, and I didn't get anything. Nor could I see if there were elevated energy levels or *anacapa* energy."

Then she bobs her head a little, as if she's correcting herself. "Actually, that's not entirely true. There are elevated energy levels, but those came from that hole in the barrier or from the barrier itself. In other words, the elevated levels existed before the probe got near those…things."

"We're going to call them ships, right?" Mikk says. "They are ships, right?"

"That's what I don't want to say." Diaz scans the room, her gaze meeting all of ours. "It's logical to think they're ships, because we're in a boneyard filled with old ships. But they could be something else—some kind of weapon, maybe, or a structure that we can't entirely see. There's a lot of missing data here."

"Nothing in the Fleet records that matches these?" Orlando asks. "As ships?"

Diaz sighs. "There might be."

"Might be?" Orlando asks. "That's not the answer I expected."

She looks at me, as if I understand her. I don't. I shake my head ever so slightly.

"What did you find?" Mikk asks her. It sounds like he understood what she wasn't saying.

"Blockages," she says. "I searched for the ships by shape, and got kicked out of the system."

"On the *Sove*," Mikk says.

"On the *Sove*," she says, agreeing with him.

We all look at each other. More need-to-know information from the Fleet? Or simply a glitch of some kind? We don't have enough data to know.

"But," Diaz says slowly, "when I had the system clean up the imagery, and fill in the blanks, this is what I got."

She swipes her hand over the tablet again. The incomplete half-circle remains, and next to it, a full circle of data rises. It shows actual ships, lined up in precise rows. The ships are huge, rectangular, and something about them seems menacing.

"This is from the Fleet systems," Mikk says. It's not a question. It's a statement.

"Yes," Diaz says.

"Do we know what those ships are?" I ask.

"No," Diaz says, "but the Fleet's computers seem to."

I frown. Or not. We've been dealing with a lot of illusion on this mission.

"Have you run the same data through a non-Fleet system?" I ask.

"That was tougher," Diaz says. "I borrowed one of the non-Fleet tablets you brought without permission. I hope that's all right."

I don't care about the lack of permission at the moment. Actually, I don't care about it at all. I am not Fleet. I don't care about hierarchy, and

143

she was just doing what I would have asked her to do if she had briefed me earlier.

She reaches into the shoulder bag she brought and pulls out another tablet. Bulkier and heavier, definitely one of mine.

"I didn't want to run the information through any Fleet equipment," Diaz says, "even to show it to you."

"Smart," Orlando mutters.

I agree. I might not have been that cautious.

She sets the Fleet tablet down, but leaves the holoimagery up, floating near her. Then she taps the other tablet, and its screen comes alive. She uses a thumb to swipe upward—I had shut off voice commands long ago on most of my tech after we met up with the Fleet. It always felt to me as if I was giving away what I was doing if I spoke something out loud.

With her swipe, another round holoimage rises. It looks nothing like the Fleet-corrected image of the ships.

Instead, it looks like a combination of the two-dimensional and three-dimensional originals. The black-gray-white colors dominate, along with some gaps in the data stream. The edges of what we're calling ships look crisper than they do on the originals, but the holes in the data remain.

"Here's what happens when I use a program on this tablet to guess what these could be," Diaz says.

A fourth holoimage rises and we all gasp. Instead of square ship fronts, what appears before us are Dignity Vessels all lined up the way that the ships in the Fleet-repaired holoimage are.

The Fleet is precise in its DV classifications. Coop, Yash, and other Fleet officers use the term "Dignity Vessel" sparingly. I've only heard them use it in reference to the ancient vessels, like one I found years ago, when I still believed that *anacapa* energy was stealth tech.

These images look like those ancient ships, not like the DV-class vessel that we're in right now.

"Okay," I say, feeling a bit shaken. "Are we looking at actual Dignity Vessels? Or at something else?"

The others look at me, frowning, and I realize I'm not being clear.

"So far," I say, before anyone can ask, "we've seen truth from non-Fleet tech and illusion from Fleet tech. Is that what's going on here?"

"I asked myself the same question," Diaz says. "I don't have a definitive answer for you. If I could run it through yet another system, I might be able to."

"But...?" Roderick says, picking up on her tone.

She gives him a slight smile as an acknowledgement. "But I did look at the data—on the non-Fleet equipment—and I think that to create this image, the program interpolated the data based on the information in its database."

"Meaning what?" Tamaz asks quietly.

"Meaning that my old equipment has ancient Dignity Vessels in it with similar compositions, maybe even similar energy signatures," I say.

Diaz is nodding.

"For all we know," she says, "the non-Fleet tech is interpolating the data so that it shows what it *believes* to exist there."

"Like the Fleet data is doing," Mikk adds.

"Yes," she says.

I feel my heartrate increase. This is exciting, in so many ways.

"So, in other words, it's all a guess." Mikk sounds disappointed. "We have vague shapes and incomplete data and no idea what we're looking at."

"I don't think it's incomplete," I say. "Both devices agree on one thing."

Everyone looks at me, but only Diaz is smiling. She's nodding again. She knows what I'm going to say.

"They agree that we're looking at ships," I say.

Ships lined up in rows. Ships deliberately placed behind forcefields and defensive weaponry. Ships that the Fleet considers valuable.

Of course I want to go in there and see those ships. I want to know what the Fleet is hiding. I want to know why those ships are hidden.

I want to know everything about them, no matter what the cost.

Mikk is watching me, his expression flat. Orlando's eyes are wide. Roderick is looking at the imagery before him, frowning. Tamaz has his arms crossed.

Diaz is working the two tablets, not paying attention to me.

Because she hasn't worked with me. She doesn't know me. Those four men do. They probably know what I'm thinking, and they're clearly worried.

"The ships are hidden for a reason, Boss," Mikk says quietly.

"Yes, they are," I say. "And we're going to find out what that reason is."

11

NOW EVERYONE IS STARING AT ME. Roderick, Tamaz, Diaz, Orlando, and Mikk. Diaz's eyes are wide. I don't think she's ever seen this side of me before. Tamaz's arms are still crossed. Roderick's frown has gotten deeper.

I'm giddy, just like I am on brand-new dives. I have to work to keep my breathing even.

I'm also relieved we're on the BS19, because, right now, BS19 is inside the *Sove*, and we have all but the most important systems shut down.

I'm glad about that, because for the first time in years, I worry that the Fleet equipment is spying on me. If one of my people had said something like that to me after we discovered the *Ivoire* and partnered up with its crew, I would have asked, *So? What's the problem?*

Only now, I feel like the problem is the tech itself. It can turn on us. It might send our very conversations to the Boneyard, and the Boneyard might throw us out.

A long time ago, Squishy, one of my divers, told me I wasn't paranoid enough. I feel paranoid enough now, justifiably so. And I want my own ship, the *Nobody's Business* or *Nobody's Business Two*, because I control the tech on those ships. I know no one is spying on me when I'm in them.

The bridge of the BS19 feels small, partly because the ship isn't moving. Even though the environmental systems are up and running, not much else is. I had deliberately shut down most of the ship, and I'm glad I have now.

I definitely stopped it from networking with the *Sove*, something we'll have to set back up if we are going to take the BS19 out again.

I'll think on that later.

My team is waiting. It disappoints me that they aren't as excited as I am. Usually they can see what I see. But right now, they don't.

Which I find odd. Maybe the team can't feel the pressure of those holoimages, but I can. The images loom large, even though none of them are as big as a pillow. The 2-D image still bothers me, because, in my mind, it's the truthful image. Something about it seems honest.

The other images, though, they fascinate me in a way that makes my team nervous.

I back away from all four holoimages, the tablets and the contradictions.

"You're going to dive it, aren't you?" Diaz asks in that tone someone uses when talking to dangerous crazy people.

"Eventually." I keep my voice calm. I have to, because I don't want her to panic. I don't want any of them to.

She glances at Roderick, as if he holds the secrets to my work methods. He knows many of them, but not all of them. If she wants secrets, she should talk with Mikk. He's been beside me through all of it.

"You weren't with me in the old days," I say to Diaz, and then wince. Of course she wasn't. In our old days, she was 5,000 years in our past, blithely living her life, unaware that she would end up so far in her future that she would never see friends and family again.

To her credit, she doesn't acknowledge that stupid sentence. Her dark eyes just hold mine as if she's trying to see inside me.

"I would find a wreck, something to dive, and then I would research the hell out of it." I am still using that calm tone, but I'm wondering if I'm being a tad too defensive. "Once I knew all the available information, then I would put the correct team together, and I would dive the wreck."

"And people still died." Mikk. His tone is as flat as his expression.

He doesn't approve. I'm not sure why that surprises me, but it does. And he's right. People died. Not just people, but friends of ours. Friends who knew the risks.

I want to say that to him, but I don't. Instead, I nod at him, acknowledging what he said. But I'm not going to go there.

Then I continue. "I'd like to say that this is important to us. But it's probably not. We can get the ships we need from this Boneyard without ever going behind that starfield."

Diaz shifts slightly. Tamaz is now frowning. Orlando has crossed *his* arms, his mouth a tight line.

I'm not going to talk to my team. I'm talking to Diaz right now. Maybe I *am* feeling defensive. Maybe Mikk's disapproval is making me more uncomfortable than I thought.

"If I really wanted to convince you," I say to Diaz, "you or Yash or Coop, I would say that if the Fleet still exists, entering that starfield is how we find out. If the Fleet is still protecting those ships, if the defensive equipment isn't old and just working automatically long after the culture is gone, then breaching the starfield is going to bring the Fleet to us."

There's a bit too much passion in my voice. I decide to clamp it down, and hope it works.

"Of course," I say, "someone could argue that the Fleet should have found us after we entered the Boneyard, and they haven't. We've been raiding their ship graveyard for months now, and we haven't heard a peep."

"The Fleet doesn't go backwards," Diaz says.

"Your Fleet didn't," Roderick says softly.

She turns her head toward him quickly, almost as if she were going to yell at him for his comment.

He shrugs. "Forgive me," he says. "Your knowledge of the Fleet is 5,000 years old."

Her cheeks flush. She closes her eyes for half a second—the only time I've ever seen Diaz react to the horrid time shift she's experienced—and then opens them. It's as if she has put on a mask.

"Think of the layers of security," she says. "There's the blank spot on the star maps. Any ship that gets beyond that, well, it gets attacked from the Boneyard when it tries to enter. We went past that layer of security and into the Boneyard by masquerading as a Fleet ship."

"Technically, we are a Fleet ship," Orlando says.

"I'm not sure," she says. "The *Ivoire* was a Fleet ship, five thousand years ago. Does that count?"

There's an edge to her voice I've never heard before, and judging by the expression of the others, they've never heard it either.

"But the *Sove*? It was a Fleet ship," she says, "and we stole it."

The word "stole" feels both harsh and accurate. I've been aware of the fact that we're stealing from the Boneyard. It feels different to take things from long-abandoned wrecks, single ships that list in the emptiness of space.

This is a garbage dump, a boneyard, a repository. It looks like it hasn't been touched for thousands of years, but, as we're learning, looks can be deceiving.

"Maybe we did steal it," Orlando says. "Or maybe you, the surviving Fleet members, took it to help yourselves continue forward."

"Except we're not doing that," Diaz says. "We're not acting like the Fleet. We're helping Lost Souls, and we're patrolling a border for the Nine Planets, but we're not moving forward. We're not moving at all."

Her voice is shaky. I've never quite seen her like this before. Maybe this is the real Diaz, the one who talks to her friends, who lets her worries and her fears out to the people she loves—if there are people she loves in this time and place.

I don't know enough about Diaz to know that. I haven't gotten to know most of Coop's crew. I try not to get to know people well unless I'm going to work with them continuously.

That introvert in me. I'm overwhelmed by what I'm already doing.

She's looking at me. There's a challenge in her eyes that I've never seen before.

"Let's assume you're right," she says. "Let's assume that the Fleet—the *modern* Fleet, if it exists—would consider us a Fleet vessel. I suppose

Captain Cooper could make an argument for that, that we're trying to find the best way to get to the Fleet."

She pauses, then frowns a little, as if she heard herself. That is a plausible argument, one that some would listen to.

I think, anyway. But what do I know, really, about the Fleet then or now? Not much. Only what the crew of the *Ivoire* has told me.

That contemplative look leaves Diaz's face, and the fierceness has returned. She says, "We're still in a part of the Boneyard that the Fleet is protecting *from the Fleet*. They don't want people of the wrong rank to know about those ships. Why?"

That's a good question, and one I don't have the answer for. The gids make me want to say, *Let's go find out!* but I don't think that reaction would be appropriate right now.

"We don't have anyone of sufficient rank to get past that starfield-barrier or whatever you want to call it." She takes a deep breath, glances at Orlando, as if she's making the point to him as well as to me.

"And," she says, "the Fleet is willing to reprogram Fleet vessels and *destroy* them to protect what's behind that barrier. And you, Boss, you think it's a good idea to go back there, to *see*, just for curiosity's sake, what's hanging out there? *How* is that a good idea?"

Put that way, I have no real answer for her. Some people don't understand curiosity for curiosity's sake or risk for risk's sake. I probably don't either, when it comes to things I'm not interested in. But there might be a whole mess of ships back there, lined up and ready to…what, exactly? Replace the Fleet should it come to a bad end?

I have no idea and the more I speculate, the more I want to know.

"What will you get from research?" Diaz asks. "If we send another probe in, we're just antagonizing whatever's in there. We're drawing attention to ourselves."

She's right. If we're being logical and doing things only for Lost Souls, we need to leave that starfield-barrier alone. But I'm tired of Lost Souls. I'm tired of working *for* something. I'm tired of being the head of a corporation.

That's becoming clearer and clearer to me as this long mission here in the Boneyard continues. I was happy to have my team together. I'm happy to be diving again.

I let out a breath. Those thoughts remind me that Diaz isn't the only one who is charged here. I am too, and I *am* feeling defensive.

Time to bring down the temperature in the room. I nod at her.

"All good points," I say. "All of them. And once we figure out what we're doing next, I'll let everyone who is on the *Sove* know. That way, whoever wants to leave can, before we ever get near that starfield again."

Mikk crosses his arms. I hope he doesn't leave. I need my team, but I don't say that. Not right now.

Diaz opens her mouth as if she's about to argue with me even more. So I speak quickly, before she can say anything.

"I'm not going to go behind that forcefield without knowing as much as we can." I try to sound calmer than I'm feeling. It's tough, because I feel both defensive and oddly joyful. I want to be back diving. Properly diving. Diving for me.

Diaz has closed her mouth, but she tilts her head ever so slightly, as if she's about to argue with me.

I'm not going to let her, at least, not yet.

"We're going to have a plan, as well as an escape plan—if we can devise one." I'm keeping my voice level. I'm proud that it can stay level when I'm bouncing inside. "We are not on a timetable. We can figure out what's back there. I'm encouraged by the images of the ships, myself."

"Because we need more ships?" Diaz's question is almost—almost—snide. I think of that as the military snide. The one that won't get you in trouble with your superiors because it's a tad too subtle.

"Because," I say, "the Fleet imagery suggests that somewhere in the database of the *Sove*, images of those ships exist. And if they exist, then we should be able to track them down."

And as I say that, I realize we should also be able to see star maps of the Boneyard, and anything else that is at a level of clearance well above the one that Coop has. That information has to exist.

If an admiral stepped on board the *Sove*, he would have access to that information. It would be stored in the *Sove's* databanks.

But we don't have an admiral, and we can't just randomly promote someone to that job.

But there had to be protocols and procedures for just that sort of thing. If the make-believe admiral whom I've just mentally put on the bridge of the *Sove* dies in battle and someone else gets promoted, then that person has to get access to the classified information.

There has to be a way to do that.

Coop would know how, wouldn't he?

And if someone didn't know, if the entire leadership team is incapacitated, then the survivors would have to get that information somehow.

Would they manufacture it? Or would they go around the clearance?

"You're thinking something nefarious, Boss." Orlando actually sounds amused.

But Mikk isn't. He's watching me as if he doesn't want to let me out of his sight.

"Yeah," I say. "I just realized that we might be able to get clearance."

"By making up our own admiral?" This time, Roderick sounds snide. But he's also smiling, just a little. He's enjoying this as well.

The rest of my team seems amused. All but Mikk. I'm not sure what's bothering him, but something clearly is.

"If that would work." I look at Diaz. Her lips are tight, her expression grim.

"I've never heard of it," she says.

"What do you do when someone with clearance dies?" I ask.

"Contact the Fleet and have them either send someone with clearance or promote someone on the ship."

I let out a small breath. Of course, that's what happens. They contact the Fleet through a secure channel, and the Fleet makes the promotion happen.

"And if you can't contact the Fleet?" I ask.

"It's a scenario officers get tested on," Diaz says. "The prescribed way is to keep the channels the Admiral or whomever has already opened going and not shut them down."

"You're not helping," Orlando says softly to her.

Diaz whirls on him. "I'm not trying to help," she says. "I think going into that barrier is suicidal. There's no point. If those are ships, so what? We can get all the ships we need from here. And if they're active ships, then—"

"Then why haven't they come after us, already?" Mikk says softly.

I look at him. Is that what's bothering him?

"Is there a team that looks after those ships?" he asks. "Are those ships being stored for reasons we don't understand?"

"I would say the answer to that is yes," Orlando says. "To the second question anyway. If there's a team, well, then going back in will flush them out."

"For what reason?" Diaz says. "We're already in a conflict that we don't want with the Empire. We're already working for a group whose only affiliation to us is that they let us—or rather, you, Boss—run your corporation in their space. There's no reason—"

"What if those ships belong to the current Fleet?" I ask. "What if they are here? Don't you want to join them?"

She turns pale.

"That's the real problem, isn't it?" I say. "If it is the Fleet, and it's active, you'll have to make a choice."

"Boss," Mikk says softly. "Enough."

Too much, really. Diaz is my ally, not an enemy. She doesn't need me to go after her, particularly in front of others.

She swallows, then licks her lips. She looks away, takes a deep breath and shakes her head a little, the way people do when they're holding back extreme emotion.

Then she squares her shoulders and turns back toward me.

"There's no choice to make," she says. "My Fleet is 5,000 years in the past. Joining this Fleet, whoever they are, is just like joining you. Only, maybe, I might understand their mission. Or not. Because it's a heck of an assumption to believe that they're still traveling forward, living the kind of life we lived when we were with them."

Her voice is thick.

"I've given this a lot of thought," she says. "I have. We all probably have. And for me, the Fleet—what I think of as the Fleet—it's gone. It'll always be gone. But…"

She looks at all of us, one by one, as if she's trying make her point to each one of us individually.

Then she shakes her head.

"Never mind," she says, "no 'but.' Just this. If we find the modern Fleet, like some want us to do…"

Some—Yash and Coop is who she means.

"…then everything blows all to hell again. Some will want to join, others will run, and some will actually have to face everything they've lost. We've lost. We can't pretend to be emissaries of a Fleet long gone. We might end up in the modern Fleet as curiosities or something else. Who knows what? And I'm…"

She shakes her head again, then gives me a weak smile.

"I'm probably afraid of that," she says.

I can understand it. I just haven't thought of it in those terms before.

I am about to thank her for her honesty, but something in her face stops me. The look she gives me warns me that if I say the wrong thing— or maybe even the right thing—she'll become more emotional than she already is.

"You don't have to help here," I say. "You can return to Lost Souls. There's a lot of work to be done there."

"I know," she says softly. "I know."

Then she waves her hand at me, as if to say, *Get on with it*. After doing so, she looks so appalled at herself that it's all I can do to keep from laughing.

Orlando grins and looks away. Tamaz bows his head.

Roderick says, "It's okay to talk to Boss like a person, you know. There's no rank here."

Diaz gives him a grateful look. She half-smiles, then nods.

"All right," I say, looking at the other four. "We have to make some decisions, and I don't think we can do that with what we have. We'll need to figure out what those ships are—if, indeed, they are Fleet ships."

"You think they're not?" Tamaz asks.

"I have no idea what they are, and you shouldn't have any preconceptions either," I say. "This Boneyard has been here for a long time, and if you're building up an army of ships, this is the place to do it."

"If you're building an army and have the ability to reprogram Fleet stuff?" Mikk sounds doubtful.

"If some other group is behind that starfield," I say, "then they already had a way into the Boneyard. And that means they have, or ended up, with a knowledge of Fleet tech. So, yes, they might be able to do that."

"I think that the ships back there are Fleet," Diaz says. She sounds like herself again.

"Let's see if we can prove it, then," I say. "Without sending another probe in there."

Mikk lets out a breath. "You're not going to send in another probe?"

"Not right now," I say. "I want to know what we're up against first. And that little snippet of information gives us a lot to go on."

His gaze is holding mine. And I can't take it any longer.

Since we're already having some kind of weird therapy session, I say in the least judgmental tone I can manage, "What's bothering you?"

"I know you're intrigued," Mikk says, "but I'm agreeing with Zaria here. I think this might be too dangerous for us."

I want to argue with him, but he has been with me forever, through things that had appeared—at the outset—to be as risky as this.

"Why do you think this is too dangerous?" I ask.

"The reprogramming," he says. Then he glances at the others, as if he wishes they aren't here. I am about to say that he can talk to me in private when he adds, "It scares me, Boss."

I take a deep breath, trying to calm the gids. I think about it for a moment, picturing that probe as it zoomed toward the edge of the Boneyard.

"If we had gone in without using the probe," I say, and almost add, *that isn't procedure. You know that, right?* But I don't say that because it's insulting to Mikk, even if Diaz probably has no idea about our procedure, "then we would have been caught by surprise. Even if we were, we could have evacuated the ship."

All of the vessels we're using, Fleet or not, have more than enough escape pods. I make sure of that.

"We don't know that," Mikk says. "What if the reprogramming prevents us from using the pods?"

I shrug. "We have a lot of time. That probe sped to the edge of the Boneyard, but it still took hours to get there. If we were surprised, we might not think of a solution in hours, but we can model all kinds of scenarios, including the one you just listed. We can have solutions."

Mikk stares at me. Then he half-smiles and shakes his head.

"You know, if someone were to ask me if you were an optimist, Boss, I would say no. It would be a gut response, and it would be wrong."

I let out an involuntary laugh. "I don't think of myself as an optimist."

"I don't think you are," Orlando says. "I think you just do what you do, and you don't let anything get in your way."

I lean back for a moment. Orlando is probably closer to correct than Mikk. But Mikk is right about one thing: I always expect to succeed. I know it might take a lot of attempts, but in the end, we'll be able to do it.

"Okay," Diaz says. "I'm confused. If we go into that starfield-barrier, what's the goal?"

Roderick, Orlando, Mikk, Tamaz and I answer her in unison: "To see what's there."

She shakes her head. "And that's enough for you?"

I think about that for a moment. She asks good questions. She gets to the heart of the matter.

And the heart is that of course figuring out what's back there is enough for me. It's all there is for me. I want to know. Once I know, I make decisions about whether or not I want to continue exploring.

In that, I would have thought that I was like the Fleet. But I'm beginning to learn that I'm nothing like the Fleet. The Fleet moves forward, because it can't stop, and it doesn't want to examine its past or anything else.

I'm intrigued by the past. I'm intrigued by everything I don't know. I want to know as much as I can, and if that means I spend years here, just learning, then I spend years. I don't need to move "forward," whatever that means. I can stay in one spot.

Which is why I initially called the Boneyard an all-you-can-eat buffet. Because there are a lot of answers here.

And that will help us—help Coop, help Yash—find the information they need.

I didn't realize, though, until we found this starfield-barrier that I also need the questions. I love the questions, in fact. Not *what happened*, so much as *what is that?*

And now we have one of those.

I can't ignore it. I don't even want to try.

I'm not even looking for benefits as I explore. I just want to learn.

And I need to find the best way to do that.

A way that won't get us all killed.

12

BEFORE WE LEFT THE BS19, I gave everyone assignments. Diaz is going to see if she can find a back door to find those ship images. Mikk is going to model all the different scenarios for escaping a reprogrammed Fleet ship. I want him to use every single thing that scares him about it, no matter how unlikely. I want him to figure out how we can escape all of it.

Roderick and Tamaz are going to examine the same information that Diaz is, only they're going to look at it from the point of view of my old tech. Why did those ships show up as Dignity Vessels and not as mystery ships?

Orlando is going to go through all the scans that we've taken of the starfield, and see if he can see anything else.

And me, I'm going to contact Coop.

I've been thinking of that all the way back to my quarters from BS19. I love talking with Coop and we try to do so at least once per week. We've found a way to communicate from the Boneyard, even with all the weird *anacapa* energy floating through this place.

My concern is this: If someone is actually behind that starfield-barrier and monitoring our tech somehow, then they'll hear me ask for clearances. I'm not sure I want to do that.

But they won't know what we need the clearances for, if I don't tell Coop. I don't really want to tell him. He backs me a lot, but sometimes he sounds like Diaz. And I'm not sure which Coop I'll get—the one who'll give me the answers I want no questions asked, or the one who will ask too many questions and maybe get me to reveal the wrong things.

If only I had someone in the *Sove's* crew who was on the leadership track with the Fleet. But with Lynda Rooney back at Lost Souls, no one here can answer my questions.

So Coop it is, with me being as vague as possible.

I meander to my quarters, thinking about those ships, thinking about all of the dangers. As I let myself into the quarters, I'm just as giddy as I was in BS19. And Coop will see those gids. He might even understand them.

I almost abort right there, but I don't. I step into my quarters.

They're the captain's quarters, which I've taken because there is a control center built into them. I can take over the *Sove* from here if I want to. I see no need to. But I understand why it's both necessary and possible.

The captain's quarters are too big for me, truth be told. The living area alone is almost as large as my single ship, the one I often used to find wrecks to dive.

When I first moved in here, months ago, I pulled up the most minimalist furniture design I could find. A couch, a few chairs, a table near the "windows," which, this being a DV-Class vessel, weren't windows at all. The captain's quarters had no portals showing space, because the captain's quarters were in the center of a middle deck. Something could attack the *Sove*, and unless that something penetrated all kinds of shields and the hull and multiple walls and decks, that something could not take out the captain's quarters.

Other living quarters—which were on a completely different deck— were vulnerable, but the captain was as protected as possible.

The quarters had the option of three or more bedrooms, combining some space from nearby rooms and areas, but I had opted for a single bedroom. I would have taken the smallest bedroom, but I have discovered a fondness for elaborate bathrooms, and the only elaborate bathroom in these quarters came with the master suite.

I got lost in the big bed every night. I actually prefer a bunk. I suppose I could have set one up, but I never did. I suffer by sleeping sideways on a bed that engulfs me.

My quarters smell of old coffee and rotting fruit. I don't leave anything on automatic here, so the garbage collection happens only when I give an affirmative command, which I often forget to do. The smell reminds me, as it does right now.

I walk through the galley kitchen, press my hand against the garbage controls, and let them cycle the garbage into the various compartments on the ship. Organic waste will be recycled and reused, either as fertilizer or some kind of nutrient compound I don't want to think about. Other items go to various departments to be broken down and reused.

Coop tried to explain it all to me once. He's so proud of the way that the Fleet managed to use and reuse everything. *It's one reason we travel the way we do*, he said to me early on. *We don't ever have to stop on land. We have everything we need, and more.*

Later, I found out that "everything" did need replenishing now and then, usually with the help of sector bases. But "now and then" in Fleet terms was after years, rather than months.

The systems were good, and I've insisted that the new ships we're trying to build at Lost Souls use them.

Doesn't mean I always remember to.

I grab a spotted apple out of a bowl on my counter, then squeeze the apple slightly to make sure it's fresh enough to eat. I have a high tolerance for overripe fruit, but I don't need to eat bad fruit on this ship. We have more than enough of everything to keep us going for a long time.

I hover in the galley for a moment, caught between wanting to sit on the couch comfortably when I talk to Coop or talk to him from the control center.

Considering what we might end up discussing, I opt for the control center.

It's in what some would call a closet, between the bedroom and the living room. The door to the control center is actually hidden. If you don't know it's there, you can't access it.

Maybe that alone should have told me about need-to-know inside the Fleet. There's a lot of hidden and secret stuff in every Fleet ship, stuff that only the captain or the commanders know, stuff my original team and I ended up finding on some ships only because we dove them.

Unless the walls around this control center had been destroyed, however, I never would have found it. It tricks the mind's eye, looking like a smooth wall. And from the corridor, the wall looks to be just the right length for what's visible.

There's a slight bend inside the quarters, a curve that's almost impossible to see. I suppose ship builders or designers could see it. But I'm usually pretty good at spotting too much space or something that is a bit off inside a ship, and I never saw the control centers until Coop showed me the one in the *Ivoire*.

I run my finger along the side of the pocket door. I like old-fashioned touch access. I hate wearing extra tech so that the doors recognize me the moment I arrive, and I'm not really fond of voice command or retinal identifications.

I suppose I could leave the control center permanently open, but I don't want to do that. I trust my team, but I don't trust anyone else. And there's always a chance, no matter how slight, that someone could break into the ship and take it over, using this control center.

I smile at myself at the thought. Maybe I am more paranoid than I give myself credit for.

The door quietly slides open, revealing a narrow room with controls on one wall. I have left a chair up near the center of the control panel, so that I can access everything without getting up. There is the option of bringing three more stool-like chairs out of the floor, but I can't imagine doing it. The little room feels cramped to me when I'm the only person in it.

But being the only person in it also makes me nervous. Usually I let someone know I'm going to use the control center. I have a worry, which I usually don't have in tight spaces, that I could get trapped in here.

So I always leave the door open, even if I'm doing something that most would consider confidential. I never let anyone into my quarters anyway, so it's never a problem. And I have all of the excess monitoring that the Fleet routinely does shut off in my quarters.

Someone on the bridge will know I'm here from my heat signature and my entry codes, but there's no way anyone can track what I'm doing all the time, which I can set up Fleet programs to allow.

I slip into my seat and activate the protocols we've set up to contact Lost Souls through the Boneyard. I make sure the contact settings here are private, so no one else on the *Sove* can listen in.

I'm hoping those privacy settings will be enough to prevent anyone else from eavesdropping, but I am keenly aware of the fact that I am using Fleet tech to contact someone outside of the Boneyard. I'm hoping that nothing has been reprogrammed in the *Sove* that would allow someone outside of the ship to listen in.

I'm half imagining people behind that starfield-barrier. I can almost feel them, paying attention to everything that we do.

I know I'm making this up, but once the idea got into my head that someone might be observing us, I can't shake it. I'm not sure what to do with it yet.

The console beeps to life. We've traveled farther through foldspace than I ever have before and that creates a communication lag that I've never experienced before. There's also a bit of a lag because of all of what Yash once called "rogue" *anacapa* energy throughout the Boneyard.

It takes a few minutes, but finally I have a connection with Lost Souls.

Because the connection comes from me here in the *Sove*, with a command center identification, I'm immediately routed to Ilona Blake, who runs Lost Souls.

She's at her desk in the main section of Lost Souls. I recognize the view of the corridor through her open door. That office was mine, ever so briefly, before we figured out that putting me in an office was akin to putting me in prison.

Her long black hair is in a loose ponytail and draped over her right shoulder. She looks tired.

"Boss," she says with a smile, but her eyes are worried. I never contact her, and I'm not contacting her now, but she doesn't know that.

She doesn't add fripperies like *To what do I owe this pleasure?* One of the things I like the most about Ilona is that she is direct and to the point.

"Ilona," I say, and nod. I'm not good at pleasantries either, so I don't even try. "I'm actually looking for Coop."

Her smile fades, and now the rest of her expression matches her eyes. "He's not at Lost Souls," she said.

"On the *Ivoire,* then?" I ask. He does that sometimes. He spends a week or so on his vessel. I always think of that as his way to maintain his sense of self. "Should I contact him there?"

I'm not happy about doing that—more communication through Fleet tech—but I will, so that I can ask him questions.

"You can contact him there, I suppose," Ilona says, "but I'd caution against it."

I frown. I did not expect to hear that from her. "What's going on?"

"They found the location of a sector base in the records," Ilona says. "They've gone to check it out."

I swallow hard. I don't even need to ask who "they" is. I'm sure it's Coop and Yash.

And I feel...I don't know what I'm feeling. I don't want to examine that right now.

Because Coop hasn't told me any of this. He and Yash discovered something they've been looking for since they arrived—evidence of the fact that the Fleet exists. Or existed, anyway, long past the *Ivoire's* disappearance from the Fleet's timeline.

"Where is this sector base?" I ask.

"Nowhere near you," Ilona says. "They say in the Fleet numbering system it's E-2."

"E-2?" I have no idea that the number system has 2s after it, but I guess that makes sense. "I assume that means it comes after Y."

Because that was the base Coop was searching for last I checked.

Ilona smiles, seemingly in spite of herself. "Yes, it does. Apparently they started over with A, but added a '2' after each letter."

"E-2," I say. I have never entirely understood how far each sector base is supposed to be from the previous base. But I gather it's a heck of a distance. "So, they're somewhere else. They went through foldspace?"

"Yes," Ilona says. "You could try to reach him, but it'll probably take more time than you're used to."

And the contact I've been doing now with Lost Souls is already taking more time than I'm used to.

I take a deep breath. Coop left me out of the decision-making for a reason. Maybe because I don't entirely approve of his search for the modern Fleet.

Maybe that's why he didn't tell me where he was going. Why he didn't tell me about the most important discovery he's made since he arrived.

The relationship is casual, I remind myself. It's not the most important thing to either of us.

And that's true. But I did think we had rapport, that we confided in each other, that we were each other's most important confidant.

That was probably an unrealistic assumption on my part. Even though he's not involved with Yash, and never will be, they're closer than he and I ever can be. They went through something traumatic together, and they continue to have experiences that I can only partially understand.

Ilona's right: contacting Coop right now is probably a bad idea, just on the communication level alone. Let's not even examine the emotional fallout for both of us.

And if he's on a mission to this sector base, then he's probably focused on what he's finding. He doesn't need an unplanned communication in the mix.

I sigh and give Ilona a smile that she will know is fake. "All right," I say. "Since I can't speak to Coop, let me talk to Lynda Rooney."

Ilona bites her upper lip. "Um…Coop took a full crew compliment, Boss."

At first, that sentence doesn't compute. Of course he took a full crew compliment; he's running a DV-Class ship.

And then I understand what she means. Or what I think she means.

"He took the original crew?" I ask.

Ilona's expression turns dark. I haven't seen that look on her face in a long time. It takes me a moment to realize that she's furious—and not at me.

"He took as many of the original crew as would go with him," she says. "He also has a few of our people. Lucretia Stone. McAllister Bridge."

I had first brought them into our team back on the mission to Vaycehn, the mission where we discovered the *Ivoire*. Since then, I've used their skills on land-based trips, and on a sad mission to what had been Sector Base W. It had been destroyed, somehow. Coop believed it had been deliberately attacked, but I'm still not sure what made him think that.

"So he plans to explore Sector Base E-2?" I ask. My voice is trembling just a little, and I realize that I'm suddenly a bundle of nerves.

Is he going to explore the sector base or use it to contact the Fleet? And if he does that, does that mean he's going to leave Lost Souls?

Would he even have told me that he was going to leave? If he found his precious Fleet, would he and the *Ivoire* just join up?

And what does that mean for the handful of *Ivoire* crew members who are here, like Zaria Diaz and Gustav Denby? How would they feel if the *Ivoire* left without them?

Rather like I'm feeling right now, I suppose. Times a million.

"Boss, you okay?" Ilona asks.

I nod. "It looks like you're not, though," I say, deflecting.

I don't like talking about my emotions. I don't like talking about anyone's emotions, but if I have to talk about emotions, I'd rather they were someone else's.

"He and I went round and round over this," Ilona says. "I forbade him from going. I told him that he had to wait until you got back."

Oh, I'm sure he loved that. Coop doesn't take orders from anyone, even me.

But I don't say that. I'd rather let her tell me the story.

"What did he say to that?" I ask.

"He told me that I'm not in charge of him. He's captain of the *Ivoire*, and his crew answers to him. They will do what he asks—which most of them did."

"Most?" I ask.

"Some have moved on," Ilona says. "They didn't even answer his hails when he tried to speak to them. That's why he needed other crew. He took some from here, and then specialists like Bridge and Stone."

"You didn't have to loan him personnel," I say.

"I didn't." Ilona spits out the sentence. "The first time he tried to take someone, I forbade them from going. So they quit and joined up with Coop."

I let out an involuntary sound of surprise. I had missed a heck of a fight. And I'm not sure how I would have fallen on it. I probably would have gone with Coop to the sector base and brought some personnel. I might have been able to calm Ilona down.

Depending. I have no idea what kind of information Coop and Yash found. I have no idea what kind of data they were chasing. It might be wishful thinking or it might be something more concrete.

And it might end up exactly the way the trip to Sector Base W did— with disappointment and sadness and anger and fear that something major has happened to the Fleet that Coop once knew.

Well, no matter what's going on with them, there's nothing I can do about it, short of aborting the mission here at the Boneyard. And I'm not going to do that.

Besides, in some ways, I'm as guilty as Coop is of keeping things out of the relationship. I wasn't going to tell him everything on this communication. I wasn't even going to tell him most of it.

"Is anyone from the *Ivoire* still at Lost Souls?" I ask. That question is more than a little desperate. I don't know what they can do for me, in reality. I need one of the officers and Coop's remaining officers are very loyal to him. They're probably all on this mission.

"No." The word is sharp. Ilona is very angry about what Coop has done.

I lean back a little, trying to process what I've learned. Neither of them contacted me, even though what Coop has done will have large implications for Lost Souls.

"He took all of his people?" I repeat. I'm beginning to think about that, not from my perspective, but from the perspective of Lost Souls. "What about the border with the Empire?"

"Oh, he felt guilty about that," Ilona said with so much sarcasm her anger remained clear. "So he made sure to send the best people that he's trained on DV-vessels to the border, so that we're protected."

He felt guilty? I'm frowning. It was my understanding that the ships on the border were staffed with mostly non-Fleet crew.

I don't say anything, though. Because if almost everyone who knows anything about DV vessels is gone, then finding anyone who can help me—anyone who might have accidentally stumbled on what I need—is clearly impossible.

"I don't suppose he said when he'd be back," I say and brace myself for the answer.

Ilona tilts her head, eyes flashing. "Oh, he didn't say if he'd be back at all."

That was the answer I was afraid of. I take a deep breath. He wouldn't just disappear from our lives, would he? Or would he? The Fleet has always been the center of his existence, and if he finds it, then maybe he will join up, leaving us far behind.

Leaving me behind.

I feel shaky, and my heart aches. I don't think I've ever felt anything like this before.

And as I recognize that, anger follows. Deep and powerful. This is why I've never gotten involved with anyone, why my diving partners are my friends, but never more than casual lovers if they're anything at all.

Human beings hurt each other, especially if their needs don't mesh.

"I'm sorry to hear that he did this to you," I say, surprised my voice is calm.

"He did this to all of us," Ilona says. Then she puts her chin down in a sharp movement, as if she's going to nod but doesn't. "But I would be remiss if I didn't tell you one other thing."

She pauses, probably expecting me to say something. But there's nothing I can say, nothing I really want to say.

"Yash asked me to make sure no one got into their lab," Ilona says. "She says there's some material in there that shouldn't be in the wrong hands."

My anger spikes. I'm so tired of limiting information. That's why I'm talking with Ilona now, because the stupid Fleet likes to segment information.

"There are wrong hands at Lost Souls?" Now I'm the one being sarcastic. Clearly my sarcasm flows from the same place as Ilona's does.

"Apparently," Ilona says. Then her expression softens. "And, to be fair, there are a few people who think they understand more than they do. I wouldn't want them to have access to some of the technological information. I'd be afraid of what they would try, unsupervised."

I nod, but my mind really isn't on that. It's on what she told me before we started discussing the personnel at Lost Souls.

"Yash asked you to keep things secure for her," I say slowly. "So you expect her to be back."

"What I expect is irrelevant," Ilona says. "*Yash* expected to come back."

I think about that for a moment. Yash has always been a closed box. She doesn't say much, and when she does, it's usually harsh or critical. We've learned to work together, and I've come to like her, but it has taken a long time.

"Did she apologize for Coop's behavior?" I ask.

"No." Ilona smiles somewhat coldly. "But I get the sense that Yash rarely apologizes for anything."

"True enough," I say.

"However, what she did say leads me to believe that while she's excited about the discovery of that sector base, she expects it to be a piece in the continuing puzzle, not the complete answer to all the questions that they've had."

I nod. I would expect that too, given what we've seen in the past.

"Still," I say, "they took the *Ivoire*, and what remains of the crew."

"Honestly, Boss, I don't blame them, even though I'm angry about it." Ilona looks down. "I would probably do the same things in their shoes. They are lost here."

"They're lost everywhere," I say. It's a complete sign of my anger that I have finally said that sentence out loud. I have kept it to myself, more or less, for years now. "They can't go back, and the Fleet—even if they find it—probably doesn't even know who they are or that they were missing. If they can even understand the Fleet and its rules. It was hard enough for them to learn ours."

I thought they had finally settled in. I was beginning to relax, to think I can go back to my life, while Coop and Yash and Ilona and the others create something new at Lost Souls.

Maybe I'm as lost as the crew of the *Ivoire*.

I let out a small breath. This conversation certainly has demolished my gids. I'm no longer excited about the discovery or the possibilities. I'm worried about Coop, and angry at him for leaving, and feeling unsettled because he said nothing to me at all.

"Is there anything else?" Ilona says. She clearly doesn't want to discuss Coop and the *Ivoire* any longer.

"Yes," I say. "I need someone to bring one of the DV vessels we've pulled out of the Boneyard back here. And on that ship, I need some non-Fleet tech."

"For what?" Ilona asks.

It might be my corporation, but Ilona does run it now. And she deserves to know…some of what we've learned, anyway.

"We're finding discrepancies between the readings we get from Fleet tech and readings we get from non-Fleet tech," I say. "So I need some smaller non-Fleet ships, and some extra non-Fleet tech."

"Important discrepancies?" she asks.

Here's where that stupid need-to-know bit comes in. Apparently, I'm playing the same game that the Fleet plays, because I can't bring myself to tell her everything.

Part of my brain says she doesn't need to know, and part of it realizes that I don't want yet another person to try to talk me out of my plan.

"We don't know yet," I say. "It could be. Or it might be nothing."

She studies me for a moment. She knows me pretty well, and she's worked with me on dives. She knows that I often hold back when I don't want interference.

I can see her brain working: does she want to ask more questions or is she going to let this one go?

It's a sign of how overwhelmed she is that she doesn't ask anything else. Instead, she says, "Be careful. We have more than enough to work on here. And if the *Ivoire* and its crew don't come back, then we have as many ships as we can handle at the moment too."

Maybe I had misread her earlier expression. Maybe she wasn't thinking about asking me more questions. Maybe she was evaluating the mission, thinking of bringing us back if she could.

Because what she just said is a sideways method to get us to shut down this entire trip and return to Lost Souls. She already thinks she might have lost Coop and the *Ivoire*. She can use the extra experienced hands from our mission back at Lost Souls.

"We'll be careful," I say. I can promise that. We'll be as careful as my team always is on important dives.

She looks like she wants to ask more, but I don't let her.

"Let me give you a list of what we need," I say. And then I do.

THE FLEET
NINE AND A HALF MONTHS AGO

13

IRENA SAT IN HER SON JOEL'S CHAMBER on the *Santé 15*. Although to call the area she was in a "chamber" dignified it, and made it something it was not. It wasn't exactly a treatment room either, more like a series of health units, cobbled together to accommodate a little boy who barely knew how to crawl.

Right now, he slept in the middle unit, and for that she felt grateful. He had been awake for the last four hours, crying, mostly—or Joel's version of crying. His lungs were being regrown from healthy stem tissue, but he was in the transition between his old underdeveloped and mostly malformed lungs to these new healthy lungs.

He didn't know how to wail, like babies do. He couldn't. He couldn't get enough air. He got enough to keep his skin from turning that weird pale blueish gray that children who didn't get enough oxygen seemed to get at his age, but he couldn't really cry or talk or do much at all.

He'd always seemed like a lazy, uninterested child to the unpracticed eye. But he was Irena and Noemi's ninth child. They knew how babies should act. In particular, they knew how *their* babies should act.

And none of them had ever been as listless as Joel.

It had taken more than a month to get the medical professionals on the *Kutelekezwa* to pay attention to what Irena and Noemi had to say. Irena might have been in charge of that ship, but when it came to the

175

medical unit, the doctors therein saw her and her wife as troubled parents, not people who could derail their careers.

A few of the doctors learned that to their peril. Irena replaced them with doctors who took her seriously. But that had taken time, and had cost Joel. Lack of oxygen caused listlessness and a whole host of other problems in adults as well as in children. She could only hope that those months without enough air hadn't cost him brain power.

So far, he'd tested fine, but there was only so much tests could do.

He sprawled on his back on the gray carpeted floor. There were cushions under the floor that changed to the proper thickness whenever someone slept on them. Not too thick for a child Joel's age, so he wouldn't roll over and smother, but not too thin either.

The area was blocked off with a slightly yellow barrier. The yellow meant that the oxygen content was just a bit higher than normal. There was an entire color scheme for the air mix that he was exposed to. The oxygen mix changed hourly, and each change was reflected in the barrier.

In some ways, the colors were a cautionary mark for the adults and medical professionals, so that they knew what to expect if they breached that barrier.

After Joel's new lungs had been implanted but before they had become operational, the oxygen content in that little area was so high that it made Irena giddy whenever she sat with him.

She wasn't giddy now, but she wasn't behind the barrier. Instead, she was just outside, in the ship's normal environment, tablets spread around her as she worked. And as she worked, she kept an eye on Joel.

It was a joy to watch him sleep.

He looked comfortable, his too-thin arms bent at the elbows and flung over his perfectly formed head. His hair was one of the few things about him whose growth hadn't been stunted. He had a thick head of black curls that almost made him look top-heavy.

Those curls, plus his dark brown eyes, would make him devastatingly handsome someday. If she and Noemi could get him healthy enough to make it through to someday.

Irena sat cross-legged on the same carpet that supported her baby boy. The carpet was thicker for her, and had risen up to support her back and spine. The carpet was also soft enough that if she let herself relax even slightly, she would probably fall sound asleep, just like Joel.

She was spotting Noemi, who had taken the brunt of Joel's illness. The baby's lungs were being regrown in place, and monitored hourly. Once they reached a certain size, then the doctors would make some adjustment (that Noemi understood better than Irena), and the old lungs would get removed.

The new lungs already brought more oxygen into his little body. The old lungs weren't being used at all, but it was, apparently, wrong at this stage to remove them. They were operating as some kind of template for the new lungs to grow against.

Irena didn't understand all the details. She didn't have to. Noemi was monitoring every bit of the procedure. They both had spoken to a dozen specialists, and found the best doctors for the task. Noemi had studied all the possible options, and once the two of them settled on this procedure, Noemi had studied it as well.

Noemi joked that if the procedure hadn't required steady hands and years of hands-on training, she would have been able to perform the procedure herself.

Intellectually, that calmed Irena. But emotionally, she was barely holding it together. She could send entire ships into battle, knowing that she might lose one or all of them, at the cost of thousands of lives.

Yet the idea of losing this little guy or even stunting his growth or his potential made her as shaky and nervous as a first-time parent.

In fact, first-time parenting hadn't been this hard. Back then, she and Noemi had worried about their every move, and they probably made overprotective parenting mistakes—mistakes they didn't have the luxury to make as the other children arrived—but it didn't matter. Their oldest, Zaire, had turned out all right.

He was going to graduate in less than a year and he had already been accepted to one of the toughest engineering academies in the Fleet. That would take him even farther away from them.

Irena dreaded telling Klara, who took the absence of each sibling personally. But telling Klara wouldn't be necessary for another six months or more.

Maybe by then Joel would be living the life of a normal child.

Although he wouldn't, not exactly. His development had slowed to accommodate his breathing issues. He had rolled over on time, and smiled early, but he hadn't started crawling yet, even though he was seven months old.

He was thinking about crawling now that he was getting more air. When he was awake, and not upset, he would roll onto his stomach, spread out his tiny hands and pull himself forward. Eventually he would figure out how to use his knees.

Every other child had.

She half smiled at herself, at the hopefulness she had finally allowed herself to feel regarding this little boy. For a while, she wasn't sure what kind of child Joel would be and whether or not he would even qualify for school.

Lung issues were serious problems on starships, because the lungs were filters, and a backup to the environmental system on a ship. She'd had crew with lung issues, usually developed on land, and they were always the first to get sick and the last to heal.

She hadn't wanted that for Joel. The doctors were telling her and Noemi that it wouldn't happen to him either. Because once this procedure ended, he would have a normal, healthy set of lungs, and the problem had been caught soon enough and repaired early enough so that he would have a normal life.

Whatever that would mean.

He snuffled a bit, which made her tense. Any strange noise caught her attention. But the snuffle was just that. The sound of a baby who had cried himself to sleep, which Joel had. The doctors had checked him out three times today already, and Joel had cried through much of it—in a Joel way. All tears and no sounds. It actually looked like his eyes were leaking.

He had no pain, though, and seemed to be protesting his confinement. Or maybe being poked and prodded so much. Or maybe that no one was holding him.

Because they had all been guilty of that: every member of the family had held him close as they realized how sick he was, cradling his frail little body as if they could protect it just by cuddling.

This week in the *Santé 15* had been the first time in Joel's life that he spent hours without someone cuddling next to him. Having someone in the room, near the barrier, was the closest that he got to an actual cuddle—unless it was doctor-sanctioned.

Irena gave her son one last look, and then returned to the work before her. She had spoken to her superiors about that Scrapheap. She had presented all of the options, including the one Gundersen mentioned, that of doing nothing.

Everyone Irena spoke to took that last bit seriously. They were going to invest a lot of time and treasure sending ships back to that Scrapheap. They had to make sure the expense was worth the trip.

No one knew for certain if it would be.

The research she and her assistants had done turned up one piece of information that solidified her decision, however. All of the Scrapheaps that existed near this one—if you could consider the distance across such vast regions of space "near"—had Ready Vessels.

She had assumed from the start that this Scrapheap contained Ready Vessels, but her superiors mandated that it did. Whether it actually did or not was now irrelevant. Because the Fleet assumed there were Ready Vessels in that Scrapheap, she had to behave as if there were.

Which meant sending a team back.

The question was: How large a team were they sending back and what should that team prepare for?

That was the decision she had to make.

She was doing it now, while watching Joel sleep.

Three regular ships would be the minimum that she sent to the Scrapheap. One DV-Class ship, and two SC-class ships with as much weaponry as the Fleet could spare.

Or she could send two warships, with a full complement, and assume that the warships would be engaging in some kind of action.

She could also send a dozen ships of varying sizes. The normal plan with a group of ships like that would be to surround the Scrapheap and go after the thieves.

But this Scrapheap was too large to surround.

The last thing she could do was send a group of ships, with a lot of Scrapheap experts, and have them go to one of three control towers that she had found so far inside that Scrapheap. Using the towers, the team could either bring down the Scrapheap or take out the thieves.

And perhaps the towers might have more information on the thieves, information that hadn't yet made it back to the Fleet.

Joel sighed and turned his little head slightly. His cheeks looked a little too red. They were probably chapped. He'd been wiping at them as the tears leaked from his eyes.

She would wait until the oxygen mix was close to normal, and then she would ring for one of the assistants. She wanted to stretch out and cuddle with her little boy. Maybe she could do that until Noemi got back.

Irena pulled another tablet closer, forcing herself to concentrate. She needed to decide who to send to that Scrapheap.

What she needed was someone who could make decisions on the fly. Someone with enough seniority to make those decisions without repercussions.

Those decisions might include the destruction of the Scrapheap, and whether or not to chase the thieves back to their lair.

The more she studied this, the more she thought about it, she wanted to chase down those thieves.

Not because they had stolen ships from the Fleet. But because those thieves knew how to use an *anacapa* drive. Knowing how to use an *anacapa* drive made them a threat to the Fleet now.

Although, as Reyes had mentioned, they wouldn't be a threat if they had no idea the Fleet still existed.

Irena sighed and ran a hand through her hair. She had to give some kind of guidance to the ships she was sending back to that Scrapheap.

The danger came if the thieves had some way of tracking other ships through foldspace. If those thieves knew how to do that, then they would be able to track down the Fleet.

But would they be stealing DV-Class vessels if they knew how to track ships through foldspace? And would they be a threat if they had to steal their ships?

She ran a hand over her face. Too many unanswered questions made her decisions hard.

She had other requests she had to consider as well. She had three historians who asked to go on the mission. They were trying to figure out what, exactly, happened to Sector Base W. When Gundersen had asked for specialized help on that matter, she had stumbled into a matter of severe scholarly debate, all based on an incomplete record.

Everyone agreed that Sector Base W had been destroyed, and the movement of Sector Base Y from the original Fleet trajectory to the one they were on now was tied to that destruction.

But who had destroyed Sector Base W and why was not in the records. There was, as one scholar had told Gundersen, a gap. And then he had repeated it, with emphasis that (she said) somewhat creeped her out: A *significant* gap in the records, maybe even one that had been deliberately made.

The scholars wanted answers that might exist in that Scrapheap.

And her superiors wanted the thieves tracked down and maybe punished, if such punishment were appropriate.

And she…she wanted to find out why the Scrapheap was so big. But that was an intellectual curiosity.

What she really wanted was to fulfill this assignment and spend more time with that little boy a few meters from her. The little boy who sighed heavily as his sleep grew deeper.

She checked the time. The air within that barrier would cycle into a near-normal mix within ten minutes.

She would have to decide exactly who would lead this mission to the Scrapheap, and in deciding that, she would decide the mission. If she couldn't find someone who had a small reckless streak, someone with a great reputation who knew how to make the difficult decisions without immediate Fleet backup, someone who wouldn't get the Fleet involved in a conflict that stemmed from *behind* them, then she would send a group of three ships and have them destroy the Scrapheap.

That decision made her uncomfortable, but it was the best one she could make. Because if she didn't have the right person in charge of this mission, too much could go wrong.

If she were younger, if she didn't have so many children, if Joel wasn't so very sick, she would lead this mission herself.

Then she smiled, understanding for the first time why she had been taking so very long to make a decision.

The decision she wanted to make was to go back there and find out exactly what was going on, and maybe lead an entire squadron to find those thieves and their stolen *anacapa* drives.

And she could do that. She didn't need anyone's permission to go that far and do something that difficult. She had that reckless streak she would be looking for in another commander.

But she couldn't leave Noemi alone with a sick child. A child who was on the road to recovery, but Irena had been warned—*they* had been warned—that this procedure didn't always go smoothly in a child this young.

Joel might have to go through the same procedure again, and maybe even again. Or this one might only partially take, and he would need to have some kind of mechanical triage while the doctors tried, yet again, to grow him another pair of lungs.

Part of her wanted to go on this mission so she wouldn't have to sit and watch over her critically ill child, knowing she couldn't do anything more than she was already doing to save him.

Part of her wanted to run away and think about other difficult things, like Scrapheaps and thieves and possible battles.

But she wasn't that woman. Or, rather, she wasn't that woman any longer.

So she needed to find someone just like her. Only younger and freer. Someone she could trust.

And that would take a search.

A search she was willing to do—after Noemi returned. After one short little nap with Joel, in a perfectly controlled environment, while Irena willed him to get better.

THE BONEYARD

NOW

14

IT TAKES THREE DAYS FOR THE *MADXAF* to arrive from Lost Souls, with someone I've never met before at the helm.

The three days is shorter than I expected when I finished talking with Ilona. I had a hunch we wouldn't get the things we needed for a week or more. And yet the *Madxaf* is here, now.

When we found the *Madxaf*, it was a dilapidated DV-Class vessel that Yash said looked relatively intact. I led the dive, because I hate the word "relatively," and discovered that the *Madxaf* was dusty and dirty (unusual, even in the ships we dive) and had two different *anacapa* drives, one of which, Yash said, was an extra.

Now the *Madxaf* looks nothing like the ship we dove. It's pristine and perfect, and seems almost brand-new. I have to admit that the folks on Lost Souls do spectacular work when they have the time to do so.

I was happy to see the ship, but I'm not happy with the newbie at the helm. I encountered her almost immediately, and we clashed from the start.

Ellen Pao is a slender woman who apparently has excellent engineering skills as well as leadership training. And, according to Ilona, Pao has a lot of skill with *anacapa* drives. She's been trained by Yash.

Apparently, the *anacapa* drive experience, more than the ability to run a crew on a DV-class vessel, is the reason that Ilona sent her here.

I don't need an *anacapa* expert, and I certainly don't need someone to challenge my every move, which Pao looks like she's going to do.

I greeted the entire crew, and then told them that they could be on reduced duty for the rest of the day and the following day, establishing that I'm in charge. Pao looked like she was going to argue, but I gave her a sideways look and she quieted.

Either someone explained to her that I'm the one who owns Lost Souls or she's easier to push around than I originally thought.

After the *Madxaf* crew has rested, I will load them up with some information we've pulled off other ships—information that has nothing to do with that starfield-barrier—and send them back.

I haven't instructed my team to remain quiet about the starfield-barrier, but I don't need to. My team doesn't seem to like Pao any more than I do.

I am going to remain true to my word, though. Anyone on my team or who is on the *Sove* and doesn't want to participate in the starfield-barrier mission can go back on the *Madxaf*. And before they leave, I will swear whoever leaves to secrecy.

If the damn Fleet can do it, I can too.

I'm feeling a lot less charitable about the Fleet than I usually am. I am angry at it, and I know that some of that anger is at Coop. We've given him time, attention, and a damn home, and he's willing to throw that away without telling any of us?

Without telling me?

I've been trying to find a way to calm down about this ever since I learned about it, and I'm not succeeding. Part of the reason for my lack of success comes from the fact that I'm dealing with Fleet tech, and Fleet secrecy, and a mission that some of the others here think is unnecessary at best and dangerous at worst.

We have combed through all the information that the doomed probe sent back to us. We have run it through every system we can find, looking for more telemetry or hints about what, exactly, happened to the probe.

On that, we're no farther ahead than we were before I first spoke to Ilona.

But Diaz has been finding information about those ships whose images showed up for a nanosecond on that last image the probe sent back. She has tried to replicate that finding by putting incomplete information into the *Sove's* systems, and twice now, she's come up with those ship images, each time from a completely different angle.

Now, she needs to test her findings on the *Madxaf*, without bringing any preconceptions with her, to see if the same pathways exist there.

And I'm going to go with her, but before I do, I have to tell her that Coop has found another sector base.

I've put this off for the last four days. I need to be honest with Diaz, Denby, and the other members of the *Ivoire* who are here with me. Not because I think they need to know right now—I don't think they do—but because I want them to hear it from me, and not from Pao.

I have decided to tell Diaz first. I will tell the others later.

I meet with her in Engineering on the *Sove*. She has carved a workspace for herself in one of the wings off the main room, and she looks like she's in her element. She has four tablets set up on one console, and four non-Fleet tablets attached to a non-Fleet board resting on top of an actual table. I have no idea where she found the non-Fleet control board, and I don't ask.

The wing smells of fresh coffee and that ever-so-slight funk some rooms get when a person spends most of their waking hours working in it. It doesn't matter how well the environmental system works, that slightly musky odor remains.

She is wearing an older Fleet uniform, one that has some shiny spots on the elbows of the shirt. The piping looks like it's coming loose as well.

I'm about to tell her that the uniform isn't necessary, and then I realize what she's doing; she's convincing the *ship* that she's Fleet, not the rest of us.

So she believes that we're being monitored as well. Or maybe it's just that, to her, small things make a difference.

I greet her, and thank her for meeting me before we go to the *Madxaf.* She nods, a slight frown creasing her forehead.

"I just found out," I say, deciding not to tell her that "just" is a few days ago, "that Coop and Yash have found a sector base. E-2, they think. They've taken the *Ivoire* and most of the crew to examine it."

I figure if I tell Diaz all at once, she'll ask fewer questions, and maybe get her anger out all at once.

To my surprise, she nods. "I know."

I'm the one, apparently, who has to guard against anger. Before I let myself blurt, *You already know?* in an incredulous tone, I swallow hard.

"You know?" I say, my tone soft and deliberately bland.

"Yes," she says. "Coop contacted me when he was planning the trip— a few weeks ago? He didn't tell you? I thought he did."

"He didn't." My voice remains bland.

"That might've been when you were injured," she says.

But I shake my head. "I saw him at Lost Souls after that," I say.

She shrugs. "I don't know timelines."

Her eyes look at anything but me. The comment about me being injured must have been a lie. She had known that I hadn't known, and she didn't want to hurt my feelings.

"Coop asked you not tell me, didn't he?" I ask.

"I—" She sighs and shakes her head. "He said he'd rather not tell you, because you might decide to go with him, and what we're doing here in the Boneyard is important. The information we gathered here helped them find E-2."

I set aside any emotional reaction I have to that. I'll explore how I feel later. Right now, I have to negotiate this conversation, which is going differently than I thought it would.

"He told you to stay here?" I ask.

She shook her head. That crease in her forehead had grown deeper, but her expression wasn't quite a frown. It was more like a deep concern, probably for me.

"He said it was my choice. He would wait for me, if I wanted to investigate the sector base with them. He made the same offer to Gustav."

So Denby knows as well? Am I the only person who hadn't been told about this new sector base?

"And the others from the *Ivoire?*" I ask.

This time, she looks up at me. "I'm not sure what he said to them. I do know that they made a point of telling me they were staying."

I frown. I may have made a mistaken assumption. I would have thought—I did think—that all of Coop's crew from the *Ivoire* would go with him on a journey to a newly discovered sector base.

I am clearly wrong about that.

"What made you decide to stay?" I ask.

"He has Yash," Diaz says. "And there are some other good engineers on that crew. Since he wanted this mission to continue, and you to have support—well, I can actually do real work here, where I might not have there."

"Don't you think exploring a new sector base is real work?" I ask, then wish I hadn't. "Especially since they're looking for evidence of the modern Fleet?"

Her head tilts a little, as if she hasn't expected that question. She can answer it a variety of ways. She can talk about how she feels about returning to the Fleet or she can talk about how she feels about Coop, although I'm not sure she'll want to do that with me.

After a moment, she shrugs.

"I figured this," she says. "If there's a lot of work at the sector base, then it'll take months. And if they can download most of the information and take it back to Lost Souls, they will. I can help filter that information when I return from this mission."

"You're not worried that they'll find the Fleet and go after it?" Oh, I sound a bit too desperate here. It's clear, just from my tone, that I'm worried about that.

"I think there's a small percentage chance it'll happen," she says. "But the way I figure it, if the Fleet still exists, it's on Sector Base J-2 or something like that."

Provided that the Fleet has the same mission now that it did 5,000 years ago. Provided that the Fleet continued behave as it did when the *Ivoire* disappeared. Provided that the Fleet didn't just stay at Sector Base E-2 and settle down there.

"I don't think the Fleet will welcome us with open arms," she says. "I know the Fleet—or at least, our old Fleet. It loses its history. So it might not even know about a ship named the *Ivoire* that disappeared on a mission. The new Fleet would have to vet us, and decide if we fit in, and we probably won't."

She lets out a small shaky breath. Either she's nervous about what's about to happen with the Fleet or she's nervous about telling me.

"I'm not sure I want to be part of the early part of that encounter," she says, "if indeed there is one. I think I want everything to settle first. Or at least, I want everyone else to go through the uncertainty. I prefer engineering problems to people problems."

Her gaze is on mine. That last sentence is a warning to me as well as information. My anger at Coop is a people problem, not an engineering problem. She'll help with the engineering problems; she won't help with the people problems.

"I can always join them," she's saying. "And I'll be honest: when you started on this whole starfield thing, I thought about it. What you're suggesting is really dangerous."

And what Coop is doing isn't? I manage to block that sentence as well.

"Then I saw the images of those ships from the probe, and the disparate information and I…" She gives me a sideways smile. "I am interested in spite of myself. I want answers just like you do, even if that's not the logical and rational way to behave."

I let out a shaky laugh, and as I do, I realize I've been holding it back through this entire discussion. An uncomfortable laugh, one that lets out tension but doesn't have a lot of humor behind it.

"Thanks for the confidence vote," I say. "I think."

Her smile becomes a grin. "Yash once told me that you're a stealth leader."

"What does that mean?" I ask.

"That you have what most leaders don't," Diaz says. "You're inspiring. So first, we react against the inspiration, because we're logical creatures, we Fleet members. And then, slowly, the inspiration sucks us in. We do it logically, though. We listen to your questions and we slowly go from *Why should I care?* to *I really wish I knew the answer to that.* I've moved from not caring about that starfield-barrier to wanting to know what the heck these ships are."

"You think they're actually ships behind that barrier?" I ask.

"Or someone went to the trouble of making us think they're ships," she says. "Ultimately, figuring out what's going on with that image from the probe is an engineering problem, and I prefer engineering problems to people problems."

There's that sentence again. I smile, despite myself.

"I prefer engineering problems to people problems too," I say, deciding to be honest. "I prefer all other kinds of problems to people problems. That's why Ilona runs Lost Souls."

Diaz studies me for a moment, then she smiles again. She seems to relax.

"What if these are ships?" she asks me. "What are you going to do then?"

"I don't know," I say.

"You have an idea," she says.

And she's right: I do.

"If those are ships," I say, "I want to know why the Fleet is protecting them behind that barrier. Although that might not be the right question."

She frowns at me. "There's a different question?"

I nod. "Is it the Fleet protecting them?"

"It's Fleet tech," she says. "It can reprogram Fleet tech."

"And it just destroyed Fleet tech," I say. "We're thousands of years from your Fleet, in a part of space your Fleet left a long time ago. Why wouldn't some other group commandeer Fleet tech for itself?"

"You think someone is mining the Boneyard like we are, only storing the ships behind some barrier?" she asks.

193

"Maybe," I say. "Or maybe they're actually behind that barrier. Maybe the ships aren't stored. Maybe they're some kind of active military unit, waiting, hiding. And if we violate that barrier, we might find ourselves in some kind of military action."

She makes a small disbelieving sound. "If that's the case," she says, "then pursuing this mission, trying to get behind that barrier, is not a good idea at all."

"I know," I say. "But if we're going to continue 'mining' this Boneyard, as you so aptly put it, then we need to know what's back there now. Because that probe probably called attention to us. If whatever's back there is aware of us now and doesn't want us here, then they might take action against us."

She nods. "They haven't yet. And if they are watching us, they just saw the *Madxaf* arrive."

"Return," I say. "We removed it and brought it back in better working order. But as we keep removing ships, whatever is behind that barrier might object."

"We're not set up to fight anyone," Diaz says. "It would be dangerous to have any kind of weapons fire in the Boneyard."

"Yes," I say. "It would."

She makes that slight head tilt again. Then the tilt becomes a headshake. "You confuse me."

"I do?" I ask. I'm really not surprised. I confuse most everyone connected to the Fleet.

Coop and I have had this discussion more than once, in fact. He told me that he now expects me to confuse him.

"You think we may have activated a sleeping giant," she says.

I nod.

"And yet you want to keep poking that giant," she says.

I struggle to maintain my expression, keeping it calm.

"And," she says, "you're excited about that."

I smile. I *am* excited. "I like taking risks," I say.

"This isn't a risk," she says. "This is beyond risky."

"Just like going to that sector base," I say, and as I say it, I realize that Coop and I have more in common than I ever thought we did.

Diaz doesn't smile anymore. She looks pained. "You're telling me that if I want to live risk-free, I should stay away from you and from the *Ivoire*."

"I'm going to give you a chance to make your own decisions," I say. "All of you, the *Ivoire* crew who are working here, and the rest of the people I brought on the *Sove*. I fully expect to be left with my original team, and no one else."

"Your team of risk-takers." She isn't being sarcastic. Nor is she really asking a question. She's paraphrasing in an attempt to understand.

She glances at some of the non-Fleet tech around us, as if it can provide her with answers.

"Does that mean anyone who stays with you is a risk-taker?" she asks.

I have no idea how to answer that. I'm not even sure I should try.

She runs her hand over the non-Fleet tech in front of her.

"We all signed up for this, you know," she says.

"This trip to the Boneyard?" I ask.

"No," she says. "The Fleet, the *Ivoire* crew. When we agreed to serve on a DV-class ship, we signed up for the unknown. We knew that we might end up in a part of the universe we didn't understand. We also knew we might never get back home. So, if someone from the *Ivoire* tells you that they can't handle risk, they're lying."

"Then what about the crew who've gone planetside? The ones who no longer want to serve?" I ask.

"From what I understand, they're done with risk," she says. "Their risk tolerance is much lower than it was. But those of us who remain? We have a high risk tolerance."

She seems to like to speak elliptically. I wonder if that's because she's not a people person and isn't used to discussing important things at this depth or if she speaks elliptically because she's with the Fleet, and speaking her mind is something that's done cautiously if at all.

"What are you saying to me?" I ask.

"Maybe you shouldn't give us a choice to leave," she says. "We'll follow orders. We'll do a great job. That's who we are."

"I know that," I say, and I'm making sure that my tone is soft again, respectful. "But I'm not Fleet. It's not my way to bring people on a mission, as you call it, if they don't want to come along. Even if they'll do a great job."

She studies me for a moment. Then her lips turn up in a rueful smile.

"You *are* a stealth leader," she says. "You just got me to argue for everyone to stay, when I thought we should all leave not an hour ago."

"I didn't intend to do that," I say, and that's true. "And I don't expect you to make a decision right now. Let's see what we can find in the *Madxaf*'s databases. Let's see if we learn anything new."

"All right," she says. She shuts down all the tablets around her. "I'm ready. Let's go."

15

I FIND MYSELF CONSTANTLY SURPRISED by the *Madxaf*. When we found the *Madxaf*, we all knew it was going to take work to make it a working vessel again, but Yash liked the ship's bones.

She wouldn't recognize them now.

At least, I don't.

Diaz and I have taken a small runabout from the *Sove* to the *Madxaf*, so we enter through one of the cargo bays. It looks empty and imposing at the same time. It has a lot of gleaming sidework, and all kinds of attachments built into the walls that I've never seen before.

In fact, if I wasn't already familiar with the layout of the *Madxaf*, I would have gotten lost, just because of how different the ship looks.

The interior walls are light gray with shining silver accents, usually indicating some control panel or a door access. The only part of the ship that's black is the floor, and even that gleams. The lights have a warm yellow cast, and the entire interior smells as fresh as the outdoors does in the handful of planetside wildernesses I've visited.

In fact, this area smells slightly fresher, as if a scouring wind has come through with a cleansing rain and freshened the air.

I'm wondering if the entire ship smells fresh because it's been refurbished and hasn't been used on a long trip. This is the longest journey the *Madxaf* has gone on.

Plus, we're on a ship built for at least five hundred people, and right now, twenty live on it. The *Madxaf* feels new and empty and unused.

Diaz and I take an elevator to the bridge. Only six members of the crew are on the bridge at the moment, working various consoles. Pao greets us, spending more time saying hello to Diaz than to me. Pao's dark hair is pulled away from her face, and she's wearing some kind of brown work scrubs. Apparently, she expected to help Diaz.

I almost say something, but Diaz gives me one of those slight shakes of the head.

"It'll be great to have assistance," Diaz says a little too cheerily, and as she does, I realize why she's saying it. Better to have someone else who has never seen those ships search for them.

Diaz might replicate the same search pattern, but having Pao help— or even do the search—would guarantee a different pattern, one that might come up with different results.

"I'm going to leave you both to the work," I say. "If you'll just point me to the non-Fleet ships you brought along, I'd be grateful."

Pao barely looks at me as she says, "They're in ship maintenance."

My surprise must have shown on my face because she adds, "They don't need maintenance, but Ilona told me to be discreet with the non-Fleet ships, and that's the best thing I could think of."

"Thank you," I say, surprisingly pleased by the decision. Placing non-Fleet ships in maintenance makes them seem unimportant at best, something to be used for parts at worst.

I am about to ask her if ship maintenance is in the usual location, when she turns to Diaz, sweeping her had toward a console that I've never seen on a DV-Class ship before.

"We can work here," Pao says, and touches the edge of the console. Screens rise and envelop the two of them in a literal bubble. The screens are black and shiny, made of nanobits.

If I wanted to spy on them, I couldn't. Fortunately, I don't want to.

The five members of the bridge look a bit curious, but then they see me staring at the bubble and return to their work. I recognize all of them because I've seen them around Lost Souls, but where and when and doing what I can't say. I can't even remember their names, if I ever learned them.

Since no one is paying attention to me, I have no reason to say good-bye as I leave the bridge.

I take the elevator to Deck Two, which is where ship maintenance is on most DV-Class vessels, and where it was when we sent the unre-paired *Madxaf* to Lost Souls. The entire journey to ship maintenance is a revelation to me.

The elevator is smooth and bright, with harsher lighting than the lighting in the corridors, and reflective silver walls. When I get out on Deck 2, I note that the design pattern holds, light gray walls with silver trim. Even though the standard DV-class ships are large, they always feel a bit closed in, tunnel-like, even in the corridors.

Here the light walls, silver trim, and warm lighting makes the corridor seem larger, and actually lifts my mood. I wonder who made the decision on the design change and if they actually were experimenting to see if a lighter color palette would improve the experience of living and working on a DV-class ship.

When I reach the entrance to ship maintenance, the doors are open. The interior is dark until I step across the threshold, and then the lights come up. The walls are smooth and a darker gray, which is, I realize, a series of cabinets that are lined up and labeled.

I'm the only person down here, so I explore a bit. The air isn't as fresh here. It smells faintly of rubber and some kind of cleaner. I have the lay-out of the ship in my head, and realize that the ship storage part of ship maintenance is to my left. I have to open a series of doors to get there.

For a moment I hesitate, worried that I'm not going to be able to open them. And yet I can, with the touch of my palm on the access panel. Because someone thought it through, apparently, and remem-bered that I own Lost Souls.

That rubbery smell grows as I step deeper into the maintenance bays, followed by the sharp stinging odor of industrial cleaners. The bays closest to this entrance are empty, but those near the ship bay have ships in them.

There are seven ships of different makes and models and none of them are mine. Which is probably good. The last thing I would want is my single ship or the *Business* or even some of the smaller dive ships I've used (and loved) to get blown up by that starfield-barrier.

Still, a tiny part of me is disappointed. I think I was hoping for familiarity.

Ilona or whoever she assigned to the task of giving me non-Fleet ships gave me a variety. I don't know what each type of ship is called, since none of them are of a make that I'm familiar with. No Fleet ships, as I said, no ships from the Empire, so most of these must have come from the Nine Planets.

I see one single ship, which I will probably not use—although, on closer inspection, it's not quite a single ship. It has room for two people up front—dual seats near the controls. The ship has a reinforced windshield of some kind and, from the look of it, some kind of shutter that will come down over the windshield.

As I stare at the ship, its specs form on the windshield itself, telling me the weight capacity, what the ship was designed for (short journeys of less than a day for one or two people), the type of fuel, defensive technology (a lot), and weaponry (none). The information scrolls, telling me that the ship is not designed for space-to-land travel, and that it needs to dock on space stations or other ships. The information begins and ends with the ship's designation, a cute name that I promptly forget.

The next smallest ship seats four. It's a space-to-land orbiter, designed to be taken from a larger ship like this one to some kind of landing area on the ground. The exterior of the ship is rounded on top, with a flat bottom that can release some kind of landing gear.

The information on this ship scrolls along its black sides. That's when I realize that the information scroll on these ships isn't part of the ship's specs. Someone at Lost Souls has added this feature, so that we know what kind of ships we have at a glance.

Unlike the single ship, this ship has a minor amount of weaponry—the kind that can defend the ship against something small that might arise around a landing or an exit from a hostile place. The ship also has a startling amount of speed, both inside atmosphere and outside. It doesn't have much cargo room, though, and like the first ship, is only designed for one day of use at a time.

The third ship catches my attention. It's about the size of one of our orbiters. It fits ten to fifteen people easily, fewer if the crew needs to travel overnight. According to its specs, it has a galley kitchen, an optional full kitchen (for long-haul runs), sleeping quarters with furniture that can be recessed so the quarters can be repurposed into additional cargo space, enough weaponry to defend the ship, and a fairly strong defensive profile.

The ship itself looks like nothing much, something that I've learned through all the decades of wreck diving, means that the ship is deliberately camouflaged, and that it has a lot of capability.

The ship is a muddy brown, with a spiky exterior—made with literal spikes. Wherever the ship's designers could add something pointed, they did. In fact, they added layers of spikes—each section of the ship is a spike, and the ship itself hardens into points on three sides.

I suspect that the fourth spike would appear when the ship is in space, instead of docked on some kind of floor.

The rubbery smell seems to come from this ship, which tells me that I have no idea what it's made of.

I walk to the back side, where the ship's main door stands open, a ramp (fortunately spike-free) spilling out of it. The ramp doesn't look very stable, but I climb on it anyway.

It wobbles under my feet as I make my way to the entrance. Interior lights wink on as I dip my head inside. The sharp smell makes my eyes water. If we were to use this vessel, we'd have to clean it again (if it has been cleaned at all).

The floor is smooth and curls inside, like an inviting path. The walls are covered with gleaming and unfamiliar technology.

I wander inside, searching for the bridge.

Instead, I find a cockpit barely big enough for one person. Branching off the cockpit—in another room—is the weapons system. In fact, all of the different systems, from weapons to defense to navigation, seem to have their own little one-person rooms.

I can't decide of that makes this ship too annoying to use or perfect for a trip inside that starfield-barrier. The ship is certainly unlike anything the Fleet has designed and unlike anything I've seen in the Empire either.

I make myself leave. I'm intrigued by this ship as a wreck diver, and I'm not sure if that emotion carries over to the woman who is going to lead a mission into the starfield-barrier.

To figure that out, I need to step away.

Finding my way out of the ship is harder than I thought. That path and the little rooms don't give me guidance. I wonder if the design is bad or purposeful. I take two wrong turns before I find the exit and can walk down the wobbly ramp.

As I step onto the floor, I sneeze. Whatever chemicals are inside that ship are pungent enough to make my sinuses ache.

The remaining four ships are variations on the runabout design that the Fleet uses. Rectangular and long, they vary mostly by the size of the interior. Two can handle nearly a dozen crew members. Another can only handle five and the last one can handle twenty, if we set up the ship properly.

None of them have much in the way of weaponry, and only two have defensive capabilities that make them good enough for my needs.

I backtrack out of the ship maintenance area. Now, the emptiness of the *Madxaf* makes me uncomfortable, which I find ironic, since I love diving empty ships.

But the newly refurbished *Madxaf* isn't supposed to be empty, the way that wrecks are. The *Madxaf* is supposed to be teaming with people, all of them working on something or living their lives.

Part of the discomfort comes from those seven ships. When I asked for non-Fleet ships, I had envisioned something like the *Business* or even my single ship. Something I'm comfortable with, something I understand. I had pictured us going into that starfield-barrier feeling strong, as if we knew what we were doing.

If we're going to know what we're doing, then we need to figure out everything these ships can do before we remove them from the *Madxaf*. I have to figure out which of the ships will work best for us.

I worry about the runabout clones, simply because they might be misinterpreted by scanners as repurposed Fleet ships. But that might not be something I'm making up. I'll have to check with Diaz about the scanner capabilities that she's familiar with.

I like the single ship, except that it means whoever goes into the starfield-barrier goes in as a team of two, and might feel that they're about to be sacrificed to my curiosity. Even if it's just me and someone else. That ship isn't big enough to handle the mission I have in mind.

For the reason of size, I'm probably going to rule out the four-seater orbiter as well. Although I haven't made up my mind about that entirely.

It depends on what we learn about the spiky orbiter. That ship is different enough that nothing will read it as Fleet. I also like that the ship's systems are separated from each other. I'm hoping that means that if one gets compromised, the others will not.

I'm deep in thought as I pass several doors, and don't realize until the very last minute that one of them is blinking at me, as if it's trying to catch my attention. I stop and put my hand on the door's control panel. The door slides open to reveal a closet, filled with non-Fleet probes.

I let out a tiny whoop of surprise. Lots and lots of non-Fleet probes, of all sizes. Along the wall of the closet are some control devices, like tablets and other things I barely recognize.

The probes are much more useful than the ships, at least at the moment. I can use the probes and probably will.

My mood, which had been declining since I visited the ships, has risen again. The excitement, which was waning in the face of all the criticism—and, frankly, in the face of Coop's unexpected decision to visit a sector base—has returned.

I reach out and run my hand on the cool metal of the nearest probe. We'll see if these probes can be reprogrammed.

If they can't, I'll be happier about sending ships into that starfield-barrier.

If they can…well, I'll worry about that if it happens.

One step at a time, as I've reminded my team. One step at a time.

16

I RETURNED FROM THE *MADXAF* ahead of Diaz. When I spoke to her before leaving, she said there were things she wanted to check before she talked to me.

I liked the sound of that.

I expect to see her in a day or so, but to my surprise, she comes to my quarters only a few hours later.

I am sitting at the dining room table, which doubles as a workspace for me. At that moment, though, I'm eating a pozole, using some fresh cilantro and watercress from the hydroponics bay as garnishes. Usually I just cut up an avocado and add a bit of cheese, but I decided to grab myself a treat as I came back.

I'm not really tasting the treat much, though. This pozole's base is a green chili, which is my favorite, and I really should pay more attention to what I'm putting in my mouth.

Instead, I've surrounded myself with a three-dimensional map of this part of the Boneyard, with a special focus on the starfield-barrier.

I've watched the images of that probe a dozen times, and I am gleaning no new information from that. So now, I'm comparing the three-dimensional views of the starfield-barrier from the Fleet tech to the three-dimensional views of the ghostly darkness from the non-Fleet tech.

I keep adjusting the settings on my views, not certain if what I'm seeing are shadows of the mines placed between the regular ships in the Boneyard and the actual barrier leading to the mystery ships inside that region of space, or if my eyes are playing tricks on me.

I know that Tamaz and Orlando are examining the telemetry, trying to see what they can find, but they haven't let me know they're ready to talk yet, and I haven't pushed them.

I have to keep reminding myself that I'm not in a hurry, that there is no reason for a tight timeline to explore that part of the Boneyard.

But my internal clock wants me to move fast, and I'm not certain if that's just because I'm still excited about all of this. I can't seem to shake the feeling that we are now being watched, but who or what is watching us isn't easy to figure out.

Diaz didn't contact me before she came to my quarters. She hit the chime outside the door and then identified herself, something that people rarely do around me.

I unlatch the door without getting up from the table, then I shrink the view of the starfield-barrier until it's screen-sized.

By the time Diaz enters, my quarters look less like a piece of the Boneyard, and more like a place someone lives in.

"There's pozole," I say, indicating the still-open container in the kitchen. I cut up more cilantro and watercress than I needed, and I left the avocado on the counter, where it's probably turning brown.

"Thank you," she says. "I haven't eaten all day."

I mentally shake my head. Engineers. They get wrapped up in whatever they're doing, and forget to take care of themselves. It seems to be one of the traits that they all have in common.

Dishes clatter, silverware clinks, and the sound of running water indicates that she got herself something to drink without asking me for permission—which is a good thing. While she's prepping her meal, I keep staring at that starfield-barrier, not really seeing it, wondering why I'm feeling watched.

She brings a steaming bowl of the pozole to the table, a spoon stuck into the side. She sets a water glass down, then returns to the kitchen before I can say anything.

I take another bite of my pozole, letting myself taste it this time—the green tomatillos in salsa verde seem fresh too, and they—along with the jalapeños—mostly drown out the taste of the garlic.

I don't slow down enough to enjoy things. I always get accused of that, and it's true. I'm not really slowing down right now either. I'm pausing to let my senses catch up with that feeling of being watched, that feeling which is really starting to bother me.

Diaz returns, carrying a tablet. She finally notices the screen-sized images of the starfield-barrier.

"Finding anything?" she asks.

I shake my head, and move the holoimages to the side. "Did you?"

"Yes," she says. "That's why I want to talk with you."

At that *yes*, my heart starts jumping. I set down my spoon.

"About the ships?" I ask.

She nods. "I had Pao search. I didn't let her use the imagery as a base either. She didn't touch any of our files. She did a search based on the description."

"And?" I ask.

She taps her tablet and a hologram rises at eye level. A three-dimensional image of a ship—a large imposing one—starts circling, as if it's trying to impress me.

It does impress me. The stats, listed below, make the ship as big as a DV-Class ship, but with sharper edges. This ship has as many edges as a runabout, and the same general rectangular shape, only much much much larger. Arrows and instructions appear in a language that looks only vaguely familiar to me.

It must be Coop's version of Standard. He—and the rest of the *Ivoire's* crew—had to learn our version of Standard. We saw no point in learning theirs.

"What is it?" I ask.

"It's a warship," she says.

I frown at her. "I thought these ships, the DV-class, are the warships."

She shakes her head. "The Fleet has warships that it rarely uses. We don't need them, since we mostly go on diplomatic missions."

I wouldn't use the word *diplomatic* much with what I understand of the Fleet. Yes, they do practice diplomacy when they want something, but mostly they travel through sectors; they don't try to colonize them.

"If you don't need them, why build them?" I ask.

"We've needed to fight in the past," she says, waving a hand. I'm not sure if she's being vague because the fights aren't relevant to our conversation or if she knows very little about the kind of fights that Fleet has gotten into.

I would wager it's the latter, and not the former.

I stare at this ship before me, looking at all the nooks and crannies, and the arrows pointing at various parts. "I can't read this," I say.

"Sorry." She toggles something, and the language shifts.

I find myself examining laser canons, torpedoes, and a lot of standard fighting equipment. But there are still words I don't understand, and I assume that they're for weapons I've never encountered.

The defensive capabilities of this ship are amazing. The ship has its nanobit exterior, which will protect it from most things, as well as a secondary armor plating that can be activated around the ship as needed. Each part of the ship has a different kind of shielding from the other part, so that a shield breach won't lead to a catastrophic breakdown of all of the shields.

Each department, each wing, each level of the ship has its own defenses, as well as secondary and tertiary bridges that will activate if parts of the ship break off.

I've never seen ship design on this scale and it's impressive.

"This is what's behind that starfield-barrier?" I ask.

"We think so," she says.

I note the *we*, but don't comment on it. Not yet, anyway.

She scoops a spoonful of soup, filled with hominy, so that the pozole looks lumpy. She holds the spoonful, then sets it back down.

"Neither Gustav nor I know much about the warships," she says. So, she's been talking with Denby about this. "We know that they exist. We know that it takes a lot of communication between a captain and the chain of command to launch the warships. It's not a decision either of us have had experience with, not even when we were in ships run by someone else."

I'm done with my pozole and I set the bowl aside. I fold my hands in front of me so I don't fiddle with the spoon.

"I can't remember the last time I heard of anyone launching warships. I think maybe I studied it in school." Diaz picks up her spoon again, heaping more food on it. This time, she slurps the pozole off the spoon and chews a little, clearly thinking.

I'm waiting, although I want to ask a million questions. That antsy feeling has returned, the one that provokes me to push for all of the answers all at once.

I know better than to do that. I need to focus, and maybe that will calm down all of my swirling emotions. The food didn't do that, and it usually calms me a little.

She swallows, then says, "As Gustav and I talked, we realized we've never even seen a warship. They don't travel with the Fleet. I remember learning about that in school—that the Fleet didn't want to travel with military vessels, afraid that any culture we encountered would think we're warriors."

"The DV-Class ships look like military vessels," I say.

"I know," Diaz says. "I didn't say that was an effective method. That was just the thinking behind it. And look at this."

She taps her screen again, and the warship model gets replaced by nine small warships, stacked around each other, three on top, three in the middle, and three at the base.

They look imposing, like a wall of ships. If I ever encountered something like that in my single ship, I would have veered off, and tried to look as insignificant as possible.

I would have thought they were on their way to attack some place or someone.

They really do look like they're heading to war.

Then she places nine DV-class vessels in the same formation. They don't look as formidable. In fact, the formation looks like a mistake. DV-Class vessels aren't designed to travel in groups like that.

The warships clearly are.

"If the warships don't travel with the Fleet," I say, "where do they come from when they're needed?"

"That's what Gustav and I realized we don't know," she says. "We have no idea at all. All we know is that if they're called up, they arrive."

"Is there a regular crew for the warships?" I ask, trying to imagine this.

"We don't know that either," she says. "Our knowledge is very limited. I tried to do a search on the *Madxaf,* and then again when I came back to the *Sove.* I even used that hack we'd found for the admiral identification. I'm not coming up with anything. I think Coop might know."

She says that last sentence tentatively, as if she expects me to react badly to his name.

"Well, let's hope we get a chance to discuss it with him," I say.

She nods, looking down. She doesn't seem to want to discuss Coop with me again, which is probably my fault.

I turn slightly in my chair so that I can see the starfield-barrier on those small screens still floating near the table.

"You're telling me those ships could be manned," I say.

"I'm telling you I don't know," she says. "I don't know any of it."

"Theorize for me," I say.

She sets the spoon down. The bowl is still nearly full. She hasn't had much time to eat.

She pushes back from the table, as if she doesn't want to be tempted by the meal.

"The Boneyard bothers me," she says. "All of these ships, many with their *anacapa* drives intact, just here, waiting for what, we don't know. And then, we've been active in here, taking ships back to Lost Souls. I mean, the *Madxaf* doesn't belong to us, if us is the Lost Souls Corporation."

I find that "us" interesting. That's the first identification she uses, not the Fleet.

"If we think of us as the Fleet," she says, almost as if she could hear my thoughts, "then I think we have a right to these ships. We're stranded here, and we can use them. That part is kind of logical. If a Fleet ship gets in trouble near a Boneyard, there are resources."

I clench my folded hands together, so that I don't interrupt her. Because there's a flaw in her logic right there: Coop and the rest of the *Ivoire* crew hadn't known about the Boneyards. They had been as surprised as the rest of us, particularly when they saw how many ships were scattered through this incredibly large place.

Coop immediately went to the aftermath of a war, thinking that's what might have happened, but we have since found some records in the older ships that show there had been a number of Boneyards before this one.

Yash had some theories about the Boneyards, and all of them were similar to the theories that Diaz is espousing now.

"Those warships, though." Diaz reaches for the spoon, as if she needs to do something with her hand, then drops her fingers to the table, as if she is rethinking eating while theorizing. "To me, they explain everything. Boneyards scattered throughout the areas of the universe where we've been. If we have to go back, then we have ships…"

Her voice trails off, and she looks at me sideways, as if she's embarrassed by what she's just said.

"Of course, we generally don't go back," she says quickly, almost as if she's saying it before I could.

"But, if we have warships waiting for us, and we need them, just ahead of the Boneyards—somewhere along the route, they can show up, and do what they need to do." She shrugs, then shakes her head. "I would guess that they're unmanned. Because otherwise, we have generations of people, living on ships in a Boneyard, and they've never been deployed for any reason."

That's my theory too. It's good to hear her say it though.

"I take it, then, the specs of the ships don't include full automation," I say.

"That they could come to someone's rescue and fight in some kind of battle without a crew?" She sounds surprised, as if she hasn't thought of that. "Every Fleet vessel that I'm familiar with has some kind of automation. But none of our ships are designed to work on their own, without someone guiding them."

"Except the big life rafts," I say. I've seen those, but never in use. They're designed to do large rescues, often of people who have no idea how to run a ship.

"Well, yeah," Diaz says, "but even those are designed to be run from another ship. Besides, they're not supposed to go very far. They're designed to go from rescue vehicle to the ship needing rescue, and nothing more."

I nod, thinking about all she's said. Now I really want to see those ships. I also understand why they're so well defended.

"How many ships do you think are behind that starfield-barrier?" I ask.

"Hundreds," she says. "It's a big space."

It is. I'm looking at the starfield-barrier, at both sets of images, as well as those smudges.

"If there are ships at the ready," I say slowly, "and they need a crew, where would that crew come from?"

Diaz looks at me, startled. She clearly hasn't asked this question.

"You had a lot of education from the Fleet," I say.

"It may not—"

I hold up my hand. I *know* that every crew member of the *Ivoire* was educated a long, long time ago. I know that what they learned may not be what the people who put this Boneyard together learned. I don't need to hear that again.

"And I know there were educational tracks—leadership, engineering…" I'm not exactly sure how to ask this question, but I decide to just go for it. "Were any of them military?"

"By your definition," she says, and by "your" she means the Empire and everyone we've encountered from the Nine Planets, "our entire culture is military."

"I know," I say. That's why I had trouble asking that question. "But there's DV-level military, and then there's these warships. Is there something like a war college?"

From the way she looks at me, I know there is not. She doesn't even understand the question.

"I don't…think so," she says slowly.

"So, do you think they would send someone like Coop to man these ships if some kind of battle was heating up?" I ask.

She lets out a breath. "It doesn't seem logical, does it?" she says. "I mean, they'd have to know how the ships operate, and be really familiar with them."

"So, do people just go to school and then you don't hear from them again?" I ask.

"What do you mean?" she asks.

"I mean, like…" Oh, I have no idea how to explain this to her. If there is a different military force, and the regular Fleet doesn't know about them, then a lot of people would go to school, find themselves on the military track, and never be heard from again.

"It happens all the time," she says, in that tone the Fleet uses with me sometimes. "We end up on different ships. It's rare to see our school friends again, once we've graduated."

Of course it is. And I have to stop pressing her. She doesn't have the answers. Only someone who has been on the leadership track or actually in leadership would have those answers.

Which brings us back to Coop.

Again.

"Warships," I say, as I look at that starfield-barrier again. "You're certain."

"As certain as I can be," she says. "It's an image generated in a nano-second by a probe that got destroyed."

Good point. I think of all of those probes in the *Madxaf*. They might find something different. The warship imagery could be as fake as that starfield is.

"We're done with that starfield-barrier now, right?" she asks. Her tone is hopeful, but her face is in a half-wince, as if she expects a blow.

"No," I say. "But you can be done with it, if you want."

She looks down at her pozole. "You scare me, Boss."

"I know," I say, but don't add, *Sometimes I scare myself.*

THE FLEET
ONE MONTH AGO

17

CAPTAIN KAYLA COHN STEPPED OUT OF HER OFFICE onto the bridge of the *Geesi*. She had finished coordinating with the other ships in her Task Unit, and they were now ready to head into foldspace.

She had to give the go-ahead, and now, she was the one who wasn't quite ready. She needed to triple-check everything with her chief engineer and her navigator.

First, though, Cohn shrank her office into a small box, and stored it inside the Ready Room to the left of the captain's chair. She was one of the first captains of a DV-Class vessel to use the floating office as her home base, adopting the program years ago when it was new.

These days, she couldn't imagine living without it. Even the Ready Rooms were dated, although she couldn't convince the brass of that. And she wouldn't convince them for some time, because this trip took priority.

Her bridge crew, plus Chief Engineer Erasyl Iosua, were completing the doublechecks she had requested. It wasn't every day that Cohn took five ships into foldspace. In fact, outside of foldspace rescue training missions decades ago, she had never taken five ships into foldspace.

So much was new on this mission, and she wanted to do it all right.

Vice Admiral Irena Mbuyi had handpicked Cohn for this mission. Mbuyi wanted someone with a lot of command experience, someone who knew how to think quickly in tough situations, someone who was willing to make a mistake that might actually cost her her career.

Cohn was never reckless in the choices she made. She always analyzed them as deeply as she possibly could. But she would never make a decision based on what was best for her career. Nor would she choose the cautious route simply because it was cautious.

Mbuyi had explained the difficulties with this mission: the thefts that triggered an old heretofore unknown Scrapheap to find the Fleet; the decision to investigate; and the possible problems that the Task Unit might encounter when it arrived.

The fact that the thieves had *anacapa* drives and old codes for Scrapheaps bothered Mbuyi enough to consider those thieves part of something that might be equal to the Fleet. The Fleet had never encountered anything like that before, but the brass had always known that it was possible.

Cohn walked over to the navigation console. Iosua stood next to Aksel Priede, the navigator. Cohn towered over both of them.

Iosua was short, chubby cheeked, and a little round. His dark eyes sparkled with intelligence, and were the only part of him that actually looked adult. The rest of him looked like an unformed adolescent, a problem made worse by his braying laugh and propensity to crack inappropriate jokes.

Priede, by contrast, was extremely serious, and looked it. His skin was darker than Iosua's and covered with frown lines. Priede looked older than Iosua even though he was twenty years younger. Some of that was his spacer's thinness. Unlike Iosua, Priede had never lived on land, and even when the *Geesi* docked in a sector base, Priede often volunteered to stay with the ship.

He preferred space to land, just like most officers in the Fleet did.

Technically, neither Priede nor Iosua should have been determining foldspace coordinates, but Cohn wouldn't have it any other way. Iosua was a foldspace wizard, not just in her opinion, but in the opinion of half the Fleet. He was always getting offered the opportunity to move to a different ship.

But he had trained with Cohn, and had been on the *Geesi* for his entire career. Cohn and Iosua understood each other, and knew how each other worked.

And Cohn knew that Iosua's willingness to work with Priede was unusual. In all her years with him, Iosua had never offered to work with a navigator before. But Iosua had told Cohn that Priede was the first person he had ever encountered who saw foldspace the same way he did.

Iosua had tried to explain what he saw to Cohn dozens of times, but she had never understood it. She saw foldspace the way she was trained to see it: as a different part of space that somehow folded the distance between two points, the way that a person would fold the corners on a blanket.

Iosua said that was wrong, but he couldn't come up with an analogy that she understood—or that anyone else understood either. He did make it clear that he thought foldspace was a different sector of space that the *anacapa* drive somehow let them access, but he wasn't sure exactly what that sector was.

And he couldn't really explain his ideas.

He had toyed with working research on *anacapa* drives and foldspace for years, but he had finally gotten rid of that notion when he learned that foldspace researchers worked on ships that rarely (if ever) went into foldspace.

He told Cohn that he would rather study in the field.

As he was going to do today. This trip the *Geesi* was taking to the Scrapheap was the longest foldspace journey the *Geesi* had taken since Iosua and Cohn had taken over command of the ship.

They had spent a lot of time together, without the rest of the crew or the captains of the other vessels, determining how best to get to that Scrapheap. There were several options, including making short hops through foldspace, with distinct stopping points in regular space.

Normally, Iosua had told her, he would have preferred that method if the *Geesi* were traveling alone. But she wasn't. She was traveling with four other ships—two fully equipped and relatively new DV-Class vessels, an SC-Class ship, and much-too-old DV-Class ship that was filled with researchers and scholars.

Cohn had wanted to jettison the old ship, the *Tudósok,* but Mbuyi wouldn't hear of it. The entire scholarly arm of the Fleet saw this trip to an old Scrapheap as an opportunity to get information about the Fleet's past, information that the Fleet itself seemed to have either never recorded or deleted centuries ago.

Unfortunately, that information was one of the things the *Geesi* could have used for this particular journey. This Scrapheap wasn't far from Sector Bases W and Y. The Fleet had recorded that Sector Base W had been destroyed, and that Sector Base Y had been moved from its original site to a site that was on a completely different trajectory for the Fleet, but there was nothing in the records that explained what happened.

Scholars knew bits and pieces of what happened—there had been a battle, maybe even a war, and Sector Base W had been destroyed. But no one knew who destroyed it or why, and no one knew who made the decision to abandon the original site for Sector Base Y.

Some scholars felt the lack of information was deliberate—that something had happened that the Fleet was ashamed of. But other scholars pointed out that the Fleet had no history of shame, and didn't seem to care about what happened in the past.

Those scholars believed that the information had been lost.

There were two reasons Mbuyi wanted the *Tudósok* on this trip: the first was to recover that history, but the second was in case whatever—whoever—was stealing from the Scrapheap had something to do with that ancient destruction of Sector Base W.

Some cultures—land-based cultures in particular—kept historical grudges, and nurtured them for centuries as part of their own culture's lore.

Mbuyi was worried that the Task Unit was going to run into one of those cultures and wouldn't know how to respond.

Cohn didn't think scholars would know how to respond either, but she wasn't going to question her superior, particularly when Mbuyi made certain that the *Tudósok*'s crew was comprised of some of the most experienced old-timers in the Fleet.

As Cohn reached the navigation console, she heard the soft conversation that Iosua and Priede were having. It wasn't about what she had thought it would be about.

"…concerns me that our star maps are centuries old," Iosua was saying. "Regions of space change. We pick the wrong coordinates and we might arrive in the middle of an asteroid field."

It was a good concern, but it was one based on normal tactics. Nothing about this mission was normal.

"I don't think we can guess where to arrive," Cohn said as she stopped on the opposite side of the console from the two men. Priede was frowning even more than usual, and Iosua looked almost downcast.

They both raised their heads in surprise when she spoke. They clearly hadn't seen her approach.

"We're going to have to guess," Iosua said. "We don't want the thieves to see us, after all."

In a situation like this, Fleet tactics called for a stealth arrival, usually one that was as much as a half-day's journey from the target.

But Cohn didn't care if the thieves saw them. In fact, it might be better if the thieves did see them. The moment the ships left foldspace was going to be impressive. One minute, there would be nothing in that region of space, and in the next moment, there would be five large and intimidating ships.

"I don't see how we avoid guessing," Priede said, but Iosua put a hand on his arm, trying to stop him from commenting further.

"Clearly, the captain has a plan," Iosua said.

Cohn smiled at him. "I do. The only thing we know for certain is the configuration of that Scrapheap ten months ago. So we use that configuration. We arrive just outside the Scrapheap."

"And have it shoot at us?" Priede asked.

"It won't," she said. "We'll be sending it our identification, as well as its own signature from those contacts. If the Scrapheap is still working on Fleet technology, and from the contact, it clearly is, then it will accept us willingly. It might partner with us if we end up facing a force of those thieves."

"That sounds hopeful," Iosua said. Cohn couldn't quite read his tone. Was he being sarcastic? Or sincere? Every now and then, he could be both at the same time.

"The partner part might be hopeful," Cohn said, "but the rest of it isn't, and you know that, Erasyl. We've worked Scrapheaps before."

"Newer ones," he said. "I trust their technology more."

So did she. But she wasn't going to admit that, not right now.

"Pick a location near the first breach from those thieves," she said. "Make sure there's enough room for all five ships. With luck, the thieves will have stationed another ship outside of the Scrapheap, and they will receive notification of our arrival."

"You're hoping to scare them away from the Scrapheap?" Priede asked.

"If they are true thieves," Cohn said, "they will scatter when the authorities show up."

"Will we chase them?" Priede asked.

"We won't know that until we're on-site." Cohn wasn't about to make a decision like that before she had a bit more information. She was hoping she would not have to engage with the thieves at all.

There was a chance that the thieves were particularly lucky pirates who had figured out how to break into the Scrapheap. She had encountered pirates around Scrapheaps before, some of whom had captured some former sector base personnel, who gave them access to the codes to get inside.

The pirates had been surprisingly easy to deal with, and had convinced her that thieves were usually not the problem that everyone saw them as.

She had discussed her past experience with Mbuyi, probably sealing the *Tudósok's* place in this mission. Since the Task Unit was going so far from the Fleet, there had to be more of a reason than simply putting terror into some pirates.

Cohn would let the *Tudósok* do its research, remove as much material from the Scrapheap's core and the nearby ships as possible, find a way to remove the Ready Ships if there were any (and if they were still of value, considering their age), and then destroy the Scrapheap.

That was the trajectory of the perfect mission. That trajectory was how the Task Unit got its official name. It was the Scrapheap Investigation Unit, a title she didn't want to use because she felt it might not end up describing the job.

Cohn thought the Scrapheap Destruction Force would have been a better fit for this mission her ship and the four others she led were on, but Vice Admiral Mbuyi had gently disabused her of that notion.

If I send a Destruction Force, she had said, *then they are obligated to destroy the Scrapheap, which might not be appropriate yet. Better to send an investigative unit, so that we might catch these thieves or at least learn something about them.*

And then Mbuyi got to the heart of the matter.

Besides, she had said with a bit of a smile, *there is the chance that these thieves will attack. The Destruction Force can handle all kinds of disasters, but they're not set up for a firefight with a ship that has similar if not the same capabilities as ours.*

She had to be prepared for the attack, and she believed she was. Her ships were state-of-the-art.

The ships being stolen from the Scrapheap were centuries old, with technology that the Fleet knew how to disable or destroy because the Fleet had built it.

"Arriving next to the Scrapheap changes some of our calculations," Iosua said. "We're going to have account for loose *anacapa* energy."

"Won't the forcefield prevent that?" Priede asked.

"Never assume all Fleet forcefields are the same," Iosua said. "We don't know when this one was added, and whether or not it protects against escaping *anacapa* energy."

He was speaking from experience, an experience that Cohn shared. She had been with him when they made the mistake of targeting a Fleet forcefield outside a Scrapheap, and that forcefield had been modified by some other culture long after the forcefield was first used.

The resulting energy backlash had nearly destroyed the *Geesi*.

"How long will it take you to revamp those coordinates?" Cohn asked.

"With a check, and doublecheck, not to mention review from the other ships, maybe an hour." Iosua sounded calm, but he wasn't. Those reviews irritated him more than he wanted to admit. The other ships had insisted on reviews as some of their terms for joining this Task Unit.

Since this Task Unit was put together, the other navigators from three of the four ships had been questioning Iosua's every decision. They didn't understand why a Chief Engineer was doing a navigator's job, and would constantly ask to talk with the Chief Navigator.

But Chief Navigator Hayden Troyes wouldn't talk with them. After years of serving with Iosua, Troyes had stepped back from foldspace planning. Troyes not only knew that Iosua was more talented with foldspace, but Troyes also encouraged Iosua's involvement.

Troyes handled navigation through real space, which the *Geesi* found itself in 95 percent of the time. But the most dangerous part of the *Geesi's* travel always happened in foldspace, and everyone knew it.

They also knew that the *Geesi*, under Iosua's foldspace guidance, was the only DV-Class ship of its generation that had never experienced a timeslip while traveling through foldspace. Not even a tiny timeslip such as the loss of a few seconds.

Cohn was hoping to maintain that record on this trip.

"If it takes more than an hour," she said to Iosua, "that's fine. We want to do this right."

She'd been saying that to him all along. The trip through foldspace was long and dangerous. In addition to toying with the idea of taking short trips through foldspace to ultimately arrive at the Scrapheap, she had also thought of telling the other ships that they could travel separately and meet up near the Scrapheap.

She preferred that strategy and had used it half a dozen times on other missions. But she had had accurate star maps for those journeys. This time, she didn't trust the map.

And Iosua was right: coming in too close to the Scrapheap had dangers she hadn't even contemplated.

She thanked both men and headed back to her captain's chair. She was going to have to inform the other captains that there would be a delay.

She wasn't sure how they would take that information. Two of them seemed genuinely interested in leaving as quickly as possible. The captain of the *Tudósok* didn't care when they left. Everyone on that entire ship seemed to look at this trip as an adventure, rather than a job.

She liked the enthusiasm, although it worried her. Sometimes enthusiasm existed only when there was no experience. She had a feeling that a lot of people on that ship had no idea what they had gotten themselves into.

Fortunately, though, that wasn't her issue. She didn't have to take care of them. She just had to guide their captain.

"Let's double-check grapplers, tethers, and *anacapa* fields," she said to Sigrid Vinters, her first officer. Vinters, a tall pale woman who accented her paleness by refusing to color her winter-white hair, nodded once.

She had probably already checked the grapplers, tethers, and *anacapa* fields, but she wasn't the kind of officer to tell Cohn that. Vinters would check again, and then she would return to her main task, which was organizing the other four ships, making sure they knew their places in the foldspace positions, and their assignments on the other end of the journey.

Some on the crew would look on that command as make-work, but it wasn't. The other difficult aspect of this trip was the fact that all five ships would be tethered to each other as they traveled through foldspace.

The *Sakhata* was in charge of the tethering. They were going to use a technique that was common in foldspace. SC-Vessels, like the *Sakhata*, often tethered with old and decaying ships, particularly ships that had no working *anacapa* drive.

Such tethering usually got those ships out of foldspace, and back to wherever they had gotten lost.

The *Sakhata* had pulled as many as ten ships out of foldspace on one mission, with six of those ships tethered to the *Sakhata*. Its captain, Vilis Wihone, wasn't concerned about traveling through foldspace with four other ships. He had done it many times.

That was one of the many reasons Mbuyi wanted the *Sakhata* on this trip. The *Sakhata* had been chosen before the *Geesi*, before Cohn had even been contemplated as the overall leader of the mission.

She had gotten the job because of her record and her lightning quick response to changing dynamics. But she lacked the kind of foldspace experience that Wihone had.

She was actually nervous, something that happened to her rarely nowadays. Usually, she had enough experience on all aspects of a mission to know how the mission would go.

But this one was filled with complete unknowns, including the captains of the other four vessels. She had studied their records, and met them repeatedly as this Task Unit finished its preliminary work.

But work records and conversations were no substitute for being in the field with someone, for understanding exactly how they would react under pressure.

Both she and Mbuyi had discussed various scenarios with the other captains, and the other captains professed to understand those scenarios, but Cohn wasn't so certain. They were all used to making their own decisions in battle, even when they were part of a task unit or a task force.

But here she had the overall command, even though, technically, she didn't outrank them. And if there were trouble in that sort of situation, Cohn would usually rely on Mbuyi to clarify matters.

But Mbuyi would be out of easy communication range.

Cohn would be on her own in all senses of the word.

She leaned back in the captain's chair and made herself take a deep slow breath to calm the nerves. This trip would happen whether she was nervous about it or calm about it.

She wasn't sure what was going to happen near that Scrapheap. She didn't even have a guess.

And that left her uneasy—more uneasy that she wanted to admit.

18

CAPTAIN VILAS WIHONE SAT IN THE BUBBLECRAFT, his hands clenched in frustration. He had left his SC-class vessel, the *Sakhata,* to inspect the tethers and grapplers of the five ships on his own.

He could check them on computer, but he had long ago learned that inspecting each tether from the outside was just as important as getting computer readings.

He was nervous about this mission. He hadn't worked with any of these captains before. He also did not like the fact that Vice Admiral Mbuyi had put Cohn in charge. But Mbuyi had made one fatal error (at least in Wihone's mind). Mbuyi had not given Cohn a higher rank than any of the other captains. They were instructed to follow her command, but they also could do what they wanted.

So he continued to follow his usual procedure. He didn't tell Cohn that he was heading outside of the *Sakhata* to inspect the other ships. He just did so.

The ship he was most worried about was the *Tudósok.* It was an old ship with an "experienced" crew, many of whom hadn't gone on a mission in years. He expected lots of screwups, starting with the tethering.

So he was inspecting the *Tudósok* first.

He maneuvered the tiny bubblecraft underneath the engineering quadrant outside the *Tudósok.* The bubblecraft was tiny and completely clear. Even the seat he was strapped into was clear, as were the straps and all of the other contraptions that held him in place. The dashboard was virtual, except for a small off-white button near the bubblecraft's only door. That button would activate a touchscreen that would slide out of the floor near his feet. The touchscreen (and the button itself) was an emergency tool, a rather ham-handed way of getting the bubblecraft to send out an emergency beacon and give him some kind of control over the systems, should the virtual command screen cease to exist.

He'd never had that happen on any mission, but his first officer had, years ago, and as a result, his entire team was a bit skittish about bubblecrafts.

Wihone ignored his team's worries. He wouldn't be in the bubblecraft long.

He peered over at the *Tudósok's* grapplers. They were old and had a completely different configuration than he was used to. The tethers were made of a material that he didn't trust.

He was going to have to treat the *Tudósok* as if it were an abandoned husk that he found in foldspace. None of the *Tudósok's* equipment worked properly—at least not properly for the maneuver the *Sakhata* was going to execute this evening.

Wihone hoped the ships would officially leave on this mission in the evening. At the moment, it seemed like it would take years before he could get the five ships of the Scrapheap Investigation Unit into foldspace. If he had had his way, the *Tudósok* wouldn't have joined this mission at all. The DV-Class ship was much too old—almost a century older than the other ships—and nothing about it was standard.

Its captain, Balázs Jicha, had never tethered his ship to any other for travel, not just in foldspace, but in regular space as well. He said he preferred not to tether, although he had no choice here.

Jicha did a lot of things his way, and that way rubbed Wihone wrong most of the time. Jicha was close to retirement. He'd spent the second half of his career training newer ship crews and taking scholars on harmless research missions.

It had been clear from the meetings they had all had with Cohn that Jicha didn't believe anything would go wrong on this particular mission. He saw it as yet another scholarly research trip, with a bit of a foldspace adventure in between. He didn't want to tether. He wanted to make the trip on his own.

Which Wihone had initially thought of as Cohn's problem, until it came time to tether with the *Tudósok*. And that was when Wihone realized the extent of the problem.

He had asked the *Tudósok* to dangle those tethers, so that he could see them in the light of the bubblecraft, not with all of the noise and distraction of an interior inspection.

He wanted to see how the tethers handled the sheer cold of space. While they dangled properly, they were already developing tiny ice crystals along one side, which told him that these tethers had been made with a moisture-rich nanobit formula that the Fleet stopped using three hundred years ago.

If those tethers were used for longer than a day, and if they ended up under any kind of stress at all, they could shatter. The grapplers would probably continue to hold, but "probably" wasn't a word he wanted to use in any circumstance.

The problem was as bad as he figured it was going to be after he had read up on the *Tudósok*. The ship was simply not of the same caliber as the other ships on this mission.

He wound the bubblecraft up the side of the *Tudósok*, and near the bridge, inspecting the edges for good places to grapple. He would attach the *Sakhata* to the *Tudósok*, not the other way around. But first he wanted to make sure the *Tudósok's* hull was up to the task.

If he had his way, he would tow the *Tudósok* through foldspace, but the other three ships would go through on their own, and meet up near that troublesome Scrapheap. He had argued for that plan, first with Cohn, and later with Mbuyi before the mission even left the Fleet.

In that final conversation with Mbuyi, he had asked her to let him command this mission. After all, he was the one with the most foldspace experience, and he knew how to deal with unwieldy *anacapa* energy.

But she had refused, citing problems that could arise with the thieves near the Scrapheap that Cohn was better suited to handle.

Wihone didn't agree. He had seen her records. Cohn was a lot more reckless than the other captains on this mission, and prone to making the "adventurous" decision.

Adventurous was well and good with the Fleet nearby, but without Fleet backup, adventurous could get them all killed.

Another reason he was out here.

Being alone in space centered him. He loved the bubblecraft, the way it made him feel like he was floating undisturbed in the blueish light of a nearby star. Right now, his little bubble was flooded with the lights from the *Tudósok,* and he didn't mind. Because he could see the stars and the wisps of a far-off asteroid belt in the distance.

The ships wouldn't travel to those places—they would enter foldspace not far from here—but they glowed like possibilities, far beyond him.

Whenever he was out here alone, he felt the potential of space, and— egotistically, he knew—he felt like that potential was placed there for him alone.

He turned his attention back to the *Tudósok.* He would have to baby it through foldspace. He might have to change the travel formation. He would love to place the *Tudósok* in the center of the formation, but he doubted that Cohn would go for that, no matter how well he explained its benefit.

So, he'd have to place it between the *Royk* and the *Mächteg,* and have them tether to it as well as to the *Sakhata.* That would give the *Tudósok* the extra stability it needed.

He leaned his head back for just a moment, letting the view calm him. The ships floating around him, impossibly huge and dominating.

He smiled just a little. He didn't love any particular region of space. Each sector was different, with its surprises and its dangers and its beauties. He loved space itself.

He was excited to see the area around the Scrapheap. He wanted to see how it compared to the old star maps. He always did that whenever he went back to older sectors of space—and he had never been to a sector so far away before.

He wasn't looking forward to the foldspace journey, not because he disliked foldspace, like so many of his colleagues did, but because he hated the situation Mbuyi had forced him into.

The one thing he had said to her that she had no answer for was the thing that kept cycling through his brain, over and over again.

He had assured her that the trip to the Scrapheap would be…not exactly easy, but not hard. He had done similar trips before with ships that were much more disabled than these.

But the trip back…

Vice Admiral Mbuyi had chosen Cohn to lead this mission because there might be fighting. The thieves might actually have several ships to back them up, ships with *anacapa* drives and laser weapons that could actually do a bit of damage to these five ships.

Mbuyi didn't expect Cohn to retreat. Mbuyi expected Cohn to fight and protect that Scrapheap.

But Wihone had been in battles before, and they never went as planned. Sometimes the stronger force with the best equipment had to retreat and regroup.

And sometimes the stronger force with the best equipment had to flee.

The only place these five ships had to flee to was foldspace.

And setting up the proper foldspace configuration to get them back to the Fleet—with tethers and grapplers and coordinated *anacapa* launchings—would be impossible in that situation.

He had said that to Mbuyi and her mouth had become a thin line. He recognized that expression.

She had used it before.

It meant she knew what he was talking about, had already thought about it, and had decided to take the risk anyway.

If that happens, she had said to him, *I expect you to do your best.*

He had bristled at that comment. He always did his best.

But he hadn't protested because he knew what she meant. She meant that he would have to improvise as best he could in the worst-case scenario.

And he would. They both knew that.

When he tried to brief Cohn on the same scenario, she had nodded and said, *I've already thought of that. We're going to try to avoid that scenario at all costs.*

He wasn't sure if that answer reassured him or not. He was glad she understood the danger, but her answer made him realize he was unclear about one thing regarding this mission: the trip home.

On his foldspace rescue missions, the trip home was always clear. He was supposed to get the living crew members back to the Fleet in the best way possible. That included his crew, and any surviving crew of a ship trapped in foldspace.

The trapped ships might have to be destroyed, especially if it was impossible to tow them back to regular space.

But the human crew members—they all needed to return to the Fleet.

Here, no one had given him that directive. He wasn't even sure which of the five ships going to the Scrapheap would take priority if he could tow only one back to the Fleet.

He never asked. Because he had a hunch that Mbuyi's answer to that question would have been different than Cohn's answer, which would have been different than his.

Mbuyi would probably have told him to bring the scholars and researchers back. Their knowledge was the undercurrent of this mission.

Cohn would have told him to bring one of the other DV-Class vessels back, because they had the latest newest equipment, and all three of them had stellar crews.

Given his druthers, though, he probably wouldn't tow any ship back unless it was disabled. He would hope that they all could make it through foldspace back to the Fleet.

Wihone didn't like the idea of leaving in the middle of a battle. He didn't like the idea of taking the *Sakhata* into a region of space where he might actually have to use the ship's weaponry. He'd only had to do that a few times, each time on the way to a foldspace rescue.

A protracted battle was something he hadn't participated in since he was a cadet, decades ago.

It made him nervous.

He smiled ruefully. He'd gotten calm, then he'd thought too much, and made himself nervous again.

The bottom line for him was pretty simple: almost a decade ago, he had become the captain of the *Sakhata*, and he had stopped taking direct orders on an hourly basis.

Once he was on a mission, he was in charge of that mission, at least for its day-to-day particulars.

He wasn't in charge of the day-to-day here. He was firmly and solidly Cohn's subordinate.

And it made him feel out of control and a bit lost.

Which was probably why he was delaying taking the other four ships into foldspace.

He had all the information he needed now.

He just had to get the ships attached to each other, and the mission would get underway.

With the sweep of his palm over the virtual controls, he peeled the bubblecraft away from the *Tudósok's* side and headed back to the *Sakhata*.

Whatever happened, happened.

And, once they were out of foldspace, he wouldn't be responsible for any of it.

No matter how much he wanted to be.

19

THE SHIPS WERE TETHERED and grappled and attached in ways that Cohn had never experienced before.

She sat in her captain's chair, a holographic formation of this little Task Unit floating in front of her. She had thought the ships would be equidistant from each other and from the *Sakhata*, but Captain Wihone had changed the formation on her. Or at least had changed her understanding of the formation.

The *Geesi* was in front, attached to the *Sakhata* with the *Geesi's* tethers and grapplers, as if the *Geesi* were towing the *Sakhata*. The *Sakhata* attached to the *Geesi* with a single grappler, one that looked thinner and less powerful than the grapplers the *Geesi* used to attach to the *Sakhata*.

The *Sakhata* was directly behind the *Geesi*. The *Tudósok* was directly behind the *Sakhata*. Those three ships were in a perfectly straight line. The *Tudósok* was attached to the *Sakhata* using the *Sakhata's* tethers and grapplers.

It was the position of the other two ships that surprised Cohn. They weren't directly across from the *Sakhata*, which would have formed another perfectly straight line.

Instead, they were farther back and closer to the *Tudósok*.

If Cohn rotated the image of the ships so that she was looking down on them, it looked like the *Tudósok*, the *Royk*, and the *Mächteg* formed a smile. The *Royk* and the *Mächteg* were directly across from each other, but with enough space between them to place another DV-Class vessel in the gap.

The *Tudósok* was behind them at enough of an angle that, if looked at from a different perspective, the four ships formed a diamond.

The *Geesi* was the vessel that seemed out of place, all alone at the front of the formation, with no ships beside it at all. If someone viewed this formation without knowing how the ships worked, that someone would think that the *Geesi* was towing the other ships, even though she wasn't.

She was clearly leading them, though.

Although she was the most vulnerable ship—not just because she was the lead vessel. But also because the other ships had more reinforcement than the *Geesi* did. The *Royk* and the *Mächteg* were attached to the *Tudósok*, using their equipment, as well as with the *Sakhata*. The *Sakhata* used one rather thin tether to attach to the *Royk* and the *Mächteg*.

Those four ships were attached to each other more securely than the *Geesi* was attached to them.

Before they set up that new formation, Cohn had pointed out that discrepancy to Wihone.

Your ship needs the least amount of help going through foldspace to the Scrapheap, Wihone said to her. *And if we get separated, you, at least, have Iosua to get you through.*

She couldn't quite tell if that last comment had been sarcasm. Wihone was the only person who actively denied that Iosua had any more skill at negotiating foldspace than anyone else who had traveled through foldspace.

Whether or not it was sarcasm and whether or not Wihone was subtlety punishing her for taking the lead on this mission, Cohn couldn't tell. She wasn't going to worry about it.

Because even if Wihone didn't believe in Iosua, she did. Which made Wihone's assessment of the situation correct: if the *Geesi* got separated from the rest of the Task Unit, the *Geesi* would find its way to the Scrapheap without an issue.

The others probably wouldn't.

The difficulties would be the entry and exit from foldspace. That vibration that took ships into foldspace made every single member of the Fleet nervous, whether they admitted it or not. No matter how hard Fleet engineers tried to figure out what that vibration was, they never could.

And she had no idea if it would separate her ship from the other four. Wihone had assured her it wouldn't, although Iosua wasn't as confident.

We don't know what the difference is between foldspace and real space, he said to her just recently. *So that vibration might be something we can't see. It might also come from an interaction inside the* anacapa *drive. All I know is that our people have never been able to recreate the vibration in the lab.*

Which bothered her more than she wanted to admit. Especially on this journey. She had really wanted to emerge from foldspace five strong, not as five ships that looked like they were limping out of some other dimension.

"Are we ready?" she asked Iosua.

"We're waiting for confirmation from the *Sakhata,*" he said, sounding as irritated as she felt. They'd been waiting for confirmation for more than an hour now.

"Tell them I'm done waiting," she said. She would have done so, but she didn't know if she could have a civil conversation with Wihone right now. His hesitation was either too cautious for her taste or he was being passive/aggressive because he didn't have official command of this mission.

Or maybe it was a bit of both. She never did learn why Mbuyi had passed him over for command.

Cohn could almost imagine Wihone's response to her statement that she was done waiting: *Ask her what she's going to do about my delay. Leave without me?*

He was right; she really couldn't leave without him. She had to work closely with him whether she wanted to or not.

"Well, how about that?" Iosua said. "The other four ships are ready."

Cohn blinked at him, startled. She hadn't expected that response at all. She had expected another delay of an hour or more.

"Okay, then," she said, "let's get underway."

Both Iosua and Priede looked at her, apparently expecting a more formal command to start this mission.

"You've locked in the coordinates?" she asked Priede.

He nodded.

"Then execute," she said.

Priede lifted one hand with a flourish, like a conductor about to start an orchestra on a symphony. Then he brought his hand down, and the *Geesi* made a slight whistle, just like it always did when the *anacapa* slowly rose to full strength.

No other ship Cohn had worked on had ever had an *anacapa* that made a noise as it engaged. As a young captain, she had taken the *Geesi* to the nearest starbase after finishing her first foldspace journey and demanded a stem-to-stern examination of the ship, as well as a focus on the *anacapa* drive.

The starbase found nothing amiss. Neither did a nearby sector base, or any of the Fleet's *anacapa* specialists. Iosua had finally provided her with his version of an explanation.

I think you're actually hearing the energy change. Some people do interact with anacapa *drives on a sonic level. You might be one of them.*

But never with other drives besides this one. And she had gotten used to that, except on days like today.

She braced herself on the edge of the captain's chair, waiting for the familiar bumps. Going into foldspace normally didn't bother her; she wasn't one of those captains who counted each journey in and each journey out. She also wasn't one of those people who considered themselves blessed to survive a foldspace journey.

Her job was dangerous and would be dangerous with or without foldspace.

Foldspace just made the job easier, especially on days like today. She would never be able to go to the Scrapheap without foldspace, so therefore foldspace was a tool, one she needed.

And as she had that thought, the *Geesi* vibrated. The vibrations were small at first, almost impossible to feel. Some members of her crew wouldn't be able to feel them at all. But she did.

Just like hearing that whistle was a signal for her, the ache that started in her lower jaw was another. She knew now what caused the ache: it was a miniscule vibration that made her teeth clench.

She had to actively work to unclench her jaw, and she had to be careful to keep her tongue away from her teeth because right about now—yes, now—the vibration became more intense.

Just at the edge of her sightline, she saw Priede clutch the navigation column—the actual one, not the holographic one. Iosua stood with his feet slightly apart, as if he were centering himself so that he stayed balanced.

In the dark screens before Cohn, she saw the rest of the team hit their foldspace stances as well. No one else stood hands-free like Iosua and no one else sat like Cohn was doing.

Several members of the bridge crew grabbed their consoles and held on, looking forward toward the screens as the vibration continued. A few kept their heads down, pretending to work as the *Geesi* bounced its way from one kind of space to another.

The vibration pattern was familiar, and in that familiarity, reassuring. Cohn was just starting to get calm when she heard the whistle again, only this time it sounded louder and almost strained.

She clapped a hand to her ear, although that made no difference, and then looked around to see if anyone else was hearing the whistle.

No one else seemed to, but Iosua looked over at her and frowned.

The vibration changed too. It should have become deeper, more like a series of bumps on a road, but it was more than that. The bumps became a rapid vibration, so intense that if she wasn't holding on to the edge of her captain's chair, she would have bounced out of it.

Iosua bent his knees, and still nearly toppled forward. He grabbed a nearby console with his right hand, something Cohn had never seen him do. Priede wrapped his arms around his console, no longer trying to hide the fear in his face.

Cohn started to give the order—*check the grapplers*—and then realized that it would be easier to do so herself.

She freed one hand, and pulled the holographic screen toward her, tapping it with her thumb.

The information came up, and then transferred—without her giving the command—to the holographic representations of the ships in front of her. They twisted slightly so that she could see the grapplers and tethers connecting the *Geesi* to the *Sakhata*.

Her ship looked fine. The tethers looked fine. The grapplers seemed a bit strained, but she wasn't getting any warnings from them, so she had to assume they were okay as well.

She examined the other ships, saw that they were not entirely visible.

Oh, the *Sakhata* was, along with all of its grapplers and tethers. But the back half of both the *Royk* and the *Mächteg* appeared to be lost in what she could only describe as a fog. Only that wasn't correct, because a fog would be a wispy gray.

The back halves of both ships simply faded into nothingness, leaving only the bright dark blue of space.

The *Tudósok* wasn't visible at all.

Cohn's heart started to pound hard. She made herself breathe evenly, which was hard. She wanted to breathe with the vibrations, and that was too rapid for her.

She had to plant her feet to keep herself braced on that seat.

Iosua had moved beside the console he clutched. His gaze met hers and his eyebrows went up slightly, as if to say, *Do you believe this?*

She didn't respond. She wasn't sure how to respond.

Instead she looked at the hologram of the ships again, and realized that more parts of the *Royk* and the *Mächteg* were visible, as well as the edges of the grapplers that tied those two ships to the *Tudósok*.

She was watching the ships arrive in foldspace, and if she had to guess, she would assume that what she was feeling was the drag on her ship from their weight.

Although that shouldn't have been possible. She shouldn't have felt any drag at all.

She lacked the words for what she was thinking. Somehow the presence of the other ships had slowed hers down, making the *Geesi* more vulnerable than usual to the transition from regular space to foldspace.

Wihone hadn't warned her about this. He had to have been familiar with it. He had brought dozens of ships out of foldspace, all grappled to his.

Or maybe he hadn't noticed the difference as he had *left* foldspace. Right now, all of the ships were entering it, which was somewhat different.

She shoved the holographic screen to one side, and gripped the armrests of the captain's chair again. The vibration had become something almost too violent to be called a vibration. A bumping, a jarring, something that if it got too much more extreme, would knock everyone off their feet, and maybe even knock her out of the chair.

The *Royk* and the *Mächteg* had finally emerged and appeared on the holoimage, the tethers and grapplers straight out, as if they were attached to something. Which, in theory, they were.

"Captain," Priede said, sounding just a bit panicked, "this is not normal."

"I know that," Cohn said, and was pleased to hear herself sound calmer than she felt. "We will get through it."

Or not. It was one of those situations that a previous commander of hers, back when she was a green officer candidate who had never really been in a life-or-death situation before, had barked at her, *You do what you can, Cohn. But sometimes, there isn't anything you can do except kiss your ass goodbye.*

This wasn't quite a kiss-your-ass-goodbye moment, but it might end up that way.

Because she had never, in all her years as a commander of any kind, ordered a ship to shut off its *anacapa* drive at this stage. She could probably do so with little or no effect on the *Geesi*, but she had no idea what such an order would do to the other four ships.

Which were visible now. Or rather, part of the *Tudósok* was. About half of the ship.

Cohn wanted to contact Wihone, ask if this sort of slow-motion entry into foldspace was normal when tethered to other ships, but she wasn't even certain she could safely do that.

She had never contacted another ship while her *anacapa* was trying to get the *Geesi* into foldspace.

And then, as abruptly as it started, the vibration ceased. She still felt it, echoing in her bones, her teeth, behind her eyes. She let out the breath she hadn't even realized she'd been holding, despite her best efforts to keep breathing.

The blood pounded in her ears, and she thought she still heard a high-pitched buzz of some kind. She made herself look at the hologram again, and watched as the *Tudósok* slid the rest of the way into view.

The buzz continued, and so did the echoey feeling left by the vibrations, as if her cheekbones and her teeth and that space behind her eyes was still vibrating, only at a softer frequency than before. Almost like a hum itself.

Priede stood up. But Iosua hadn't moved yet. His gaze met hers, and he looked alarmed.

Which, oddly, calmed her. She contacted Wihone.

"Are we all here now?" she asked, not quite sure the best way to communicate her meaning.

"Not quite," Wihone said, sounding as clear as if he were on the bridge with them. "The *Tudósok* isn't quite with us."

She wasn't sure exactly how he knew that, but then, she hadn't asked her team to investigate how the other ships were doing on their way into foldspace. The *Tudósok* looked all right on the hologram, but that didn't mean it was.

And then the echoey feeling in her teeth and cheekbones and behind her eyes ended, almost as if it hadn't been there in the first place.

Although she used the word "almost" because she had the beginnings of a headache forming in her sinuses, a side effect she sometimes experienced after a prolonged transition into foldspace.

"We're all here now," Wihone said, and as he did, Cohn frowned slightly at Iosua. So the feelings she had were vibrating into the *Geesi* from the *Tudósok*? Or had something else happened?

She stood, her legs a bit wobbly.

"All right," she said to Wihone. "I'm going to move us to the exit coordinates at a slower pace than we had planned. The transition into foldspace was rough, and I want to give us a bit of time to recover."

"As you wish," Wihone said, which irritated her. She shouldn't have spoken to him so that the whole bridge could hear. Now they knew he didn't agree with that order.

Not that it mattered. They were *her* bridge crew, not his, and they did need a bit of time to investigate things.

That continued vibration was odd, and she wanted to know if the vibration had been amplified by the tethers and grapplers. She would have Iosua and Priede work on that, or at least assign it to someone who might be able to figure it out, maybe before the ships exited foldspace.

She wanted all five ships and their crews to be in the best shape possible when they arrived at the Scrapheap, and if they felt the way she felt at the moment, they wouldn't be.

"I want a full systems diagnostic on this ship," she said to Carmen Gray, who did most of the catch-all work on the bridge crew. "Every inch of this ship needs a good going over. I want to make sure nothing separated or cracked on that trip into foldspace."

"What about the grapplers and tethers?" Gray asked. She had her fingers wrapped around an actual tablet, one of her preferred methods of research. She was tiny and intense, her braided eyebrows matching her black eyes.

She clearly wanted to investigate the grapplers and the tethers, and Cohn wanted her to. But Cohn wasn't sure if the investigation would get in the way of the tethering, at least at the moment.

She needed to consult with Wihone. All they had discussed about tethers and grapplers was that they would remain tethered while they were all in foldspace.

"I'll let you know," she said to Gray.

She would talk to Wihone, maybe get him to examine the tethers and grapplers. After all, he had done so before they left, in a silly little bubblecraft, all by himself. That behavior alone would have disqualified him from leading this mission, at least as far as she was concerned, but she could use it now.

Still, they were in foldspace, all five ships. Together. They had gone over one major hurdle. They still faced several, but this was a small victory.

Or maybe it wasn't so small.

Her heart was still pounding a little too hard. She hadn't been scared, but she had been uneasy. She still was.

This journey was different. She had known it was going to be, but it was even more so than she had thought. And she still had at least three more trips tethered to the other ships.

That was three more than she wanted to do.

But she would do it, if the situation called for it.

She had no other choice.

THE BONEYARD

NOW

20

MIKK AND I ARE THE ONLY TWO on board the Fleet runabout that we've taken from the *Madxaf.* I didn't ask Pao's permission to take it. No one knows that we have, in fact. We've decided to conduct most of this mission as if it were top secret.

I'm not entirely sure why we're going to such lengths to maintain secrecy, but part of me feels it's necessary.

I'm beginning to trust these hunches.

We're not talking much because we're on a Fleet vessel. It was Mikk's idea to use a Fleet vessel for the first part of our plan. The rest of this plan is all mine.

I have finally figured out how we are going to use the non-Fleet probes, and maybe even the seven non-Fleet ships that Ilona sent me. I haven't shared the full plan with anyone, but I have spoken to Mikk about some of it.

We have decided to try another duplicitous move, at least as far as the starfield-barrier is concerned. We haven't told anyone in the team about that either.

The runabout we've chosen is refurbished, which surprises me. I really have no idea what Lost Souls has been doing, but I'm impressed by it now. It looks like everything on the *Madxaf,* from the small ships to the quarters, have been rebuilt, better and stronger than they ever were.

The *Madxaf* is a gem, and if that's what Lost Souls is doing with the DV-Class vessels we're finding, then we should bring more to Lost Souls. And, the follow-on thought is, that I should give up this crazy quest to figure out what's behind that starfield-barrier.

But I can't. What if those warships are unmanned? What if the defenses are automated?

What if they can be shut off?

Suddenly we have a squadron of warships. We can take them and defend the Nine Planets. We can mine their tech. We can…leave them here and study them, which is my bent.

And if Coop ever returns from his new sector base mission, then he will have a ready-made squadron to do whatever he wants with them.

This runabout that Mikk and I have commandeered has more power than any runabout I've ever piloted. It also has some minor weaponry— the kind that could take out a ship of similar size, if used properly.

I don't plan to use the weaponry or the defensive capabilities. I want this trip to look like we're exploring a slightly different region of the Boneyard.

I'm doing all of this as a test, not just of me and Mikk and the non-Fleet probes, but of the Boneyard itself. I want to know what it monitors, what it doesn't monitor, and whether or not it will "think" about what we're doing.

We are going to make some complicated maneuvers, and if a simple program runs the defenses of the starfield-barrier, then the results should be pretty predictable. But if an active intelligence runs the defenses of the starfield-barrier, then we won't be able to predict the outcome.

The runabout is one of the smaller models, which is another reason Mikk and I picked it. The cockpit is small, but seems large because we've recessed all of the seating for any extra personnel. We've left the door open to the galley kitchen, because we'll be away from the *Madxaf* for most of a day.

I'm piloting. Mikk is in the back of the cockpit, prepping the probes that we brought. We brought six. Two are decoy probes, if we can call them that. They're going to be in position to see if the Boneyard destroys them.

We expect to lose the three others over the next few days.

If none of them gets destroyed, then we will reprogram them.

I'm taking the runabout as far from the *Madxaf* and the *Sove* as I can, and still maneuver inside the Boneyard. I'm steering the runabout toward an intact DV-Class vessel. We will send the sixth probe into that DV-Class vessel, if we can find an entry point.

We will use that vessel as a decoy, to hide what we're trying to do from the Boneyard itself.

Mikk and I spent most of a day figuring out which DV-Class vessel was going to be the best for this little trick. We're going to release all six probes at the same time, but only one of those releases will seem intentional.

The other five are going to "fall" out of the runabout, as if we've had some kind of accident on ship. In fact, Mikk is going to attempt to scoop them up, and fail.

It takes us most of the morning to get to the DV-Class vessel. It's nowhere near the starfield-barrier, which is something that we did on purpose.

In fact, the DV-class vessel is on the other side of the starfield-barrier from the location of the release of the very first probe nearly a month ago now. Even if a human is watching us, they won't think that we're going after the starfield-barrier, at least, not at this moment. Maybe later.

Most machine intelligences won't consider what we're doing part of a mission to examine the starfield-barrier. At least, most machine intelligences that we're aware of.

Mikk finishes prep long before we reach the DV-Class vessel. I steer us around some smaller vessels, which, according to the scans I'm running, have active *anacapa* drives. If I were to dive this area, I would "hear" random *anacapa* energy. It would probably be very musical outside of the runabout.

I would be happier diving, truth be told. It's very tight between these vessels, and even though the runabout is small, maneuvering it through these narrow passages takes most of my concentration.

When we finally reach the DV-Class vessel, I scan it as best I can from a distance. The scans come back the same as they did when we ran them on the *Sove*. The DV-Class vessel is intact. To get a probe inside will take a tiny bit of luck—an open laser missile slot, an unlocked airlock, an open environmental system vent.

I search for any opening on the ship, and after nearly thirty minutes begin to despair. Our ruse will work better if we can get a probe on board this thing.

Finally, I find an open portal on an exterior engineering panel. That will do. I tell Mikk to get ready.

He grins at me. "I'm not used to being this kind of clumsy," he says.

He's wearing an environmental suit, but doesn't have his hood up. He's also wearing four tethers.

This runabout has an airlock, and he's going to "launch" the probes from there.

Even though he doesn't think it necessary, I put on my environmental suit as well. I've been diving long enough to know that the trip where you think nothing can go wrong is the trip where something absolutely will.

My suit isn't really engaged though. I haven't done my usual prep on it, and my hood is down.

Mikk's got a container filled with probes, which just looks odd to me. Normally we launch probes the way that we would launch a weapon—through a tube.

Here, though, we're going to toss them out the exterior door.

The probes don't sit comfortably in that container. They're pear-shaped, with little sticks on the top that Mikk's been calling antennae. They tumble over each other as he moves them. I can hear them clink against each other. Putting them one on top of the other will scratch them, but Mikk has reassured me that the scratches won't harm any of the probes' functions.

He goes into the airlock, and I make sure all of the cameras are on. He attaches all four tethers to the inside of the airlock, then puts his hood up. With his left hand, he pinches the edges of the hood, both to seal it and to test the environmental system. When he knows it works, he gives me a thumbs-up.

This is the scary part. He's going to open that exterior door, throw the first probe out, and then "knock" the container of five probes over the lip of the door. He's going to reach out and try to gather them—or at least make it look like he's gathering them. Instead, he'll push them away.

My heart is pounding. I hate maneuvers that I'm not a part of, especially weird maneuvers. But he's more familiar with these probes, and he wants to make certain they're handled correctly.

He cradles one probe awkwardly under his left arm. If he moves too far in one direction or the other, the probe will slide away from him— the problems of gravity—but he doesn't dare use the sticking properties of the environmental suit to hold the probe in place. He just shifts the probe a little bit each time it slides.

It takes him a moment to get everything settled. He double-checks the tethers, and so do I. He's as attached to the interior of the ship as he's going to be.

He apparently comes to the same conclusion because he places his gloved right hand on the door release. He should have the gravity in his boots on, but no gravity on the container of probes.

The door opens and the environment leaves the airlock. The container starts to float. Mikk ignores it.

I'm breathing through my mouth until I realize I'm doing it—and I realize that because my mouth has gone dry. I close my lips, make myself take a deep breath, and tell myself to remain calm.

I'm suddenly glad no one is monitoring me, because my heart rate would be very high.

That makes me glance at Mikk's readings. His heart rate is normal, as if he's not doing anything unusual at all. He's always like that whenever we work together. It's as if he dons calm along with his environmental suit.

I wish I could be like that, but I never have been. Although it's one of the reasons I like working with him. He seems unflappable—at least when he's in that suit.

He grips the probe by the pointy end near the antennae, hefts the probe as if it still has a bit of weight, and leans forward, so any video imagery of that area of our runabout will show images of him.

Then he flings the probe as hard as he can. It flips, end over end, tumbling away from the runabout, heading toward the edge of the DV-Class vessel.

I stop eyeballing the probe as it moves away from the runabout. Instead, I watch Mikk, who backs into the airlock and jostles the container. Purposefully, I know, but the movement looks accidental—unless you look closely. Then you see his right hand underneath the container's bottom corner, tilting the container forward.

That movement is all he needs to get the container to spin slowly. As it moves forward and out, the probes move away from it, moving on their own trajectories.

But they are close enough for him to grab them. He does—or "tries"— fumbling the closest one and sending it sideways into two others. He reaches for all three, and nearly tumbles out of the airlock himself.

My breath catches. He's tethered, so he won't really fall from the airlock. Even if one tether gives way, he's secured.

Plus he still has the gravity on in his boots. He doesn't really fall so much as pinwheel his arms to "catch" himself, like a beginner on their first time outside a ship.

He grabs the edges of the exterior door, and visibly breathes hard. I know that's for show as well, because I can monitor his readings, and he's still calm.

As he pulls himself back into the airlock, the probes swirl around the door. He can grab them if he wants to, but of course he doesn't. He swipes at one of them, bumps it, and sends it tumbling away from him.

He's having more of a fight than either of us expected. The probes don't want to tumble so much as float where they are.

That's because they're well balanced, designed to move forward in zero-G, with a minimum of fuss.

Finally he leans out again, grabs at the two closest probes, and deliberately misses. They float away from the ship.

It takes all of that effort to get the probes out of his reach. His shoulders slump and he steps back inside.

Then the airlock door closes, and he leans against the interior door as if he's exhausted.

His readings are only slightly elevated. He hasn't exerted himself much at all.

I glance at the original probe. It's still moving swiftly toward the DV-Class vessel. Time for me to act.

I switch that probe on, and it instantly stops barreling forward. It hovers.

I change its trajectory so that it travels toward that opening I've found. I also turn on every system inside the probe, so that it records what it experiences, in a dozen different ways, from what it "sees" to what kind of energy patterns it's finding in the Boneyard itself.

My heart rate is still elevated, and my right hand shakes as I make sure all of the systems are operating properly on that probe.

Behind me, the airlock door opens.

"Well, that was harder than I expected," Mikk says, as he pulls his hood off. He's untethering himself. "The damn things didn't want to leave the ship."

"They're too well designed." I'm not looking at him at the moment. I want to make sure our decoy probe operates properly. I guide it to that tiny opening, and the probe trundles inside, as if it was designed to go into that hole.

We'll get a secondary benefit out of all of this. We'll actually see how the interior of that DV-Class vessel looks.

Mikk has removed the tethers. He leaves them in a pile on the center of the runabout's floor, and walks over to me, his boots clumping for half the walk before he remembers to turn off the boots' gravity.

I leave a screen open, monitoring all of the information coming from the decoy probe. Then I open a secondary screen. My fingers are shaking too.

I haven't been this nervous in a long time.

Mikk reaches me. "You haven't activated a second probe yet?" he asks.

If I activate one, *when* I activate it, we're going to purposefully breach that starfield-barrier. Nothing will change that, no matter how many games we play, no matter whether or not we get caught.

I am not able to blithely pretend that we are accidentally breaching the starfield-barrier. We aren't. And what we're about to do is very dangerous, more so now that we have an indication that the ships behind the barrier are warships.

"Having second thoughts?" Mikk asks. His voice is gentle, which I don't expect.

My finger hovers over the screen. The shaking has stopped.

"Second thoughts is the wrong description," I say. "When we decided to breach the Boneyard, we thought it was abandoned. But now we know at least part of it is active."

"We don't know that," he says. He remains hovering behind me. "Those systems might be automated too."

I nod. That's part of what we're trying to figure out. But the idea of warships, that leads me to believe that these Boneyards are active in one way or another.

I've already gone head to head with the Empire. Do I really want to do that with the Fleet?

"Besides, Boss," Mikk says as he sits down next to me, "it's too late to have second thoughts."

"It's never too late to have second thoughts," I mutter. Mikk actually taught me that a long time ago. Mikk and Karl. They both loved adventure, and they would both occasionally urge caution.

And what good did it do Karl? He died anyway.

"We're in the Boneyard," Mikk says. "We've already breached the starfield-barrier once."

"And got rebuffed," I say.

Mikk shrugs. "I'm not going to argue with you, especially since you're trying to force me to argue in the position you held not a day ago."

I was right: there is amusement in his voice. He knows I'm not playing him. That's not who I am. But he's also not used to me hesitating.

"What's really behind this?" he asks me.

"Warships," I say before I can even think. "Dozens upon dozens of warships."

"Which," he says quietly, "we need."

I look at him sideways. His eyes meet mine, his mouth a thin line.

"You've changed your mind about this mission," I say. "Because of the warships?"

He nods. "We're going to have that fight with the Empire again at some point. It would be nice to have more than a few Dignity Vessels and a bunch of half-assed ships from the Nine Planets."

"You think the Fleet *abandoned* warships?" I ask.

"Not intentionally," he says. "I think they've moved on. The Fleet doesn't go backwards. How many times have Coop and Yash and everyone else told you that? This is pretty far backwards."

It is.

I nod, just once. "If the Fleet is defending this," I say, "then Coop gets his wish."

"You're not investigating so that Coop can meet the Fleet," Mikk says. Is there a question in his voice? I can't entirely tell.

"No, I'm not." I look at the information coming from the decoy probe. It's worked its way into the Engineering section of the DV-Class ship. Lights actually blink off and on on some of the consoles. This ship wasn't properly deactivated.

Oh, goodie. More problems, if I accept them as such.

"Boss?" Mikk sounds confused.

Apparently, I wasn't paying attention to what he was saying.

"We're set up to do this," he says, and there's emphasis in his voice, as if he has just repeated himself.

We are. I nod again. Then I activate the second screen.

Mikk straightens in the chair beside me, leaning forward ever so slightly. This is the real key, getting one of the probes into that starfield-barrier.

We have a system. And we're going to use it.

I'm going to use it. I can't let any doubts get in my way.

I activate a second probe. It beeps on. I can see it on the runabout's regular screen, a tiny blinking light just past the ship's exit, right beside the floating, abandoned container.

With the flick of a finger, I activate the program that Mikk installed into the probe.

It flashes green for just a moment—accepting the instruction—and then it zips around the container, heading toward the starfield-barrier.

That probe's mission is to map the mines in that empty space between the image and the actual starfield-barrier. The probe is not programmed to go inside the barrier at all.

As Mikk and I planned that mission, we knew that the probe might get destroyed. It might hit a mine or it might get hit by one. We're ready for that.

Still, my heart continues to pound. I'm not used to taking these kinds of risks anymore.

Or maybe, I'm just out of practice being courageous and a bit reckless. I have been running a corporation and letting someone else, Coop, mostly, make decisions for me.

The decisions I have made led to Karl's death, Elaine's permanent injury, and my own near-death.

I let out a breath. Am I scared? Do I believe in myself less than I did before?

Or have I simply learned about consequences? Maybe I've learned just how painful they can be.

I raise my head as the probe heads toward that starfield-barrier. My gaze meets Mikk's. He looks as solemn as I feel.

"Second thoughts?" I ask him.

He grins, surprising me. "Always, Boss."

"Yet you do these things with me," I say.

"Yes," he says. "I do. I've never regretted doing that."

"Not even when Karl died?" I ask.

Mikk looks away, then brings his gaze back to mine.

"Not even then," he says.

21

WE STAY NEAR THE DV-CLASS VESSEL while the probe explores the ship. That exploration is more interesting than I expected. Most of the ships we've encountered in the Boneyard are completely powered down, but this one isn't. It seems to be in a sleep mode, or waiting mode, something I've never seen before.

The lights are on low in the corridors, and some of the consoles in engineering beeped on as the probe passed them. I'll need to talk to Diaz about this, to see if this is what DV-class ships look like when the crew is off the ship, but the ship has not been properly decommissioned.

I don't contact her from the runabout, though. I am going to wait to talk until Mikk and I get back.

We're not leaving for a few hours at least. We're still pretending not to notice that one of the probes that "accidentally" tumbled out of the runabout has sped off to the starfield-barrier.

We're already getting updates from that probe as well, but we're deliberately not monitoring them on the runabout's screens. Mikk has checked the tablets that he brought, the non-Fleet tablets, which are linked to the probes.

That probe is sending back information as it travels along.

We can set the decoy probe inside the DV-Class vehicle to provide us with the same kind of long-range information, and we will do so shortly.

I'm getting tired of hanging out in this part of the Boneyard, especially since we have no plan to dive this DV-Class vessel.

The decoy probe doesn't run into any trouble as it moves its way through the ship. The decoy probe moves forward as if it knows where it's heading. It doesn't. We just set it on explore mode.

The real probe, the one we intended to send, still hasn't reached that black area of the starfield-barrier. The other probes still float just outside this runabout, but the container has tumbled farther away.

Mikk has removed his environmental suit and put the tethers away. I made us lunch—sandwiches with some kind of spread I couldn't identify, but which Mikk assured me was good. It wasn't. But it was food.

And I'm hungry again already, ready to get back to the *Sove*. Only we're not going to examine any of the probe information on the *Sove* itself. We'll do so on one of the seven non-Fleet vehicles, just in case.

The decoy probe has traveled straight through the DV-Class ship without running into a single problem for more than four hours now. Usually the probes power down or get stuck somewhere.

Mikk notes that, then says, "You going to call it back here?"

That's standard Fleet procedure. It's also standard procedure for me from the old days, when I was short on money.

"I think we set it on long-range and let it explore," I say, as much for the record as for Mikk. "We'll pick it up when we come back."

If we come back. Although now I'm thinking we might.

Mikk calls up the operating system for the decoy probe and changes a few of the instructions. He also points, as surreptitiously as possible, to an icon that indicates the other probe has sent more information. He's asking if I want it.

I don't, not yet.

"I changed it," he says. "We going to head back or dive this tomorrow?"

I laugh. Mikk knows better. That question is truly for the record.

"We don't have a large enough team," I say. "Besides, I think the crew has already picked out a different DV-class ship to explore, at least before this one."

Although I might discuss this one with them. That database might answer a bunch of our questions, in ways that other ships haven't. Even if we don't bring this ship to Yash.

An unexpected find, on this odd little mission.

Mikk studies me for a moment, then says, "You want to pilot us back?"

"I do," I say. Then I point at the Fleet equipment, hoping he understands that what I'm about to say next is for the record, not because I'm upset with him. "You don't seem to be on your game today."

"Yeah," he says. "I haven't had an experience like that one in the airlock in years."

"We haven't been diving much," I say, relieved that he understood what I was doing. "So we're all a bit rusty."

I sink into the pilot's chair, get comfortable, and call up the controls. I'm going to fly this thing myself, because I need to focus on something. I need to keep my mind off that probe winging its way to the starfield-barrier.

I do chart the trip back, though, making sure we take a different route than the one we took to the DV-class vessel. There are two other DV-Class vessels nearby that are possible candidates for Lost Souls, and I want to scan them.

They look newer than the one the decoy probe is still exploring. For the life of me, I can't entirely figure out how these ships got here, and in what order. It still looks random.

Which makes the warships inside the starfield-barrier even more unusual. If they exist. If what we saw is actually there.

My heart rate increases again. Almost the gids. I'm really excited about this information, and I'm not exactly sure how to get it all.

But we will.

I change my mind about piloting us back to the *Sove*. I take the quickest route I know. The quickest and the safest.

I really want to see what the real probe is sending back.

And I want to see it now.

22

BY THE TIME WE GET BACK TO THE *MADXAF*, the real probe has entered that treacherous area in front of the starfield-barrier. My stomach is in knots, and it takes all of my self-control not to monitor the probe on any Fleet equipment.

Mikk and I land the runabout inside the *Madxaf's* ship bay, and try hard not to sprint to the non-Fleet ships. Fortunately, Pao and her crew don't ask what we're doing. Apparently, they all consider me in charge of the mission they're on, even though this is Pao's ship.

Mikk has gathered our non-Fleet tech and has stuffed it into a carryall, since the container he originally used is floating in the Boneyard. I touch the carryall as he's packing it. I expect the smoothness of nano-bits. Instead, my fingers find a slightly coarse fabric, something I've never felt before.

I raise my head ever so slightly and mouth, "Fleet?"

He shakes his head, also slightly, and I mentally salute him. He's a lot more on top of the Fleet/non-Fleet stuff than I am. He thought ahead enough to bring a non-Fleet carryall for the equipment as we head back.

The tablets clink together, making me wince. I turn away, stack the Fleet tablets on the navigation panel, and leave them there for now. I promise myself that we will return for them later, since we do need to evaluate the work that the decoy probe is doing in that DV-Class vessel.

Mikk is already halfway out the exit for the runabout by the time I join him. He's in that airlock, looking bemused.

So far, the Boneyard hasn't reacted to what we're doing, which is a good thing.

But we need to see how it's reacting to the real probe. We step out of the airlock, and down the ramp that has extended from the runabout into the ship bay. The environment here is cooler than it was inside the ship and has a fainter version of that sharp solvent smell that I noted in the ship maintenance area.

Mikk hefts the carryall over his back, and then glances at me, as if to say, *Hurry up!*

But neither of us discuss what we're doing. I shut the runabout's door from the outside. The ramp eases up, and the runabout hums as it powers down. Then I follow Mikk to the door.

From the ship bay to the ship maintenance area is less of a walk than I had thought it would be. I'd never gone from one to the other on a DV-Class vessel.

Still, Mikk has set a good pace, one that I have to struggle to keep up with. Ever since I got injured, my physical capacity has declined. The med techs—all of them, from Nyssa Quint to Jaylene Paskvan—have told me that I lost muscle mass during recovery, and muscle mass is tough to rebuild in space.

I realize, as I breathe a little too hard as I follow him, that I have not put the effort into exercise that I should have. It's something I should have paid more attention to, because when I'm actually diving wrecks and such, I need to be strong.

I pretend I'm in the same shape I always was as I struggle to stay on Mikk's tail. He's not sprinting, but he's walking damn fast. We reach the ship maintenance area at long last. Mikk opens the door, and finally waits for me.

His eyebrows go up as he sees me.

I know I'm a bit of a mess, my breathing ragged, and sweat dripping down one side of my face.

I make no excuses, and he doesn't say anything.

I guess we're both pretending I'm in the same shape I've always been in.

We step inside the ship maintenance area, and that rubber/solvent smell makes me sneeze. Mikk rubs his nose, as if the smell bothers him too. But we're quiet as we hurry through the doors, finally arriving at the non-Fleet ships.

I pick the ship-to-land orbiter, the one that seats four. I don't want to be distracted by the non-Fleet ship itself. Right now, I want to look at what's happening with the probe, and we need that extra layer of non-Fleet equipment around us, so that we can see what's happening.

The orbiter is about half the size of the runabout we just left, but the main area for the crew is roughly the same size. The orbiter has a small kitchen area, but it's built into a wall, and there's no seating for it. Essentially, there is one space for the human crew, and a tiny area, which can be closed off, that operates as both equipment holding and a small cargo bay.

We don't open that door. Instead, we step inside the main area. It's rectangular, and there are two sets of controls. The long navigation panel is in the very center. A shorter control panel is on the wall opposite the ridiculous kitchen.

The four seats are plush, square, and comfortable, exactly the kind of chairs I dislike in any cockpit. Whenever someone can sit comfortably, they automatically lose just a bit of awareness, awareness they usually need to navigate any region of space.

I take all of that in as I immediately go to the long panel of controls.

Of course, they're in a language I've never seen before, but as my fingers brush the smooth panel in front of me, that same scroll that the team prepared for the ships appears here.

I swear.

"What?" Mikk asks.

I wave my hand at the scroll. It's nice and wonderful, explaining what area operates what thing, but I have no idea what kind of tech created that scroll. If it's Fleet tech, then all of these damn non-Fleet ships are contaminated.

"I didn't want Fleet tech in here," I say. "Not in any of these ships."

He smiles, and eases the carryall off his back.

"It's not Fleet tech," he says. "Don't you pay attention to anything at Lost Souls?"

I frown at him, because he already knows the answer to that question. I don't pay as much attention as I should. Or as others think I should.

"Ilona manages Lost Souls," I say, defensively.

"I thought maybe you checked to see what kind of tech your people are developing." He opens the carryall, and starts pulling tablets out. "The scroll is one of the earliest items Lost Souls developed. It comes standard in all ships you build, so that anyone who buys the product knows how to run it."

"Oh," I say. Now that he's mentioned that, I think someone told me about it. Something about it being a simple, but profitable bit of tech that's earning us a lot of money.

At least, I think it's this kind of tech.

"Let's see the real probe," I say, not wanting to remain on this topic any longer.

He picks up two tablets and sets them on the nearest chair. Then he orders up a hologram, showing the tracking telemetry, as well as a visual of the probe itself.

The real probe has just hit the rim of that black area. It's got the entire dark area of space to cover before getting to what I had once called the ragged edge of the starfield-barrier, but which I now think of as the actual barrier itself.

"Has the probe slowed down?" I would have thought it would have gotten farther along by now.

"No," he says. "It's just approaching from a different angle."

I grab one of the tablets, and jostle it open. I have to give the tablet a direct command, but I finally get to see a two-dimensional map of the journey the probe has already taken.

And there it is: the thing that confused me. The probe didn't enter the black area between the ships and the starfield-barrier directly. It traveled across what I would call the rim of the blackness, hanging just outside before finally entering not too far from where the original probe had entered.

I shove the tablet toward Mikk. "I don't recall programming the probe to enter there," I say.

He leans over the tablet, frowning. "We didn't."

He opens the other tablet he's holding, and the telemetry from the probe fills the screen with numbers and equations and little figures.

Even at normal speed, Mikk can scan that stuff and get a sense of it. I can't. I either need it to slow down, or have it translated into visuals.

"Look at this." He taps the scrolling telemetry.

"What am I supposed to see?" I ask.

"I programmed a sense of self-preservation into it," he says. "If it thought it was going hit something physical, it was supposed to travel around it. See?"

Now that his finger has pointed out the pattern, I do see it. All along that edge, the probe thought it was going to hit something physical.

I move the other tablet closer to me and call up the telemetry, looking for that pattern. Of course, I study it at a much slower speed than Mikk does, but I'm seeing the same thing.

The probe read the difference between the ship storage area and the blackness as some kind of wall.

However, the area where the initial probe went into the blackness didn't register the same way.

I open a three-dimensional screen, putting it against the mostly blank wall before me. (The shutters are down over the portal, and this particular vessel doesn't have screens to show what's outside the ship.)

The three-dimensional image shows the visuals from the probe. They're in color, but I only know that because the edges of the starfield-barrier, in the distance, are glowing a golden yellow, threaded with some red.

Closer to the probe, everything is in shades of black and gray. The edge that it's skating along is a pewter color that is hard to see through. As the probe moves past it, I see bits of white light, the occasional golden halo, and some dots that actually look like flame.

"Is that another barrier?" Mikk asks.

"I think it's the same barrier," I say. "I'm beginning to think there's a malfunction or a hole in the barrier. Maybe it was that comet trail?"

"It would be a heck of a coincidence that the hole in the barriers started when we arrived," Mikk says.

"We don't know when it started or what's causing it or whether or not it is just growing and growing," I say. "I don't think we can jump to any conclusions yet. I'm not even sure that is a barrier."

"Maybe we should activate one of the other probes," Mikk says.

"We probably should," I say. "But we should bring it closer to the entry point for the original probe, and not have it travel along the edge."

"I was thinking the opposite," Mikk says. "I think we should see if it gets the same reading."

I don't want to waste the probes. Our initial plan was to get a map of the mines and weaponry inside that dark area, and then a map of that edge. We decided that, if the first few probes get destroyed, the last two probes would travel inside the starfield-barrier itself, one at a time. We fully expect the first probe to go in to get attacked or reprogrammed like the Fleet probe.

But we hope—I hope—that the barrier will ignore it entirely.

"Maybe we should see if it can move directly into that black area from where it's at, instead of traveling all the way around," I say. To do that will take quite a reprogramming feat, but Mikk loves working on the probes and I think he's up to it.

He gives me an irritated look. "I wish you had come up with that earlier."

"Earlier, I didn't think there was a barrier on the outside of that black area," I say.

"Yeah." He sounds both bemused and annoyed. "It'll take some work to get the reprogramming done."

We have a timeline, but it's unofficial. We didn't want to make it solid, depending on what we discovered. But we figured that, once we launched the first probe, we only have a day or two of grace before the Boneyard notices what we're doing.

If the Boneyard notices what we're doing.

"I'll monitor all of this if you do the reprogramming," I say. As if I would do the reprogramming. I'm not as good at it as Mikk is. I don't have the interest.

I'm being confronted on several levels today about the things I'm not interested in. Probably because I'm dealing with a lot that does interest me.

Like the mystery of this starfield-barrier.

"Any idea of the trajectory you want?" Mikk asks me. "How do you want that probe to get to what we think is the opening?"

"The fastest way possible," I say.

"Won't that be obvious?" Mikk asks.

"I have no idea." I'm getting tired of thinking about this potential intelligence behind the Boneyard. Even if there is one, it's probably not monitoring every small piece of equipment.

Even if it is, there's no obvious pattern to the way we're using the probes. Not yet, anyway. Once that second probe gets to the opening, it'll be clear that this little grouping of probes is getting into the dark area, but that'll be in hindsight. That's why we have to move somewhat quickly.

"At some point," I say, "we have to stop worrying about what this unknown and maybe nonexistent intelligence thinks, and just try to figure all of this out on our own."

Mikk grins at me. "Uh-oh," he says. "Apparently the idea of being watched is suspiciously close to following rules."

Which, unless I've made those rules, is something I dislike doing. I smile back.

"Yeah, there's that," I say. "But we've decided to do it, so we can't hesitate along the way. Because we'll waste this opportunity if we do."

"Direct shot it is," Mikk says. "I'm leaving in the admonition to avoid every solid surface."

"Probably even more necessary on this one," I say, "since the direct route will take it around some actual ships and ship parts."

He nods, already preoccupied. He's sorting through the carryall, finding the tablet he has attached to one of the probes left behind.

We've done a lot to fool that maybe non-existent intelligence, including using a different command system for each probe.

Instead of watching him, I open yet another holoscreen, and have it start designing a map of the dark smudges behind that pewter barrier that the real probe has picked up. The smudges and the light and the bit of flame are irregularly placed, but my eye detects a pattern.

Or perhaps I want there to be a pattern, just because I like order.

We'll know more when we have another probe doing the same kind of mapping.

I glance at the real probe—which I should probably call the first probe now. It has finally moved inside the black area. It zigs almost immediately, in the same place the Fleet probe that we sent in zigged. Then this probe zooms upward, around and down again. It's avoiding things that the Fleet probe didn't seem to notice or consider.

I glance at the images the probe is sending us. There's a bit of a lag on those, just enough to show what caused it to zig minutes after the zig was completed.

That something looks like a flame. The other items, appearing rapidly as the probe speeds up, look like smudges. I glance at the telemetry, hoping for readings that are more than the visuals, and I let out a hiss of air as I realize we're getting them.

Energy readings. The smudges have stronger readings than anything that shows up as light or flame. It makes me wonder if they're shielded.

"Got it," Mikk says. It takes me a minute to realize he's talking about reprogramming the other probe.

"That was fast," I say.

"Easier than I thought," he says. "I'm sending it off now."

"Good," I say, still frowning at the first probe. It's now following the same path that the Fleet probe took. I had expected the first probe to hit something by now or to be destroyed.

However, the first probe seems to have looked like it has a clear path to that opening. Then the probe zigs downward again, and veers sideways before turning back ever so slightly.

Then it veers sideways again, before making an even sharper upswing. In the last minute, it has changed direction several times and has stopped moving forward.

I wish I was getting information from it faster than I am. Because I'm not seeing what's causing it to change direction.

Then I do. More smudges, even darker than the ones farther back. They're smaller too, and unless I miss my guess, they've moved toward the probe.

I curse, and send a command to the probe to send us all of its data immediately. Usually probes send data in batches, just in case the dumps are too much. But this time, I want as much as I can get right now.

"It's off," Mikk says.

I glance at him, confused, then I blink hard. The second probe. He just checked. The second probe is on its way.

"I'm having trouble with the first probe," I say.

More smudges have moved toward it. They're small and from this distance, they look like one big weapon. If I look at the telemetry and, specifically, the energy readings, I realize that they're not one big weapon but several tiny ones.

And I'm only assuming that they're weapons. I don't know what they are exactly.

Mikk sets aside the tablet governing the secondary probe and moves toward me.

"I can program it out of there," he says, referring to the first probe.

"Yes," I say. "Do what you can."

He slides a different tablet toward himself, and starts inputting commands. The probe moves around and around in tighter circles, like a person being tormented and trapped by small birds. As I consider the analogy, I realize that it's spot-on. The black smudges are tormenting the probe, trying to push it into a smaller and smaller space so that they can...what? Attack? Cover it? Destroy it?

If they want to destroy it, why haven't they done so by now?

My heart is pounding, and in a distant part of myself, I'm bemused that I am rooting for the probe as if it is a live creature. Although, whether or not it's alive, it is an important information-gathering tool, and I'd rather have it intact as long as possible.

I stare at the attack and the poor probe, circling, circling. It doesn't have a governing intelligence, and so it can only react as programmed.

Right now, it has no escape route programmed.

Then I see one, a small opening near the entry into the black area.

"Mikk," I say, "there's a way out for the probe. Program in these coordinates."

He nods and I give him the coordinates for the small opening. He inputs them, his fingers moving quickly.

The probe stops circling and zooms, with purpose, out that little opening, away from the smudges.

They converge on the area the probe left, and for a moment, I wonder if they even realize it's gone. Then they combine—I don't know what word is better than that—and trail after it, turning white as they do so.

Mikk curses, and just when I thought my heartrate can't rise any more, it goes up dramatically. It's almost hard to catch my breath.

So the comet trail that we saw initially, that was these smudgy things? And they were pursuing something else? Something that isn't tied to us?

We had initially thought the trail was the edge of the barrier or some sloughed off nanobits. But it might be something completely different.

We'll have to investigate that later.

Mikk is motionless beside me, staring at the probe. "I can't make it go faster," he says.

And I understand what he means. The probe is moving at a fast clip—faster than I've ever seen a probe move—but that's not as fast as the unified smudges, the comet trail, whatever we're calling that thing. Because now that they're organized into one long tail of white, they've sped up.

For a brief moment, I think the probe is going to reach the edge of the blackness and return to our part of the Boneyard. But just a few seconds after I have that thought—feel that tiny bit of hope—the comet trail envelops the probe.

"It looks like the stuff outside the Boneyard," Mikk says. "Only white."

And he's right: the way the comet trail encases the probe looks like the same maneuver we'd seen with that Fleet probe, after it had been reprogrammed and emerged from the Boneyard itself. Encased, and then destroyed.

Only this time, I can't see the probe. The white dominates everything. The white curls under itself, and moves toward the starfield-barrier—the edge that our very first Fleet probe actually got into.

Once the white reaches that edge, it goes inside. The tail of that comet trail dissipates, as if it is actually smoke.

"I'm not liking this," Mikk says.

"Yeah," I say, because that's true. But it's also true that watching the comet trail—eat (for lack of a better word)—the probe made me giddy. We're getting answers to questions that we had, such as what is that comet trail, but those answers lead to more questions.

Mikk is fiddling with the tablet in his right hand. The other tablet, the one that governs the second probe, remains untouched on the console.

I don't pick that tablet up, not yet, but I will. I'm not sure if we should send that probe into the blackness. Not until we get some answers.

"Was the probe sending us information when it got engulfed?" I ask, because I know what Mikk is looking for. He's looking for answers to the new questions we have.

"Yeah," he says. "It's still sending us information."

"How is that possible?" I ask. "It's gone."

"We don't know that. Those—things—they took it into the starfield-barrier."

We look at each other. Mikk's face is flushed, looking darker than it did just a moment ago. He's worried, but emotional as well.

"Let's stop the second probe from going inside," I say.

He glances down at the second tablet. He's clearly forgotten about it. "Too late," he says.

I make myself let out a breath. My poor giddy heart can't handle this. If I were on a dive, someone would call me back inside.

I don't want to waste that second probe. And clearly something sees these probes as interlopers. Either we send one more probe in, as planned, or we stop right now.

Then I have a horrid thought.

"Can whatever is inside that starfield-barrier track where the probe's information is going?" I ask.

"I can do that with probes," Mikk says. "So I have to assume whatever that is can do what we can do."

I stare at him for a second, then I hold up a finger. I'm not going to communicate from inside this orbiter. I hurry toward the exit, push it open, and step into the ship repair area. I go to the communication panel on the wall, and contact the bridge, hoping I'll get Pao.

Fortunately, I do.

"Make sure shields are on full," I say to her. "Prepare for some kind of attack."

"What's going to attack us?" She sounds calmer than I feel. She probably *is* calmer than I am.

"We don't know yet, but something might. And send the same message to the *Sove*. Make sure the entire crew is on each ship."

"Boss," Pao says. "What's going on?"

"We'll show you later," I say. "Just make sure we're defended."

"Okay," she says, although the word cuts off as I close the communications panel.

I'm going to trust her to get that job done.

I've got to trust all of my people.

Because we might have initiated something bad, and we need to be as prepared as possible. We need to be ready to return home.

23

MIKK IS COLLECTING AS MUCH INFORMATION AS HE CAN. He's got three tablets in front of him, along the navigation console. He's under the delusion that if he doesn't pour the information from the first non-Fleet probe into the computer system on board this orbiter, then the overriding intelligence of the Boneyard or whatever we're thinking this might be won't be able to track us to the orbiter inside of the *Madxaf.*

I know—and I know that Mikk knows—that's wrong. Whatever is tracking us—if something is tracking us—will be able to locate us easily. Heck, I can locate us easily.

But I need Mikk to work, so I'm not going to challenge his assumptions, at least right now. I'm the one pulling information from his tablets onto the orbiter's computer system, just so that we have a backup. And I'm trying to monitor the second probe on several different holoscreens.

The second probe is traveling along a direct line from the place where it tumbled out of the runabout into the opening of that black area, the very place the first probe we'd put in there was trying to escape out of not fifteen minutes before.

The second probe is close. It's moving at a constant speed, dodging ship parts and the edges of vessels stored in the Boneyard. Soon, if something doesn't get in the second probe's way, it'll cross into the opening of that dark area.

Now that I've had a chance to think about things, I'm relieved that the second probe is moving into the dark area. Since the smudges have formed a white comet trail and attacked the first probe, they won't be outside the dark area. We'll be able to see if the Boneyard or something in that area replaces the smudges or if they're a finite unit.

Mikk isn't looking at the information which is still coming from that first probe. He's compressing the information, so that we can take as much of it as possible. Pretty soon, he's going to have to transfer some of it off the tablet, just for the sake of storage.

Because I'm working behind him, and I can see that there's a lot of data coming our way, more than I expected, even though I'm the one who set up the probe to do a full data dump when the smudges approached.

The second probe turns a sharp corner and heads into the dark area. My breath catches. I slide the second probe's tablet toward me, and open one more holoscreen, so I can see the visuals as the probe sees them.

There are white circles and things that look like flame, just like there were from the point of view of the first probe.

But I'm not seeing smudges, and as the second probe travels into the dark area, the second probe doesn't bob and zig like the first probe did or even like the Fleet probe did. This second probe goes straight into the main part of the darkness, occasionally moving to one side or another to avoid one of the white circles.

Nothing is chasing this second probe. There are no smudges and certainly no comet trail. The second probe seems to have a clear path to the ragged edge leading into the starfield-barrier.

"Hey, Boss," Mikk says, an odd tone to his voice.

I glance at him.

"The information coming from the probe," he says, "it's fading."

"Fading?" I ask.

"Yeah," he says. "The way your voice fades when you go to sleep while you're still trying to say something."

Or the way your voice fades as you die, I think but do not say. I'm suddenly feeling squeamish about mentioning death around Mikk. We're skirting on the edge of something, as he warned me just a few hours ago.

"Normally, I'd boost it," he says, "but I don't want to contact the probe if I can avoid it."

That's Mikk's way of asking me if he's doing the right thing.

"Good call," I say.

I'm still looking at that second probe. It's not hitting anything, and it's not moving all over the black area, like the first probe did.

My stomach flutters nervously. If we send in two ships…or maybe even another probe…as we try to go into the edge of that starfield-barrier, then we might have a chance of avoiding an attack, at least outside of the barrier.

But there's a lot of risk. We don't know what's happening to the probe in there—not yet, anyway—and we need to, before we ever send a ship with a crew inside.

"Is that probe being reprogrammed?" I ask.

"If it is," Mikk says, "it's taking a long time."

"It's not Fleet equipment," I say. "In that instance, reprogramming would take a long time. Or longer, anyway."

"Maybe," he says. "It's more like the probe is being…I don't know… strangled, maybe? Only a thread of information is coming through right now. I expect that to fade at any moment."

I nod. I want to dive into the information, but I also what to see what happens with the second probe, which is moving straight toward the starfield-barrier.

I copy more of the first probe's data from the tablet onto the orbiter's systems. But I'm watching the second probe at the same time, wishing I had set up a program that would compare what the second probe is encountering with what the first probe encountered in the same area.

I can do that later, of course, but I want to see it now.

I want to see all of it now.

"It's—there's no more information coming our way, Boss," Mikk says. He sounds a little choked up. I get the sense he almost told me that the probe is dead.

I look over his shoulder at the opening in the starfield-barrier, the spot where the comet tail entered. On the screen I'm looking at now, I can't see the second probe at all.

I'm not sure what I'm waiting for—and then, I know. I'm waiting for the first probe to come zooming back out, the way the Fleet probe did.

But the first probe doesn't come back. I wonder if something inside disassembled it or destroyed it or shut it down.

I want to know if something in there is examining it.

Maybe the answer to those questions will be in the data. Is there a way to know if the probe is being disassembled?

I turn back to the holoscreen I created for the visuals on the second probe. As I turn toward it, I see the path of the second probe. It's right at the edge of the starfield-barrier. No smudges come near the probe, and there's no comet trail.

My heart is hammering again. These changes in the treatment of the probes both excite me and discourage me. I'm worried that I'm missing something, and I'm worried that I'm viewing it all through the prism of what I want, rather than what's actually happening.

But at the same time, this little encounter with the non-Fleet probes and the starfield-barrier is going better than I expected.

Finally, my gaze rests on the visuals the second probe is sending back. Something is glistening before it, the way that some shields glisten when viewed with the right equipment.

There's also a trace of white, but it's not moving toward the probe. Instead, the white is dissipating, the way that it had dissipated outside of the starfield-barrier after capturing the first probe.

The second probe continues to move forward, crossing into what we think of as the starfield-barrier. There's no more white, and there's no first probe either.

But there are edges of other things, larger things. I reach down to expand the visual field, but Mikk captures my hand.

He's been watching this too.

"We're not going to contact the probes when they're inside that barrier," he says, as if he's the one in charge and not me.

That wasn't my ruling. It wasn't my idea. Even though he's expressed that idea earlier, it's not something I agreed to.

But he's right. We need to let this play out.

The probe moves in deeper, and it scans the area before it, with all of its equipment, including the visual. I don't look at the full data download.

I just look at the visuals.

And they match that single image we got from the Fleet probe.

Ships. Warships. Fleet warships. Lined up in perfect rows. Looking like they're waiting for something, or someone, to launch them.

Looking like they're prepared for battle.

Looking powerful and strong, and real. So very real.

"Son of a bitch," Mikk says ever so softly.

"Yeah," I say. Son of bitch, indeed.

24

THE SECOND PROBE MOVES DEEP into the starfield-barrier. It scans everything it passes and sends the information to us. Nothing that we can see shows us what happened to the first probe, and it's not visible, but, as Mikk reminded me once his voice came back, the probes are small and the warships are large.

The second probe has changed its visual input to take in as much as possible rather than concentrate on the areas closest to it. It's almost as if the probe senses its own danger and wants to get us as much information as possible before it vanishes for good.

I'm anthropomorphizing a probe. That's not like me. But I want this entire mission to work. And I'm not understanding all of it.

And...ah, hell. I'm also thinking of the probes as ships, with people inside.

Because I know how close I came to sending our ships in, our people in, without doing my usual due diligence. If I had done that, I would have doomed at least one ship, maybe two, and I never would have made it to the third.

I am working as hard as I can, standing next to Mikk, who is moving the information he received from the first probe to yet another tablet. I still haven't told him I'm backing it all up on this ship.

My gaze toggles back and forth between the journey of the second probe, its telemetry and the visuals.

Warships, warships, and more warships, all the same size and shape, all facing the same direction, none of them seeming to notice the very tiny probe traveling between them.

To be fair, the probe isn't even the size of a pebble from the perspective of one of those ships, and since the probe matches the one that got enveloped by the comet trail/smudge-things, then the warships might know (or someone might know) that the probe isn't a weapon, and therefore isn't a threat.

Maybe the Fleet doesn't care that we are receiving information from that probe. Or maybe the Fleet hadn't planned for something like this, that a single probe would breach the starfield-barrier, and be sending back images.

I rock on my toes, feeling the gids rise again. I make myself breathe, and rub my hands over my upper arms. The pattern here—one probe going in, getting captured or destroyed, and the other not suffering any consequences at all—is giving me hope.

We might be able to go behind that starfield-barrier anyway. I'm already planning the first mission with these ships. One on autopilot, that will draw the smudges away from an area, and the other with a crew that knows what it's up against, one that can go into the starfield-barrier and maybe view the warships.

I know I'm getting ahead of myself. Before we can do any of that, we have to know if those warships have crews. We have to know what else is behind that barrier. We also have to know if we've just experienced some kind of fluke with the two probes.

I also want to re-examine that comet trail we saw before we sent in the Fleet probe, and see if we can find another ship inside it. I have a to-do list a mile long, all of a sudden, because I want all of this information right now.

I feel like I do when I'm confronted with a gigantic wreck, filled with mystery. I set up all of my diving rules because of near misses. I nearly died a dozen times when I dived alone, so I stopped doing that. And then I nearly died—and my people nearly died—when we got preoccupied with whatever we were seeing, and forgot how much oxygen we had or what kind of distance we had to travel to return to our ship.

I never lost anyone on those missions, although I can't count the number of times I would sit alone in my cabin after those dives, berating myself.

Near misses were worse than deaths. Deaths happen. We come across something we've never seen before, something we can't predict, and it harms the first person to go in. Or maybe the second or the third person, like Jypé and Junior when I encountered my first Fleet ship. I know—I still know—that space and its unknowns win every time, no matter how we plan for them.

But we can mitigate what we do know.

"What?" Mikk asks. He's looking at me. "What did you say?"

Apparently, I've spoken out loud. Maybe I was just mumbling. Maybe I was saying exactly what I thought. I do that when I'm concentrating sometimes. I say things or pieces of things.

It comes from working alone for so very long.

"We have to run this like a dive," I say.

"I thought we were," he says.

I'm shaking my head. We're running parts of it like a dive, and parts of it like a Fleet mission. I've been around Coop too long. I've been thinking about rules and regulations and crews, and I'm endangering too many people.

We need to run this like an actual dive—and that starfield-barrier is what we're diving. The ships are what's inside the wreck, the way that we would find broken consoles or floating possessions left behind by long dead crew.

I let out a breath, suddenly feeling stronger. I know how to run this mission now.

We are going to separate out the dive team, so that I don't endanger the lives of everyone who is working here in the Boneyard.

Which means I was wrong: I do need a ship of my own. I have these seven ships, but I would like something just a bit bigger, and a bit more familiar. I will need one more ship from Lost Souls.

Much as I would love the *Nobody's Business* or *Nobody's Business Two*, I don't think they'll work. I need something Fleet, but also something familiar. I know what I want. I'll just have to convince Ilona to send it to me.

She probably will when I send the *Madxaf* back to her, after I've moved the non-Fleet vessels and the remaining probes to the *Sove*.

"You're scheming," Mikk says to me. This time, his voice holds approval.

I smile at him. "I know how to do this now, Mikk," I say. "I know exactly what we've been doing wrong."

THE FLEET
ONE MONTH AGO

25

MAYBE IT WAS THE FORMATION. Vilis Wihone had never used this formation before when he traveled out of foldspace. On previous journeys he had kept his ships in a typical diamond formation, every ship equidistant from his ship, the *Sakhata* always dead center.

Whether the ships formed a flat diamond or a three-dimensional one, the formation had worked. Even when he had to form something akin to a cube, with several ships around his, he had never experienced a transition like that one before.

The vibrations left him with a slight headache. He had never felt vibrations like that before, so deep and hard, almost as if something had grabbed the *Sakhata* and shaken it violently. No one on his bridge crew had fallen, but there were reports of unsecured items falling in various departments, as well as crew members tumbling down one of the corridors.

He had his engineering team make note of all of that, so that he could investigate it later.

He wanted to suggest an easy solution to the difference. He had never towed ships *into* foldspace before, so perhaps that was what caused the problem.

If he were a different man, he wouldn't even acknowledge that the formation had been a problem, but he wasn't that man. He had wanted the *Geesi* out front, not because it made the formation sturdier, but because the *Geesi* would have to be the first to handle whatever they found near that Scrapheap.

Since Wihone wasn't leading this little mission, he hadn't wanted to take point, and have the *Sakhata* crew see what a problem was before any other ship did.

He knew it was petty. He wasn't proud of himself for being that petty. But he had been.

And maybe they were all paying for it.

He let out a small sigh, glancing around the bridge. His bridge crew, the best he'd ever worked with, still looked shaken. Even though nothing had fallen here, everyone had grabbed onto their consoles a little too tightly, and a few crew members had looked scared.

He hadn't been scared, but he had been worried. Strike that. He *was* worried. Those vibrations bothered him more than he cared to think about.

"We need to check tethers and grapplers," he said to his first officer, Uxue Aruni. She stood to his right, one hand still braced on her console. The slight twist to her narrow mouth told him that she had already given that order.

It was standard for the *Sakhata* to check tethers and grapplers after leaving foldspace. She had probably assumed that the order stood for entering.

He didn't like the assumption. Even though he gave a speech to all incoming crew that included the line "foldspace is just like real space," he wasn't sure he believed it. There were variations in foldspace that bothered him, things that he didn't entirely understand.

Although he could probably say that about real space as well. He hadn't studied real space like he studied foldspace.

"Are you going to examine the tether personally, sir?" Aruni asked. She had a way of keeping her rich alto flat, so that it held no emotion at all. She thought that using little emotion would keep her own opinions close, but it had the opposite effect: whenever she used that tone with him, Wihone knew she didn't approve of what she was discussing.

Normally, he would have investigated the tethers, but he wasn't going to do that right now. The ships were going to be in foldspace for nearly two days. He could investigate later if need be.

"No." He kept his own tone flat. "Get the other captains for me. I'll be in my ready room."

The ready room on the *Sakhata* was tucked in a corner off the main part of the bridge. The ready room was actually recessed, almost a protected space since the ready room was surrounded on three sides with various types of storage.

He preferred the newer ships, with ready rooms that could grow to fill a space if the captain so desired. But he hadn't qualified to serve on those ships—all of which were DV-Class vessels.

And, if he were being honest with himself, he didn't want to command a DV-Class vessel. He liked working SC-Class ships, going in and out of foldspace. The job appealed to a sense of recklessness that his advisors had noted when he started on the captain's track.

Because he did have a tendency toward what they called "recklessness" and what he called "adrenalin-fueled moments," they assigned him foldspace. That way, they wouldn't be able to interfere with any potential mistakes.

The reasoning was if he made it back to real space in any form, he had accomplished his mission, one way or another.

In other words, success in this part of the Fleet outweighed any mistakes he might have made because he was "reckless."

The new formation might have been reckless.

He wasn't sure, and it wasn't like him to doubt himself this early in a mission. But the vibrations had disturbed him. He had never felt anything like that, and he wasn't sure what caused it.

He made his way across the bridge to his ready room. As the door slid open, he saw the four other captains standing in a semi-circle. They were all present holographically, but the holos were solid—he couldn't see through them at all.

As a result, it seemed like all four captains were there with him. Mihaita al-Aqel stood closest to the door, hands clasped behind his back.

He wore a brown tunic and matching pants, which were not regulation. But Wihone had worked with al-Aqel before, and knew that al-Aqel preferred comfortable clothing to uniforms, even for his staff. Every now and then someone reported him, and each time, Command dismissed the arguments, claiming that captains could run ships as they saw fit, so long as the ship ran smoothly, which the *Royk* had done for fifteen years under al-Aqel's command.

Al-Aqel was several inches taller than Wihone and thinner as well. Al-Aqel's angular features made him seem even taller. He kept his brown hair trimmed closely to his skull, which accented his light brown eyes, eyes that seemed to miss nothing.

He had such a presence that even though he wasn't really here, he seemed to fill the ready room.

Although he wasn't alone in that. Cohn's hologram stood on the other side of the door. She always dominated any room she was in. Her lips were in a thin line, her arms crossed. She seemed to be an even more solid physical presence than al-Aqel, and Wihone wasn't sure how that was possible.

The only captain who didn't seem like a force in the room was Gyda Fjeld of the *Mächteg*. She had the roundish form of someone who let her physical training slide, something Wihone did not approve of. For all his so-called recklessness, Wihone believed in discipline above all else. That was how a solid ship was run.

Fjeld had the palest skin Wihone had ever seen, and eyes that seemed almost silver. Perhaps those traits, along with the close-cropped hair that she kept a pale pink, made her seem even more invisible than she was.

Wihone had worked with captains like her, though, in leadership courses. There were several schools of thought on leadership, and one of them was to step back and be a nearly invisible presence, unless more was needed.

Wihone knew the remaining captain did not prescribe to that theory. Balázs Jicha was the only captain not standing. His image looked odd, because it was a full-body image of him seated on only part of a chair. The rest of the chair did not show up on the hologram, so it looked like he was floating in the middle of the room.

Wihone wondered if Jicha had devised the odd appearance on purpose or if he didn't care. Or perhaps he had given it no thought.

Wihone didn't pretend to understand Jicha. Jicha had a round face and soft features, even though he wasn't overweight like Fjeld. He just seemed soft and a little careless. His salt-and-pepper hair was tightly curled against his skull and his eyes were a little milky, their whites more yellow than actual white.

But his gaze was sharp, and Wihone got the sense that Jicha never missed anything. He was the captain who annoyed Wihone the most and the one Wihone understood the least. Wihone suspected those two things were related.

As the ready room door slid closed behind Wihone, Jicha leaned back in his chair, away from his holoimager, which cut off the back of his head.

"That was the worst entry into foldspace I have ever experienced," Jicha said. "Now that we're here, can we untether and travel on our own auspices? We can leave foldspace through the same coordinates, which would have just as desirable an effect as leaving all at once."

He was directing the comments to Wihone as if Wihone were in charge. And, honestly, in this part of the trip, Wihone was in charge, more or less.

Wihone let his gaze travel to Cohn's face. She didn't seem annoyed by Jicha's comment. In fact, she seemed slightly bemused.

"It's Captain Cohn's call," Wihone said, and he couldn't quite keep the bitterness out of his voice. Apparently, he wanted this command more than he had realized.

"You are free to untether if you so desire," Cohn said to Jicha, surprising Wihone. "You have an experienced crew, and you have more years on the job than the rest of us. If you think it's safe, then by all means."

"Um…" al-Aqel started to speak up just as Fjeld said, "Captain, my understanding—"

"But," Cohn said over them, "if something goes awry, that's on you, Captain Jicha. We will not be able to search for you or come back for you. And it will take days, maybe weeks, to contact the Fleet for assistance."

Jicha leaned forward, the back of his head visible again. His eyes narrowed, as if he was about to argue.

Wihone braced himself. He hadn't called everyone together to fight. He wanted to discuss the vibrations.

Apparently, Cohn saw Jicha's expression too, because her eyes glinted.

"I'll be frank with you, Captain Jicha," she said, her words clipped. "As far as I'm concerned, yours is the expendable ship. Vice Admiral Mbuyi is the one who wanted the *Tudósok* on this mission. The rest of us were uncertain about the value of your contribution. If things go as I hope they will, then Vice Admiral Mbuyi will be right, and you will be able to do a lot of research. If things go badly, which seems likely, you'll be hanging back and observing. If you arrive at the Scrapheap ahead of us, then you'll be dealing with whatever is still there—or rather, *whoever* is there—without any assistance. And that might be difficult."

Jicha's expression hardened into something nasty. Apparently he also believed that he should be in charge of this mission, or maybe, in charge of his ship. He didn't have a history of working in tandem with other ships. In fact, the job he'd held over the past decade or so had precluded him working with other ships.

Scholar ships, even large ones like a DV-Vessel, worked alone most, if not all, of the time.

Wihone made note of Jicha's expression. Wihone was also unhappy that he didn't have full command of this mission, but he understood how to play nice, even though he hadn't exactly been warm either to Cohn.

Fjeld hadn't reacted at all to Jicha's request nor to Cohn's response. But al-Aqel winced when Jicha made the request, as if al-Aqel expected Cohn to respond differently than she had. And after al-Aqel tried to speak up, he straightened his shoulders and his eyes flashed, as if what he saw disturbed him.

All of those movements were small, however, and not something the others probably noticed.

Except maybe Cohn. Not much seemed to get past her.

"Vice Admiral Mbuyi said the *Tudósok* was the point of the mission." Jicha punctuated each word, the endings clipped, as if the words themselves were weapons.

So Cohn had gotten to him after all.

"The vice admiral had told me something similar," Cohn said. She sounded almost cheerful, which Wihone wouldn't have expected, given the sharpness of Jicha's comment. "If the thieves are long gone and we cannot track them, then the work of the *Tudósok* will make this mission worthwhile."

Jicha's eyes narrowed. Fjeld shifted slightly, another of those small movements like the ones al-Aqel had executed. He wasn't moving at all.

Neither was Wihone. He hadn't expected any of this when he called the meeting.

"However," Cohn said, "if the thieves remain, they pose a great threat to us. We—or rather, I—will expect the *Tudósok* to take part in any physical action we'll have to take against the thieves. I would prefer to have you arrive at the same time that we do. But if you want to go this alone, you're welcome to it."

Jicha started to nod, and part of Wihone wished Jicha wouldn't respond yet.

Cohn didn't seem to care about Jicha's response. She continued, "You should know, however, that if you untether, I will make sure you exit foldspace first. You will arrive in real space alone and unprotected. With luck, you will arrive just moments before us."

Her words hung in the room. Everyone knew that foldspace didn't favor the lucky. It didn't favor anyone. There was a chance—a good chance—that the *Tudósok* could arrive an hour or two ahead of the rest of the Task Unit. Or two hours afterwards.

Cohn's expression softened, but her eyes didn't. "As I said, it is entirely your decision, Captain Jicha. I will respect whatever you choose."

Silence hung in the ready room. Wihone thought of walking deeper inside the room, but he would have to pass the holograms of both Cohn and al-Aqel, stopping beside Fjeld so that he could take his chair.

Movement at this moment no longer appealed to Wihone, no matter how much he wanted to rest his legs.

The silence had gone on much too long when Jicha's frown deepened. "You want me to decide now?" he asked.

"Yes," Cohn said.

Cohn's simple response surprised Wihone as well. If he had been in charge, he would have said something like *I thought you had decided already*. But that simple response was much more effective.

It seemed to flummox Jicha.

Jicha's gaze turned toward Wihone. Their eyes didn't quite meet because Jicha seemed to have his holoimager set up improperly.

"Can you guarantee that we won't go through another series of vibrations like that?" Jicha asked.

"No," Wihone said. He was about to add more—the vibrations were why he had brought the captains here, after all—but he decided to take a cue from Cohn instead, and give only one-word answers to the question.

Jicha was still speaking to Wihone. "I've never experienced anything like those vibrations before and I don't want to do it again. So if it was caused by the tether—"

"We don't know what caused it." Fjeld spoke up, her voice surprisingly deep and authoritarian. "I experienced something similar years ago, and my ship wasn't tethered to anything."

"So the problem is the *Mächteg*," Jicha said.

"I didn't say I was in the *Mächteg* the first time this happened." Fjeld gave him a smile similar to the one that Cohn had had. "I wasn't. I wasn't even on a DV-Class vessel. I was in officer training on a routine fold-space mission when we had an entry into foldspace so violent that half of the crew got injured. This one was mild by comparison."

Her comments intrigued Wihone. He was going to want to talk with her. He needed to know where she had entered foldspace and what kind of vessel she had been on and if anything else had been similar to this mission.

"Reacting out of fear," al-Aqel said to Jicha, "is precisely the wrong reaction."

"I'm not afraid," Jicha snapped.

Wihone heard the defensiveness in Jicha's voice, and if Wihone heard it, then everyone else had as well.

"Please." Al-Aqel smiled thinly. "I've studied your file. I've studied everyone's. It's quite clear, Captain Jicha, that you took on the scholars because the missions would be easy. I do understand how battle sometimes leaves scars, but had I been you, unable to get past the scars of the past, I would have resigned my commission and retired years ago."

"I'm not afraid," Jicha said again, with even more emphasis.

No one spoke for a moment. Wihone's gaze met Cohn's. She still looked bemused, as if she had hoped for something like this. Or maybe not hoped. *Expected* something like this.

Unlike al-Aqel, Wihone hadn't studied the other captain's histories, nor had he studied the histories of their ships. Wihone hadn't even thought of it, although he would wager that Cohn had.

Maybe Wihone hadn't been the right person for this job, not because he lacked the experience, but because he had never considered doing the kind of research at least two of the other captains had done. Maybe he lacked a subtler kind of leadership experience, one he hadn't given any thought to at all.

He shifted slightly, and felt something inside himself relax. He wasn't going to protest his position any longer. He wasn't even going to think about it anymore.

He couldn't tell how the others reacted to Jicha's outburst. Fjeld watched, her gaze sharp. She clearly didn't miss much. Al-Aqel's eyes were slightly hooded, as if he was trying to contain some emotion, but what that emotion was, Wihone couldn't tell.

Jicha was sitting up straighter than he had before, his entire body coiled as if he were ready to spring out of his chair and defend himself with his fists.

Cohn's expression hadn't changed at all. She glanced at all of the other captains, meeting their gazes one by one. Her gaze met Wihone's second to last. He thought maybe she was sending him a message—maybe a challenge to see if he still wanted to protest her leadership.

Or maybe he was reading too much into this.

Then Cohn's gaze left his and met Jicha's.

"I would like you to make your decision now," Cohn said to Jicha. "We have much to discuss, and do not have much time to waste."

Jicha's mouth tightened, as if he was holding back his initial response. And judging by the glimmer in his eyes, that response would not have been civil.

His mouth moved a few times before he said, "I don't like being pressed into making a decision with no information."

The words were clipped again, each one articulated precisely and firmly and just a bit louder than necessary.

"You have all of the information that the rest of us have," Cohn said.

"We don't know what caused those vibrations!" This time, Jicha spoke faster, his voice slightly raised. This time, he sounded defensive.

"That is correct," Cohn said. "We don't know. None of us know. Which means that we all have the same information, and we choose to remain tethered."

That was an assumption, since she hadn't polled the remaining captains. But it seemed like a safe assumption to Wihone, judging by the expressions of the others. They seemed disgusted by Jicha.

"We need the decision now," Cohn said, all the amusement gone from her face, "because we need to know how we will proceed."

"I don't like making decisions on incomplete information," Jicha said.

"That explains a lot," al-Aqel said just loud enough for everyone to hear.

Jicha turned toward him, face mottled. "You have no right—"

"Gentlemen, please." Cohn's voice was calm. "Captain Jicha, you have had quite a luxury captaining a ship of scholars."

Jicha turned toward her, his hands clenched.

"Most captains do not have the luxury, ever, of making decisions based on complete information. Perhaps you recall that from your earlier assignments." She did not make that into a question. Her response was smooth and firm, and there was just a hint of toughness underneath.

She was much more polite that Wihone would have been. Had Jicha been one of Wihone's subordinates, he would have been given a warning.

But Jicha was no one's subordinate. Cohn didn't even outrank him, except as the leader of this Task Unit.

So she was shaming him, which seemed to make him angrier.

"I need your decision," Cohn said evenly. "And I need it now."

Jicha looked toward Fjeld. Maybe he expected her to support him. But her expression hadn't changed. Or hadn't changed much. Her lips were twisted ever so slightly, in disapproval, or so Wihone thought.

"We will stay tethered," Jicha said. "But I hope *someone* will be working on that vibration problem."

By someone, he clearly meant Wihone.

"We need to do something else first," Cohn said, shifting slightly so her hologram wasn't facing Jicha. She could adjust her own input at any point if she didn't want to look at him, so the shift was just for show. "We need to check the tethers and grapplers."

"I'm already on it," Wihone said.

"We're checking ours," al-Aqel said.

"As are we," Fjeld said.

Jicha crossed his arms. "I would like to wait—"

"You will not wait for anything," Cohn snapped. "You are part of a team now. If you and the *Tudósok* do not wish to work with us on the Task Unit, then you can return to the Fleet by yourself. Those are your choices. You will follow my orders immediately or you will remove yourself and your ship from this Task Unit. Is that clear?"

Jicha looked a little to his left. Wihone couldn't tell if he was looking away from Cohn, or looking directly at her.

"Is that clear?" Cohn repeated, the words softer than they had been.

"Yes." Jicha sounded like a surly teenager.

"You will check your tethers and grapplers immediately," Cohn said. "We will wait while you order your team to do so."

Jicha sighed, then planted his hands on the arm rests of his chair. He stood slowly, as if his entire body ached.

Wihone had never seen another captain move like that. Jicha was considerably older and al-Aqel had mentioned something about his history. Perhaps Jicha had been seriously injured. Or injured many times. After a certain point, the rebuilt and rehabbed areas ceased functioning in the same way as the rest of the body.

Jicha stepped out of the frame.

"If I were you," Fjeld said, "I would just send them back."

Al-Aqel nodded, and so did Wihone.

Cohn's expression did not change. "Noted," she said.

"We will be inspecting the tethers attached to the *Tudósok*," al-Aqel added. "All of us. We are attached."

"I know." Cohn's tone remained flat.

Wihone was about to say that he too would be inspecting all of the tethers, whether the other captains did so or not, but as he opened his mouth, Jicha sat back down.

"Done," he said as the chair groaned beneath him.

Cohn nodded, then she turned toward Wihone. It looked like she was looking directly at him, unlike the effect from Jicha's holoimager.

"You contacted us," she said. "I assume there's more to the contact than a reminder to check the tethers and grapplers."

"Yes." Wihone paused for a moment, noting how his own attitude toward Cohn had changed in this entire interaction. She had masterfully taken command of all four captains, something she hadn't done when they met the first time.

Of course, the first time, Vice Admiral Mbuyi had been in the room as well and had been in charge. There had been no real meeting since, although all five captains had been in the same conversations more than once.

Everyone was waiting for Wihone now. He said, "I wanted to talk about that vibration. I've never experienced anything like it, and it was *not* caused by the tethers. We've examined our readings, and there's nothing unusual that we could find in our foldspace entry. I was hoping one of you found something."

"We didn't have to have a meeting for this," Jicha muttered.

"We examined our readings as well," Cohn said, "and found nothing. I thought perhaps the vibrations came from the fact that some of our ships were in foldspace and some had not yet completed their arrival, at least from the perspective of the *Geesi*."

"We've never had that problem in the past," Wihone said, although he had never sent one ship ahead of all the others before. He was going to keep that to himself at the moment, until he was able to examine more of the readings.

He didn't think that would make a difference, though.

"You always brought ships out of foldspace into regular space," Fjeld said. "Never the other way around. Do you think that is the difference?"

Wihone was about to answer, when al-Aqel spoke.

"If so, we have nothing to worry about as we leave foldspace," he said. "And, if all goes as planned, we won't need to tether on the way back."

Wihone swallowed his annoyance. He was gaining more and more respect for Cohn. Keeping these captains corralled was more difficult than he expected.

Wihone was also aware of the fact that he couldn't give exact orders. So he chose his words carefully.

"We should tether even on the way back," he said. "We should use every precaution we can for a journey of this distance through foldspace."

"Even if it causes that vibration?" Jicha asked. "I wasn't sure our ship would survive."

And they were the last ones to arrive in foldspace. Wihone wondered if their vibration pattern was similar to the *Geesi's*.

"Send me all the information that you have on what happened for your ship during the transition from regular space to foldspace," Wihone said to Jicha. "We will analyze it, and see what we find."

"We should all do that," Cohn said. "I want you to send information on the transition to Captain Wihone, and to me as well."

Wihone glanced at her. He knew she had some of the best foldspace minds in the Fleet on her ship, but they weren't foldspace experts like he was.

Although an extra set of eyes wouldn't hurt.

"Perhaps you can put your scholars to use," al-Aqel was saying to Jicha, "and have them investigate if such vibrations have been a problem in the past."

"They don't specialize in engineering problems," Jicha said. "They're strictly working on a history of the Fleet."

Fjeld shook her head slightly, as if she couldn't believe what she was hearing. Cohn's expression was carefully neutral, but Wihone remembered how not long ago she had told Jicha that his team was expendable.

Clearly, and for good reason.

"Well," Wihone said to Jicha, "any information they might have from the Fleet's history would be welcome. And Captain Fjeld, I'd love to hear more about your foldspace experience as well."

"I will send you the files," Fjeld said somewhat primly. "It was well documented at the time."

"We've already run simulations," Cohn said, "and they do show that we are on the correct trajectory, and that the vibrations did not cause predictable problems."

If she was mentioning trajectories and predictable problems, then she was saying, without alarming anyone, that nothing had gone awry in the traditional way in foldspace. They weren't off-course, and as far as they could tell, they hadn't lost time.

But lost time usually showed up once the ships left foldspace, not before.

"However," Cohn was saying, "you contacted us, Captain Wihone. Do you believe the vibrations are a problem?"

Time to be honest. Wihone glanced at Fjeld, who was studying him, then he turned his gaze back to Cohn. She seemed calmer than all of the rest of them.

"The vibrations might be a problem," he said. "If we experience them as we leave foldspace, and they cause a lot of damage, then we might not be at our full capacity as we arrive in real space."

And if they encounter the thieves or hostiles or the Scrapheap itself attacks, the ships might be subject to even more damage.

But he didn't have to say that part for Cohn. She understood. So did Fjeld, who nodded, and al-Aqel, who closed his eyes ever so briefly. Jicha's eyes were moving as if he were watching the reactions of his colleagues, and trying to understand them.

And then, almost on cue, he said, "Maybe we shouldn't tether, then."

Cohn raised her chin ever so slightly. "We settled that."

Or maybe not, depending on what they discovered with the vibrations. But Wihone knew better than to say anything about it.

The vibrations might mean nothing, or they might make this entire trip even more difficult than it already was.

"Let's get our best people on this," Cohn said. "Each captain will instruct their foldspace engineers to coordinate with…"

And she paused ever so briefly. For a moment, Wihone thought she was going to say that they should coordinate with her man, Iosua, and Wihone braced himself.

"…Captain Wihone here, who will coordinate all of the information." Cohn gave him a small smile, as if she had known what he thought she was going to do.

He gave her a nervous smile in return.

"You will then report to me," she said, "no matter what gets discovered. Or if there is nothing conclusive. I want all of this before me in twenty-four hours."

"It's not enough time," Jicha said. "I know how scholars work, and—"

"This is not a scholarly mission," al-Aqel snapped. Apparently he forgot he wasn't the one in charge, or maybe he was just so irritated that he couldn't remain silent any longer. "This is how we do things on *real* missions, or have you forgotten?"

"Captain al-Aqel," Cohn said. "Enough."

Al-Aqel shot her an irritated look, then leaned back slightly, as if he was acquiescing. Or maybe just recalling that she was in charge.

"Captain Cohn," Jicha said, and his tone was actually polite. "We could take extra time. We're not on any kind of clock here. We could let our investigations run their course before we leave foldspace."

Cohn leaned her head slightly to the right as if she hadn't thought of that.

"What say you, Captain Wihone?" she asked.

"I don't want to spend any more time than necessary in foldspace," he said without even thinking about it.

"I thought you believed foldspace wasn't dangerous," Jicha said.

"I never said anything like that," Wihone said. "We have spent millennia using foldspace, and we still don't understand it. What little time we spend studying it has always given us inconclusive results. I personally don't mind foldspace. I'm not afraid of it, and I find it intriguing. But I also know it's dangerous, and that we should always treat it with respect."

"I am treating it with respect," Jicha said. "I would like to respect the warning it gave us, and make sure we have as much information as possible."

"We don't know the warning came from foldspace," Fjeld said.

"And yet you experienced something similar entering foldspace once before," Jicha said.

"If your scholarly friends had taught you anything," al-Aqel said, "you should have learned that assuming one factor in evidence does not make that factor the cause. We don't have time for a thorough examination of what Captain Fjeld's journey and ours have in common."

Wihone half expected him to continue, but he didn't.

The problem was that Jicha was right; if they were to do this right, they should take all the time they needed rather than run on some imaginary timetable.

"I don't like being in foldspace any more than you do," Cohn said to Wihone, "but I will defer to your greater experience with foldspace. Captain Jicha has a good point. We are not under extreme time pressure. If you believe we should investigate more, then we will."

Wihone frowned at her, stunned at her level of trust in him. Did she think he would make the right decision or was this decision too dicey for her? Would she rather have it on the record that she had defaulted to him, so she wouldn't get blamed?

Jicha's bad mood had rubbed off on Wihone.

"There are no good choices here," Wihone said. "We have no idea if extra time will help us figure out the vibration problem, and we don't even know if that problem is tied to foldspace. What I do know is that ships which spend a long time in foldspace are more likely to suffer problems when they emerge from foldspace."

"Problems as in loss of time?" Fjeld asked.

"Significant loss of time," Wihone said. "Not just minutes, but hours or even days."

Or more, but he wasn't going to say that.

They were all watching him now, including Jicha. Jicha seemed more alert than he had at any other previous moment in the meeting.

"I know what days in foldspace will do," Wihone said. "I know that the level of risk of some kind of issue grows with each passing moment in foldspace. I don't know what the risks are with the vibrations, but that seems to be less common, and so I'm willing to experience more vibrations."

Cohn nodded. She tilted her head, and Wihone couldn't tell if she was thinking about what he had said or if she was listening to the advice of someone else.

That was the only downside to doing meetings this way; he couldn't tell if someone was listening in.

"Would a change in formation help?" she asked. And the question surprised him, even though he had been thinking about it. He had expected her to make a decision.

"It might," he said. "I don't know. I don't know if ships would always have that kind of reaction going into foldspace and something different coming out."

Cohn nodded again, a slight frown forming between her eyes. "I've been thinking about the formation," she said. "If we emerge out of foldspace and encounter a hostile force, the formation wouldn't be good for us. If, for example, the *Geesi* finds itself in the middle of a battle while tethered to the rest of you, but you haven't left foldspace yet, then a myriad of things could go wrong."

A shiver ran down Wihone's back. He hadn't thought of that. And he should have. Because there were demonstrable incidences in the history of the Fleet of ships getting lost in foldspace during a battle, particularly if some kind of weapon interacted with the *anacapa* drive.

Al-Aqel looked sharply at him, and Jicha's mouth twisted into a slight smile. Apparently, he was happy that someone else was getting all the attention from Cohn.

Fjeld's expression hadn't changed at all. Wihone was beginning to wonder what it took to alarm her.

Because Cohn's scenario alarmed him.

"We'll have to assess that," Wihone said. "I'll look at the formation. There's no good way to exit tethered."

"Yeah, that's what I thought," Jicha said.

"Because," Wihone said, maybe a bit more loudly than he should have, "even if we're in some kind of straight line, there's still a chance that at least one ship will lag a second or two behind."

"That doesn't sound good," Jicha said, and he might have been speaking for everyone.

It wasn't good, and Wihone had experienced it more than once. He thought of it this way: The *Sakhata* would yank a ship out of foldspace, preventing an even more serious catastrophe. He had no proof that his belief was accurate, but it felt right.

Given Jicha's attitude, though, it would be better if Wihone kept those assumptions to himself.

"Exiting one by one is also dangerous." That was Fjeld. "We've established why and, frankly, I do not wish to end up stuck, alone, either in foldspace or near that Scrapheap."

Cohn nodded, but didn't commit. Wihone watched her work, and decided he could learn even more from her. He almost wished he could apologize to Vice Admiral Mbuyi for his arrogance in thinking he was the better person to lead this team.

"The Scrapheap sent us maps of itself," al-Aqel said slowly, almost like he didn't want to insert himself into this discussion. "Which means they are relatively recent."

Just an hour ago, Wihone would have snapped at him, saying that they already knew that bit of information. But he was getting a sense of al-Aqel, and was realizing that al-Aqel built his arguments bit by bit.

"Perhaps we should exit foldspace in a different place than we had planned." Al-Aqel had folded his hands together. Of all of the captains, he was the only one that Wihone would have guessed was alone in the room where he was speaking. "Perhaps a day or so away from the area where the thieves broke in."

Jicha's frown grew. Fjeld raised her eyebrows. Wihone nodded, and wondered why he hadn't thought of that.

Cohn didn't nod. Nor did her expression change. Instead, after giving it what seemed like a moment's thought, she looked at Wihone.

"Let's take that option into account as we discuss formation," she said to him.

Wihone nodded again, uncertain when they would discuss formation. Probably after he investigated the vibrations.

"You know what I like about Captain al-Aqel's idea?" Jicha said. "I like that we arrive and then we can assess what's going on. Maybe that was what was bothering me all along."

That didn't sound like an apology, but at the same time, it was less aggressive than Jicha had been throughout this meeting.

No one looked at him, although Wihone disliked the fact that the man had been right twice now. Maybe Wihone had been wrong to write him off as an idiot, and maybe al-Aqel had been wrong to assume Jicha was damaged from whatever had happened in his past.

Maybe Jicha was more cautious than they were, and maybe he had a different leadership style.

In this single meeting alone, Wihone had learned more about leadership than he had learned in all of his leadership classes combined. And it had been years since he had served under anyone. He had a lot of time to study then, but usually it had been in reaction to that leadership. Negative experience was the phrase he had used to describe it in the past.

Cohn's leadership was much more subtle, and positive.

She acknowledged Jicha with a slight movement of her head. Wihone had no idea if Jicha had seen that or not, and Wihone wasn't even certain if that mattered.

Her gaze then met Wihone's. "We have about forty-eight hours to figure out the vibrations. By then I will have a decision on formation as well. Unless Captain Wihone has more to discuss, I think we're done for now."

That last was almost a question.

"I have nothing more," he said.

"Good. Let's get to it." And then, somehow, she made all of the other captains vanish at once.

Great way to prevent them from discussing her. Wihone supposed they could contact each other again, although he doubted any of them wanted to do that. They would have discussed her, though, if she had left first.

He took a deep breath. The ready room seemed four times bigger than it had a moment ago.

He hadn't even made it past the door. He had stood there, like a young officer, for the entire meeting.

Maybe that was why he had felt so unsettled.

Or maybe the vibrations were more of a problem than he suspected.

Now, he would have a bit of time to find out.

26

THE DATA WEREN'T CONCLUSIVE, but then data rarely were conclusive. And when data were conclusive, it was usually bad.

Wihone leaned back in the captain's chair and rubbed his eyes with the thumb and forefinger of his right hand. Personal screens glinted around him like shields, even though he didn't need to be protected from anyone.

The bridge was mostly empty. The night crew was working—the foldspace night crew, the ones who knew exactly what to do if something went wrong, the ones who knew how to contact him so that he would wake up alert and ready to solve the problem—if, indeed, they needed him to help them solve it.

He had been working for hours, and he hadn't even taken a break for dinner. As he surfaced from the data, he realized that he had a slight kink in the left side of his neck and his back ached from sitting too long. His eyes burned from staring at the screens, and when he blinked, he actually saw reflections of the information floating around him.

He had data; he just wasn't sure what to do with it.

He stood, his back cracking, his knees sore. He really hadn't moved at all.

He needed another brain on this, and that brain couldn't be his own engineering staff. He wanted to reserve them for other problems, in case he interpreted this wrong.

The person he needed to talk with was Cohn. She needed this data as much as he did. Maybe she would have some opinions about it.

He reached over to the communications panel on the right armrest of his captain's chair. His finger hesitated for a moment—he truly had no idea what time it was, but the night crew was on, so it was late.

Then he smiled at himself. He was acting like an underling rather than a co-equal commander of a co-equal vessel. Cohn was not his superior officer. And even if she was annoyed at being awakened, that would have no impact on him or on his career.

Old habits died hard. He had been a rules-bound officer until he became a captain. Then he had relaxed just enough to comfortably command his own ship. But, apparently, that rules-bound officer still lived inside his more relaxed captain's self.

He moved his hand away from the communications panel. He would talk to Cohn from the ready room. That way, if she was like any of his captains of old, he would be able to ease her into wakefulness by giving her information.

Plus, he could talk freely there. Even though his crew knew what was happening, frank talks with other captains didn't need to concern them.

He folded up all of the holoscreens until they were tiny dots that could be called up when he sat back down. He didn't like closing the screens permanently, because it often took time to figure out exactly where he had been with his analysis.

He made his way to the ready room, twisting his head and moving his arm, trying to get that kink out of his neck. He truly had been lost in the data if he hadn't noticed that forming.

As he stepped into the ready room, he instructed the computer to contact Cohn through a secure channel. He also marked the communication important. He had briefly considered calling it urgent, but urgent would send the wrong message. He was going to save urgent for something life or death.

He started to sink into the chair next to his desk, then changed his mind. The last thing he needed was to sit right now and have his muscles seize up all over again. He leaned against the desk, his hand on its smooth cool surface as the computer chirruped with a response to his summons.

"Wihone?" Cohn sounded alert and on-point, but the lack of visuals suggested that she had been asleep. "I assume you have something."

"Yes, Captain," he said. "I didn't think it could wait."

A sideways apology had always worked with the captains in the past. He hoped it worked now. It certainly worked with him as well.

"Did you find the source of the vibrations?" she asked, before he could gather himself.

"Not yet. But I did find something unusual." Which was why he wanted to talk with her.

His fingers curled around the desk's edge, biting into the skin just enough to keep him alert.

"Is it something you can tell me, or do you need to show me?" She sounded a bit reluctant about that last part. She probably wasn't dressed. He shook his head ever so slightly to get that image out of his mind.

"Let's talk first," he said. "Then you can look up the information or have your people review it to see if it even seems relevant."

"Have your people reviewed it?" she asked.

That was a side road he didn't want to go on at the moment.

"We have an interesting issue with our *anacapa* drives," he said, knowing that would get her attention.

"An issue?" she asked.

He might have been overstating by using the word *issue*, but he wasn't going to hedge that out loud.

"The three newer DV-Class vessels have *anacapa* drives that come from the same source," he said.

Anacapa drives looked like bits of rock. Even though the Fleet had been recreating them for millennia now, the Fleet had been unable to make the initial created drive a certain size. It was almost as if they grew—well, they did sort of grow—and some occasionally grew larger than others.

The Fleet had always dealt with that by cutting smaller drives out of the large ones.

"Three ships on this mission have the same sourced drive?" she asked, sounding as incredulous as he had felt when he first found the information.

"Yes, ma'am," he said, then quietly cursed himself for sounding like a subordinate. "Captain Jicha would have been proud of me, because I immediately looked up the history of those drives. The source was huge, one of the rare boulders that we got in the last batch of drives."

She might not have known about drive batches, at least in detail. Every captain knew about them, of course, because the manufacture of drives was an important part of training. If someone on a leadership track couldn't touch an *anacapa* drive with their bare hands, then that person could not handle any ship with an *anacapa* drive. There were other leadership roles in the Fleet, but they weren't in what the Fleet considered "important" categories, such as captaining a major vessel.

Wihone monitored drive design changes (which were always miniscule) and drive batches. He'd seen what malfunctioning *anacapa* drives could do. Often, when ships had to be rescued from foldspace, they got into trouble because of their *anacapa* drives.

He tried to mitigate that as much as possible with his vessel, and he wanted to know every single tool available to him when he did foldspace rescues.

Cohn hadn't responded to his statement, not yet. He wished he could see her face, so that he knew whether or not she was thinking about what he was saying or if she hadn't heard him properly.

"The other thing," he said, "is that it appears, from the records available to me right now, that the ship Captain Fjeld was on when she felt that vibration going into foldspace also had a drive from the same source."

"She said she was a young cadet when that happened," Cohn said. "Long before she captained anything."

He had expected that comment, but it disappointed him just a bit. It showed that Cohn was indeed someone who didn't pay attention to drive batches, and maybe she was one of those captains who didn't pay a lot of attention to the drives themselves.

"That's not unusual," he said. "Large *anacapa* boulders can serve as sources for *anacapa* drives for several generations."

"How do you track it?" Cohn asked, and then he heard rustling, as if she waved a hand. "Never mind. I don't want to know."

He was glad that she didn't, because tracing the source of a drive took some work. He had the information on the *Sakhata* because he did so much security and foldspace work, but the information wasn't easily accessible in most ships, even larger ships like a DV-class vessel that had to spend months, sometimes years, on its own.

"I can show you at some point how it's done," he said. "It's not relevant now. If I had more time, I could see if other ships with the same sourced drives have had troubles heading into foldspace."

"I suppose we could take the extra time…" She sounded uncertain, which surprised him. He had never heard her sound like that before.

"I'm not asking for more time," he said. Silence. He tightened his fingers around the edge of the desk, then loosened them. He twisted his neck again, wishing that kink away. He glanced through the clear door of his ready room at the crew on the bridge.

He couldn't see anyone. No one worked the mid-levels of an SC-class vessel's bridge when the bridge was sparsely populated. Most people either worked in the back or down near the captain's chair.

If he twisted, he could see the crew, heads bent or frowning in deep concentration. He always had at least one person monitoring the changes in foldspace when the ship was in foldspace. He didn't know who that one person was on this night shift crew. He probably should have known, but he'd been so focused on the vibrations and the journey toward that Scrapheap, that he had allowed his first officer to make the duty assignments.

"Let me get this straight," Cohn finally said. "You see this information as concerning."

"That the ships' drives share a source?" he asked. "Yes, I do."

"Because…?" she asked.

"The because is difficult," he said. He needed to be as up front with her as possible. "I'm guessing on everything. I'm working off a brand-new theory, at least for me. And, given what I've researched, one that no one else has come up with either. I want to be clear on that."

"All right." She didn't even sound hesitant. Half of a captain's job involved educated guessing, especially in the middle of a mission.

He took a deep breath. He was going out on a limb, and he knew it. But, given his expertise, given what he was seeing, the possibility he was dealing with seemed likely.

"I'm wondering," he said, "if the vibration isn't an amplification of something that occurs naturally when a ship goes into foldspace."

"An amplification?" she asked. "I don't recall experiencing that kind of vibration before."

"There's always a bump and a skip going into foldspace," he said, carefully modulating his tone. Some captains didn't notice that. Some *crew* members didn't notice it, not after the first few times.

Those crew members absorbed what they considered to be normal.

"Oh," she said. "That's what you mean by vibration."

He nodded, then realized she couldn't see him. "It can be minor when some ships go into foldspace."

"I know for a fact that vibration has been studied a lot," she said.

It had, because it was inexplicable. There was nothing to bump or skip over when a ship went into foldspace. And logically, nothing should cause a vibration at all.

All of the study had come up with nothing, at least as far as he knew. And he checked whenever he was back with the Fleet or near a sector base.

"It has been studied," he said, "and there is a theory that the *anacapa* drive itself causes the vibration."

"So several drives from the same sourced material might amplify each other." Her tone was musing, as if she was thinking about it, rather than talking to him directly.

"That's my current theory," he said. "But I'm not going to be able to prove it one way or another."

"Because of the mysterious nature of *anacapa* drives?" There was some amusement in her tone. Apparently she, like everyone else in the Fleet, had had that vague and unsatisfying discussion before.

"Well," he said, not willing to go down that digression either, "in this instance, there are other factors at play."

"Other factors." She sounded like she was musing again.

"Yes," he said. "Here are the problems that we're facing. We might not have any issues emerging from foldspace. There might not be any vibration at all. But when we return to foldspace after the mission we might feel it again."

"Why is that a problem?" she asked.

"Because," he said, "the changes I'm going to suggest might not make any difference at all, and we won't know it until we try to return to the Fleet."

"Oh." She put a lot of weight into that word. "So we could end up with the same problem, even after we've made changes."

"Yes," he said.

"All right," she said. "I understand. With that on the table, let me hear your plan."

He straightened, about to stand, when that kink in his neck flared. He caught himself just before he gasped in pain.

He was rather relieved that she couldn't see him any more than he could see her.

"What I want to do," he said, "is this: I want to tow two of the DV-class vessels out of foldspace."

It was a bit of a risk. Towing ships used a lot more energy, and sometimes caused extra wear and tear on the ship that was doing the towing.

"You don't want us tethered?" she asked.

"I do want the ships tethered," he said. "I want two of the ships to disable their *anacapa* drives."

She didn't respond. The silence was driving him crazy. He wanted to see her face, to see if he could figure out what she was thinking.

He knew some of it. She was worried—just like he was—that he was handicapping the ships. If there was some kind of trouble or even if a tether broke, those ships would be on their own. Sometimes it took work to reboot a disabled *anacapa* drive. The ships might end up trapped in foldspace or lose time, so that they might arrive hours or days after the main part of this caravan.

There was also the possibility that all five ships might arrive into the middle of a battle, and the two disabled DV-class ships would be at a disadvantage there as well. They would be able to maneuver out of firing range, but not back into foldspace—at least, not until the drives rebooted.

"Would disabling the drives do any good?" she asked. "Wouldn't they still amplify the vibration?"

It was a good question, one he didn't have an answer for. Or, at least, one he didn't have a good answer for.

"I don't know," he said. "If the active drive is causing the vibrations, then I don't think that there would be amplification. But if the presence of the drives alone causes it, then there would be."

Cohn sighed. A holoimage winked into view. She was wearing some kind of off-white loungewear, and her hair was down and back. Her eyes had deep shadows underneath them.

He couldn't see anything around her, so he figured she was in her quarters.

He stood up, trying not to wince as the movement hurt his back.

"You don't have to stand," she said.

She must have seen the look of pain cross his face. He leaned back against the edge of the desk.

Her gaze met his, and she looked…bothered. He didn't know a better word for it than that.

"Fjeld says that the experience she went through was worse than the one we went through." Cohn crossed her arms. "Since she was on one ship with a single *anacapa* drive, that argues against the amplification theory."

He noted her body language. She didn't want to tow the ships, but she wasn't willing to tell him yet. Apparently, she thought he could be convinced.

"Yeah," he said. "I thought of that. And I would just be guessing as to why she had that experience or what the difference was in that *anacapa* drive. For all we know, there's something in the *anacapas* themselves that resonates as we go through foldspace, and some *anacapa* drives have more of that something than others."

"But you don't think so." Cohn's body language hadn't changed.

"I don't know," he said. "I'm just guessing, Captain."

He adjusted his shoulders just a little and winced again. He had really stiffened up while working on all of this.

Then she uncrossed her arms, and pressed hands against her torso as if she was wiping off the palms. He had no idea what that meant on a body language scale. Maybe she was just as tired as he was, and aching because of the tension.

"If we tow the ships," she said, "what does that entail?"

He blinked in surprise. He thought all captains had to serve on a foldspace rescue vehicle for at least one year.

"I take it you've never done it," he said, trying not to let his incredulousness show.

Her eyes glinted, but he couldn't quite read the expression. So much for visuals helping.

"I served on a foldspace rescue vehicle for two years," she said, as if she had heard his thoughts. "We never towed anyone."

He almost asked if they failed to rescue any ships in that period of time, but he didn't. He wanted to focus on what they were doing. He only had a limited period of time to figure out what those vibrations were, and how to mitigate them...if she didn't take his suggestion.

So, rather than ask more questions, he just nodded.

"We've towed all kinds of vehicles in all states of disrepair," he said. "But healthy ships, ships that simply missed their foldspace window or whose captain no longer trusted their *anacapa* drive after it got them becalmed or some such, they disengage the *anacapa* drive and leave all other systems functioning."

"So weapons are online," she said.

"And all defensive systems," he said. "As well as our regular drives. It's the *anacapas* that get disabled."

And then he whistled softly to himself.

"What?" she asked, her gaze sharpening even more.

"I never checked the small *anacapa* drives," he said.

"The communications *anacapas?*" she asked.

They were little slivers of an *anacapa* drive, some smaller than his pinkie. He hadn't thought of them either, although he wasn't going to admit it.

He had meant the full-size *anacapa* drives all over these ships, from the extra drive that almost every ship carried now, to the drives—if any—in some of the smaller ships.

"Yeah," he said. "And the full-size drives. I need to know what each ship has in its ship bay, as well as the identifier for the extra drive that some of the ships are carrying."

"All right," Cohn said. "I'll make sure every ship gets that information to you immediately."

He nodded, his brain already several steps ahead of this conversation.

"Captain," he said, "that's an explanation for what happened to Captain Fjeld on that bad trip into foldspace."

"That there were other *anacapa* drives?" Cohn asked.

"There could have been several, all from the same source material."

She smiled at him. "Now we *are* speculating."

He smiled in return, and just doing that relaxed him a little.

"We are," he said, "but we have a working theory right now. Something that makes sense."

"Until it doesn't," she said, her smile fading a bit. She had worked with *anacapa* drives as long as he had.

"Until it doesn't," he said, and left it at that.

27

IN THE END, THE IDEA OF TOWING BECAME MOOT. It turned out that each ship, including Wihone's SC-class vessel and Jicha's ancient DV-class vessel, carried additional *anacapa* drives from the same source material.

Cohn thought that unusual. Wihone did not. He had said that ships built around the same time often had *anacapa* drives from the same source material. All he had initially looked at had been the parent ships, but when he looked at communication *anacapas*, the backup *anacapas*, and the *anacapa* drives in some of the smaller vehicles, he found nearly a dozen more drives.

Which left Cohn with a choice: she could shed the drives and the extra ships, pull three of the five communications *anacapas*, and leave them all in foldspace, maybe to pick them up on the return, or she could leave well enough alone, and cross her fingers, hoping that the vibrations leaving foldspace wouldn't be as bad as those coming into foldspace.

She spent a rough afternoon in her quarters, pacing and drinking coffee, arguing with herself. She didn't want to bring this to the other captains for some kind of vote, but she knew she had three options.

She could abort the entire mission, and that would fall on her. It would harm her career trajectory, but it wouldn't harm the others. It would also leave her feeling vaguely dissatisfied, as if she had fled from her duty, even if, possibly, it had been the right thing to do.

She could untether all of the ships as they left foldspace, and hope that they arrived at the same time, but that had all of problems she had outlined to Jicha before.

Her final choice, the one she discussed with no one, was that she pile some of the extra *anacapa* drives and all of the small ships onto Jicha's vessel, and have him wait in foldspace until she sent someone back to get him.

But that was no more fair than anything else she thought of, and it avoided the point of her mission.

She didn't believe, deep down, that she would encounter the thieves. And if she didn't, she needed Jicha's ship and his scholars to do the promised research while she investigated the Ready Vessels, to see if they were worth saving.

Then she needed to destroy that Scrapheap once and for all.

Given all of that, she really had only one choice, and it was the choice she was facing now.

The ships were tethered together in the same formation they used to enter foldspace. She had chosen that configuration after as much thought as she had used on the *anacapa* drives, ultimately coming to the same conclusion: this was what they had done before, and it had worked.

She didn't want to mess with success.

She stood in the middle of the bridge on the *Geesi*, watching the screens on the wall. She also had one small screen floating in front of her, downloading a lot of telemetry that she was currently ignoring.

To her right, her team had set up a three-dimensional holographic image of the Scrapheap, using the data that the Scrapheap had sent them. Three red dots showed the three facts that the Fleet knew about the thefts.

The first dot showed where the thieves had entered the Scrapheap. The second dot showed the spot inside the Scrapheap where the thieves had removed one of the DV-class vessels. And the third dot showed the area near the Scrapheap where the Scrapheap had fired on the thieves.

A blue dot, much farther away, marked the coordinates that Cohn had given all of the other ships. She had taken al-Aqel's advice to arrive far from the thieves' location, a piece of advice she had initially thought overcautious, but now which seemed like the most sensible thing she had heard.

She found it privately amusing that she no longer worried about the thieves. She was much more concerned with the vibrations.

She had spoken privately with her engineering staff about the condition of the *Geesi*. If the vibrations were exceptionally severe, she wanted to know what kind of damage the ship would sustain.

Her staff believed that the *Geesi* would come through the vibrations just fine, no matter how severe they were, but they were worried about Jicha's older ship, the *Tudósok*. She had offered to send some of her people to his vessel to make sure everything was ready for the exit from foldspace, but he had turned her down.

I do know how to captain my own ship, Cohn, he had said, and signed off.

She knew that he did, and that he had a good team on board, but she wanted an excess of caution from the captains, and all she seemed to get from him was pushback.

She wasn't going to worry about it. Nor was she going to worry about the tethering, not this time.

She had a series of events to get through, and she would do so: the exit from foldspace, establishing a somewhat hidden area for the ships to remain, and set up contact with the Scrapheap itself.

She wanted to know what had been happening while she had been traveling. She hoped that the Scrapheap would be able to give her that information.

She glanced at her team. Vinters stood near the Scrapheap hologram, hands clasped behind her back, her pale hair piled on top of her head. Iosua stood near the captain's chair, his short form almost hidden by the chair's back.

Cohn wanted Iosua there because she wanted him to have all of the pertinent information about the exit from foldspace. She also wanted him to have access to the highest level of controls.

Priede stood at his side, ready to make adjustments if the *Geesi* arrived in the wrong location—which was possible given the gaps in the information the ships had received.

Cohn had set their arrival point far enough away from the Scrapheap so that there would be no chance the ships would arrive *inside* of the Scrapheap—or so she believed, given the information she had.

Troyes had double-checked all of her theories and all of her math, as well as the coordinates she had chosen. While Wihone had spent the last forty-eight hours tracking down the source of the vibrations along with an assist from Iosua, Troyes had spent those same hours checking and rechecking the information that had come out of the Scrapheap initially.

"Are the other ships in position?" Cohn asked Carmen Gray. Cohn had installed Gray across from her, for just this reason. There was a lot of information Cohn could look up on her own, but she wasn't going to do that.

"Yes," Gray said. "And all of the crews have checked in. The tethers are secured, and everything onboard those vessels is secured."

That was the other order that Cohn had given: she didn't want anyone injured by flying debris should the vibrations become something even greater than they had been before.

Everything that could be attached was. And extraneous things were stored, the way that they got stored in zero-G.

Many of the crew members who didn't have a function during the transition out of foldspace were strapped in or had shut off the gravity in their locations on the various ships and were working in zero-G, just because it was easier for them.

She left that up to the various commanders in different sections of her ship, and she knew that al-Aqel had done the same on his. She had no idea what the other captains were doing, and she didn't care, so long as no one got hurt.

She just wanted to get through this journey out of foldspace with all five ships intact.

"All right, then," she said. "Let's leave foldspace."

Normally, she would have plugged in the coordinates herself. But she hadn't been on a foldspace journey this long as captain, and she didn't trust herself to handle the small details as well as Iosua.

"Executing," he said, unnecessarily, since she could see the transition on all of the screens before her.

And she could hear the whistle of the *anacapa* drive. The whistle seemed sharper than usual.

On the telemetry, it was just a series of numbers, but on the screens, the transition looked solidly black, with sparkles along the side. She had seen a dozen different "views" of the exit from foldspace and they all looked slightly different.

She wasn't sure she appreciated the darkness at the center of this one.

The vibrations started, small at first like the shaking of a finger, and then they grew so strong that her teeth began chattering.

Iosua had turned on the gravity in his boots so he would remain in the same position, but Priede hadn't, and he vibrated across the bridge until he caught himself on one of the navigational panels.

Vinters also didn't move, although her hair started to tumble out of its fasteners. Apparently she had the gravity on in her boots as well.

Cohn was going to leave the gravity in her boots off, but she changed her mind as she started to vibrate across the bridge, just like Priede had done. The shift from bouncing and sliding to being rooted in place made her lose her balance.

She swung her arms to keep herself upright, then grabbed a panel in front of her.

The vibrations seemed worse than they had going in, but she wasn't sure if her perspective was accurate or if she was simply more aware of what was going on.

Because she had her boots' gravity on now, her experience of the vibrations had changed from actual bouncing to an almost internal shivering. She could feel the shiver in her bones. Her heart pounded, hard, as if it was working extra hard.

The whistle had grown louder and so painful she could feel the sound behind her eyes. This time, she didn't put her hands over her ears because she didn't have a hand to spare.

She had felt this before, a long, long time ago, back in her engineering classes when they had moved to the *anacapa* sections of the class. Not the whistle. She had only experienced the sound on this ship.

But in class, she had wrapped her arms around a drive, just like she had been bidden, and her entire body shook and ached, deep inside.

But, unlike several of the other students, she had been able to hold on. She hadn't cried or screamed or had such an intense physical reaction that she had been sent to the *Santé*.

There had been both joy and pain in her ability to hang onto the *anacapa*. Joy that she could go forward, but almost a burning pain as the surface rubbed against her skin.

Very similar to what she was feeling now.

She inhaled sharply, felt a wobble in her lungs as she did so, and dug her fingers deeper into the console she was holding. She needed to concentrate on getting through this journey into foldspace, but she also wanted to hang on to her realization as well.

It felt like they were all inside that *anacapa* energy. Wihone had been right: the presence of the drives somehow amplified the reaction. Or spread the *anacapa* energy. Or did something that changed how the entire crew felt.

She glanced at her team. The bridge crew had all gone through the same testing she had, but some of the others on this vessel hadn't. She had no idea if their reaction to the increased *anacapa* energy was as devastating as the reactions had been in that long-ago class.

Then the *Geesi* stopped vibrating. The entire bridge crew stayed in the same position for a moment, as if no one believed that the vibrations were over.

The whistle had faded, but the pain remained, a dull ache throughout her face.

The Scrapheap appeared on the screens before her—or at least an edge of it, its force field glistening. It covered the entire area in front of the *Geesi*. It had been a random act that had gotten her ship to the Scrapheap, right-side up, and facing the Scrapheap itself.

Her heart still pounded so hard that she wondered if anyone else could hear it. Priede stood up straight, although he only let go of the console before him with his left hand. He kept the right one balanced on the surface.

Iosua didn't even seem to notice the Scrapheap. He was monitoring the telemetry and the other readings from the rest of the ships in their little convoy.

Vinters put a hand to her falling hair, then grabbed the fastener and undid it, letting the hair tumble around her face. That lasted for only a few seconds before she grabbed her hair in one hand and pulled it back, using the fastener to keep the hair in place again.

She did it all while staring at the images of the Scrapheap.

"That thing is big," Gray said.

Cohn glanced sideways at her. Gray didn't seem affected by the vibrations at all. She was standing in the same position she had been standing in when the *Geesi* had entered foldspace. Apparently, she had had the gravity in her boots on as well.

Cohn mentally saluted her. Gray was posing as unflappable, even though her right hand betrayed her. It was clutching the edge of her console, much like Priede's hand clutched his.

Cohn didn't respond to Gray's comment, nor did anyone else. They had all seen the information the Scrapheap had sent them. They had known how big it had been when it contacted them—or, at least, how big it had seemed.

But Gray was right: seeing the edges of the Scrapheap through the cameras was impressive, and startling, even though they had all expected it.

Cohn returned to her spot, her ankles and calves aching as she walked with the extra gravity on. She didn't shut it off, though. Not yet.

She needed to check two things.

First, she checked what was going on with the remaining ships in the Task Unit. Even though the *Geesi* wasn't vibrating and had come through foldspace unscathed, that didn't mean that the others had as well.

And she was right: the next three were coming through together, only half visible. But, unlike the last time, the vibrations in the *Geesi* had stopped, even though one ship was still inside foldspace, and the other three weren't entirely out.

She made a mental note of that. There wasn't much she could do about it at the moment, but she would report both things to Wihone and Iosua.

The next thing she checked was the Scrapheap itself. It wouldn't do to have the *Geesi* this close, and have the Scrapheap think that the *Geesi* (and the other ships) were about to attack.

She opened a small window on her holoscreen, searching for the automated contact information. She had called it up earlier so she would be prepared for this, and good thing.

The Scrapheap had been pinging the *Geesi*, asking for a response. But the pings had come through a channel the *Geesi* rarely used.

She answered the ping with all known forms of Standard, as well as a code that she hoped would work.

"Captain," Priede said, his voice sounding a little more on edge than usual, "we have pings—oh, wait."

"I saw it," she said, "and answered."

Priede shook his head. "The systems they're using, wow. They're old."

And out-of-date and barely accessible with the equipment that Cohn was used to using. But the Fleet never tossed out old systems. They built pathways and doorways and backends on most of their equipment to handle older information and older tech.

She had never understood the reasons why before.

She certainly understood it now.

She glanced at the ships. The three were through foldspace and into regular space, but, just as happened with the entry into foldspace, the *Tudósok* wasn't visible.

Yet. She had to remind herself that trip into foldspace had worked. The trip out of it would work as well.

She started to contact Wihone, then stopped. He would be taking care of the *Tudósok*. She would worry about what happened after it happened.

First, she had to make sure there were no problems with the Scrapheap.

She checked that odd channel and saw approvals, along with more codes, and a few questions. The questions concerned the type of ship she was commanding and the history of her command. She'd sent her command codes earlier, but clearly those hadn't resonated.

So, instead, she sent back a packet of information gathered from the Scrapheap itself, along with a message that informed the Scrapheap that they had come from Sector Base K-2. The Scrapheap should be able to compute how much time had passed and maybe, just maybe, figure out that they were using different equipment now.

Or maybe she was expecting too much from an ancient automated system.

"Well, that took forever." The voice came through the comm system, broadcasting to the entire bridge, maybe the entire ship.

She didn't need identification to know that the voice belonged to Captain Jicha.

"It did," she said, understanding his annoyance. "Is your ship all right?"

She almost asked if it was intact, but she could see that it was, glistening at the end of its tethers as if it had been newly cleaned.

"That was a hell of a ride," he said. "We're going to have to talk about re-entry. But we're here now."

She checked the channel he was using to see if he had contacted the other captains as well as her. He hadn't, so she added the others.

At the moment, she didn't mind that her bridge crew could hear everything being said.

"Everyone else all right?" she asked, without preamble, to the other captains.

"The vibration was worse," al-Aqel said. "But we were prepared for it this time. No damage."

"We didn't sustain any damage either," Fjeld said, "but we are checking on a deep level to make sure no systems were weakened in the journey."

"We read the vibrations as almost exactly the same," Wihone said. "I used a straight measure on it. The ship is fine."

"I used a measure too," Jicha said, "and we were two times worse than before. My people are going over everything now, but we need some solutions before the trip back."

"Noted," Cohn said. She would worry about the trip back when the time came. Right now, they were at the Scrapheap and ready to begin that part of the mission.

She glanced at her team. They were working as if this were a normal afternoon. Iosua hadn't moved. Everyone else was doing what she had asked before they had left foldspace—making certain that the ship had no extra damage from the journey.

The Scrapheap glinted before them, its forcefield formidable, even if it was old. She looked at the information the Scrapheap had sent to her. It was filled with codes and procedures and reminders about The Way Things Were Done.

She would sort through all of that later. Right now, she had to get the other captains ready for their encounters with the Scrapheap. Oddly enough, this would probably go best for Jicha, with his older vessel.

"I've already been in contact with the Scrapheap," she said. "It uses older codes and some tech I haven't seen in use, ever, in my career. I will send you the channel that it will contact you on, and the protocols I used."

"I'd like to untether before we deal with that thing." Jicha again. And he was right; they needed to untether as soon as possible.

"After we make sure everything is in good shape, we will untether," she said. She didn't want to hurt the ships by pulling tethers too fast. "I suggest that you interact with the Scrapheap sooner rather than later, since we know it fires on interlopers."

"Noted." There was sarcasm in Jicha's tone. Apparently, he had noticed how she deflected decision-making with that one word.

She wasn't going to let him irritate her, though. They were here, and they were intact, and they hadn't been attacked upon arrival.

All in all, a good start to this part of the mission.

"Let's do the housekeeping work," she said, "and then we will figure out what our next steps are."

She already had an idea what her next step would be. She would see if the Scrapheap could give her information about what had occurred since the first breach by the thieves.

But she didn't tell that to the other captains, not yet. She wanted to be the one to investigate that information. She wanted to know what exactly was happening.

She wanted to have as much information as she could, before she figured out what they would do next.

THE BONEYARD
NOW

28

IT HAS TAKEN NEARLY A WEEK to put all of my plans in place. A week in which I vacillated from believing strongly that I'm making the right decisions to wondering why I ever deviated from my initial plans.

Just this morning, an old SC-Class Fleet vessel that we removed from the Boneyard nearly two months ago returned to the Boneyard with only a skeleton crew. They're the delivery service. They brought more probes, both Fleet and non-Fleet, environmental suits, tablets and small weapons that can be used either by someone diving a wreck somewhere or by someone hanging outside a ship.

The SC-Class vessel, which has the designation *Veilig* and which Lost Souls has been calling *That Security Ship* because we haven't had an SC-Class vessel before, isn't completely refurbished. Ilona complained about that. But I'm not sure the *Veilig* will survive what we're going to do, so I'm somewhat pleased that it hasn't had been completely upgraded.

It's upgraded enough for a skeleton crew to use and, at my request, all of its weaponry and defensive features were either repaired or augmented. While this ship isn't ready for battle with all those warships behind the starfield-barrier, it can defend itself while we activate its *anacapa* drive to send us home.

We've already sent the *Madxaf* back to Lost Souls. We moved the ships from ship maintenance on the *Madxaf* to ship maintenance on the *Sove*, along with all of the probes. The *Veilig* brought four more small ships—again at my request—only these too are Fleet vessels, and they haven't been repaired or upgraded. They're usable, but just barely.

I haven't told Ilona that they're going to be destroyed, but I think she knows.

I have a sense that she disapproves from a distance of everything that I'm going to do, but that she isn't arguing with me because she knows arguing won't do any good.

I also have the sense that she's humoring me, as a way of keeping me out of her hair. As long as the *Sove* continues to dive vessels and find tech that will be of value to Lost Souls in the future, I have the sense that Ilona doesn't really care what I do.

Which is more than fair, since I really don't care what she does either.

I've spent the past week digging into the information both probes sent back. The second probe stopped sending telemetry and data about twenty-four hours after it crossed into the starfield-barrier.

Until that point, the second probe proceeded without attracting any attention at all, and if my suspicions are correct, it is probably still gathering data and trying to send that data to us.

The probe just got too far away from us, back to the area where the starfield-barrier is strong, and the secondary barrier, the one around the black area, seems to be intact as well.

For any kind of signal to reach us, that signal will have to be powerful, and while the probe can gather a lot of information, it doesn't have a lot of power.

What it did send us is both invaluable and chilling. For the hope I have in saying—both to my team and in my own mind—that going into the starfield-barrier is just a dive, I can't quite get past the rows and rows and rows and rows of warships, waiting quietly for something or someone to activate them. It's a bit unnerving.

I have no idea what kind of war the Fleet thinks—or thought—it will fight, but whatever it is, there's a lot of firepower behind that barrier.

We also combed through the information the first probe sent us. That information is just as valuable as the information the second probe sent, but is wildly different.

And the end of that information is different too. At one point, the second probe just stopped sending. The first probe seemed strangled by that comet trail stuff, and the information feed bears that out. It's broken up. It's just bits and pieces of information without much tying it all together.

We have a lot of information, from both probes, to comb through. We have a lot of questions, which thrills me and worries me at the same time—which, I remind myself, is perfectly normal for this kind of dive.

So I focus the research into sections.

I want to know how those smudges work. I want to know why the Boneyard hasn't attacked us or even seems to care that we're removing vessels from it. I want to know what happened to my two non-Fleet probes.

I figure we'll have all of that in due time.

But first, I'm concentrating on the next phase of my plan. I have designated my old crew, plus Denby, to help me figure out the starfield-barrier. When the time comes, we're going to dive it, maybe in the *Veilig* or maybe in a smaller ship. I haven't made that determination yet.

Mikk is feeling a bit out of sorts, since I changed the entire plan on him. We were going to hurry our way into the starfield-barrier, worried about that overarching intelligence, and then I put the brakes on everything, and we're going slow again.

But now that I'm thinking of this as a dive, there's just too much information to sift through, and too much uncertainty. If the starfield-barrier were an asset-rich wreck, I would proceed just as slowly as I am now, if not more slowly.

I would put together the proper team. I would make certain we have the right equipment. I would take away all of the unknowns that I can take away, before we ever commit one human life to that dive.

Which means I have to slow down.

But it also means I can handle setbacks better. If we run into something, like the Fleet probe getting reprogrammed and then destroyed, we analyze it and understand it before we ever send a person near that wreck again.

I'm patient when I'm planning a dive. Apparently, I lose that patience when I'm dealing with Fleet procedures.

Which sort of makes sense, considering the fact that I don't like living under Fleet regulations, and I've been doing it for months. We keep Fleet hours. We eat on their timetable. People have actual jobs. There's a posted schedule.

All of that works well as we're working toward something for Lost Souls, but this dive—this starfield-barrier—it's not for them. I can't even justify it as something for Lost Souls.

It's just for me, and whoever else is curious.

Which, thank goodness, is my usual team.

I bring them to the *Veilig* after the skeleton crew has left. The skeleton crew gave me, Mikk, and Orlando a tour of the systems, showing us what has been repaired and what hasn't. They also showed us the new weapons systems and the *Veilig's* defensive capabilities.

The one thing that hasn't been fixed—and the one thing that Ilona, among others, was most apologetic about—was the *Veilig's* capacity for speed. Its *anacapa* drive works well, and it can move long distances without using the drive, but the *Veilig* can't scurry away from anyone or anything. The engines don't have that capability, at least right now.

Ilona hasn't been to the Boneyard. She doesn't know how close ships are together. And she hasn't seen the warships inside the starfield-barrier, because I haven't told anyone outside of a trusted few about that discovery.

She is probably thinking that the *Veilig* is going to have to hurry away from some kind of threat, and that would be true in normal space, particularly normal space around here. A lot of pirate vessels check on the Boneyard regularly, as we learned back when we first discovered it.

But there's nowhere to hurry inside the Boneyard. Speed is actually a detriment here.

So we're doing fine with the additional weapons, the strong defenses, and a working *anacapa* drive.

I wouldn't call us safe, exactly, but we have everything we need.

Ilona sent us the *Veilig* fully stocked, as if the entire crew of the *Sove*, as well as everyone they've ever met, was going to spend the next year on the *Veilig*.

We're running the *Veilig* with a crew of eight, and we could probably survive on those provisions for the rest of our lives. But I'm happy to have them, because it's one less thing for us to think about as we prepare for this dive.

Even though I have to familiarize myself with this ship's systems, its layout is a standard one. Standard layouts help me—when I'm diving, and when I'm planning a dive. In a dive, I know where something should be. As I am getting to know the *Veilig*, I'm finding that most of the controls and the layout are as I expect as well.

The *Veilig* is one of those SC-class vessels that has a bridge shaped like a bowl. The captain's chair—which is a magnificent thing, solid and black and comfortable as a bed—is in the very bottom of that bowl. It's a design that Coop has told me he hates—apparently he served on a ship like this once—but I've got a fondness for it. That chair feels protected, and I like captain's chairs that I can sleep in. I don't like going down long corridors to my quarters when my team is in the middle of something.

I expect we'll be in the middle of something soon.

One of the neat features about the *Veilig*, though, is that its standalone table-like control panels are retractable. They fold into that angled floor. So the first thing I did after the skeleton crew left was recess more than half the standalone panels.

When they get recessed, their functionality moves to an upright panel, reconfiguring it. I leave us six panels, two in the back for weapons and defense, and two for research of all types, and two for navigation and command.

We'll also use holoscreens, but this will give us the best situation to work with.

I've also dropped the wall screens around two of the walls. They can show us in two or three dimensions what's going on outside the ship or whatever else I need to see in real time.

I leave the fourth wall, the one with the exit, alone. But the third wall is our map, rather like the Ball of Knowledge that we have on the *Sove*. I brought everything that was in the Ball of Knowledge to the *Veilig*, as well as all that we've been pulling out of the three probes—the information the Fleet probe sent us, which we keep isolated on its own panel, and the information from the other two non-Fleet probes.

We've combined the information from the non-Fleet probes into a map, showing the placement of the weapons or mines or whatever we want to call them. They're scattered all over that dark area, and they seem to be of varying sizes and capabilities.

We don't know what all of that is, at least not at the moment.

The Fleet probe zigged away from most of those, but it also zigged away from things that the non-Fleet probes read as empty space. So I've made one small map combining all three, and marking those zig spots, just in case they are something.

We're going to approach that empty area as if it's a true minefield, and not a floating weapons area. Although it's probably both, given how those smudges work.

I will be releasing more probes to see if the smudges have returned to the same position or if they are gone for good.

We've been trying to find out what, if anything, the comet trail/smudges attacked when we first noticed the comet trail, and we have some readings.

The comet trail/smudges might have attacked a probe or a small ship, and it might have appeared in that dark area from outside the Boneyard, suggesting that whatever it had been had had an *anacapa* drive that brought it into the area without us seeing it.

But we don't know for sure, and figuring that out isn't as important to me at the moment as getting every single mine or weapon mapped.

Our next mission is to send in two more probes, to double-check that response we got from the two non-Fleet probes.

Before we do that, though, I'm going to do something Mikk doesn't like. I'm going to send in a Fleet probe.

I'm replicating our entire experiment, right from the beginning.

The Fleet probe is already in place. I had the *Madxaf* drop the probe before it left. The probe was programmed before it got dropped. It's running on automatic, and will, in twelve hours, try to get inside the starfield-barrier.

It will send its information to the *Madxaf*, even though the *Madxaf* isn't here—just a little misdirection that Pao and I set up—and Mikk and I will piggyback on that signal to find out what's really going on.

All of us are on the bridge. Normal Fleet policy is that someone man the bridge at all times, and that's a good and smart policy, but it also means that with a crew this small, someone will miss important parts of the mission.

Because we're in the Boneyard and—at the moment—not suffering any attacks or dealing with anything overtly hostile, I feel we can all keep the same hours and be in the same place at the same time.

I have the captain's chair, the only comfort I want. It's upright and set on extra hard, because I don't want to relax, even subtly. I'm not using one of the control panels. I'm using a holoscreen designed specifically for the captain. The screen curves around me, like a shield, but I have it programmed as clear.

The net effect is that I can see all the telemetry and any other information I request as if it's floating across the front of the bridge. That effect used to make me uneasy, but I've gotten used to it—maybe even prefer it.

Mikk is to my right, bent over the controls, a stool that he had programmed to rise out of the floor pushing against his thighs. He's not sitting, even though he apparently had planned to.

He's a lot more nervous than I would have expected.

Tamaz and Roderick have taken over the research panels, which has left Fahd at loose ends. He hovers near Tamaz's shoulder, looking like the man I met a long time ago, quiet and timid. Fahd isn't really timid anymore, not with this group, but he puts it on like a shield.

Like Fahd, Nyssa isn't really on a panel either. She stands near the exit, arms crossed, watching all of this. She's one of my best divers, but she'll probably remain on the *Veilig* even if we dive, because her medical skills outweigh her diving skills.

Orlando has taken the other navigation panel. He hasn't said much about this mission, but he seems excited by it, maybe because we're diving again. He both lost and gained confidence after he saved my life. He lost confidence in me, and in some of the diving that we do, but his belief in himself has grown tremendously.

Denby stands far behind me and up near the top of the bowl. He has taken over one of the weapons and defense panels, and I find that to be a big relief as well. Because he's the only one of us deeply familiar with Fleet weaponry and defenses. He knows what ships should be able to do and what they actually can do.

He has spent every waking moment on the *Veilig* familiarizing himself with its defensive capabilities, and now he's slowly working his way through the weapons systems. Once he has learned all of it, he will train the rest of us—some more than others.

It feels odd to set up a dive and think about defenses and weaponry. In my past, I would occasionally encounter an outside ship, sometimes a ship that wanted to defend a wreck, and I would abandon the idea of diving that wreck.

So this aspect of the dive is distinctly different than anything I have done before.

I move away from the captain's chair, take a step deeper into the well of the bridge, and look at my crew. I actually smile at them, which makes Orlando's eyebrows go up. Apparently, I never do that at this stage of a dive.

Fahd steps into the center aisle so that he can see me better. Nyssa uncrosses her arms and straightens her back. Denby raises his chin. The other three watch me warily, just like Orlando is.

"Before we send out the first probe," I say, "I want to remind you all that you can leave at any point in this long mission. I will understand."

I won't understand, not entirely, but I will forgive them. Or maybe I won't do that either.

Mikk grins and shakes his head, but his eyes aren't smiling. "Boss, you know that none of us will do that. If we were going to leave, we would have done so already."

I don't know that and neither does he. A long time ago, Squishy left me in the middle of a dive and then reported what we were doing to the Enterran Empire. Up until that point, I would never have thought that Squishy would ever leave me in the middle of a dive.

My smile fades, but I nod curtly at him, unwilling to say anything negative right now.

"We're going to send two probes," I say, "so that we replicate what happened before, right down to the timeline. Is everything ready?"

The question is pro forma. I know everything is ready. I set it up myself. Mostly, I want to know if the team is ready to receive information from that probe in real time.

Everyone nods or acknowledges me with a grunt or a short "yeah."

"You ready to piggyback on that signal?" I ask Mikk.

"More than ready," he says, and I can't quite tell if that's a dig against me or if he just wants this dive underway.

"Then activate the Fleet probe," I say.

"Okay, Boss," he says, and the images wink out of the wall screens. Now there are two different visuals. The first is of the area before us—the blackness as well as the starfield-barrier. The second is of the little region of the Boneyard where the *Madxaf* dropped some of its probes.

A little blue label appears just to the right of the drop zone.

Probes often have designations within the Fleet itself, and we do have this probe's designation encoded into our systems. But for our purposes, we have labeled this probe FP2, Fleet Probe #2. We've relabeled the information on the first Fleet probe as FP1.

That blue label is part of the Fleet's designation, but our systems have tacked a black FP2 over the blue, for ease of identification.

We can all watch the probe make its journey on the big screen before us, but I choose not to. This will take a little time, so I sink into the captain's chair, call up a small screen and zoom in on FP2.

I'm getting visuals from two of the other probes—a neat feature of higher-level Fleet tech. Those probes aren't officially activated, yet they're recording the area around them, in preparation for their eventual service.

The visuals focus on FP2, which is a tubby little probe, slightly different from the first probe we sent. This probe is rounder, squatter, and slightly smaller. Its internal mechanisms are exactly the same as those of FP1, which is what I care about.

FP2 blinks on, golden lights circling its center like running lights on an orbiter. The top of the probe blinks white, and the bottom blinks a darker gold, so that we can get a sense of the probe's orientation as it travels away from the pile of probes. Right now, the top of the probe faces us, and the bottom faces the side of a ruined runabout.

FP2 rights itself—the top in the direction that all the ships inside the Boneyard use as up—and with a jaunty twist, almost like the tipping of a hat, it maneuvers its way out of the pile of probes.

We lose the exterior imagery almost immediately, which Mikk replaces on the big screen with what FP2 is sending back to us. He runs the telemetry on the left and the visuals on the right.

I'll look at the telemetry later. I make a different change on my own screen. I move to the tracking screen, so that I can see where, exactly, FP2 is in relation to the rest of the Boneyard.

The *Madxaf* dropped FP2 nowhere near the origin point of FP1. We had a lot of discussions about whether this was a good or a bad idea. I was the one who finally determined that FP2 needed a different origin point.

Yes, we are trying to replicate an experiment, but the part we are trying to replicate happened after the probe got inside the black space before the starfield-barrier, not on its journey in.

I'm still just a bit paranoid about that overarching intelligence that might or might not be part of the Boneyard, and I believe it's better that we have a different point of origin for the probe.

One of the many things we did program into FP2 is its entry point into the black area ahead of the starfield-barrier. We have FP2 enter in the exact same area as FP1 did.

It doesn't take FP2 long to get to that point. It charges forward, glowing blue on my screen, but red on the one that Mikk has open in front of him.

Most of the wall screens are taken up with the visuals from FP2, which are showing bits and pieces of ships. The moment it crosses inside that black area, though, it shows the starfield that we have seen a hundred times.

The unmoving, unchanging starfield, even though FP2 heads directly toward it.

So FP2's sensors are as screwed up as the other Fleet sensors are. FP2 "perceives" that area as a starfield and nothing else, at least in the information it's sending back to us.

I am standing in front of the screens, hands clasped in front of me, almost as if I'm praying. The moment I notice that I'm doing that, I let my hands fall to my sides. I don't want to seem more tense than I already am.

But, as FP2 heads into the blackness, my hands creep upwards again. I stop them, only to find that moments later, I've clenched my fists. Finally, I thread my fingers together, clasping my hands in front of me like a kid trying not to touch something on a table.

FP2 zigs, just like FP1 did. FP2 goes around what seems to be nothing on its sensors, no readings, no nothing, almost as if there's a programmed path into the blackness.

Which was something we never investigated—whether or not the path that FP1 took was a familiar one, one that was programmed into the systems like that fake sensor reading was.

I look at Mikk, about to say something, and then change my mind. He's staring raptly at his own screen which, from my angle, seems to show only telemetry. He's frowning. I'm familiar with that frown. It's one he uses when he's trying to figure out a puzzle, not when he's dissatisfied with something.

FP2 follows the same path that FP1 did, including all of the same zigs and zags that FP1 made. As FP2 approaches the opening in the actual starfield-barrier, I thought I caught a glimpse of that white cloudy stuff we had seen earlier. The thing that enveloped the non-Fleet probe.

But the image vanishes almost as quickly as it appeared—if it was there at all. I grimace at it, make a mental note, then decide that there's too much noise inside my head.

I make an actual note on one of my screens—for that and for extra research, to see if the Fleet probes are following a programmed trajectory.

Orlando glances at me, as if he's trying to figure out what I'm doing. I give him a smile that might actually look like a grimace. He tilts his head a little, a small movement that he occasionally uses to reassure someone around him, and then he focuses on FP2.

As it crosses the barrier into that glistening starfield, my breath catches. That sense I had earlier—that these probes are actual creatures—fills me one more time. I know I'm sending this little mechanical servant to some hideous fate, and I'm uncomfortable with that. Both with the fate and my own anthropomorphizing of the probes.

But I can't seem to stop it. Probes have helped me on all of my dives. I've relied on probes, and I've lost most of them. But I've never sent them directly into something that could—and probably would—destroy them.

"Dammit!" Mikk says beside me. His curse is loud enough to echo in the near-silence of the bridge.

I almost ask what he sees, but stop myself. The screen in front of me has gone dark. FP2 has stopped sending information.

I glance at the wall screen. The telemetry stopped mid-line. It's too far away for me to scan with any kind of understanding, but it's clear that the information being sent back was interrupted.

"I'm flagging that spot," Tamaz says, but no one responds.

We'll all remember where that spot is. What we should see is what changed, if anything, what we can do, or what's different.

And we're not seeing anything.

"We've completely lost contact," Roderick says. "I've been pinging it."

"Pinging it does no good," Mikk says. "It didn't do any good the first time either."

His fingers are moving across the screen in front of him. He's entering commands, commands that I'm not seeing.

If he's not pinging FP2, then I have no idea what he's doing.

Then, for a brief second, more telemetry appears. It's only a little bit, not enough to fill one side of the screen, and then it stops again.

"What are you doing, Mikk?" Roderick asks. "I can help."

But Mikk doesn't answer. He's biting his lower lip, his brow furrowed. I want to help as well, and as I lean over to see if I can tell what he's doing, Orlando curses.

The curse is long and creative, something Orlando only says when he's not paying attention to what comes out of his mouth. He's staring at the overall map, and I look at it too.

FP2—the tubby little probe—is hurtling out of the starfield-barrier. My stomach clenches. Part of me had hoped that this time the result would be different.

"Can you get us a clearer visual?" I ask Orlando. I ask him, and not Mikk, because Orlando was the one who noticed—or it seemed like Orlando was the one who noticed.

"With what?" he asks. "There's nothing in that emptiness."

"I'll see what I can do." That's Tamaz. "We have some ships nearby, things we've dived. I'll see if we can activate them."

And as he says that, the paranoia I've been fighting on this mission rises. "No," I say. "That's not a good idea."

"You want information or not?" This time, it's Mikk, and his words are curt. "If you do, then get the damn information however you can. I thought that's what this entire dive is about."

I know he's using the word "dive" on purpose. He's using it to get my attention, to remind me how we used to do things, how we *should* do things when it's just us, and not anything to do with the Fleet.

I let out a small breath. "Mikk's right. See if we can track that probe as it makes its way past us."

"Shouldn't we collect it?" Roderick asks. "If we can figure out what they did?"

"That's a hearty no, and it's from me," Mikk says. "The last one exploded."

"Because it was sent *out* of the Boneyard, and then the Boneyard shot it," Roderick says. "If—"

"No," Mikk says. "We're in a Fleet vessel."

His words hang. We are in a Fleet vessel, and while that would argue for Fleet tech not attacking us, it also argues against that whole theory. Because Fleet tech is attacking Fleet tech for a reason we don't understand. I have a plan to see if the tech behind that starfield-barrier will treat a Fleet ship the same way it treated the probe, but I don't want to vary from that plan.

I don't want to get us killed.

"Let the probe go," I say. "Let's see if the same thing happens to it as the first probe."

"Track it, then?" Orlando asks.

"As best we can," I say. "And scan at the same time. See if we can get any readings off it."

"What about the *Madxaf*?" Roderick asks. "Shouldn't we contact it, and see what it's getting?"

"Not yet," I say. That's the caution again. But this time, the caution seems appropriate—even for the old me. "Let's wait to see how this plays out, and then figure out if they got different information than we did."

"The data stream to them was interrupted," Tamaz says. "I can guarantee that."

"We don't know that for certain," Mikk says. "I programmed the probe so that if something clogged the data flow, the data would travel through a different channel."

"Can you find that channel?" I ask.

"I'm not going to look right now," he says. And I have a hunch that's his surfeit of caution speaking. I'm not going to argue, though.

Instead, I watch FP2 as it zooms out of the black area and heads into the main part of the Boneyard. I open another screen which shows the route of FP1 as it headed out of the Boneyard. I then overlay that route with the route FP2 is taking.

It's exactly the same.

"We have some time now," Mikk says, and leans back. I know what he means. He means that it'll take a while for FP2 to get to the edge of the Boneyard.

My gaze meets his. He seems tired, or maybe that's just discouragement. It bothers him that he can't figure out exactly what's happening with the probes.

I want to remind him that one of the reasons we're doing this is to find out what's happening with the probes. We need to know what's happening inside that starfield-barrier so that we can protect against it when we go inside.

But I'm not going to say that. In theory, he knows it. In practice, it's discouraging to watch a second probe get destroyed in the exact same way the first one did.

Orlando has shifted positions. He's now standing slightly closer to me.

"Don't you think it odd," he says in a tone just a bit softer than the one he has been using, "that the Fleet would set up something that would destroy equipment?"

I look at him.

He raises his eyebrows, then sweeps his hand toward the wall screens.

"I mean," he says, "look around. We're inside a gigantic ship graveyard, filled with parts that will never get used. They're abandoned."

"We don't know that," Mikk says. "We don't know if they get used."

We don't, in theory. But in practice, it seems to me that there's so much here and the Fleet is so far away—if it even exists at all anymore—that these ships around us are just so much waste.

"My point," Orlando says with just a bit of emphasis, leaning toward Mikk as he does so, "is that the destruction of these probes is not the standard procedure for the Fleet."

Except we don't know that either. I turn toward Denby. He's focused on the console before him, frowning, and seemingly not part of the conversation at all.

"Gustav," I say, "is that true? Does the Fleet ever destroy its own equipment?"

He lifts his head, as if coming out of a long sleep. He blinks once, then his frown deepens.

"Sure," he says. "Yeah. When the equipment is dangerous."

"Meaning what?" Orlando asks.

"Meaning," Denby says, "that the equipment will somehow harm a ship or the Fleet itself."

"But what if it can be fixed?" Orlando asks.

"Depends on where the danger occurs," Denby says. "In the field, a lot of times, we jettison and destroy things."

Then his gaze meets mine.

"I thought you knew that," he says.

I shake my head. It's logical, of course. The Fleet's actions are often logical.

"Does this count as 'in the field'?" I ask.

"'This'?" he repeats.

"The Boneyard," I ask.

He looks at the screens that surround us all. FP2 is already past our little part of the Boneyard and heading at top speed toward the same section of the Boneyard that FP1 left from.

"As far as I can tell," he says, "we're not near the actual Fleet."

I nod once.

"So," he says, "if those warships are still active, then, yeah, I guess this counts as in the field."

The entire team looks at me, all at the same time. A shiver runs down my back, strong enough that they can probably see it.

If what Denby says is correct, then we're not diving an old, abandoned space graveyard filled with new ships. We're diving an active storage facility for military vessels.

Which makes what has been happening to the Fleet probes a warning to back off.

I square my shoulders. I'm not ready to back off. I don't know for certain that this is a warning or that the Fleet considers those probes dangerous. I don't yet know what's going on, and, as I've always reminded my teams, making assumptions is sometimes as deadly as going into a bad situation without scoping it out first.

"Good to know," I say to Denby, and return my attention to the screens around me. I don't want the team to say anything more. Not at the moment. I want them to get back to work.

We can abort this mission at any point. We can and we should. That's one of my own rules as well.

I'll keep it in mind as we progress with my plan. I will make the right decision—and I can only hope that, should there be severe danger, I will make that decision quickly enough.

29

It's discouraging to watch FP2 travel through the Boneyard. The little probe moves as fast as FP1 did, heading to the exact same exit point. We are able to activate three ships other than the *Sove* and our own to track FP2, but none are close enough to see much more than the tiny exterior, traveling by at a speed no probe should ever use—especially in a place as populated as the Boneyard.

This time, I watch as much as I can. Finally, when we do get a somewhat closeup view of FP2 from one of the nearby ships, my discouragement grows.

FP2 had been a jaunty little thing, tubby and burbling, its lights spinning rapidly around its middle almost like a cheerful *let's go!* signal. But those lights are off now. Only the big golden light remains on. That light blinks slowly, which it hadn't done before. It's almost as if that light has become a target—and maybe it has.

By the time FP2 leaves the Boneyard, I'm sitting in the captain's chair. I'm not finding it comfortable. I'm sitting on its edge, the puffy part of the seat pressing into the backs of my knees, and I'm leaning forward just a bit.

I want the outcome to be different this time. I want little FP2 to keep heading away from the Boneyard to territory unknown.

But the same thing happens.

Our exterior beacons catch FP2 as it exits the Boneyard. The beacons swivel at the exact same place as they had before, tracking the movements of FP2 as closely as they tracked FP1.

This time, though, I'm not watching FP2's imagery from the beacons. This time, I've set up the telemetry from the beacons, and I'm watching the energy levels outside the Boneyard. This time, I see the slow energy spike as the weapons on the exterior of the Boneyard power up.

When the black lines appear, I'm not surprised. The weapons readings at the exterior of the Boneyard reach their peak energy readings—the same ones we found when we reviewed the information we had gotten from the destruction of FP1.

The black lines extend outward, almost like tentacles, and envelop FP2. I want it to fight, even though I know it can't. I want it to explode and destroy those black lines, even though I know it's not programmed for that.

Technically, I didn't want it to be programmed for that. I would have told Mikk to reprogram it that way if I had wanted that change. But I wanted to see if the situation replicated and it did.

The black lines completely cover FP2. It stops moving, just like FP1 did. FP2's little blinking light goes out first. Then it expands, as if it's a balloon being filled with water.

Just like FP1, FP2 turns completely black, then blue, and then orange. It continues to expand until, like a balloon being overfilled, it explodes.

The black lines do not disappear with the explosion. They catch all the little pieces, just like they had before. Only this time, I'm watching the telemetry, and this time, I receive an answer I didn't get earlier.

There are tiny energy spikes within those black lines. They're not containing the explosion and collecting the pieces, returning them to the Boneyard. The black lines are collecting the pieces and then exploding them, little bit by little bit.

I have no idea how small the pieces have to be before the black lines stop attempting to destroy them. I'm not exactly sure how the process works.

The first time I saw them, with FP1, I had thought the lines disappeared, but they don't. They recede, and that only takes about five minutes.

Five minutes to remove any trace of FP2, any idea that it existed at all.

The little probe, and all of its very valuable information, are gone.

Dangerous.

The Fleet destroys dangerous equipment in the field. And then wipes out any trace of that equipment, because the equipment itself might be infected with something.

I stand up, wipe my hands on my pants, and look at the various screens. Some still show the starfield-barrier. Others show the blackness between the barrier and the part of the Boneyard we're in. A few show the edge of the Boneyard where FP2 exited, and the screens around me show the area outside of the Boneyard where FP2 exploded.

All seems normal now. Nothing different, nothing unusual. There's no way to know that a tiny probe was just completely destroyed.

"Anything different in the starfield-barrier?" I ask Tamaz. I had given him the assignment to monitor all the energy levels around the starfield-barrier as best he could, to see if he could see anything that we might have missed the first time.

Part of me hoped that we would see that other weapon, the cloudy white one that attacked the non-Fleet probe.

"No," Tamaz says. "I'm not seeing anything at all."

"That's a little creepy, don't you think?" Nyssa asks. "I mean, something just got destroyed, and you can't even tell."

"It's designed that way," Denby says. "You send a probe somewhere, and then show up, can't tell what happened to it. That protects not just the area the probe went to, but the destruction."

"It doesn't protect it at all." Mikk turns, half angrily. I put out a hand, low so only he can see it, to remind him to remain calm. He gives me a vicious glance.

He clearly hates the destruction of the second probe as much as he hated the destruction of the first one.

"If you go by the information feed," Mikk says, "you'd go to the starfield-barrier to recover your probe. You'd want to see why it stopped sending information."

"And then you'd get destroyed," I say quietly.

Mikk looks at me.

"Think of what Gustav told us," I say. "The Fleet destroys dangerous equipment. If the probe came from a Fleet vessel, and the Fleet vessel showed up to see what was going on with that probe..."

"No," Denby says. "I refuse to believe that the Fleet would destroy one of its own ships, filled with its own people."

I look at him, and so does the rest of the team. The bridge is quiet, except for the hum of equipment.

Denby ostentatiously shrugs. "That's not the Fleet I know. It can't be."

I consider arguing with him. I consider pointing out all the risks the Fleet does take with its personnel. I consider how often the Fleet has left stranded people in foldspace behind. There's even a possibility that the *Ivoire* was abandoned by the Fleet. We have no idea if the Fleet conducted a search for them.

But I don't say anything. I want this team to work well together. I need them to. Because firing off FP2 is just the beginning of this dive.

Time to change the subject.

"Gustav," I say, "do you think it's possible that the Fleet has maps of each Boneyard in the files?"

"I've never seen anything like that," he says.

"Classified maps," I say. "Maps you can see with the right security clearance."

He shakes his head, but instead of answering directly, he says, "Why?"

"Because both probes followed the same path out of the Boneyard," I say. "And they were both going too fast to avoid anything in their path, should there be something surprising in their way. So they were following directions."

"The map is probably inside the starfield-barrier," Mikk says. "It was probably downloaded when the programming changed."

"Probably," I say. I don't want to contradict him because he's angry enough already. "But there's also a possibility that whatever happened to those probes wasn't a rewrite of their systems, but an activation of something stored inside of them."

"I'd've seen it," Mikk says.

"Maybe not," Denby says slowly. He knows how mad Mikk is too, and doesn't want to cross him. Or maybe that's just Fleet behavior. Maybe Denby sees Mikk as a superior officer.

I do know that not settling rank in a mission that I lead bothers anyone with Fleet training, no matter how much they try to hide it.

"That kind of program," Denby is saying, "would be small. It wouldn't take much information at all. It's actually a defensive system."

He has all of our attention now. I turn so that I can see him better. His eyes are brighter than they were before, as if this idea gave him a lot of hope.

"That doesn't make sense," Mikk says. Or rather, growls. He's still too riled up for my tastes. "No defensive system would work like that."

"Actually, it makes sense to me," I say, because it does. But I don't want to explain what I think when Denby actually knows how these things work. "But I'd rather hear your thoughts, Gustav."

"They're not thoughts," he says. Now he's sounding a little cranky. "It's an old defensive technique, a way of saving small ships if the crew is gone or if they're on land or they're incapacitated when there's a big attack. You send out a pulse—the Fleet or a DV vessel or an admiral or someone with the appropriate rank—sends this pulse, and the pulse overrides whatever else the probe or small ship was doing. The purpose is to get the probe or the ship out of the area quickly."

"Which is why the probe went so fast," Nyssa breathes.

"Maybe," Roderick says, looking at Mikk.

Mikk, who is getting even more tense than he was a moment ago. "You're telling me that none of that information was lost? That if we had intercepted the second Fleet probe, we would have learned more things?"

"I'm not telling you that for certain," Denby says. "I am saying that saving information, and maybe incapacitated lives, is the point of that little program."

I think about that for a moment, wondering if I need to change our plans. I could send in one more Fleet probe.

Everyone is looking at me, as if expecting me to say something. Everyone except Mikk, who is glaring at Denby as if Denby were the one who put that program inside the probes.

I need to calm Mikk just a little and get him to focus.

"Okay," I say, "so that's a defensive system the Fleet uses, which is kinda brilliant."

Mikk grimaces. Orlando looks at me and raises his eyebrows, as if saying, *Do you really want to irritate Mikk more?*

"But that program's existence still doesn't explain how both probes knew where to go," I say. "I wouldn't be worrying about this if they followed different paths, but they didn't. They traveled along the same path."

"Maybe they hit something at an angle," Nyssa says. "Maybe it's the way they went into the starfield-barrier that influenced how they came out. You know, from the force of the blast or whatever reprogrammed them."

Denby looks at her, apparently about to correct her, when she adds, "Or activated the program or whatever."

He smiles, just a little, which I don't think she sees.

"That wouldn't work," Mikk says. "They were built differently, so they would have wobbled their way to a different trajectory. And I can't believe that they would miss all the ships and weapons and everything without some kind of map."

He sounds calmer now. I got him to think about something else. One of the best ways to deal with Mikk is to give him a puzzle and let him focus his mind on it.

"If there is a packet," he says, enunciating each word as if it offends him, "then maybe there's some other little packet of directions that gets activated as well."

"Sounds complicated," Tamaz says. "If something like this is automatic, wouldn't whatever got activated be simple?"

Mikk nods. So does Roderick.

Denby nods as well.

"There's no way that the Fleet would know where a ship is going to end up when it gets in trouble," he says. "So maps don't make sense. What makes sense is that the activation sets all sensors on alert. The probe will probably 'see' everything, for lack of a better word."

Now I'm nodding. That does make sense.

He continues, "The probe then heads out on the shortest possible route, the one that keeps it away from any danger that would hit it *inside* the Boneyard. I'll wager, if they hadn't gotten hit by those weapons, the probes would still be heading away from this Boneyard at top speed."

I frown, and wonder if he's right. My memory tells me that he is. Neither probe slowed down once they got outside of the Boneyard.

"Well, that makes sense," Tamaz says, and we all look at him. He seems surprised.

"Sorry," he says when he realizes we're all looking at him. "Just musing."

"What makes sense?" Mikk's voice isn't as taut as it was earlier.

"Why the non-Fleet probes didn't get attacked," Tamaz says.

"They would've gotten attacked," Mikk says. "They just didn't have any packet to activate."

He still sounds angry. Just not as angry as he was.

"Which means that the starfield-barrier is only there to stop Fleet ships from getting in," Nyssa says.

"Yeah." I have already had versions of that thought. They're niggling at me, worrying me. The Fleet against itself.

Years ago, when we all trooped to what had been Starbase W, and we saw its destruction, Coop had said that a war would have caused that. And when he first saw the Boneyard, he was worried that these were the remains of Fleet ships, destroyed after a fight with other Fleet ships.

I only asked him about those reactions a few times. Mostly, he declined to say anything, but once, he said that he believed only Fleet ships could so thoroughly destroy Fleet property like that.

I figured it was arrogance, but maybe he knew something he wasn't telling me. Maybe he had an idea of history or of something brewing inside the Fleet, some kind of rift he wasn't telling me about.

"What do you think, Boss?" Orlando asks.

I blink at him. If he has been talking to me, I haven't heard it.

"About what?" I ask.

"Sending another Fleet probe in, like Mikk just suggested," Orlando says.

I'm not going to look at Mikk, because to do so would mean that I haven't been paying attention, which, apparently, I haven't.

"No," I say, before I even have a chance to consider.

"No?" Mikk asks. "Just…no?"

I nod, feeling my cheeks heat. I should have marshalled an argument. I really don't have one.

"That thought crossed my mind too," I say, "but I think we should stick to the plan."

"Still afraid of that intelligence here in the Boneyard, the one we might have made up?" Mikk lets sarcasm into his voice.

Denby stiffens. Most people don't talk to each other like that on Fleet missions.

"Yeah," I say. Then I shake my head. "No." And correct myself one final time. "Maybe."

Once again, I have the full team's attention. I smile at myself as much as at them.

"What I mean is this," I say. "If there is an intelligence like that, we might have tipped it off with the second probe. But if we didn't, the third would definitely tip it off."

"And if there isn't an intelligence like that," Mikk says, cutting off the edges of his words in his barely contained annoyance, "then we're denying ourselves a wealth of information. I say we send in another Fleet probe, capture it on the way out, and extract the information from it."

"How can we trust that information?" Orlando asks quietly.

Mikk's gaze flattens. "What do you mean?"

"The sensors are compromised," Orlando says. "The readings we've been getting from Fleet equipment are false. That's why we've brought non-Fleet equipment here. So, yeah, we might get more information, but it might be all wrong."

Mikk looks at me, exasperation all over his face. He expects me to agree with him, and I might have, if I hadn't just seen another probe destroyed. But I agree with Orlando: I don't think we can get accurate information from any Fleet equipment.

"We're sticking to the plan," I say, "but with one modification."

Mikk closes his eyes and looks away, without waiting for the modification at all.

So I don't direct my next sentence at him. I look at the majority of the team to my right and just behind me. My gaze meets Denby's.

"Gustav, do you know of any way that you can access that packet inside one of the probes, now that you know what you're looking for?"

"He doesn't have clearance, Boss." Mikk, turning now. He seems even more exasperated.

"I don't," Denby says sadly. "I can't just poke around..."

His voice fades as he gets an idea. He wears all of his emotions on his face, which I find fascinating. I wonder if we had just gotten him early and years of service in the Fleet would have trained that out of him, or if that's who he'll always be.

"Gustav?" Nyssa asks.

He looks at her as if he has just realized she's there. He shakes himself. "Sorry," he says. "I got an idea."

Clearly. But I don't say that.

"I think we might be able to find the packet a different way," he says.

Mikk takes a step toward him, as if movement will shake the ideas out of Denby. "And what is it?" Mikk asks, letting all of his annoyance into that sentence.

"They have to be placed into the probe's systems, right?" Denby asks. "And they have to be repaired or replaced if they're not there."

"Maintenance mode," Tamaz says.

"Maintenance mode," Denby repeats and then he smiles. "Or, more accurately, repair mode."

The Fleet term, of course. But it's better to use Fleet terms on Fleet equipment.

Mikk looks at me. His expression is calmer, and his eyes are less stormy than they were.

"And if we find it, we remove it?" he asks.

"Yes," I say.

"So we send in another Fleet probe," he says.

"Not yet," I say.

"Because we haven't solved the false information problem," Tamaz says, thinking he's being helpful.

"Well, no," I say. "If we remove the packet from the probe's systems, and then we send the probe in, and it doesn't get returned to us, we were successful. Which means we can search for packets like that inside all of our Fleet equipment."

"Protecting us when we dive," Roderick says.

I smile at him. I like that he used the word "dive."

"Exactly," I say. "That's exactly what we're going to do."

30

WHAT THE TEAM INITIALLY MISSED was that we were still going to follow the plan. I had to do quite a bit more talking and some convincing to get them to prepare for the non-Fleet probe.

I want this dive to remain on time—my timetable. I can't lose the sense that we have a limited amount of time to make this dive, before we get caught.

I give us a short break, because we need one. Mikk's anger showed me that.

Most of the team doesn't want a break, though. Mikk uses it to calm down. I use mine to review the footage of the Fleet probes, and find that I agree with Denby—they were heading nonstop away from the Boneyard when it attacked.

Denby hasn't taken any time away at all. He corralled Tamaz, and together they've been examining Fleet probes. I asked both men if they wanted me to get Diaz working on the same problem, back on the *Sove*, and they said no. They'd bring her on if they felt they needed her.

But, like me, they want to keep this mission as quiet as possible.

It does feel like we're operating outside of Fleet rules. Even though we're on a bigger ship and we're working on a completely different project from any I've done before, I feel as if we're reaching into my past—what I considered to be my lost past.

I'm happy with the risks, happy with the danger, happy to feel *alive* again. I hadn't realized just how stifled I felt at Lost Souls, and working under Fleet structure.

What we do next is activate another non-Fleet probe. In the spirit of Fleet nomenclature, I dub the probe NFP2, and hope it has as much good luck as the previous probe did.

We pluck this probe out of the pile of probes Mikk and I dropped days earlier. The probes haven't moved too far from the area where we dropped them.

We activate this one and send it directly to the opening in the blackness, with an eye toward the same spot in the starfield-barrier.

The non-Fleet probe—NFP2—heads directly there, taking the same route as its predecessor, sending us similar information.

The entire team is on the bridge, just like we were the last time, although this time Denby grumbles that he was better served in ship maintenance, trying to find the packet in the Fleet probes.

I'm pleased that he's grumbling—it means he's comfortable enough to operate outside of Fleet rules. Mikk, on the other hand, isn't pleased about the grumbling at all. His frown gets deeper with each word that Denby utters.

Finally, Mikk snaps, "If there's a weaponry issue, we need you to see it in real time."

I'm about to say something to Mikk about teamwork, but as I open my mouth, Denby nods.

"Sorry," he says. "I have just gotten a little too focused on my work."

As have we all. I smile a little. I'm glad Denby's on the team now. An aspect of everyone here is that they're a bit overzealous. That makes them good divers and even better team members.

NFP2 heads into that black area between the regular part of the Boneyard and the starfield-barrier. And, as the other non-Fleet probes did, it's sending us all kinds of information that we can't see with Fleet technology. Glowing lights, areas that look like tiny fires, and of course, the smudges.

This time, the smudges don't attack NFP2. They follow it at a distance, as if they're a gang of thieves who are about to attack an unwary traveler. The NFP2 doesn't seem to care that it's being followed, although it registers their presence.

It hasn't sped up or moved aside, as Mikk programmed it to do, because apparently, it doesn't see the smudges as a threat.

I bring up one more screen, then cross my arms, watching. I expect NFP2 to make a few wrong moves, get caught in a loop, and need reprogramming help, just like its predecessor, but none of those things happen.

Instead, it zigs and zags exactly the way that the very first Fleet probe did. And then NFP2 speeds up as it heads toward that opening in the starfield-barrier.

"I'm not sure I like this," Orlando says. "You think those smudgy things recognized the probe as something they've seen before?"

"I do," I say. That's only logical. They had enveloped a similar probe before and carried it into the starfield-barrier. This time, they're watching to see what the probe will do.

As are we. Mikk is unusually quiet. He stands beside me, arms crossed. Tamaz and Roderick are at the same stations they were at before, but Nyssa is closer to them than she is to Denby this time.

Orlando has several screens up, as does Mikk. They're both seeing these smudges as weapons, although I wonder if they're some kind of sensor that we're not familiar with.

I suspect there's no need to engulf this probe, because they have already identified its predecessor. Maybe not where the probes were made or even who owns them, but as objects.

A similar one has breached these barriers before, and now this one is going in.

If the tech here only sees the Fleet as a threat, then these probes will mean very little to it.

I watch the moving images on the map on the screen before me, hands clasped behind my back. I have to remind myself to breathe. I find these probe interactions with the starfield-barrier ridiculously tense.

Normally, I just see probes as information gatherers, but these probes—all of them—have been under attack in one form or another.

This is the first probe we have sent to the starfield-barrier that hasn't experienced some kind of direct threat.

NFP2 goes around the sparkling edge of the starfield-barrier, and heads inside. I let out a small breath of air, then feel a bit dizzy. I've been forgetting to breathe, despite my best efforts.

I glance at the telemetry NFP2 is sending back. The scroll continues along one of my screens and all over Mikk's. Then my gaze travels to the visuals we're getting from NFP2.

And my breath catches.

Row after row after row of warships. Only NFP2 doesn't seem to be going along the length of them, but in front of them.

I don't want to examine the telemetry at the moment; I want to watch what NFP2 is sending back. So I say, "Mikk, did you program something different in this probe?"

"No," he says. "It's the same as the other non-Fleet probe."

"But it's traveling in a different direction, right?" I ask.

Orlando shifts a little too, so he can see what I'm looking at. Behind me, no one speaks. The hum of the machinery seems incredibly loud.

"It is," Mikk says. "All I can think is that something blocked its way."

"You don't know?" I ask.

"Not without examining the telemetry." He sounds as reluctant as I feel. "You want me to?"

"Not right now," I say.

I want to watch these images as long as I can. I expect the feed from NFP2 to fade at any moment.

"How the hell many warships are there?" Roderick says from behind me.

"More than I want to think about," Orlando says quietly.

"What does the Fleet need them for?" Mikk turns toward me, so I know he can see Denby as well. For some reason, he expects Denby to know the answer to that question.

"I—I'm not—I—" Denby is shaking his head. Obviously Mikk's attitude is really getting to him.

"It's okay, Gustav," I say. "Unfortunately, you are the only representative of the Fleet on this ship."

"I'm not here as a representative of the Fleet," Denby says. "I like to think of myself as part of your team."

He sounds hurt. Which is why I don't like working with other people in any way, shape, or form. I always say something wrong or hurt feelings or do something completely unintended.

I did not mean to hurt his feelings. I was actually trying to reassure him.

"You are a valued part of my team," I say, lowering my voice so that I don't sound confrontational or insincere or whatever the others expect me to sound like. "I meant that you're the only person with actual Fleet knowledge on this ship, not third-party Fleet knowledge. That's all."

Denby nods, but his gaze remains on Mikk.

Mikk raises his eyebrows just a little, as if to say, *The question still stands.*

"I don't know what the Fleet needs those warships for," Denby says. His voice is quavering just a little. He's clearly trying to hide just how upset he is. "I learned about them when you did, and try as I might, I can't find out more about them. And I gotta say, Boss, one of the reasons I'm here is I'm beginning to realize that the Fleet's decision to ignore its history really bothers me. I mean, we have a gigantic database from all of the Fleet ships. In that database, I should be able to look up the history of all the Fleet has done, what areas it traveled to, what places it's seen. I can't do that."

"Can't?" Mikk says.

This time, I reach out a hand, trying to keep him quiet, and I did, sort of. I stifled the last two words of that confrontational phrase. *Can't? Or won't?*

Denby seems to have heard them anyway. "I *can't*," he says. "I don't think any of us can, because I don't think the information exists."

I look at my screens. NFP2 is still sending back images. Warships on its left, stretching above it, below it, before it, and behind it. On its right there is only the faint sparkling of a forcefield.

The ships are all facing the same direction. NFP2 is in front of the long lines of ships, as if inspecting them for some admiral.

"I think maybe we should talk to Coop before we go in there," Nyssa says. "He might know—"

"He didn't even know this Boneyard existed." I should probably listen to her, but I'm not going to. I want to go in there and see these ships for myself, maybe even board one, if that's possible.

My heart is pounding.

"But he might know the history," she says, her voice faint.

I decide to ignore that. She knows better than to argue that. Coop doesn't know what happened out here any more than we do. He'll be as shocked by this as we are.

He would have told me that the Fleet had warships.

Wouldn't he?

But a niggling little voice inside my head reminds me that he didn't tell me he had found a Fleet sector base, that he had actually *traveled* to that Fleet sector base, that he might use that sector base to help him track the Fleet.

Am I refusing to tell Coop of this discovery now because I'm angry with him? Am I refusing to talk with him, to seek information from him, because I feel betrayed?

I stare at the ships. It takes the probe nearly a minute to travel along the face of one of them, and I would need to check the telemetry to know if the probe has slowed down or of the warships are just that big.

If I tell Coop about this, a dive into the starfield-barrier becomes about finding the Fleet. About using those warships to discover where the modern Fleet is, and what that modern Fleet will do with him, the *Ivoire*, and its remaining crew.

If I tell Coop, I lose control of this dive.

Because I'm not doing it for the Fleet.

Nyssa is still staring at me. The rest of the team is standing awkwardly, so that they can see me and the telemetry as it scrolls on the various screens around us.

They're keeping their eyes on me as well.

"Coop might know the history," I say to Nyssa, acknowledging her comment. "I doubt that he does, but he might. He might have been trained in how to operate warships."

Now, Orlando has looked up. Mikk's frown deepens. Tamaz and Roderick lean toward me, but continue to watch their screens.

Denby has frozen in place.

"We can find that out later," I say. "Right now, we're just exploring."

"So many questions," Nyssa says. "I just feel like we should answer as many of them as we possibly can before we go into that starfield-barrier."

"Have you ever thought that some of the answers are in those ships?" Mikk says a bit too harshly.

Nyssa leans backwards, as if his words were actual blows.

"Mikk," I say, using that voice—the one I used to have to use at Lost Souls when I needed to calm people down. "What the hell?"

He looks at me. "Either we dive this thing or we don't. Either we're all doing what needs to be done, or none of us are. Right now, we can't have people just guessing or making decisions worrying about other people."

I almost smile. He wants to get back to the old way of diving as much as I do.

"We are," I say. "It's just—"

I sweep my hand toward the warships. We're still getting telemetry from NFP2, which surprises me. And it's still seeing ships.

"—those ships are intimidating," I finish.

"The entire Boneyard is intimidating," Mikk says. "When has that scared you before?"

He uses the word "scared" to get a rise out of me, but it doesn't. I am scared, on some deep level. And on the same level, I think of that fear as healthy. It's making me go slower than I normally would.

But his question clarifies something for me.

"We get one shot at this before Coop and the crew of the *Ivoire* get involved," I say. "One shot to dive this the way *we* want to, not the way they do."

"What's wrong with their involvement?" To my surprise, that question came from Nyssa, not Denby.

In fact, he's the one who answers it before I can. "They'll change the focus," he says. "They seem to think the Fleet is the same as it was when we left. And it's not."

His words hang.

He knows that. I think Coop knows that, deep down. And Yash too. I know they're all trying to adjust to something huge in their lives. Something I can only imagine and not really understand.

Denby went through that change too—coming 5,000 years into his own future—and he just got emotional about not being part of my team. Does that mean he's adjusted better? Or that he's simply more realistic about what faces all of them?

"There's hundreds of ships," Roderick says, looking at the images, not at the rest of us. "Maybe thousands."

Maybe thousands.

They have to be empty. They can't have crews, just sitting in the Boneyard for all eternity, waiting to be called up.

"Thousands of ships, ready to activate," Mikk says, glancing at me.

"If they saw us as a threat, they would have activated by now," Orlando says.

"Would they?" Roderick glances nervously at Tamaz. "I mean, right now, we're just a speck."

Mikk says, "They reprogrammed—"

"Or whatever," Denby says.

"—the Fleet probes," Mikk continues, as if Denby hasn't spoken. "They clearly saw those as a threat."

Somewhere in that conversation, I ceased watching my team. I'm staring at those warships, rows after rows after rows of them, as if they were in a dress parade, waiting to launch.

I'm tempted to move forward without the next test. I'm tempted, but I'm not going to.

"All right," I say, without taking my gaze off those warships. "We need to collate all of the information that we have. We need to see if we can create a map of that dark area, and then we need to see if we can understand what those energy readings are."

Orlando nods. So does Mikk. Denby takes a deep breath.

"I'm going to keep searching for the packets, if you don't mind," he says to me, and I want to cheer. He didn't ask *Permission, ma'am* or any of the other verbal tricks he has used in the past to ask me a question.

Instead, he told me what he's going to do, and then asked permission. Kinda sorta. The way that the rest of my team does when they know they're going to do something I don't want them to do.

"I'd prefer that," I say.

"What happens after we finish going through the information?" Nyssa asks. But I know she's asking for more than half the team. Because I've told Mikk my full plan, figuring he could poke holes in it the best, but I haven't told everyone.

"We're going to send in ships," I say to her.

"We're going in?" she asks, and her voice wobbles, almost unnoticeably. I smile gently. "Not yet," I say. "We're sending in automated vessels first."

And we'll see if the Boneyard or the starfield-barrier or the warships destroy those vessels the way the probes were destroyed. Or worse.

She nods, swallows hard, gives me a nervous smile. "All right," she says. "More steps."

"Necessary ones," Mikk says.

"I know," she says quietly. "I know."

THE FLEET
NOW

31

COHN SAT AT THE CAPTAIN'S TABLE in the officer's mess. She had a cinnamon roll before her, and a large cup of coffee that still steamed. It had been too hot to touch when Iosua had brought it to her on a tray.

He was sitting beside her, a tiny tablet on the table before him. He also had a cup of coffee—chicory coffee, which was something she didn't entirely understand—but instead of a cinnamon roll, he had a slice of heavily frosted orange cake off to his left.

Wihone sat across from both of them, hands folded in front of himself. He didn't have any coffee—*can't abide the stuff,* he said when offered—but he had made himself a pot of chamomile tea, which smelled, to Cohn at least, a bit like watered-down piss.

She had decided to use the mess as a meeting area, because she didn't want this meeting to look too official—one captain to another. She hadn't let anyone else know that Iosua was here. She had insisted that he enter through the kitchen.

The chef was working the regular mess because Cohn had locked this one down late last night, marking it for cleaning. The routine cleaning was a day early, but no one would notice. Many of the officers on board never used the officers' mess, preferring to eat in their own quarters or in the regular mess.

The regular mess was three times the size of this one, and ran along one of the sides of Deck Six. One entire wall of the regular mess was windows, which could be shielded if need be. But the view was always spectacular, and Cohn half-wished she was there right now. That side of the ship faced the Scrapheap, which looked like a glistening row of lights, beautiful and formidable, with only the ghosts of ships behind the glowing forcefield. She had eaten in the regular mess daily in the three days since the ships arrived, primarily because of the view.

But here, in the officers' mess, there was no view. The mess was on the same deck as most of the officers' quarters, and used a different kitchen than the regular mess. The officers' mess was in the center of the deck, protected on all sides from anything that might damage the ship. There was a communications room to one side, for privacy, and the same kind of closet-sized remote bridge that existed in the captain's quarters, although this one had to actually be activated from a special control on the bridge before it could be used. Although the remote bridge would activate automatically if the bridge itself was destroyed.

Unlike the regular mess, though, the officers' mess had greenery. Actual plants and trees filled the space, and the overhead lighting replicated sunlight. Each booth and table had some kind of plant nearby, usually separating the booth or table off from a nearby table.

The table she sat at with the two men was in the center of the room, and surrounded by various kinds of dwarf palms, none of them taller than six feet, and all of them with branches along the sides. It was hard to see past the palms, and they tended to block any sound, which was another feature that she loved.

Right now, though, she found the palms annoying. Even though it had been her idea to come here, she wondered if they might not have been better off working in Engineering or on the bridge, rather than on tablets.

But at the moment, she didn't want to alarm her crew, so she had opted for this.

Wihone was fiddling with the handle on his mug. His fingers would caress it, and then he would move his hand as if touching the handle irritated him.

Cohn hadn't told him what this meeting was about, but he clearly had an idea, since he and Iosua were here.

"I spoke to Vice Admiral Mbuyi late last night," Cohn said to Wihone. Iosua already had this information. "I told her we were here. There was a hell of a lag in our communications, which we expected."

Wihone's fingers found the handle of his mug. "How long?"

"About three minutes," she said. "It made for an interesting conversation, made more interesting by a factor I had not expected."

Wihone's eyebrows curved into a frown. He shot a glance at Iosua. Cohn refrained from looking at Iosua. He'd been vibrating with something like anger all morning, because he felt his perfect record had been destroyed.

"Something happened in foldspace," Wihone said. It was not a question.

Cohn nodded. "It appears we've lost time."

"How much?" Wihone asked. His expression hadn't changed at all. Cohn got the sense he'd expected this.

"The vice admiral expressed her surprise that we had contacted her hours after leaving the sector base," she said.

"Hours?" Wihone said. He gripped the mug with both hands, his knuckles white. There was a lot of tension in his fingers.

Cohn hoped the force of his grip wouldn't crush the mug.

"Two hours to be precise," Iosua said.

"But…" Wihone was clearly doing the math in his head. They had left, moved to the proper foldspace coordinates, as determined by the entire team, inspected the ships, hooked up, and then went into foldspace—days after leaving the sector base.

Then he nodded, as if he had figured it out. He seemed like he was about to ask a question, but stopped himself.

He looked at Iosua, not at Cohn.

"So when exactly are we?" Wihone asked Iosua.

"Your guess is as good as mine," Iosua said. "We have no way of knowing what the actual date is here."

"Unless we trust the information we've gotten from the Scrapheap," Cohn said. "Which puts us almost a month ahead of when we went into foldspace, not two hours after we left the sector base."

Wihone bowed his head. He rubbed a hand over his mouth and closed his eyes, then let out a big sigh.

"A few weeks is dealable," he said quietly.

"Really?" Iosua asked, and there was an edge in his voice. "Because the *Geesi* has never lost time."

"Erasyl," Cohn said softly. "You promised."

She didn't need to add more. Iosua was furious that they had gone through some kind of time vortex through foldspace. He seemed to be blaming Wihone and the other ships.

But Wihone didn't seem bothered by Iosua's reaction. Wihone's gaze met Cohn's. "Good thing we were tethered," he said. "Imagine if we hadn't been."

She shuddered. The *Geesi* would have arrived…at the right time? A month ago? And the other ships would have arrived…a month later?

These kinds of discrepancies made her brain hurt.

"You spoke to the vice admiral in real time," Wihone said. It wasn't quite a question. "But there was a lag."

Cohn nodded. "You think that means something?"

"I have no idea what it means, since she's experiencing you in a different time period than you're experiencing."

"Maybe," Iosua said. "We have no idea if the timeline in the Scrapheap is correct."

His words hung between them.

"You haven't told the other captains yet, I take it," Wihone said.

"I don't want a panic," Cohn said. "You've handled this before. I haven't."

He nodded, then looked away. He shoved the tea aside, and took a deep breath.

Then he let it out slowly as he looked at her. He looked sad.

"There's no good time to tell any of the crews what's going on. If you tell them too soon, that's what they'll focus on," he said. "If you tell them too late, and they find out on their own, they'll be furious at you. You have to figure out what serves the mission."

She nodded. She had a sense about all of that, but she hadn't thought it through quite that clearly.

"The only ones who know this are the three of us," she said.

"I'd say tell the other captains, but I worry about Jicha. He doesn't seem real smart or flexible," Wihone said.

"He's very smart," Cohn said. She didn't tell Wihone Jicha's history, how Jicha had saved a ship almost entirely by himself, at great personal cost, long before he ever became a captain. "He's just…" She wasn't sure about the word. Protective? Cautious? Risk-averse?

In the end, she didn't add any word to describe Jicha. She could get away with not telling anyone for a while. She was the one who was supposed to be in touch with the vice admiral, which the vice admiral had set up so that she wouldn't end up in the middle of any kind of power battle between the captains.

Unless someone spoke to a friend or family member with the Fleet—which was not standard procedure—there was no way anyone would find out about the time discrepancy. And Cohn did consider the other captains professional enough to come to her first should something go wrong.

"I'm not going to say anything yet," Cohn said, looking at both men. "But I will need theories—or facts, if we can get them—on whether or not we will regain this time if we travel back the way we came."

"I doubt it," Wihone said.

"There's different schools of thought on that," Iosua said, almost at the same time.

"I think it depends on the ships," Wihone said.

"Do you think the vibrations caused this?" Cohn asked him.

He shrugged. "I know as much as you know on that."

Iosua's lips had thinned. He was still vibrating with barely contained anger.

"Do you disagree with the plan, Erasyl?" Cohn asked him.

"Not yet," he said. "But once we know what's going on with this Scrapheap, I want to revisit your decision to keep everyone in the dark."

"Fair enough," she said. She knew that would be a few days at the earliest.

The Scrapheap had dumped months' worth of data on them the moment they had arrived. She had given much of it to Jicha and his crew, but she had also spread out some of it to the other ships. In particular, she wanted evidence of the thieves. She wanted to know what—if anything—they had taken since the data the Scrapheap had sent initially.

And then she needed a plan. She still expected the thieves to be gone. But she wanted to know what they took and what they were doing here.

She also needed to inspect those Ready Vessels.

She didn't need the time distraction, not yet.

She almost smiled. It was ironic to think that she and the other ships had enough time to investigate what was going on, but they did. They didn't have to solve their time discrepancy for weeks, maybe months, depending on what they found here.

And she trusted that Iosua would be working on the problem the entire time.

She looked at him. His normal cheerful features had solidified into a deep frown.

"No matter what you assign me, I'm still going to work on this time conundrum," he said.

She nodded. "I know. What I'd like to know first is if the Scrapheap has kept accurate time measures. Because their measurement could be off. We might only have lost a day or two."

"And you think that's better than a month?" Iosua asked.

"I do," she said.

"A day is something the crew can deal with easily," Wihone said. "My crew has, in the past."

Iosua shot him a glare, but didn't add anything. "If we want to know what's going on with the Scrapheap's timekeeping," Iosua said, "we can't do it from the data dump. We need to go into the tower itself."

"I expect to," Cohn said. "I will put you on that team, when I have it assembled."

"You see no point in hurrying." Wihone had this habit of stating questions as if he was explaining her to herself. She wasn't sure if she found it annoying or not.

"Do you?" she asked.

"I'd like to know what we're facing," he said.

"That's what we're doing," she said. "We're going through the information. Then we'll take action."

And as she said that, her comm link buzzed.

The only person who could contact her right now was Vinters. Which meant something was happening.

Cohn opened the link. She didn't need to do anything else.

"We need you on the bridge now, Captain," Vinters said. And then she signed off.

Cohn put her hands on the table and used them to lever herself up.

"Well, I guess we're done here, gentlemen." She picked up the coffee and the uneaten cinnamon roll, walked them to the storage and recycler units, and placed them in the container set aside for her leftovers. "I will not be telling anyone about the time changes, yet. I will let you know when I do."

Wihone was right beside her. He put his untasted tea on the recycler pad. Iosua gulped his coffee down, winced, and set the empty mug on the cleaning pad.

"I'm coming with you," he said to Cohn.

"I would hope that you both do," she said as she pivoted and headed out of the mess.

She deliberately did not speculate on what she was going to see on the bridge. But she knew whatever it was had to be important for Vinters to interrupt the meeting.

Important probably meant the thieves.

And Cohn was ready for them.

32

THE *GEESI'S* BRIDGE WAS HUMMING. Cohn hadn't seen that much positive energy on her bridge since this mission began.

Her team was always professional, but sometimes they took pleasure in their work, and sometimes they just did their work. Up until this moment, they had been doing their work.

Right now, however, they seemed to do more than take pleasure in the work. Right now, they seemed excited.

Priede turned toward her as she entered the bridge, Wihone and Iosua behind her. Priede was grinning.

"They haven't left, Captain," he said.

She assumed that meant the thieves.

Vinters, who was standing near the captain's chair, frowned at Priede. She hadn't wanted him to speak, although Cohn wasn't sure why. There were screens open everywhere, and holographic representations of different parts of the Boneyard decorated the entire bridge.

Troyes was standing near the navigation panel, hands clasped behind his back as he studied something only he could see. Gray was standing near her console, also studying something, but bouncing slightly on the balls of her feet.

Everyone else was looking at Cohn, as if they couldn't wait to see her reaction.

"Well, show me," she said to Vinters.

Vinters ran a hand over her long white hair. It had been pulled back away from her face, making her features seem harsh.

"They've been here the entire time," Priede said. "We think—"

Vinters waved her left hand, silencing him with that single gesture. She seemed impatient with him, which wasn't like her at all.

Cohn walked down the aisle, toward Vinters and the captain's chair. Cohn could sense Wihone walking behind her more than she could hear him. Iosua had broken off and joined the navigators.

When Cohn reached the captain's chair, Vinters activated the screens around it.

"This happened right before I contacted you," she said, then glanced over Cohn's shoulder at Wihone, as if his presence bothered her.

Cohn was going to ignore that. She wanted to see what Vinters had for her.

The images in front of Cohn resolved into a small three-dimensional representation of that area near the Scrapheap where the thieves had initially entered. Cohn had those places memorized. She knew what that part of the Scrapheap looked like, and how the thieves had entered. She had studied their techniques herself, which was one reason why she wanted to go into the three towers inside the Scrapheap. She wanted to see if the control towers themselves were compromised.

But right now, she was staring at that empty exterior in front of the Scrapheap, the forcefield glistening just like it did near here.

"What am I looking at?" she asked Vinters.

"Wait for it," Vinters said.

The rest of the bridge crew was watching as well, but they weren't looking at the holographic representation. They were watching Cohn.

Wihone had moved to her side.

She was about to ask again what she was supposed to see when the forcefield on the Scrapheap opened and a tiny probe zoomed out of it. The probe looked ancient, but she recognized the design:

The probe was Fleet.

The probe was moving at a high rate of speed. The forcefield closed and as it did, the defenses activated. They sent killing ropes to the probe, caught it, and enveloped it.

She knew what was going to happen next; she'd seen similar defensive weapons in action. The ropes heated the probe, then separated it into its component pieces and devoured them, so that no information in that probe could be used anywhere else.

And the probe couldn't be traced either.

It was an emergency measure, usually done to protect some location, like a Scrapheap. But Cohn had never seen those measures used on Fleet equipment before.

She did know, however, that the Fleet often destroyed equipment that was deemed dangerous or had been contaminated or had been sent into secure areas.

The ropes remained in place until all parts of the probe were obliterated. Then they retracted.

"Again," she said.

Vinters played the images again. Cohn didn't see any difference, but something was nagging at her.

"One more time," she said.

This time, she noted something that the probes passed, something she hadn't noted before, no matter how many times she had studied this section of the Scrapheap.

"What's that?" she asked, pointing at a small unfamiliar square structure. It floated, equidistant, from another small square of the same type.

Those weren't Fleet equipment. Their design didn't flow. All of the Fleet's designs, whether boxy or curved, had a certain elegance to them. These things did not.

"What's what?" Vinters asked.

"Go back," Cohn said, waving her hand at the images. Vinters reversed the images, slowly, so that Cohn could stop her at the right spot.

The squares showed up again, and going this slowly meant that Cohn saw yet another square. And one more.

"There," she said, pointing at the squares. "What are those?"

"We'll scan them," Gray said.

"No need," Wihone said, almost in Cohn's ear. His closeness startled her. She hadn't realized he was almost leaning against her. "The Scrapheap itself should have scanned them. The information should be in the data."

"We have a lot of data," Gray said. She glanced at Cohn, as if trying to see whether Cohn agreed with Wihone. "Months and months—"

"And maybe years," Troyes added.

"My people have been trying to categorize the information so we can search it," Wihone said. "I'll contact them."

"I also sent the packets of information to the *Tudósok*," Cohn said. "They should have a way to search as well."

"No need." Priede gave Vinters a sharp look, as if he were proving himself to her. "I know what they are. I investigated them when we got here."

"Why would you do that?" Iosua asked, then glanced at Cohn, as if he had suddenly realized that he might have interrupted her as she was about to ask a question.

She hadn't been. She understood what Priede had been doing, even though she hadn't assigned him the job.

He had been trying to find the thieves, and in doing so, he had identified all of the objects near their original point of entry.

"What are they?" Cohn asked, before Priede could be distracted by Iosua's question.

"They're markers, buoys if you will. They have cameras and sensors and other tracking equipment," Priede said.

Cohn felt a small thrill. "They're not Fleet," she said.

"That's right," Priede said. "And they've been in place less than a year."

Cohn smiled. Priede had made this part of her job easy. She had thought she was going to have to collate information from all of the other ships.

"You said the thieves haven't left," she said to him.

Vinters tilted her head, giving Cohn a warning look. "Captain, we're dealing with the probe—"

"I am dealing with the probe, Sigrid," Cohn said.

"We can't assume those buoy things are connected to the probe, especially considering one is Fleet equipment, and the other is not," Vinters said.

"We don't make buoys like that," Cohn said, still looking at Priede, who was shifting. He wanted to answer her original question. "We have no need for them."

"But we do," Vinters said. "We make markers all the time, for sector bases and starbases—"

"And they're part of the base," Cohn said. "We don't carry that kind of equipment as standard on our vessels."

Only on vessels that were scouting for a new sector base, and even then, the markers were different. They weren't square boxes that sent information to ships. They were relays that sent information directly to Command, so that Command would know what was going on in the region.

Priede was nodding his head. "That's right, Captain," he said, unnecessarily. She knew she was right, and so did Vinters. "The thieves haven't left."

So, he wasn't overexplaining. He was answering her original question.

"How do you know that?" she asked.

"It's in the data. They've been inside the Scrapheap, finding ships and removing them," he said. "They've been doing that for months."

"And they put out these markers?" Cohn asked.

"I would assume so," Priede said. "The markers showed up after they did."

Vinters was shaking her head. "Assuming isn't—."

Cohn held up a hand, much like Vinters had done earlier. "Those markers might tell us exactly what we need. Can we access their signals? Find out what they're sending and to whom?"

"Probably." That was Wihone now. "We have research capability times five."

Cohn glanced at him. He looked very intense. She smiled. "Times five or more. This can keep our scholars busy."

"I'd rather it be engineers," Iosua said.

"You have other issues to investigate," she said. "We need to figure out these thieves."

Iosua frowned. He didn't seem to realize that there was more urgency to figuring out the foldspace issue than there had been just an hour ago.

If they had found the thieves, and it appeared they had, then they needed to roust them from the Scrapheap, and get on with the mission. They might be able to return to the Fleet sooner than Cohn had expected.

"We don't know if the probe belongs to those thieves," Vinters said.

"Not for a fact, no," Cohn said. "But it's logical that the probe does. We have evidence that they used ancient code and evidence that they're using our old ships. It stands to reason that they would use our probes as well."

"But for what?" Wihone had moved slightly. His arms were crossed. He seemed uncomfortable being sidelined, but to his credit, he didn't say anything.

"I don't know what they're using the probes for," Cohn said. "They might be sending them into ships. But a reaction like that, exploding the probe, that suggests something else to me."

Everyone on the bridge turned toward her. It seemed odd to her that they hadn't figured this out. But they had less information on how the Fleet worked at the upper levels than she did.

She inclined her head toward the images. "This Scrapheap has Ready Vessels."

"We don't know that for certain," Vinters said.

"Oh, I think we do now," Cohn said. "And that probe crossed into the wrong area. It probably got too close to the Ready Vessels."

"That's no reason to destroy a probe," Wihone said. "Maybe it was reprogrammed."

Cohn gave him a hard look. She would have thought that all captains knew about the extra security and protections for Ready Vessels, but apparently not. She knew that the Fleet kept information on Ready

Vessels on a need-to-know basis, but she hadn't realized that captains had different levels of training on them.

"It was reprogrammed," she said. "By the Scrapheap. And then the Scrapheap destroyed it."

He shook his head. "Why would it do that?"

"Ready Vessels are supposed to be secret," she said. "Or were, back at the time this Scrapheap was developed."

She looked at those markers, and let out a slow breath. She had a much larger problem than she expected to have.

The thieves had been stealing from the Scrapheap for months now. And the thieves had found the Ready Vessels.

She no longer had a choice of actions.

Her mandate from the Fleet was clear:

Those thieves had to be destroyed.

THE BONEYARD
NOW

33

Two days of work before we have enough information to add to our various collections. Two days of work before I decide that I'm comfortable enough to send in our first automated vessel.

The night before we plan to send in the vessel, I finish my own work in my oversized captain's quarters. I want to concentrate and that's the only place on the *Veilig* that I can be assured of remaining alone.

I sit at the dining table, designed—at minimum—for four people, and which, in my use of these quarters, has never had more than two (and that by an uncomfortable accident). I've made myself a sandwich with wheat bread brought to us from some experimental kitchen lab at Lost Souls, some kind of not-meat that tastes like chicken, and some crunchy purple peppers from the hydroponics bay in the *Sove*. I'm halfway through the damn sandwich when I realize I would rather have had soup or some hummus or anything else. I set the sandwich aside, planning to get something else, but I don't rise from the chair.

I'm concentrating on all the information, trying to put it together into something cohesive, something I want to understand.

First, I catalog the failures.

So far, Denby hasn't found the packet inside the Fleet probes—or any Fleet equipment for that matter. He's been working very hard, searching for something that might be that tiny string of information, but he can't find it.

Mikk has urged him to contact Diaz, and have her work on the problem. Denby has refused. I don't know if he's refused because Mikk gave him the instruction and the two of them have spent most of this trip butting heads, or if Denby's refused because he actually thinks he can find the packet—if it exists.

All I know is that if they can't resolve this, then I'll contact Diaz myself.

Other failures include Roderick's search through the Fleet records that we do have to find any history of the warships. Or even of how they're deployed.

We have found the warships listed in ship types on some old Fleet databases, but there's evidence that someone or something tried to scrub those databases.

What we have found about the warships are snippets—recommendations in some old commander's file that he move to warship duty. Commendations for admirals for their work with warships. Engineers who've moved to an entire unit on a sector base, a unit that focused on warships.

I see these mentions as possibilities. The information is in the records, but it's broken up, hard to find, and might take more computational power and resources than we have.

I can be cautious, and not do anything until I have all of the information. But I'm still working as if we're going to dive the starfield-barrier sometime soon.

Because we've had so many more successes than failures.

I finally do stand up and take the sandwich to the galley kitchen. I pull everything off the bread, but keep the bread on the plate. I toss the uneaten parts in the food recycler, so that everything can be mashed up and reused in various pastes and quickly assembled meals. They don't taste as good as fresh, but sometimes I like the processed stuff.

I grab some hummus and spread it along the bread, knowing the hummus will mingle with the leftover bits from the purple peppers and not-meat. I don't really care. I just want to eat something I don't have to think about much, because I'm thinking hard enough already.

Successes include the one I care about the most: a map.

We have a map of the weapons or mines or whatever those things are in the section of the darkness just in front of the starfield-barrier. We know where the stationary ones are, at least in the area we've sent probes through. We're not sure what those mine-weapon things are or what they do, exactly, but we know that they're dangerous enough that the Fleet probes avoid them on purpose.

So, we will too, of course.

It's the smudges that have captured my attention. I've spent some time studying them, and so has Tamaz. We've determined that they operate more as a unit than as individual weapons. The unit they create is like a beaded shield, only the beads separate at times and go their own way, for reasons we don't entirely understand.

When those beads return to the main part of the shield, they don't always return to the same position. They form whatever shape the smudge-thing seems to need at that point.

They're flexible and mostly invisible to our eyes, until they activate. And then they turn white.

The comet-trail shape is just one of their shapes. They can engulf or string themselves out in a straight line.

They didn't seem to do any damage at all to the non-Fleet probes—at least as far as we can tell—but the Fleet probes avoided them as well.

I was the one who found a way to identify the smudges in place. They have an ever-so-slight energy signature, one that we can register from any scan on Fleet equipment and non-Fleet equipment.

The energy signature grows when the smudge joins its fellow smudges and forms a smudge-thing. And then, when they all turn white, the energy signature quadruples in size.

We can't figure out what causes that. Tamaz and I have gone over and over and over the scans, but we can't determine what these are exactly or how they operate. Or whether or not they're automated.

The other thing we haven't been able to figure out is whether or not the Fleet probes went past or through smudges. The telemetry off the

Fleet probes is so tainted, we have no idea if what we're getting from those probes is real.

And this is one area where we really need to know what's before our ships or probes. And so of course, it's one area that we can't quite see.

I am comfortable with what we have, however. At least at this stage. We're not going to risk any of our lives on what we do next.

I settle back into my chair, going over Tamaz's latest work on the smudges. I take a bite of the hummus sandwich, wincing a little at the purple pepper remnants that crunch as I chew.

This sandwich doesn't taste that good either, and I'm beginning to think it's not the food.

Or maybe it is: maybe I just don't like fresh food, particularly when I'm stress-eating around a mission. I usually eat fruit that's just a little too old, like spotted apples, or I eat processed stuff I don't have to think about.

I make myself take another bite of the sandwich anyway, and chase it down with warm recycled water. That water tastes appropriate, anyway. A little too warm, a little too stale, a little too flat.

I move some of the information around on my screens, and peer at Tamaz's ideas. He believes the energy signatures of the smudges are unique to them.

We have no evidence that he's right. We also have no evidence that he's wrong. He's guessing, at this point, and so are we. But we're limited with the information that we have.

He set up a program that easily and quickly locates that signature, while shielding the scan. Often, if a ship is being scanned or a piece of equipment is being scanned, the scan is traceable.

He believes this scan won't be.

I hope he's right.

No matter how hard I poke, I can't seem to find a flaw in his work.

But I'm no engineer. I am good at cobbling things together and investigating them. I'm good at figuring out how other things work, and I'm good at finding my way around things that shouldn't be gotten around.

However, I lack a lot of other skills, and I'm not sure they'll come into play here.

If I were sending my team into that area between the regular Boneyard and the starfield-barrier right now, then I would have Diaz or someone—maybe even Yash—see if there are other flaws in Tamaz's work.

But I'm not sending a team. I'm sending an automated ship.

If our automated ships get through without attracting a smudge or hitting a mine-weapon, then we're going to be good to go.

I feel a small shot of adrenaline at the thought. We're almost to the dangerous part, the diving part, the part that I am the most interested in.

But we're not quite there yet, no matter how much I want to be.

I'm working harder at keeping myself steady, moving slowly, than I am at evaluating Tamaz's work or the information that Mikk keeps sending me on a regular basis.

I'm aware that I'm being a lot more cautious now than I ever have in the past. Some of it, I'm sure, is just a bit of common sense. Squishy told me, during that last dive she actually worked with me on, that I was messing with things I didn't understand. She was right, and it cost two lives.

But at the same time, some of this caution might simply be fear. Or history. All those deaths because I made the choice to try something. All that loss.

Not to mention my own injury. If I were interviewing myself, trying to figure out my motivations as though I were a stranger, I would ask if that injury had an impact on my courage.

I have been asking that, quite honestly.

And, deep down, I don't know the answer. I'm not sure where courage crosses the line into recklessness or if they're simply two different words for the same thing.

I've kept myself restrained for years now, long past Karl's death, which was, in some ways, a bigger blow than Jypé and Junior. And even staying restrained hasn't been as big a cure-all as I thought. That dive where Elaine got permanently injured, where we both almost died, that one was constrained and organized and as thought through as any of my dives get.

I push the half-eaten sandwich away, take another sip of the water, and then shut down the screens in front of me.

I should turn the statement I've been making to everyone else on myself.

I can leave now, if I want to. If I believe this is too much of a risk. If I feel that there's no point in endangering lives.

After all, we know what's behind that starfield-barrier. Hundreds, maybe thousands, of warships.

We don't know what condition they're in or why they're there or whether or not they're being monitored or maintained.

But we know they're there.

And I can bring that information to Coop and Yash, who will jump on it, and make decisions that I would never make.

I stand up, and take the remains of the sandwich to the recycler.

Are Coop and Yash the crux of the problem? Am I doing this because I'm afraid of what they'll do?

Am I trying to protect them?

Or myself?

34

HALF OF MY TEAM CROWDS AROUND THE COCKPIT of the runabout we've chosen for this part of the mission. This runabout is ancient and has design features I'm not used to, especially the one that made the entire front of the cockpit into windows, not screens. I actually debated whether or not to use this runabout because those windows, while lovely, are vulnerable to outside attack.

But, I finally reasoned with myself, we're not going to be on the runabout. It's going to be automated. So even if something shoots at the cockpit, that something won't kill anyone. And there are shields on this thing, albeit weak ones.

I had the choice of two other runabouts that could be automated, both from the *Sove*. But those runabouts could be useful for other missions. This runabout is barely travel-worthy. It's certainly not the kind of ship I'd let any of my crew on for longer than an hour or two.

Even so, I hadn't expected it to smell musty, and to have had its environmental systems off entirely before Zaria Diaz brought it to us. Although Diaz has had the environmental systems on for hours now, the musty smell continues.

I hate it, so I walked around the runabout to see if I could find the source of the smell, and I think it's coming from the sleeping quarters.

Someone actually put carpet in there instead of flooring. The bed itself is stored inside the wall, and I'm reluctant to pull the bed to the floor, because I suspect that, if the carpet is mildewy, the bed is as well.

Oh, well. If this runabout suffers what I suspect it will suffer, the smell won't be a problem for long.

Actually, we only have to put up with it while we're setting up, and that's uncomfortable enough. The navigation panel is small and rounded, and it isn't easily adjustable. I could spend the next two days trying to figure out how to make the panel larger and adjust its height, or I can simply squeeze next to the team and work that way.

It's a bit more complicated than that—we're all moving around, trying to get our work done, trying to adjust so we can both observe each other's work and get out of the way.

Mostly, we're working in silence, although Diaz keeps giving me sideways glances as if she's trying to figure me out. Again. Diaz is standing in front of that rounded cockpit, with me and Mikk on one side, and Roderick and Tamaz on the other. Denby has called up an auxiliary system near the tiny galley kitchen.

But we all step back on occasion, sometimes just to have a moment when we're not brushing arms with each other, and sometimes because we need to look at the various screens in front of us.

I deliberately picked the smallest runabout because of the part of the mission it will fulfill. I wanted to use a ship that's big enough to catch the attention of that possible intelligence we all seem to believe is in the Boneyard, and yet one that's small enough that it will fit into some of the narrow gaps that the probes have gone through.

We want to make absolutely certain we follow the same trajectory as the probes that have gotten inside the starfield-barrier.

I almost see that trajectory as a road, leading directly inside the starfield-barrier, to those warships.

I brought Diaz here so that she can double-check some of our plans, primarily the system Tamaz set up to scan for the smudges. I want her to look for any problems with it.

Before I got to her, though, Denby did. He told her about the possible packets inside Fleet equipment, and gave her a Fleet probe to take back to the *Sove* with her. He has already put that probe in the Fleet-built single ship that she'll be using to return.

Diaz says she will make the search for the packet a priority, and after she said that, she gave me an odd look, as if I've done something wrong.

I had Diaz run a basic systems check before she brought this runabout here, and I requested that she program the runabout to use its automatic pilot to bring her to the *Veilig*.

The automated system worked perfectly. Diaz monitored it the entire way, making sure that nothing could go awry. She says she has more faith in this runabout's automated systems than she does in some pilots.

No one on my team laughed at that comment, which she apparently meant as a joke. Our lives have often rested on the skills of a human pilot, one who could make unexpected and seemingly stupid decisions on the fly.

Diaz hasn't been on a mission like that, so she doesn't really know what that's like.

Mikk and Roderick actually exchanged glances after she said that, and she looked at me, clearly wondering what she said wrong.

I haven't told her, of course. I just want to move forward. And moving forward means setting up the systems properly.

All of the systems. I am setting up my work, mostly on the smudges and the trajectories, alongside Tamaz. But occasionally, I walk over to Denby, primarily to get away from the press of those bodies near me. But Denby does need to touch base with someone just to keep his frustration at a minimum. He knows what he's doing, and he also knows that he's searching for something Fleet engineers have deliberately kept secret.

Now, we're making him work on that small access panel near the galley. He has opened a holoscreen that replicates what's in the panel, just so he can see better. If we had time, he could've worked on the navigation panel, and set up his search properly.

Honestly, I could give him more time, but I'm not willing to. I am ready for this part of the mission to get underway.

The day before we boarded the runabout, Denby told me he thinks he's doing the search wrong. I asked him what he plans to change in his methodology, and he said, *That's the thing, Boss. I have no idea what to change.*

Which is probably why he wants Diaz's help. A fresh set of eyes sometimes makes all the difference.

Normally, I'd put Mikk on it as well, but Mikk still believes that the Fleet has reprogrammed the operating systems on the fly.

Mikk is still worrying about that. He's been trying to figure out how to protect the runabout against it.

I don't want him to. I want to send in this runabout without any extra protections, just like the Fleet probes.

What we have done is place a small rectangular download device underneath the navigation board. The download device is non-Fleet tech, the kind Yash and I used to download information from that runabout we dived after I got injured.

I'm hoping we'll be able to access any information from this runabout as it heads out of the starfield-barrier—if it manages to get inside the starfield-barrier.

We're doing all we can to ensure that it will get inside. Tamaz is downloading all of the specs on the weaponry, mines, and smudges into the runabout's systems. Roderick is working on the shields, making sure they'll go up at any sign of trouble. They're on a different automated system than the automatic pilot.

We've been working hard until just a few minutes ago, when Mikk started a heated discussion with Diaz.

He wants to know if it's possible to shield the runabout's operating computer, separate from the shield that forms outside of the runabout itself.

Diaz has spent the last fifteen minutes scrolling through systems. She doesn't believe it's possible, outside of some kind of personal shield, which would form around the pilot and the navigation systems. That, though, would only protect against an attack in the same room.

Finally, I shut the discussion down.

"I don't care," I say, although that's not entirely accurate. "I want to be able to replicate what we do here, and having that kind of shield on the computers seems like a small-ship thing, not a SC-Class vessel thing."

Diaz raises her head. Her dark hair is tucked behind her ears and there are shadows under her eyes. She's been working hard, although at what I'm not entirely sure.

I've lost track of the *Sove's* mission as I've gotten deeper in this one.

"Replicate?" she says. "This isn't the only automated ship you're taking into that starfield-barrier?"

"I don't know yet," I say.

There must have been something in my tone, because her eyes narrow. "You're taking a crew into that starfield-barrier?"

She's speaking quietly, as if she's trying to figure out whether or not I've gone insane.

"There's a percentage chance that I will." I'm not going to lie, because that would cause problems later on.

"How big a chance?" she asks.

"I don't know." Again, honesty. "It depends on what happens with the tests we're doing."

"And this ship is being tested." Diaz nods. "Got it."

I had Tamaz brief her before he arrived on the runabout with all of his information. I didn't want Mikk to do it, because Mikk has wedded himself to the idea that the Boneyard is actively fighting against us—or anything that goes behind that starfield-barrier.

I'm not willing to commit to that interpretation yet, and I didn't want Diaz thinking it either.

"Then," Diaz says, "we should only use systems that the *Veilig* has as well."

She realizes, then, that if my team does go into that starfield-barrier, we will do so on the *Veilig*.

"There's nothing special here on the runabout, is there?" Roderick asks. "It's just a standard ship, right?"

"Its autopilot is antiquated. The *Veilig's* is newer," Diaz says. "Maybe I should update—"

"No," I say. "If we take the *Veilig* into the starfield-barrier—and that's a big if—we won't be using the autopilot. For any reason."

She looks at me, and frowns just a little. Sometimes Fleet procedure mandates autopilot, particularly when trying to replicate something that had been done before. Autopilot is a lot more accurate at following a set series of procedures than a human pilot, particularly when the human pilot might miss activating a system by one-hundredths of a second. That hundredths of a second could be the difference between success and failure.

She tilts her head a little, as if she's having an argument with herself about what to say to me. She tucks her hair behind her ears, even though hardly any strands have fallen loose. A nervous habit, then.

"Okay," she says, in that *I see you're still crazy* tone she was using earlier. "Then all of the systems match well enough. I won't rig anything special."

I almost ask her what else she planned to rig differently, but then I don't. She's right: she shouldn't do anything special for the runabout.

We just need it to go to the starfield-barrier and report.

She is going to program the navigation system for us, though, although Tamaz has been working with her on the trajectory. It's pretty simple, since we have the telemetry from all of the probes, and they went the same way.

It's the return trip that's the problem.

If there is a return trip.

I'm letting Mikk help with the programming of that. He and I discussed whether or not we should have the runabout return the way that the Fleet probes did, on that path that eventually took them out of the Boneyard.

We eventually decided that we wanted the runabout to return by a different path. That way, we will know whether or not it's been reprogrammed or damaged or attacked by whatever is behind that starfield-barrier.

It will return the way it came. Diaz is helping program that, although she points out that we don't know enough about the weapons-mines and smudges to know if they will do something different if approached from the starfield-barrier side.

Diaz's hands float across that navigation board with a surety that I envy. I don't have that confidence with any ships except the *Business* and the *Business Two*. I am constantly learning new systems, new ship designs, new everything.

I guess I miss that familiarity as well.

"All right," Diaz says after a moment. "Everything you wanted is programmed into this runabout."

She has clearly phrased that sentence with care. It's masterful, hinting at her disagreements with my plans without an outright on-the-record statement. It also means the work I wanted done is done.

"Thanks." I step back from the navigation board, brushing against Mikk as I do.

"You want me to double-check?" he asks so softly that I know he doesn't want anyone else to hear him.

"Not necessary," I say quietly.

He nods once, although his mouth pulls back in an involuntary grimace.

"I still haven't found the packets," Denby says. "Maybe we should wait—"

"No." I'm done waiting. We're sending this ship in. Denby and Diaz can search the probes and the other ships we have for those mysterious packets—if they exist at all.

I run my hand along the edge of the navigation board, my fingers brushing against the download device we had placed underneath. In theory, that device will send us information all through this entire mission.

In theory.

I know better than to trust any of this stuff entirely.

I take a deep breath, about to compliment the team on a job well done.

Instead, my nose tickles, and I sneeze, startling myself and all of them as well. Roderick lets out a nervous laugh.

"I've never been in a ship with this kind of damage before," he says.

"That you know of," Tamaz says. "On the old ones, the environmental systems are always off."

He has a great point. My nose is still tickling, and if I don't leave soon, I'll have a sneezing fit, something I've never experienced in space before. On land, sure. That's one reason I'm not fond of land-based missions. But out here, never.

This runabout wouldn't really be a great loss.

Or maybe I'm just thinking that way because we've been in this Boneyard, with thousands of unused ships, for much too long.

"If we're ready to go," I say, my voice a bit strained against the sneeze, "we should go. Good work, everyone."

"Yeah, sure," Denby says quietly.

"You've copied the entire operating system, right?" Diaz asks him, not in a pointed way, but just to make sure.

"Yeah. First thing I did when you brought this thing," he says.

"Then we don't need to stay here to find those packets," she says.

"We can't prevent any damage," he says.

"But we have a baseline," she says. "We'll know what, if anything, got changed for the next time."

She's so optimistic. I'm not sure our little backup will work. I don't say that, though, because the mood on this ship is odd enough.

Mikk backs away from the navigation panel as if it has burned his fingers. He looks at me.

"We've never done anything like this before," he says to me, and his eyes actually twinkle. The old Mikk is back. He loves new procedures as much as I do, even destructive ones.

"First time for everything," I say.

"Yeah," Diaz says, not realizing that Mikk and I are having a moment. "I'm not real fond of the potential destruction."

I'm not fond of it either. I don't usually send things into harm's way. But I'm not going to send any crew into that starfield-barrier without a lot of tests first.

That's my own personal version of caution. Do something exceedingly risky while minimizing as much of the risk as possible.

That's not the Fleet way, which is why it's always uncomfortable to have Fleet personnel near one of these missions.

"Let's go," I say to the team.

Time to take one of those risks...and see how it's going to pan out.

35

THE ENTIRE TEAM GATHERS ON THE BRIDGE of the *Veilig* to watch what will happen to the runabout. For a while I thought Diaz wasn't going to join us, that she was just going to head back to the *Sove*, but she has gotten caught up in the search for the packets, so she is on the bridge as well.

She plans to compare the information from the runabout's systems before the mission to its systems after the mission.

As if we're going to recover the runabout easily.

For that reason and, honestly, because she's Fleet at heart, I've relegated her to the back of the *Veilig's* bridge. She's standing beside Nyssa. I've asked Diaz not to participate in our information gathering and she has agreed albeit with quite a bit of confusion.

I just want my usual team on this, so I don't have to worry about Fleet rules. I might make decisions that make no sense to someone with Fleet training.

The *Veilig's* bridge design helps segregate her out. She's above us near the exit. The working floor is clearly by the captain's chair, and everything else is behind us. It's probably hard to see the screens from Diaz's location, but I'm not too concerned about that.

If she wants to see closely, she can call up the images on her own equipment, like a few of the others are doing.

Mikk is at his usual spot at my side. Orlando is on the other side, even though he hasn't really helped with the prep for this part of the mission. Roderick and Tamaz are in their usual spots toward the back.

Only Denby is in a different position. He's just behind me, with screens up around him so that he can monitor our weapons and defensive systems here on the *Veilig*. I've modeled several scenarios, both in my head and with the computers in my quarters, and even though the computers claim a scenario in which the *Veilig* gets attacked isn't even possible, I think it might be.

I just don't have evidence for those computers that there's actually an operational intelligence in the Boneyard, even though part of me believes that there is.

If there is an operational intelligence, then it will notice that the runabout came from our ship, that the runabout had *traveled* to our ship from the *Sove*, and that both the *Sove* and the *Veilig* now have crews.

All of that could lead something or someone to attack us directly, and we need to be ready for it.

If that does happen, I will bring in Diaz. She will help us fend off whatever comes our way.

I have the wall screens on, all showing different views of the black area and the starfield-barrier. The wall screens run from left to right, in the direction the runabout will travel.

So to our left is this part of the Boneyard. The next screen shows the regular Boneyard between us and the black area. The next screen shows the beginning of the black area, and so on, all the way to the edge of the starfield-barrier, which is all our sensors can show.

At Mikk's suggestion, though, we have the wall screens behind us on as well. One shows the path leading out of the Boneyard, and the other has live feeds from our external cameras outside the Boneyard itself.

In addition to those screens, small screens encircle me. I have them just below my sightline, so I don't have to move my head to see what's going on with the larger screens.

"Okay," I say, feeling oddly nervous. "I'm going to send the runabout to the starfield-barrier."

It feels portentous, like this is one of those moments that will change all of our lives. I've felt like this before when I've started a dive, usually because of the danger of the dive. But I'm usually happier. I have my suit on, and I can't wait until I'm floating between my ship and whatever I'm exploring, held in place only by a tether and my own abilities.

This time, I'm standing on a bridge, surrounded by screens and very nervous people. This kind of exploration doesn't give me the gids. It just makes me uncomfortable.

I'm the one who activates all of the runabout's systems, and I'm the one who raises the bay doors here on the *Veilig*. I split my screens several ways so that I'm viewing both the runabout's interior and its exterior. It's a weird dichotomy—the runabout's control panel and what the runabout sees, and then what's actually happening inside the bay.

One screen shows the navigation panel lighting up as the autopilot engages. Another screen shows the route programmed into the autopilot. A third shows the interior of the bay as the doors lift, revealing the Boneyard behind, the curious blue color that it has that isn't quite the color of space, the ships that are hanging nearby, ships we haven't yet explored.

A fourth screen—the one directly in front of me—shows me what I would see if I were piloting the runabout. That screen is split between the actual view through those weird windows and all of the telemetry that shows up on the instrumentation.

Since the program has now been activated, I don't want to change anything on the instrumentation, so I watch the windows as if I'm on the runabout as it leaves the bay.

The runabout rises upwards, then moves ever so slowly to the bay doors. The view of the outside ships comes closer and the lighting changes through those windows, growing darker but still having a glow that seems to come from the Boneyard itself.

And then, the runabout launches into the Boneyard.

I have to thread my fingers together. Watching someone else—some-*thing* else—pilot the runabout makes my hands twitch. No matter how good the program or how good the other pilot, I always want to be hands-on.

This program makes the runabout move just a hair too quickly for me. The distance between its sides and the ships it passes is too small. More than once, I think that the runabout is going to slam into one of the static ships, only to have the runabout move slightly to the left or right as it heads forward.

I consider shutting down the pilot screen, since it's adding to my feeling of nervousness, but instead, I move the screen downward, so that it's no longer in my line of sight.

What is in my line of sight now are the wall screens. I turn my head slightly so that I can see the Boneyard proper. The runabout is moving through it like a ball on a field of boulders, avoiding the most important obstacles and nearly hitting others.

Somehow, it finds its way forward, and then it begins to speed up.

I want to grab Mikk's hand, call his attention to the change, but I know he already sees that. We programmed that change in speed into the runabout.

He and I had long debates about speed as we started into this. At first, we thought maybe it would be best to have the runabout travel at the same speed as the Fleet probes had, but then we decided against it—both of us for different reasons.

The reason I decided against it was this: If we had a runabout (or some other ship) with a crew go into that starfield-barrier, we would travel faster than any probe would. Even though the point of this is to replicate much of what the Fleet probes (and the non-Fleet probes) have done, I can't ignore the fact that my ultimate goal is a mission with a crew—with me—on board.

Mikk decided against going at the probe speed for a different reason. He believes that the overarching intelligence of the Boneyard would notice a ship of size going that slowly more than it would notice a ship traveling at normal speed.

He's probably right, and for that, it's a much more valid reason than mine. So I stopped saying anything about mine, and let him feel like he had prevailed.

He's been feeling so out of control on this mission, and just a little worthless. He's been feeling that way since the first probe exploded. I'm convinced that's why he has been butting heads with Denby. Denby is the new guy, and not one of the Six, so he's not "special," in any way. He's safe for Mikk to argue with.

Mikk is standing stiffly beside me now, his face a mask of calm. He's clearly not calm, because his fists are clenched as he watches the runabout move forward.

He's watching on the big screen, just like I am, his breathing ever so slightly ragged. He wants this to work, but I'm not sure he knows what "to work" means any more than I do.

Orlando is monitoring the telemetry and not watching the runabout move at all. I don't turn around to see what the other five team members are doing. I just let them do their jobs, since it's too late to change anything.

The runabout speeds up as it reaches the edge of the blackness, and my breath catches. I want the runabout to travel smoothly, but I've worried about this part more than I can say.

What we've seen on the sensors differs from Fleet sensors to non-Fleet sensors, and I worry that there are other things in that blackness, things that neither set of sensors has picked up.

We tried to account for that by using a setting in the autopilot that gives the runabout itself the ability to maneuver away from a new obstacle in its path. We hoped—I hope—that the added maneuverability will be enough.

But last night, as I faded in and out of a restless sleep, I had half-waking nightmares about the runabout hitting something we haven't seen inside that black area, and the resulting explosion triggers explosions all over the Boneyard.

The nightmare haunts me now, as I watch the runabout zig its way into the blackness. One of Orlando's screens shows a rendering of all of the weapons/mines/smudges that we've found. They're all marked the way that they were when he initially showed them to us—with flames and orange imagery and other markings for the various types of weapons that we've figured out so far. He has superimposed that rendering over a map that shows the runabout's trajectory in real time.

So that what looks like zigging and zagging for no apparent reason when looked at without the rendering becomes logical twists and turns when we see what the runabout is avoiding.

It's avoiding a lot. That area between the actual Boneyard and the starfield-barrier is strewn with hazards. So far, the runabout has avoided all of them, and none of its twists and turns seem illogical or created by obstacles we can't see.

Mikk is watching various different sets of telemetry. He hasn't looked over at Orlando's rendering since the runabout started to go in.

Roderick is keeping an eye on the energy levels around the runabout, hoping—I think—to see any weapon powering up, as if something is going to fire on it.

I'm trying to take it all in, but mostly I look between Orlando's rendering and the video coming from the runabout itself.

Since the runabout has crossed into that weapons-strewn dark area, the information it's sending us has slowed down, as if something is blocking (or trying to block) the communication. The video slows and glitches now. Sometimes it freezes on a single image, and I have to glance at Orlando's rendering to see if something else is causing that freeze.

I can, I suppose, look up at the actual visuals or the map that we're running on one of the larger screens or try to figure out the telemetry that Mikk is monitoring.

I can also ask the rest of the team what they're seeing, but I rather like the quiet. It feels appropriate somehow.

All except for the pounding of my own heart. I've been on edge for days now, and it has reached its culmination now. I want this trip with the runabout to work, and I want to keep moving forward with this mission. I want it all to happen at once.

Then I smile at myself. Rapid heartbeat. Impatience. Shallow breathing. The gids have finally shown up.

I let out a small, relieved laugh. Mikk glances at me, and raises his eyebrows in surprise.

I shake my head ever so slightly. I don't want to explain my reaction. He continues to study me for a moment, clearly confused, and then looks back at the telemetry scrolling before him.

The visuals coming from the runabout show the starfield-barrier as an unchanging star field, the same way that the visuals from the first Fleet probe appeared. Even though we know that the runabout is slowly getting closer to the edge of that starfield-barrier, the runabout visuals are remaining static.

Except for a few smudges to the sides of the runabout. Those smudges look like dark angry clouds that the runabout is weaving its way through.

On Orlando's rendering, the smudges are larger than other smudges, and behind a few of them hover those flaming weapons or mines or whatever they are.

The runabout avoids all of that, though, traveling forward at a clip that I find a bit excessive, even though I programmed the speed into the autopilot. Maybe traveling at this speed was the wrong thing to do after all.

The runabout doesn't slow as it approaches the starfield-barrier. The make-believe starscape before it glints a little on the visuals. Not like stars glint when seen through atmosphere, but the way an illusion becomes clear as you get close to it.

I think I can see the actual barrier through the make-believe one, but I'm not sure if that's because I know what's there.

My heart rate has increased threefold, and I have to remind myself to breathe. I'm feeling lightheaded. If I were on a dive—if I were on this dive—in my suit and being monitored from the ship, a member of my team would be telling me to calm down or cut the dive short.

I am not cutting this trip short because I'm nervous. I should calm down, though, because a tense and lightheaded leader is not what this team needs at the moment.

I swallow hard, then breathe deeply. The breath is loud enough to attract Orlando's attention. He looks at me and smiles.

He's monitored enough of my dives to know what's going on with me at the moment. His knowing expression is exactly what I need right now, more than the deep breaths, more than the admonition to be calm, more than forcing myself to focus on what's before me.

I have a good team. We have a good plan. We're going to learn something.

The runabout veers to one side, slightly off the trajectory we set up for it.

I scan the rendering for whatever caused the runabout to veer, but I don't see anything. I'm not going to scan the telemetry, because I want to watch what's actually going on, not what has happened even moments in the past.

"Anyone see what caused the runabout to change course ever so slightly?" I ask, hoping one of my team has done the work I decided not to do.

"More smudges," Denby says.

"More smudges?" I say. "More smudges than usual? Or than...what?"

"Than we've seen before." He sounds preoccupied, maybe even a bit annoyed at my question. His annoyance doesn't bother me at all. I'd rather have him deeply involved in his work than easily distracted.

The runabout is still moving forward, and it has returned to the planned path. It's not that far from the opening in the starfield-barrier, although, according to the visuals the runabout is sending back, that opening isn't visible at all.

The muscles in my back have grown tense. *I'm* even more tense than I was. Mikk stands beside me, entire body stiff. Orlando is leaning forward as if he can grab the runabout and force it through that opening in the barrier.

The visuals freeze at that moment. Of course. I should have planned for it. We knew there was interference in that area long ago, and I should have been emotionally braced for it. I wasn't, though. I'm more than slightly disappointed that I can't see anything live.

I pull up the screen that I had lowered because it showed the information coming from the runabout, as if I were piloting the runabout. That information has frozen as well.

"Is something trying to reprogram it?" I ask. I'm not sure if I'm directing the question to Tamaz or Denby or Mikk.

No one answers me, probably because none of us have the answers.

The runabout heads into that break in the starfield-barrier, the place where the smudges dragged the non-Fleet probe, and the spot where—a few seconds later—both Fleet probes had changed direction before heading out of the Boneyard.

At that thought, I bring up the cameras from the buoys outside the Boneyard and have their visuals appear on yet another screen, which I move out of my direct line of sight.

I know I'm being conflicted here. I don't want to acknowledge that the runabout will probably head outside the Boneyard in the next few hours, but at the same time, I want to be prepared for it.

I stare at the little dot on the map before us, and on the blurry images that we've already gotten, the ones that have frozen. I glance at the telemetry readings that Mikk is following, then look away.

The telemetry has stopped.

"Roderick," I say, "are you still getting a download from the device on that runabout?"

"Some," he says. "I can't upload any images, though."

"How about telemetry?" I ask.

"Nothing worthwhile," he says.

I almost tell him that I'll be the judge of that, but that sounds more like a Coop statement than a me statement. I'm not that big an expert on things like telemetry, not in real time.

I look at the exterior cameras we have trained on the starfield-barrier. Only a few, just like the other times, but they've proven useful in the past.

And they're useful now, because what I see makes me frown.

The runabout hasn't gone inside the starfield-barrier. It has stopped just outside the barrier.

"Are those images accurate?" I ask, waving my hand at the images from the exterior cameras near the barrier. Those images are on the center screen directly in front of me.

"Which...?" Mikk starts, then looks up, sees my waving hand, and frowns. "What the hell?"

He bends down, starts working on two of his screens, and doesn't say any more.

"Is the runabout inside that barrier or not?" I ask, waiting for someone to answer me. Anyone, really.

"From what I can tell," Roderick says, "it's not."

"No," Denby says, sounding more confident. "It's not inside."

"It's not inside," Mikk says, with some surprise in his voice. "I can't figure out what stopped it, though."

I'm torn between trying to sift through the telemetry and staring at the image before me. Only the image, that barely visible runabout against the starfield-barrier, isn't moving or changing.

I glance at the other images, the ones that the runabout sent back—and those are completely frozen. And the ones from the cockpit of the runabout have vanished, leaving a dark gray blankness on the screen.

My stomach clenches, and the hair prickles on the back of my neck. I don't like this. I expected trouble, but I didn't expect anything to be significantly different.

This is significantly different.

Then the runabout moves forward—or is it a lateral movement? I wish I could zoom in using those exterior cameras. I can't tell exactly what direction the runabout is moving, only that it is.

Then it turns a golden yellow, followed by a bright orange, and then a dark red. It seems to expand.

"Oh, no." Mikk's tone mirrors the one in my head.

"It can't explode there," Denby says. "It's too close to the other weapons."

"And the barrier." That's from Diaz. She has come down the aisle and is standing near me, looking at everything.

I'm not sure how they know it's close to anything, because we're not getting enough information.

"Pull as much from that device as you can," I say to Roderick.

"Already am," he says, "but it's not worthwhile. I'm getting a heat error."

"Heat error?" Nyssa, from the back. She sounds terrified.

"The device has overheated." Diaz's tone is dry, and a bit dismissive. "I wouldn't expect anything more to come from it."

The runabout expands and expands some more, as if the very interior is growing. What we're probably seeing are the effects of internal explosions, being contained by the runabout's shield. It hasn't grown, but the materials it's made of are shooting outward, being caught and held into place by the shields.

Which will cease to work shortly.

I'm holding my breath. I make myself breathe in, and the lightheadedness fades, just a little. I put my fingertips on the control panel before me, just to give me a bit of grounding.

A number of my smaller screens are grayed out as well. But there's movement on a couple of them, although none of those have a direct line of sight to the runabout. I'll deal with whatever information they have later.

Instead, I stare at the runabout, expanding, changing colors, growing darker and darker. I expected this—outside of the Boneyard, not inside. And not so close to the starfield-barrier.

Then the runabout turns a whitish gray and vanishes from the exterior cameras.

I let out another breath—apparently I'd been holding that one too—and run a shaking hand over my forehead. Well, had the damn runabout had a crew, that crew would've been struggling against equipment that was dying, against an overheated interior, against explosions, and ultimately, they would have died.

Horribly.

I can almost picture it. I know what it would have felt like to be in there—

Movement just below my sightlines distracts me. I look down and see...

I squint, not sure what caught my attention. My mind refuses to organize the information into something I can believe. I bring the screen up directly, that prickling on the back of my neck growing.

The images I'm seeing are coming from the buoys outside of the Boneyard, the ones I set up earlier to monitor the runabout when it got sent *outside* the Boneyard to explode.

The images assemble themselves into something comprehensible, something I don't want to acknowledge.

I'm seeing a ship heading toward those buoys. Not a runabout, and not coming from the Boneyard.

I blink hard. The ship looks big, but I know that sometimes perspectives get screwed up when looking through exterior cameras.

Maybe what I'm seeing *is* the runabout. Maybe some kind of weaponized *anacapa* drive moved the runabout outside of the Boneyard.

I squint even more at that ship. It doesn't have the blocky shape of a runabout. It looks bigger, much, much bigger.

I glance at the wall screens to see if I can get different information. No matter what I'm looking at, I don't see the runabout. I don't even see runabout residue.

"It looks like they're cleaning it up," Tamaz says.

His words barely register. I'm not sure what he's talking about.

"Who are *they?*" Diaz asks because she's an engineer. Engineers are such precise people.

"The smudges," Tamaz says. "They're cleaning up the debris from the runabout."

Just like we saw outside the Boneyard with the probes. No piece too small to collect.

"Did that explosion damage the barrier?" Orlando asks.

"I can't tell from here," Mikk says. "I can't see anything."

None of them are looking at the buoys. My entire team is looking at the place where the runabout had been. I look too. It really is gone, and, as Tamaz says, the smudges seem to have spread out along the edge of the barrier. Maybe they are cleaning up.

I'm not sure, though. That might simply be an interpretation—and not a correct one.

But, at least, the explosion—or rather, destruction—of the runabout did not cause any other explosions inside that starfield-barrier.

Yet, anyway.

One problem dodged.

So far.

But I seem to be the only person who has noticed what's going on outside of the Boneyard.

"Hey, everyone," I say. My voice sounds as shaky as I feel. "I think we have a different problem."

I call up the image from my small screen onto one of the gray wall screens.

I'm still expecting to see a version of the runabout there, but with the image enlarged, it's clear that the ship I'm looking at is much, much, much too big to be a runabout.

I hadn't realized that I'd also been hoping that if the ship wasn't a runabout, then it was a pirate ship, maybe even the lead vessel of a group of pirate ships, like the ones we saw back when we first discovered the Boneyard.

But this…

"Is that what I think it is?" The voice belongs to Denby, and it's strangled and shaking and very, very small.

"I don't know," Diaz answers him, her tone crisp, and businesslike. Not at all a voice I've ever heard from her before. "What do you think it is?"

"A DV-Class ship," Denby says. He's come to that conclusion a lot quicker than I have. I'm still having trouble accepting what I'm seeing.

"That ship doesn't look like any of ours." That's Mikk, oblivious to their emotions. Or maybe he doesn't care about them.

Because he's right. It doesn't look like any DV-Class ship I've seen, inside the Boneyard or out. Which is probably why I've been having trouble accepting what I'm seeing.

The ship does have the same basic shape, rather like a bird in flight, but its edges aren't as sharp. They're a lot more fluid. And it's not one color—not black like the DV-Class vessels here. Its color shifts and mutates along its surface, rather like a series of multicolored lights play across a white surface. The base color is—or seems to be—white, but then it becomes a pale pink, then a reddish brown, and then black, and then a bluish black, and then a light blue, and then a whitish blue, and then gray—

The color shifts are mesmerizing, and I'm not sure they're real. Is any of this real? Is that a phantom vessel, just like we've seen phantom images from the Boneyard?

I call up my own console. I don't even ask the others what they're looking at. I'm trying to get direct readings from the buoys—or as direct as we can get.

It wouldn't surprise me that the Fleet would respond to an incursion like ours by using more tricks. Something that would appear to be a ship that's coming to...what? Attack? A single ship, with all of this in the Boneyard? That makes no sense.

And then, as I have that thought, two more ships slide up to the first ship. One of the two is an SC-class vessel, which looks like the *Veilig* with a few exterior modifications—the roundish shape, the black exterior, the hint of power in all of its movements.

The other vessel is similar to the lead vessel. A DV-class configuration, more or less, but not a DV-class ship as we know it. The color shifts on that ship as well.

Are these ships even Fleet? Or are they something else?

I sort through the telemetry, looking for energy readings and imagery and heat signatures, and life signs, and I'm finding all of that. And as I do, I realize that I'm looking through our *non-Fleet* technology at Fleet (or Fleet-like) ships.

And most of the ghosts we've seen in our sensors have been on Fleet equipment, not on our non-Fleet equipment.

"What the hell, Boss?" Mikk asks me.

I raise my head to tell him that these ships are real when two more ships join the others.

Five ships, one of the new ones a recognizable DV-Class vessel. The others a variation on the same. And that SC-Class, too. All of them hovering outside of the Boneyard, near where we *entered* the Boneyard the very first time, and showing up right after the runabout exploded.

My heart is pounding. I'm not sure what any of this means—not intellectually, anyway. My entire limbic system seems to know, though. It's in fight-or-flight mode.

Although the explosion of the runabout might have caused that response.

This reaction is worse than the gids. I'd never let anyone dive if they were experiencing what I'm experiencing right now. It's close to panic. I'd be forcing whoever it was to come back along the line, return to the ship.

Even if it were me. I'd like to think I'd make myself do that too.

Tricks, I remind myself. *I need to use beginner tricks.*

I used to panic way back when I began diving. Every new diver does. Especially when she travels alone into unknown territory, with no backup, like I used to do when I started out. Yes, it was stupid, and I stopped doing it—

After I panicked like I am right now.

I thread my fingers together and force the pads into the bones in the back of my hand, forcing pain, feeling it, letting it remind me of where I am and what I'm doing.

I expected some kind of reaction from the Boneyard itself. I wouldn't even have been surprised if we got fired upon *inside* the Boneyard. But I expected it to be like whatever hit the runabout—sudden and from a hard-to-see source.

I did not expect ships. In particular, I did not expect ships that were coming from *outside* the Boneyard.

Has it notified someone? The Fleet, maybe?

I exhale slowly. Very slowly. Then make myself inhale. The very act of breathing calms me.

Mikk watches that, his lips pressed together. The *what the hell* must've been involuntary.

"I did not expect this," I say honestly.

"Me, either," he says softly. He spoke mostly for me. I think we were both ready for an attack from within.

This one, though, this feels even more menacing. I have no idea how many ships will come after us. I'm not even sure if they *are* coming after us. But it's logical, given what we've just done. We sent probes and a small ship into that starfield-barrier where they have warships. Or rather, where *someone* has warships.

And now, ships—that look like Fleet vessels—have arrived at the Boneyard.

"Maybe they're going to drop off a ship?" Nyssa says, and I can hear it in her voice. That bit of hope, that wish that things aren't quite what we think they are.

"That's not how they'd drop off a ship," Mikk says with authority he doesn't really have. We don't know, exactly, how the Fleet puts ships in the Boneyard.

We do know that, in this area of the Boneyard, a new ship hasn't arrived in centuries.

"If things are the way they used to be," Denby says slowly, "that's a scout patrol."

"A what?" Roderick asks.

"A group of ships the Fleet sends to investigate something that has gone wrong," Denby says.

I turn just enough to look at Diaz. She shrugs, then bites her lower lip.

"Zaria?" I ask, despite her obvious reluctance to speak.

"I don't know," she says. "We can't assume we know—."

She just stops speaking, mouth open. I turn back, see that there are no images at all on the screen. There is nothing, as if the buoys are no longer receiving telemetry.

"What the hell?" I ask.

"They destroyed the buoys," Orlando says. His gaze meets mine. His eyes are wide, his skin paler than I've ever seen it.

Now, he's panicked. They all are.

But a calm settles over me, just like it does when something goes wrong on a dive.

We're not going to be able to see anything. We have no idea what they're doing now, or what they plan to do. We won't even know how many of them there are.

Or what they want.

So we have to assume that they want us.

THE FLEET
TWO DAYS EARLIER

36

A SHIP OF SCHOLARS PROVED A LOT MORE USEFUL than Cohn expected. They cracked the codes into the control towers of the Scrapheap long before the researchers on the other ships could even get organized.

Jicha had informed her of the breakthrough in the middle of the night, expecting her to be asleep. But Cohn wasn't sleeping much—just enough to keep herself alert. She had too much work to do, and too much to organize to sleep for the requisite eight hours straight. Four hours plus several short naps was about all she could handle at the moment.

Which meant that she was able to pay an unannounced visit to the *Tudósok* not long after Jicha contacted her.

The *Tudósok* was unlike any DV-class vessel Cohn had ever encountered. Its walls were not plain black or gray or even a layered white. They were covered with artwork, most of it etched into the nanobits.

Even the interior ship bay doors had a mural that formed as they slid closed. She hadn't noticed it when she landed the single ship inside the *Tudósok,* but she had noticed it when she exited. The mural was a painting of four smiling young people, bent over paper, holding some kind of fancy pen, as they were surrounded by floating words and musical notes. The mural caught Cohn's attention for a moment, distracting her, before she shook herself and headed away from the exit doors.

The bay itself had multicolored catwalks and a bright green floor with glowing white parking lanes, also something she had never seen before. The air mixture had a faint lemon scent, which she found soothing even as she found it odd.

She also found it odd that no one contacted her after her ship slid into the bay. She expected some kind of automated greeting or a warning from the crew or even someone from security showing up as she disembarked, but she saw none of that.

She had never been on a DV-class vessel that seemed so informal and so lackadaisical at the same time.

Apparently, she thought as she made her way across a bright turquoise catwalk that curled around several small ships, it would be up to her to contact Jicha. The silence unnerved her. She had figured, from her perusal of his files as well as the conversations she'd had with the vice admiral, that Jicha was a good captain.

Maybe he wasn't. Maybe lapses like this were what had put him on a scholar ship in the first place.

It took her nearly ten minutes longer than it should have to reach the entrance into the ship proper. The catwalks were pretty and quite arty, but they prevented her from traveling along the quickest point from one part of the bay to another. Or maybe she had missed a shorter path, distracted as she was by the colors and the found art, like the tiny violets decorating the handrails overlooking a group of runabouts.

Usually she appreciated attention to detail, but this seemed like a waste of time to her, the kind of detail that distracted rather than made life on a starship easier.

To her surprise, the exit door was a bright orange, with no found artwork at all. Except a silver filigree doorknob that receded when she waved her hand across the sensor, forcing the door to open.

The door slid back, revealing a corridor done in shades of ivory and gold, with words calligraphed in black—some kind of nonsense about finding comfort in the search for knowledge.

She recognized the quote from her school days. It was something one of her professors had said repeatedly, and had ended up annoying her more than comforting her. But apparently, someone who designed or decorated this ship had approved.

"Checking up on me, Captain?"

The deep voice startled her, but fortunately for her own self-esteem, she didn't jump. Instead, she turned slowly to her right, which was where the voice had come from.

Jicha leaned against the wall, arms crossed, one foot braced against some scrollwork running a few inches above the floor. The corridor's gold carpet had matching scrollwork along its edges, making Cohn just a bit seasick.

Jicha was taller than she remembered, and thin in an unhealthy way. His hair was too long for regulation, and he wasn't wearing anything close to a uniform, not that it mattered. It was the middle of the night. His gold shirt and ivory pants looked like they were chosen to go with the corridor's décor, rather than something he wore often.

Although the shirt was wrinkled, almost as if he'd been wearing it for more than a day.

When he saw her scrutiny, he smiled. "Did you think no one noticed your arrival?"

"It had crossed my mind," she said.

His smile turned a little bitter. "I run a tight ship, Captain. I just run it differently than you do."

She looked at the decor. "Clearly."

He pushed off the wall with his back foot. "You want to see the information from the control towers."

"I do," she said. "But you could have sent that. What I really want to know is how to talk with them."

He walked slightly ahead of her down the corridor. "I don't think you need to contact them. What do you want to know? I'm sure we already have the data here."

"It's not data I'm after," she said.

He stopped, and turned. He didn't quite tower over her. His back was bent at an odd angle, as if he'd never completely healed from the injuries he'd taken as a lieutenant on the *Izlovchi.*

"What are you going to do?" he asked.

"I'm going to get those thieves," she said. "But first I need to know what this Scrapheap is capable of."

He frowned before turning around again. He walked quickly down the corridor. He hadn't asked where they were going; she assumed he was taking her somewhere where they could study the control towers inside the Scrapheap.

"That should be in the data," he said.

"It is." This conversation would have irritated Vinters and a few others on her team. It didn't bother her. Jicha was used to being in charge. She'd run into that with every single captain on this journey.

She had to respect their way of doing things, and slowly train them into respecting hers.

"If you know…" he said, letting the rest of the thought go unsaid.

"I know what the Scrapheap's specs say." Her voice remained level. She didn't want him to think she was overexplaining, but really, he should have thought of this. "But, after this long period of time, I have no idea what the Scrapheap can actually do."

He nodded once, an acknowledgement rather than an agreement. "Here I thought you were going for the Ready Vessels," he said, "until I realized we don't have clearance."

"We have clearance," Cohn said. That was the first time she had told anyone. But the other captains needed to know in case something happened to her.

She found it amusing that the first captain she confided in was the one the other captains trusted the least.

"From the vice admiral?" he asked as he rounded a corner. "Why didn't you tell us?"

That was the correct question, as well. She followed him down the new corridor. It dead ended into two elevators. Their doors were painted gold and covered with calligraphed words that reassembled themselves into a personalized greeting as Jicha approached.

He ignored the greeting. She stared at it, because it included her. She knew that the ships constantly scanned the interiors. She just wasn't usually reminded of the scanning so blatantly.

"I didn't tell you about the clearance," she said, "because I wasn't sure when or how we would need it."

The elevator door on the left slid open. Fortunately the interior was little more than a box. All of this decoration was beginning to annoy her, and it was nice to go somewhere without it.

"I'd been asking the vice admiral for clearance from the moment I knew the *Tudósok* was joining this mission." He crossed his arms and leaned against the wall, just like he had done in the corridor. Maybe that lean wasn't because he was pretending to be relaxed. Maybe he needed to stand that way to ease the pressure on his back.

"You should have gone through me," Cohn said. "I secured all the permissions we needed as well as codes and identification procedures that go back centuries. Just in case we couldn't easily communicate with the Scrapheap."

He looked at her sideways. The look was an assessment or, rather, a reassessment. She had clearly gone up in his estimation.

She didn't want to know how far down she had been.

He gave her that curt little nod again, which was much better than a *well done*. A *well done* could have been taken as patronizing. This was not.

The elevator door opened to reveal another corridor, this one decorated in light greens and golds. Instead of scrollwork, calligraphy ran at eye level.

She didn't bother to read it. She wanted to remain focused. The strange décor was distracting enough.

Jicha opened a door that she hadn't even seen, off to her left, and went inside. She followed.

The room was small and filled with all different kinds of engineering tech, as well as floating screens that seemed to beg for attention. There was only one chair—or there had been, until Jicha called up another, and it rose out of the floor.

This must have been his workspace. It was cluttered and stuffy and felt personal somehow.

One of the things she had taken to be a floating screen was actually a small three-dimensional representation of the Scrapheap. Its center was black, because that was where the Ready Vessels were stored. The three control towers formed a triangle around it.

The other ships stored in the Scrapheap showed up as dots of various sizes. She recognized the program Jicha had used for the representation. If she touched any part of it, she would be able to see that section in depth.

Except, most likely, the Ready Vessels themselves.

"Sit," he said, sweeping his hand at the new chair. "What do you want to access?"

He wasn't going to let her access any of it, not without his help. And that probably made more sense than figuring it out on her own.

She didn't sit, not yet. She was still watching the Scrapheap model as it floated by.

"The thieves have been stealing DV-Class vessels for months now," she said. "They've been working here."

She touched the model near one of the control towers. As she suspected, that section of the model grew larger, forming its own model.

Now, she could see the vessels inside clearly, and, glowing gold, a DV-class ship which also had a star placed on its icon.

"You've already found their ship," she said, pleased by what she saw.

"Technically, it's our ship," he said.

"They took it away, and brought it back," she said.

"Without much of a crew." He sat down on the stool that had been there all along. It was tilted at an angle that seemed to make his back straighter. "They're exploring other ships, probably to take them out of the Scrapheap."

"Ever since those early visits, they've been using our ships to travel back and forth. One showed up not long ago," she said.

He nodded, and this time, it wasn't a quick acknowledgement. It was to get her to move along. He had the same information.

Although she wasn't sure if he did.

"And now, they're exploring the area around the Ready Vessels," she said.

"You think they know the vessels are in there." It was a statement not a question.

"Actually, I don't know what they know." She studied that little area of the Scrapheap, much as she had done in her own quarters, earlier. "We need clearance to get to those vessels. I can guarantee you that they don't have the clearance."

He rocked the stool back so he could look up at her. He was twisted at an odd angle that had to be uncomfortable. She took pity on him, and sat down.

He rubbed the back of his neck as he said, "We could just let them continue probing the area around the Ready Vessels until they send in something manned. They won't come back after that."

She nodded. "I thought of that. But I want to know who these people are, don't you?"

His smile was as twisted as his back. "Not really," he said. "I'm much more interested in delving into the records on board all of those ships. Confrontation is not my style."

She laughed. "Confrontation is absolutely your style."

His twisted smile grew wider. "Point taken. I meant I'd rather be finding information than finding thieves."

"And yet here we are," she said. "We found thieves. Now I want to find out who they are and where they're from."

"So letting them destroy themselves is not an option."

"That's right," she said. Then she twisted her stool so that she faced him instead of the three-dimensional rendering. "They're using Fleet vessels and Fleet equipment."

"Albeit old," he said.

"Albeit old," she said. "But the Scrapheap is old. If we had encountered them in space in one of our ships, we would have had a variety of tools for pulling information from them."

He whistled ever so slightly. He clearly hadn't thought of that. He hadn't been on a working mission, one that didn't require scholarship, for a very long time.

"But with an old ship, you don't know if we have that option," he said.

"We do," Cohn said. "We have the option, if we can get close to them."

Then she expanded the model of the Scrapheap—the part that the thieves were working.

"But getting our ships in there easily isn't possible," she said.

"They've been bringing their ships in and out," he said.

"Near where they found the ship," she said. "There's a gap. We could try for the gap, I suppose. But then we go in with only one ship. I want to know if we can use the Scrapheap itself to pull information."

Jicha pulled one of the floating screens closer to him. "Well," he said with half a grin. "Let's see what we can find."

She grabbed one of the floating screens, and went directly to the operating system for the Scrapheap control tower nearest the thieves.

The thing she had to remember was that she had a lot of options. She could use the tools in the Scrapheap, if there were any. She could have all five ships use their *anacapa* drives to more or less surround the thieves. She could activate some of the Ready Vessels and bring them into the Scrapheap itself.

She liked that final option the least, because it revealed the presence of the Ready Vessels.

But she wasn't going to let that stop her. Judging from the way the thieves kept probing the area around the Ready Vessels, the thieves already knew about the Ready Vessels. Abandoning a plan just to hide the Ready Vessels wasn't a good idea.

She just needed the best plan. One that would let her know who the thieves were, and one that stopped them.

For good.

THE BONEYARD
NOW

37

FOR THE FIRST TIME IN MY MEMORY, my team freezes. They're not used to being under attack—and that's what we are. Our buoys are destroyed. I have to assume that the owners of those ships know that we're inside the Boneyard.

I have to assume they're coming for us.

Mikk, still standing beside me, is looking from the screens that show the edge of the starfield-barrier where the runabout had been, back to the dark screens that had been showing the information from the buoys.

Orlando has toggled backwards, and is staring at the images of the ships that were outside the Boneyard. Tamaz has come down the aisle until he's standing just behind Orlando, so he can see the same information. Roderick hasn't moved either, and he seems as shocked by this as Mikk is.

I can't see Nyssa. I assume she hasn't moved from the back of the bridge. Diaz has walked down so she's beside me, and she's shaking, as if she can barely hold her emotions inside.

Denby is the only one doing anything. I can hear his breath whistle through his teeth as his hands move across the screens in front of him. I don't know what he's doing, but he seems to have a plan.

Even he looks nervous, though.

I'm not. But I am concerned. I pull up one of my unused screens and immediately contact the *Sove*.

Salvador Ahidjo is the one who responds, using audio only. And I didn't expect to hear him. I worry that the *Sove* is mostly empty.

"Is everyone on board the *Sove*?" I ask.

"We're setting up for another dive," he said. His deep voice sounds perplexed and reassuring at the same time. "Who do you need? I thought Diaz is with you."

"She is," I say. "I need everyone to stay on board the *Sove*. Relay that information right now."

"Okay." He sounds doubtful, and he's silent for a moment, probably as he's letting everyone on the *Sove* know that their mission is called off.

I monitor them and the edge of the Boneyard, and the starfield-barrier, and the entire area around us. The area feels charged, but that's probably just me, since I'm one of the few people active on the bridge of the *Veilig*.

Diaz puts her hand on my arm. "I need to get over there," she says. "They need me now."

"There's no time," I say.

Diaz shakes her head a little. I can't tell if she's disagreeing with me or with the situation. She glances at the screens, her gaze stopping on the one that shows this section of the Boneyard.

She's probably looking at the *Sove* which, in Boneyard terms, is right beside us.

Then Ahidjo clicks back in.

"What's going on, Boss?" he asks. And I can't tell if he's asking that because he wants to know before he gives the others anymore orders or if he's truly curious.

Not that it matters. He has to act, and he has to act fast.

"We've been found," I say. "The *Sove* needs to get out of here. Now."

"Found by whom?" he asks.

Well, that is the question, isn't it? We're assuming we've been found by the Fleet, but we've seen no evidence that the Fleet still exists.

"I have no idea who found us," I say, "but they have five very large ships and they just took out our buoys. I need the *Sove* to get back to Lost Souls immediately."

"And bring help back?" he asks.

I silently curse myself. I should have prepped everyone for this contingency and I haven't. Even though I believed that there could be an overarching intelligence in the Boneyard, I figured if that intelligence attacked us, I thought we could just leave the Boneyard and go outside of it, like we had when the Boneyard attacked us before.

I never thought we would have to leave the vicinity. But that's our best option right now.

"No, don't send help," I say. "We'll meet you at Lost Souls. Get out of here. Now."

Beside me, Diaz has a screen monitoring the *Sove*. She's double-checking what Ahidjo is telling us. And bless her for that, because I hadn't thought of it. He might have thought everyone was on the *Sove*, and someone might have been doing some preliminary work for a dive, someone he didn't know about.

"They're good to go," she says to me, and she sounds sad. They are more her crew than mine.

"Salvador," I say, "get out of here."

"Yes, Boss. Sorry. I'm relaying the information—"

"I don't give a damn about procedure. I want the *anacapa* drive activated and I want you gone. *Now.*" I can't be more forceful than that.

I have no idea what I'll do if they refuse to follow my orders. Get Diaz to command them? Fire on them myself? I can't force them to leave.

That's the one big problem with my method of running ships. When things get truly difficult, my orders have no teeth.

"They're charging up the *anacapa*," Diaz says. Her voice wobbles just a bit. The increase in *anacapa* energy inside the Boneyard makes all of us nervous.

"I'm not seeing any activity near the entrance to the Boneyard," Orlando says.

"I'm monitoring the telemetry." Mikk seems to have gathered himself. "I'm not seeing anything either."

I don't care what they're seeing or not seeing. I don't want anyone to damage the *Sove*.

"We should be leaving too, right?" Diaz asks.

"Not just yet," I say. Even though she's right. We should leave. But we're not going to. Not until I have a sense of who is out there and what they're doing.

I want the information before I see Coop again. Because I know he'll grill me about it. Or worse, he'll want to come back here immediately.

The *Sove* waivers, and then all of its telemetry disappears.

"It's gone," Roderick says. "The *Sove* is gone."

I feel some of the tension leave my shoulders. Diaz tilts her head back, her eyes closed. Everything she had for this trip was on that ship, along with her team.

I can't tell if her reaction is relief or frustration, and I don't have time to figure it out.

"Are we getting any sense of who they are?" I ask Orlando.

"Those ships were weird-looking," he says. "If I were designing future DV-class vessels, I'd make them more different than that."

Tamaz snorted, as if he can't control a laugh. "You're not designing future vessels."

"I'm just saying they're not what I expected if they are Fleet," Orlando says.

"We have no idea who they are," Fahd says. "I mean, we would look like Fleet if we encountered someone who was familiar with them."

He has a good point. We're using Fleet vessels. Maybe someone else is as well.

"That formation is familiar," Denby says. "That's a scout formation, and that's a scout maneuver."

"We have to operate as if they are Fleet," Diaz says. "Which means, Boss, your call is the right one. We have to get the hell out of here."

"Let's prep for that." I glance at everything around me—the screens with the destroyed runabout, the starfield-barrier, the holograms, the mission that we're about to abandon.

I'm reluctant to leave, not because I want information for Coop. I want it for myself.

I want to know if we're going to be able to return.

I want to keep diving.

"Let's get our shields up," I say. "Denby, let's power up weapons just in case."

"Already done," Denby says.

Diaz swivels her head toward me. She looks shocked. Orlando is shaking his head.

I understand their concerns. We shouldn't use weapons here, not with all that wild *anacapa* energy, but we'd be fools to have the weapons powered down.

Although I'm not sure if we'd be fools to use the weapons as well.

We have no good choices, and yet I want to wait…for what, I'm not sure. Some kind of confirmation about the identities of who we're facing.

I'm half hoping they'll contact us, introduce themselves, ask us to leave, ever so politely.

If they even know we're in here.

"Boss." Mikk speaks so softly only Diaz and I seem to notice he said anything.

I look at him. He waves a hand over the screen before him. I can't quite read what it says.

"What are you seeing?" I ask.

"Some of the vessels around us," Mikk says, "they're activating."

"What?" I ask. The vessels around us are damaged, shut down, inactive.

Except that one DV-class vessel we had used as a decoy when we were working the probes. It seemed like months ago, but it was only about a week ago. That vessel was inactive, but not damaged. And it hadn't been shut down properly.

Mikk and I both noted that.

"Like the DV-class ship we still have a probe in?" I ask Mikk.

"Yeah," he says, and then curses.

I understand how he feels. We should have followed up on that, but I've been too busy with this dive, with the starfield-barrier.

"Can we get any readings from the starfield-barrier?" I ask. "Or the ships beyond it? Those warships?"

"Are you worried that they're powering up too?" Fahd asks.

Hell, yes, I'm worried about that. If we're suddenly facing an entire force of large ships, we have no hope at all.

But the real question is hope of what.

"What can the ships around us do?" Nyssa asks from the back. "They're damaged."

"Not all of them," Orlando says quietly.

The one Mikk and I had seen didn't look damaged—at least not obviously damaged.

"I'm going to see if that probe is still sending information," Mikk says. "If it has been, we've been collecting it. I can scan it and see if the ship has powered up."

It takes my mind a moment to process what he's saying. He's talking about the probe in that DV vessel we saw.

"I'm not sure that's a good idea," Tamaz says. "We don't have that kind of time."

"Won't take a lot of time," Mikk says, sounding distracted. "We should know what's going on."

I suspect I do know what's going on. It seems clear to me. There is some kind of intelligence behind this. The Boneyard had been watching us, and it had contacted someone. I'm going to assume that someone is the Fleet.

Coop will be happy, and he'll want to contact them.

"All the ships around us are powering up," Denby says. He sounds a bit breathless. "And everything from weapons to defenses are coming online."

"We have to leave, Boss," Diaz says.

She's right. We have to leave. And I'm standing in front of the captain's chair, grinning like a fool.

"Yeah," I say, and the uncertainty I'm feeling is in my voice.

"What the hell is the hesitation?" Orlando says. I'm surprised that he's the one who snapped at me, but he is.

"I want to contact them," I say.

"And say what, exactly?" Orlando asks. "Hello, we like stealing your ships?"

"If we say we're Fleet, we're not stealing," I say.

Diaz is shaking her head.

"I can try to contact them," Denby says.

"There's no one to contact," Mikk says. "There's no one on those ships."

"The ones outside the Boneyard?" Diaz asks.

"The ones inside," Mikk says. "Someone or something has automated the ships around us. Their response is going to be uniform, and it's going to come at us all at once."

So much for talking to anyone. That will have to wait.

"The *anacapa* ready?" I ask.

The ships around us actually have lights on the interior now. My screens show me a shift in position on several of the ships.

"We're ready," Diaz says.

"Weapons are powering up, Boss," Fahd says, and since he's not in charge of the *Veilig's* weapons, he means the weapons around us.

"Go," I say. "Get us out of here now."

I don't have to give the order twice. Diaz has taken the helm from Mikk while he was dealing with that probe, and he doesn't seem to mind.

She moves faster than I ever could, her fingers moving across the holographic controls at a speed that I can barely follow.

Clearly she has already inputted the coordinates that will get us to foldspace, and I'm glad she has. She's done this out of the Boneyard more than I have.

I just stand back and let her work. I'm also monitoring the telemetry from the other ships. Two right next to us, including the ship that the *Sove* was going to dive next, are completely powered up. Their weapons have been activated—and I remember what Coop told me, how the *Ivoire* was fired upon as she went into foldspace, and that's why she ended up becalmed.

My heart rate increases, and I want to tell Diaz to hurry, but I know that she's already hurrying. She's moving as fast as she can.

The *Veilig* shakes ever so slightly.

"Have we been hit?" The question comes from Nyssa. I want to correct her. A ship this large doesn't vibrate when a weapon hits its shields. A ship this large shouldn't vibrate at all—

Except when it goes into foldspace.

We move only a little forward, but we are entering that weird little pocket that opens into foldspace.

"They're firing." Denby sounds calmer than I feel.

I look at the actual screens, the ones showing the area around us, and at least a dozen ships are firing at the same time.

"Oh my god," Nyssa says, but the rest of us don't speak at all.

I don't even tell Diaz to hurry. There's no point. We're getting out of here as soon as the *Veilig* gets into foldspace, and nothing we can do will speed that up.

My screens have gone dark, just like everyone else's—except Mikk's and Diaz's navigation screen. We're crossing into foldspace now.

My hands have formed fists. The bumping that I've grown used to barely exists in this ship. It vibrates just a bit more. I hear a little bit of a hum, but nothing else. No teeth-rattling, no actual bumps.

It's the smoothest entry into foldspace that I've ever experienced.

And then the ship smooths out. There are no ships around us.

There's nothing except unfamiliar stars and silence.

"Are they behind us?" Nyssa asks, and for once, it's a valid question. Because one of those ships—one of those nearby ships—could have piggybacked into foldspace with us.

"No," Orlando says. He still sounds tense. "We're alone."

Diaz punches more coordinates into her holoscreen, and activates.

Then she reaches behind herself, groping for the armrest of the captain's chair. When her hands encounter the armrest's edge, she leans into it, as if her legs have given out.

She swallows, then looks at Denby. I've never seen her so pale. Her dark eyes have engulfed her entire face.

"Did we get hit?" she asks, and this time, she's not trying to hide the fear.

He's shaking his head. "I don't think so."

She grabs my arm. Her fingers dig into my skin. "Boss, I want to enter foldspace again. Usually, you're supposed to wait, but I don't want to."

I understand it. I have no idea what the procedure is or should be.

"Can the *anacapa* drive handle another trip so soon?" I ask her.

"The drive can," she says. "We're just usually more cautious about it."

I nod. I appreciate caution. I do. But I just saw something I hadn't seen before. Somehow those ships outside the Boneyard, or the Boneyard itself, activated ships *inside* the Boneyard. Who knows what else the Fleet (or whomever) can do?

Screw caution. Right now, we need to put as much distance between ourselves and those ships as we can.

"Let's do it," I say. "Orlando, monitor the space around us. Make sure that none of those ships has magically followed us."

"It's not magic," Denby mutters softly, but not softly enough, because Mikk glares at him.

"It might as well be," Mikk says.

"Enough," I say. "We can fight at Lost Souls. Right now, we need to get home."

THE FLEET
NOW

38

COHN STOOD WITH HER ARMS CROSSED. Everyone on the bridge was working hard, coordinating their efforts—all except Iosua who was monitoring a series of feeds that were coming from the Scrapheap. Images of the Scrapheap decorated the entire bridge. Floating holographic images reproduced much of the area before Cohn, so that it almost seemed as if the Scrapheap had moved to the bridge.

Cohn wasn't looking at the Ready Vessels or the forcefield that protected them. She was looking at a small circle of ships in nearer to this entrance, where a single SC-Class vessel remained.

The other four ships in her Task Unit had followed orders. They were now twice as far from the Scrapheap as they had been a few moments ago, and they were spread out along the edge, just in case the SC-class vessel holding the remainder of the thieves used their *anacapa* drive to exit here.

The *Geesi* monitored the entrance itself. She had moved her ship just as far away as the other ships, which was twice the Fleet-recommended distance away from a Scrapheap in turmoil.

Turmoil she was going to create.

"Got everything?" she asked Iosua.

He smiled. "Yeah," he said. "They just inputted the foldspace coordinates."

"All right," she said. She glanced at her team. Vinters had the entire bridge crew on alert. "Make sure the timing is perfect."

"It is," Vinters said. "We're powering up now."

The Scrapheap had all of the controls she had hoped it would have, and they still worked. She had tested the control tower closer to where her Task Unit had arrived, activating some of the guard ships through-out that sector of the Scrapheap.

The ships had powered up and, surprisingly, their weapons and defensively systems seemed to function just fine.

She hadn't fired any weapons because she didn't want to alert the thieves to her presence. But she really didn't need to, not even to test.

"Let's do it," she said, and tried not to smile.

She was enjoying this part a bit too much.

Twenty DV class vessels in the vicinity of the thieves' stolen SC-Class vessel powered up. From the telemetry that Cohn was monitoring, the SC-class vessel wasn't doing anything different.

Then Iosua said, "They noticed."

"Good." Cohn sounded as self-satisfied as she felt. "Activate shields on the vessels."

"Already done," Vinters said.

"The thieves have activated their *anacapa* drive," Iosua said. "It'll take a good minute for it to be ready."

"Get the weapons systems online," Cohn said to her team. "And make sure that none of those weapons has a chance of hitting that damn ship."

Even though her team knew the plan, she had learned long ago that it was good to repeat the crucial instructions. Better to insult the intelligence of her team than to have just one of them misunderstand what was coming next.

"There's no chance, Captain," Vinters said quietly.

"Good," she said. "Are we ready, Erasyl?"

"Not quite," he said. "They should have activated by now. I'm not sure what the hesitation is."

"Is their drive functioning properly?" she asked.

"It seems to be," he said, sounding a bit perplexed.

"Then we don't worry about their response," she said. "We make them do what *we* want."

"Powering up weapons," Vinters said.

"Good," Cohn said. She let her hands drop, and then she threaded her fingers together, watching the various screens in front of her.

On her personal screen, that damn SC-class vessel was outlined in red. Now, she wished she hadn't done that. She wanted the readings to show what was actually going on, rather than some kind of marker she really hadn't needed.

"We're actually going to have to fire," Vinters said, sounding surprised.

"Then fire," Cohn said.

The SC-vessel took that moment to launch itself into foldspace. The opening showed for a half second before the ship vanished entirely.

And as it did, weapons fire filled the area around where it had been. Each DV-vessel had targeted one of the others. Explosions bloomed throughout that section of the Scrapheap, ships turning red or white and shattering into a million pieces.

"What the hell?!?" The voice—predictably—belonged to Jicha. He was broadcasting to everyone. "You're destroying the entire Scrapheap."

Cohn had to check her grin in case he had activated visuals of her bridge.

"I hope not," she said. "The modeling showed that only the ships in this area would be destroyed."

But energy traveled along ropes of light that she hadn't seen before, moving from ship to ship to ship. She had been warned that explosions in the Scrapheap could trigger other reactions. Some of the models had shown it as well, but she hadn't seen anything like that before when she had destroyed Scrapheaps.

The energy expanded outward, destroying ship after ship after ship. And, if she admitted it to herself, destroying more ships than she had planned on.

Her grin faded. There was no way the entire Scrapheap would go. It was too big, and its entire middle was covered in double and triple forcefields.

Just as she had that thought, the explosions reached the edge of the first interior forcefield, bumped against it, and bounced the energy waves back into the destroyed area. For a moment, it seemed like the waves would reverberate all the way to the entrance that she guarded—which, she had to remind herself—she had planned for.

That's why the ships were as far away from the Scrapheap as they could be. She knew of ships that were nearly destroyed by the energy waves coming out of a Scrapheap. She had made certain none of the ships in her Task Unit were going to suffer because she had made this choice.

The energy wave receded, leaving a gaping hole in the pile of ships where that SC-vessel had been.

There were no more ships, and according to the readings she was getting on her own screens, no *anacapa* energy readings in that area either. Just emptiness where there had been ships and thieves and ship parts moments earlier.

She let out a silent breath, then felt the smile creep back.

"You're lucky that wasn't worse," Jicha said, still sounding stressed.

"I'm not lucky," she said, although, privately, she admitted only to herself that there had been a bit of luck involved. Those forcefields might not have held up. She had been relying on very old technology to function as if it had been built last week.

He said, "Those ships—"

"Those ships," she said calmly, "were irrelevant. There's an entire Scrapheap full of ships for you to explore. Besides, my team made sure we made backups of their networks. You'll have your information, and we won't have to wait for you to examine the Scrapheap to get all of it."

There was a chirrup as he disappeared from the comms. She grinned even wider, mentally patting herself on the back.

She had been right not to tell the other captains, right to keep this part of the plan to herself. She had saved so many arguments, had prevented a lesser decision by committee. Had, in fact, achieved everything she needed.

"So," she said to Iosua, "where are they headed?"

"Some place called Lost Souls," he said.

"And where's that?" she asked.

"Way the hell away from here," he said. "Not far from Sector Base V."

"V?" she asked.

V. She hadn't expected them to go so far back. The Fleet hadn't been in that area in thousands and thousands of years.

And if she thought of it in Fleet terms, she would say that it wasn't worth pursuing these vessels.

Except that they were stealing. They had *anacapa* drives. And she had revealed herself to them, in Fleet ships, manipulating Fleet equipment.

If they knew what the Fleet was, then they knew who had found them.

"How sophisticated is this Lost Souls?" she asked.

"I don't know," Iosua said. "I haven't combed through all of the information yet. But it seems to be a new base of some kind, and they're definitely refurbishing our ships."

"Have you figured out what for?" she asked.

"No," he said.

"Can the Task Unit destroy them?" she asked.

He raised his head. Iosua wasn't a tactician, so his answer probably didn't count. But she wanted his opinion anyway.

"It would take work," he said. "But they don't seem to have the crews to handle all the vessels they've stolen."

Her smile was back. "We have surprise on our side," she said.

"Surprise isn't everything, Captain," Vinters said.

"No, it's not," Cohn said, "but it's a hell of a good beginning."

She glanced at the now-empty part of the Scrapheap. It looked like a gigantic hole had been blown in the middle of perfectly aligned ships, which, in effect was exactly what had happened.

No more explosions were happening inside. Everything seemed calm and untouched, like nothing had gone wrong.

"Contact Captain Jicha for me, will you?" she asked Vinters. "Tell him he can start examining those Ready Vessels."

"Don't you want him to confer with the rest of the ships?" Vinters asked.

"No," Cohn said. "He can do his research, and we'll do ours."

She needed to know everything she could about this Lost Souls, about the people who were stealing from her, and how she could make certain no one ever did it again.

It would take a bit of time to do the research, but time was on her side. Time would make the thieves complacent.

And time would only add to the surprise.

LOST SOULS
NOW

39

We exit foldspace only a few hours later. The vibrations we felt going in were huge compared to the ones we felt as we left. If Diaz hadn't told me we were exiting foldspace, I would never have sensed the transition.

Lost Souls glows ahead of us, an arc of multicolored lights and arching decks. I hadn't realized just how lovely the design is. I always believed that since we cobbled our space station together, it would look cobbled together, but it doesn't.

It looks like it has been there forever, a beacon of all that is light and good and hopeful.

I let out a breath. I really hadn't expected to be so happy to return to Lost Souls. I almost would have said that I'm happy to be home, but I know myself: I'm happier on a ship, diving, than I am on any base, even one I've built from scratch.

I'm standing near the captain's chair on the *Veilig*, but I didn't pilot the ship out of foldspace. Diaz did. She's sitting on that chair now, looking pale and tired and more than a little frightened.

"Are we...?" Denby asks the question, and we all know what he means. We're at Lost Souls. It looks vaguely unfamiliar to me, but that could be because I've been gone for months.

I have no idea if it looks unfamiliar to him or to any of the others.

Although his question suggests that he's worried we've arrived years ahead of when we left.

"We're okay." Diaz breathes the words. "Only a few hours have passed."

Sometimes the ship's computers show that we've moved forward properly when we haven't. Or rather, computers have shown that others moved forward properly when they had actually lost dozens if not hundreds of years—or in the case of the *Ivoire*, thousands.

So, I have to assume that because Diaz said we're on time, we really are. That means she's somehow communicated with Lost Souls.

I glance at the screen before her, the one she's been using as navigation. Sure enough, she has received a number of automated messages from them, all of them timestamped.

I let out a breath I hadn't even realized I'd been holding.

We made it back alive, undamaged, and without anyone behind us. Now, we have to go through all the data we brought with us, and make some decisions.

We know some version of the Fleet still exists—that holy grail for Yash and Coop. We know that we irritated that version of the Fleet when we were in the Boneyard.

We don't know if the Fleet arrived because we were trying to dive the starfield-barrier or if it took that long for them to arrive because they were so very far away.

I wish I had been able to talk to them. I wish we'd been able to find out more.

Because I have no idea what kind of danger we're in here. We left so fast that I don't know if we left something behind, something that makes us easy to trace.

But that's a problem for the future, a problem that it looks like we'll have time to prepare for.

Sometimes the universe grants small miracles, even before we realize we need those miracles.

I reach around Diaz, and activate the comm on the captain's chair. I'm pinging Ilona Blake, and it takes only a moment for her to respond.

"The *Sove* just arrived," she says, taking one more worry away from me. "What the hell did you get yourself into?"

Diaz looks up at me, annoyed. Fleet members—former Fleet members—still hate the informality and the forgetfulness that comes from the lack of a strong command structure.

"We don't know yet," I say. "But we brought a lot of information back with us, and we have something that both Coop and Yash will want to see."

"I'll let them know," Ilona says. "We'll all have a debrief in a few hours."

A debrief? With everyone? Then Coop and Yash have returned. I let out a small breath, feeling some relief I hadn't expected.

"A few hours," Ilona says, "should give you time to go through all of the arrival procedures."

Which means she wants us to go through decontamination. I would protest, but I'm the one who set up the procedures, back in the day.

"All right," I say. "I can't wait to see you all."

And, oddly, I can't wait. I have missed them. But it's more than that. We've learned a lot on this trip. Unexpected things. We've learned about the warships and some of the capabilities of that Boneyard. And we've caught a glimpse of what could only be the Fleet.

Our futures are about to change, in ways I can't yet predict.

I put a hand on Diaz's shoulder. She starts. I almost pull away, but I don't. I squeeze her shoulder first, the closest I come to hugging anyone.

"You did great," I say. "Thank you."

She smiles tiredly at me. Then I let her go and turn so that my entire team can see me.

"Thank you, everyone," I say. "You were all amazing."

They look at me in surprise. I usually don't praise my team, especially when we haven't finished a mission.

"We're not going back, are we?" Tamaz asks. He sounds disappointed.

"I don't know what we're going to do," I say.

I want to continue diving that Boneyard or, more accurately, I want to investigate those warships.

But I don't plan to tell the team that. Not yet. I don't want to get their hopes up.

"We have a lot of things to research before we return," I say, and then shake my head ever so slightly. Well, that was a slip of the tongue.

"So we are going back." Mikk gives me a small grin.

"If we do the proper research," Orlando says to him, speaking around me as if I'm not even there, "then maybe by the time we're done, the Fleet or whatever the hell that was will be gone."

"Or maybe Coop knows how to work the Boneyard," Nyssa says.

"Not likely," Denby says. "We had no idea it was there."

I raise a hand. We're not going to get anywhere discussing this right now. There are too many variables, too many unknowns.

"We're going to Lost Souls," I say. "You all take a much-deserved rest. I'll debrief everyone."

"And then we dive into the research," Mikk says. He sounds eager. In fact, they all look eager.

I guess they didn't like the way we left that Boneyard any more than I do.

"And then we dive into the research," I say, agreeing with him.

With luck, that research will tell us what to do next.

With luck, we'll be back at the Boneyard, ready to defend ourselves, as we figure out how to manage that treasure trove.

With luck, we'll never see those ships that found us again—unless we seek them out.

Which I have a sneaking suspicion that we will.

Or some grouping of us will.

But that's in the future.

Right now, we need to dock at Lost Souls, debrief everyone, rest, and work. I'm ready for that.

It feels like the proper next step.

It feels like we're moving forward. And that feeling is a bit addictive. No wonder the Fleet has dedicated its entire culture to moving forward.

There's so much opportunity ahead of us.

And I know we'll figure out a way to make it work.

Here's a preview of the next book in the Diving Series.

This book is tentatively titled *The Chase,* and some parts of this preview might be subject to change.

The book takes place immediately after *Searching for the Fleet.*

1

THE *BILATZAILEA* ARRIVED IN THE MIDDLE OF A BATTLE.

Captain Kim Nyguta stood on the *BilatZailea*'s bridge, hands clasped behind her back. The moment the ship arrived, it received all of the telemetry from the battle, so she spread it across the five holoscreens before her.

Someone had breached Base 20 on Nindowne. Immediately, the Armada Jefatura dispatched a flotilla, but the Jefatura had to have known or suspected something major, something they weren't telling the captains, because that flotilla included the *BilatZailea* and a sister ship, the *EhizTari*. Both were foldspace tracking vessels.

The *EhizTari's* presence annoyed Nyguta. All the Armada needed in a battle like this one was a single foldspace tracking vessel. Whoever had issued this order had never worked with a foldspace tracking vessel.

Either that, or this battle was more significant than she thought.

It didn't seem that way when she arrived. The battle was already underway, and it was complicated. Much of it occurred in the space around Nindowne, and seemed to be directed at a single skip.

Skips weren't major threats, especially when faced with Dignity Vessels and Security Class Vessels. An orbiter, properly equipped, could take out a skip—unless the skip was something special.

She studied the skip from the moment she arrived. The skip wasn't much to look at. Boxy, with runners along its side, and shuttered portals.

It was well-piloted, but if it was like other skips of its kind, it had no real weaponry and inadequate defenses.

She couldn't really believe that a skip like that was any kind of threat. She'd seen skips like it before—the Armada had repurposed several—and none of them held more than thirty people. Even that was uncomfortable.

She hadn't checked the telemetry, but if she had to guess, the skip probably held ten to twenty at most.

Her team was monitoring the skip, as she had instructed them when the *BilatZailea* came out of foldspace. She had made the short trip using the *anacapa* drive, because she needed to arrive quickly—and there was no quickly from where the *BilatZailea* had been deployed.

She also hadn't wanted the *BilatZailea* to be seen by the enemy. At that point, she had had no idea that an entire flotilla had been called to take on a single, small ship. She had thought she would be handling cleanup, chasing dozens of ships into foldspace.

She hadn't wanted the enemy to know that a foldspace tracking vessel was anywhere nearby. The *EhizTari* hadn't been as cautious, which irritated her further. It hovered around the edges of the battle, looking conspicuous—or maybe she just thought the damn thing was conspicuous.

Which furthered her annoyance at being partnered with another ship on a mission that made partnering difficult—especially since she had never partnered with this vehicle. She didn't even know who the captain of the *EhizTari* was.

She tried not to let her annoyance at the *EhizTari* show. She wanted her team to focus on the task at hand, even if the task seemed surprisingly small.

Her bridge team was one of the best she'd ever worked with. They were behind her, their workstations staggering upwards and curved around her, almost as if she stood in the center of an amphitheater. Screens decorated the walls—screens she normally called useless, because the *BilatZailea* spent most of its time in foldspace, which didn't have relevant views.

Although, she had to admit, she'd been using the screens off and on all day, from the moment she'd arrived. She wanted to see this possible Fleet vessel whose crew had somehow invaded Base 20, and was now under attack from almost all of the Armada vessels in the sector.

The backs of her knees pushed up against the stupidly designed captain's chair. The *BilatZailea* had been designed as a Fleet foldspace search vehicle a long time ago, and modified to become an Armada foldspace tracking vehicle. The engineers had left the stupid captain's chair, with the idea that Nyguta might have to spend days in it while she was working.

Instead, she spent days bumping up against it because she preferred to stand when she was on the bridge.

She watched the fighters stream after the skip. It had left Nindowne's orbit just as she arrived, skating past all the space junk the Armada left in place around the planet, so that ships thought twice before even trying to enter orbit.

The skip was moving at a faster clip than she had expected. Instead of heading away from the flotilla, the skip had headed toward it, confusing the fighters at first.

Then they rallied, and swarmed around it, firing, the shots somehow going wide or missing it entirely. The shots didn't seem to bank off of it, though, so it didn't have unusually great shields.

Apparently, it just had an unusually great pilot.

That skip had to be heading somewhere. She scanned the ships nearby, and saw one she didn't recognized. It had a label in Old Fleet Standard. *Shadow.*

That made her skin crawl. She had no idea how an old Fleet ship got in the middle of a flotilla.

Then the skip vanished.

She leaned forward and had her screens refresh the action before her, but even as she did so, she saw—out of the corner of her eye—that some of her team members were doing the same thing.

"Did it just disappear?" she asked, worrying that it had gone into foldspace without opening a foldspace window. No ship that she had ever seen had done that before. Would that make the skip harder to track? Was that why the Jefatura had wanted both the *BilatZailea* and the *EhizTari*? Because the skip had new technology?

Then, before her crew said anything, she looked for the *Shadow*. Instead of a ship called *Shadow,* she saw what had been a Fleet Dignity Vessel, repurposed into an Armada vessel.

She cursed.

"The damn skip was ghosted," she said. Not just the skip, but that other ship as well. The *Shadow*.

"Yes," said Mikai Rockowitz, her second-in-command. He wasn't so much answering her as providing quiet confirmation.

He was a balding, wizened man who never wanted his own command. He reluctantly became her second, only after she begged repeatedly, mostly because he knew as much (or maybe more) about foldspace tracking than she did.

"It is far from the fighters," he said, as he sent her coordinates for the skip.

She didn't need them. She had already spotted the real skip, trundling forward at a much slower speed than its ghost.

She had been right, though: the pilot of the skip was unusually gifted.

Ghosting was difficult. The pilot, while under attack, created a false image of the ship, and that image had to hold up while the attackers went after it. Usually most ghosts vanished the moment laser weapons fire hit. This ghost ship had survived hundreds of shots, and confused two dozen fighters, which were seeing it up close.

And, on top of it, the pilot had ghosted a destination. That took incredible know-how and the ability to work on the fly.

In spite of herself, she was impressed.

But the pilot tipped his hand. His skip wasn't heading toward a base somewhere. The skip was heading toward another ship.

There was no way that ship would be near the flotilla. The ship had to be waiting somewhere protected.

If she were hiding a large ship—probably a Dignity Vessel named *Shadow*—she would place it near a moon. Not near Nindowne, though. And there was only one planet with a moon nearby.

She looked there, and saw the destination ship.

It was an ancient Dignity Vessel ship, but it wasn't called *Shadow*.

It was called the *Ivoire*.

She let out a breath.

The actual skip had sped up. It appeared to be vibrating—either from the speed or maybe some damage sustained earlier. If she had to guess, she would assume that the skip was about to break up.

It might not even make the *Ivoire*, given how ragged the skip looked.

The fighters realized their error and corrected, and, she noticed on the screens before her, a few ships had finally managed to follow the correct skip.

The fighters fired on it as they closed in. They shot at it, but either the shots went wild or something was protecting it.

The skip propelled itself toward the *Ivoire*, and for a moment, she thought it was going to ram the side. And then she realized what was going to happen.

"Prepare to launch into foldspace," she said to her team.

"Yes, Captain," said Rockowitz. He was probably already prepared, given his tone of voice. She hadn't given that order as much for him as she had for the rest of the team.

Something was niggling at her. Maybe the presence of the *EhizTari* had nothing to do with incompetence. Maybe the presence of the *EhizTari* showed that the Jefatura thought that Base 20 had been breached by Fleet personnel.

All that the Armada had known when Nyguta had received her orders was that the personnel who had entered Base 20 had used Fleet equipment. Those people had some ancient Fleet identification devices.

From there, the Armada had assumed—maybe hoped—that the invaders were actual members of the Fleet.

Nyguta felt a shiver of excitement. For millennia, the Armada had hoped to find the Fleet again, to extract a revenge long in the making.

She wanted that as much as anyone else, but she couldn't let it color her thinking. Not now.

Right now, her best course of action was to ignore the *EhizTari* and do the work as if the *BilatZailea* were the only foldspace tracking vessel in the vicinity.

Besides, the captain of the *EhizTari* hadn't responded to hails, which wasn't that uncommon in this kind of situation. Unnecessary communication was discouraged and, at the moment, neither vessel knew if they were even needed.

Now she knew: she would be tracking an ancient Fleet-built Dignity Vessel which, more likely than not, had a powerful *anacapa* drive.

The *BilatZailea*'s *anacapa* drive was powerful as well, and in prime condition. The *BilatZailea* might have a problem, though, if the *Ivoire*'s drive was as old as the ship herself. Because that drive could malfunction in ways no one completely understood.

Nyguta silently cursed under her breath. The Armada's Legion of Engineers still hadn't completely deciphered all of the secrets of the *anacapa* drive. The Fleet didn't know how the drive worked either—or at least, hadn't known it millennia ago, when they abandoned the Armada's founders.

The Fleet had stolen the *anacapa* drives thousands of years ago, and had been able to replicate them, but not reverse-engineer the technology itself.

The Armada had made reverse engineering the *anacapa* technology a major part of its raison d'être, but hadn't yet completely figured out how the tech worked.

If the *Ivoire*'s *anacapa* had brought them to this time period, and they were seeking a way home, then following the *Ivoire* into foldspace was doubly risky. Nyguta had tracked ships that had been displaced in time through foldspace, but that was tricky as well. The key was to find the ship while the crew was still alive, without trapping her crew in the process.

She'd managed, but it hadn't always been easy.

Tracking in real time was different. She wouldn't have a chance to think through the options.

The *Ivoire* fired on the smaller ships around it, and she watched that with trepidation as well. So many things could cause a launch into fold-space to go awry, and getting caught in weapons' fire was one of them, particularly if the *anacapa* drive was activated as a ship got hit.

She had to stay out of the line of fire, monitor the *Ivoire*, and follow it, should it jump. Ideally, the *BilatZailea* should enter foldspace at the exact same point as the *Ivoire* but she wasn't certain if she could do that.

"Contact the *Indarra* and *Hirugarren*," she said to DeMarcus Habibi. He was slender and soft-spoken, and had served on a dozen ships before joining hers nearly a decade before.

As a result, he knew someone on almost every ship, and could reach the right person to help her execute her commands quickly. He had served on the *Indarra*, which was a redesigned Dignity Vessel. He knew the captain of the *Hirugarren*, which had started its existence as a Ready Vessel.

They had long since been co-opted by the Armada and had more than enough firepower to defend the *BilatZailea*, so Nyguta could con-centrate on the foldspace tracking.

Habibi looked up at her, his brown eyes sharp. He probably knew what she was going to say, but he let her say it anyway.

"They'll need to flank us as we approach the *Ivoire's* position," she said. "We want to enter foldspace as close to that spot as possible."

"And the *EhizTari?*" Habibi asked.

"We'll let them handle their own journey." She wasn't going to worry about any of the Armada ships. She was going to concentrate on her own.

Her team was tracking telemetry and coordinates and *anacapa* energy. They would know the instant that the *Ivoire* started its transition into foldspace.

In the meantime, she would watch what was happening to the *Ivoire*.

A cargo bay door opened on the side of the *Ivoire*. If Nyguta were in charge of attacking this unknown enemy, she would attack them right now. They had to drop shields to get that skip inside.

The fighters and the other ships had to know that. She expected to see more laser fire, but she didn't.

Partly because the skip came in fast and hot, hot enough that unless the *Ivoire* had some kind of plan in place, the skip would ram through interior walls. The cargo bay door slammed shut just as fast, and something winked around the *Ivoire*—most likely the reinstatement of the shield.

"Now," she said to her crew.

The *BilatZailea* sped forward, heading toward the *Ivoire*'s position. The *Indarra* and *Hirugarren* flanked her, just as requested.

A foldspace window opened to the *Ivoire*'s side, and the *Ivoire* launched itself through.

Then the *EhizTari* zoomed past the *BilatZailea*.

Nyguta muttered, "Idiots," and hoped none of her crew had heard.

Although they probably would agree. The *EhizTari* was trying to enter the same foldspace launch window as the *Ivoire*, a truly dangerous and mostly reckless move.

But the launch window closed, and the *EhizTari* overshot the coordinates. It turned around, creating its own foldspace opening at the exact same moment.

Rockowitz cursed. Habibi said, "We really should warn them—" But stopped himself as the *EhizTari* disappeared into their own foldspace launch window.

"Maybe it'll work," Nyguta said, as much to herself as to her crew.

She couldn't think about the *EhizTari* right now, though. She had to focus on her own mission.

"All right," she said to her team. "The *Ivoire* has gone into foldspace. We have the exact coordinates, right?"

The person responsible for combining everyone's information into one set of coordinates was Jaci Intxausti. She tucked her long silver-and-black hair behind her ears, and frowned.

That frown caught Nyguta. Intxausti usually didn't make faces before answering questions. Perhaps the information contradicted itself. That happened at times, and while Nyguta could program for it, she preferred not to. It was better to use a human eye on it, because the machines were more likely to either use an average or some other formula to choose the most likely set of coordinates.

Relying on the tech for decision-making was what made other foldspace tracking vessels less accurate than the *BilatZailea* was. When Nyguta got conflicting information, she threw it all out and started again.

"Jaci?" Nyguta said, wondering if she had to repeat the question.

"I have the coordinates," Intxausti said. "I was checking to see if there was any unusual *anacapa* energy since that ship we're chasing was reported lost five thousand years ago."

So her team had researched the name. Without a request from her. Which was why this team was the best she'd ever worked with.

The *Ivoire* had been lost in time, probably through foldspace. That made it both less interesting (she had been hoping to find the Fleet) and more interesting.

"Maybe," said Tiberius Kibbuku, one of the researchers. He rarely spoke up, so a "maybe" from him was as powerful as half the sentences the rest of her team spoke. "Maybe it had been lost."

Nyguta was about to follow up, but Intxausti spoke first.

"Less of a maybe than you'd think," Intxausti said. "I investigated the moment I saw the identification. I used several Fleet databases from several time periods. The ship matches every descriptive point, including the name."

Kibbuku looked like he wanted to argue, but Nyguta didn't have time for that. She held up a hand, silencing him and directed her question at Intxausti.

"Problems, then?" Nyguta asked.

"Not that I can tell," Intxausti said, "but I don't have time to do a thorough examination. If the ship is here, it got lost in foldspace like everyone thought."

"Maybe," Kibbuku said again, a bit more forcefully this time.

Nyguta didn't look at him. She wanted to hear Intxausti out.

"And," Intxausti said, "if it did, that means there could be something wrong with the *anacapa.*"

She put a slight emphasis on the word "could," which led to Nyguta's question.

"But you don't think so," Nyguta said.

"I wouldn't be going in and out of foldspace if I knew I had a malfunctioning *anacapa* drive, would you?" Intxausti asked.

"That's not definitive," Kibbuku said, and he was right. Intxausti's point was speculative, but the speculation was a good one.

If this was the *Ivoire* and if it was piloted by the same crew that had gotten lost in foldspace, then they wouldn't venture in and out of foldspace easily, even if they were being followed.

But that was a lot of "ifs." For all Nyguta knew, for all her team knew, the *Ivoire* had been abandoned and then stolen by yet another group.

Although that didn't really explain the Fleet signatures that the Jefatura had picked up in the alarms around Base 20.

Figuring out what the *Ivoire* was mattered less than their mission. Which the *EhizTari* was already fulfilling.

"Are you worried about following the *Ivoire* into foldspace?" Nyguta asked.

"I certainly wouldn't have tried to use their foldspace window," Intxausti said, the judgmental tone in her voice matching the one in Nyguta's head. Even though she hadn't known as much about the *Ivoire* when the *EhizTari* tried to launch itself through that window, she still thought it foolhardy.

"Neither would I," Nyguta said. "But are you worried about tracking them?"

Intxausti looked at Kibbuku, not Nyguta, which surprised her. The look was one of consultation, not disagreement.

"There's a lot we don't know," Kibbuku said.

It seemed like he was saying the obvious, but he wasn't that kind of man. Instead, he wanted everyone to make the same logical leaps he did. And sometimes Nyguta wasn't up for it.

"About the *Ivoire?*" she asked.

"About foldspace, *anacapa* drives, and tracking," he said. "If they're malfunctioning, and we get too close, are we in danger?"

He shrugged, not willing to add the last sentence. The one that included *we don't know.*

They didn't know, and they didn't have the luxury to figure it out.

"Well," Nyguta said, "if they are creating something dangerous through their foldspace window, we might not be able to track them at all. Have you thought of that?"

Her question was a bit aggressive. His eyes met hers. She usually didn't talk to her team that way.

"I think we've waited long enough for our own safety's sake," she said. "Take us to the coordinates, Jaci, and open a foldspace window."

Intxausti didn't respond verbally. Instead, she executed the command.

The *BilatZailea* reached those coordinates in less than a minute, and as it did, a foldspace window opened. Nyguta braced herself, something she normally didn't do when she went into foldspace.

The *BilatZailea* entered the window, vibrating slightly as it did so. Nyguta let out a small sigh. The vibration was normal. The Armada's engineers had managed to tone down the entry—which used to be a lot bumpier and sometimes violent—but still hadn't been able to get rid of the vibration.

No one knew what it was about foldspace that differed from regular space or why entry into (and out of) foldspace caused something akin to turbulence. Nyguta paid attention to the changes, thinking they might have an impact on foldspace tracking, but so far, nothing had made much of a difference.

Something, though, had led her to believe that entering foldspace this time would be more difficult. Maybe the discussion with Intxausti. Maybe a sense.

Everything had been odd on this trip.

She didn't think foldspace would be any different.

2

NYGUTA SHUT OFF THE WALL SCREENS. Seeing the exterior of the *BilatZailea* in real time made no difference now. She had left the battle behind her, and she couldn't see the *EhizTari* at all. Nor could she see the *Ivoire*.

Which was not unusual.

Foldspace tracking wasn't about actually following a vessel through foldspace. She had never done that, except during training. And that had been difficult in a variety of unexpected ways.

She actually preferred to track a vessel through foldspace using instrumentation, *anacapa* energy readings, and good old common sense.

"Clear the signature of the *EhizTari*," she said to her team.

She didn't want the mistakes of the *EhizTari* to contaminate her search and, as far as she was concerned, the *EhizTari* had made mistakes from the moment she tried to enter foldspace with the *Ivoire*.

Nyguta had no idea who was captaining the *EhizTari* at the moment—it had been stationed on Base 21, and had taken a foldspace journey just to get to Base 20. Given the way the *EhizTari* had behaved, Nyguta didn't want to know.

She just hoped that whoever commanded the vessel would get their team through this mess unscathed.

No one on Nyguta's team responded verbally to her order, but, on her holoscreens, she noted that the *EhizTari's* energy signature vanished. Good.

Now it was time for her entire team to get to work.

Her team knew their jobs. They had tracked through foldspace fifty times before, at minimum, although never so soon after a ship had entered.

Nor had they always had the exact coordinates where the ship had gone into foldspace. She had some advantages here, although she wasn't sure how she was going to use them—*if* she was going to use them.

Her job was threefold: she needed to monitor what her team was doing; she needed to track the *Ivoire* on her own, as she had done from the beginning of her career; and she needed to keep an eye on the goal which, in this case, was finding and possibly subduing the *Ivoire*.

She wasn't going to worry about subduing the *Ivoire* yet. The moment she saw the *Ivoire* again, she would send its coordinates back to the Jefatura, and they would send a ship to that point. Or several ships, depending on how intransigent the *Ivoire* was.

Some ships (especially older ones) needed a bit of time to recover from a foldspace journey, and she wasn't sure if the *Ivoire* was one of those.

This was where she felt the lack of prep time. Usually she had hours, sometimes days, to prepare for a foldspace tracking job. And she had never tracked a ship that didn't belong to the Armada. With Armada ships, she had their histories, their quirks, and usually, she had a theory about why they had disappeared in foldspace.

The *Ivoire* hadn't disappeared. It had fled. And it was, in theory, an ancient Fleet ship that had ended up in the wrong time period. Or it had been the subject of a mutiny and vanished from the Fleet's records. Or the ship she saw wasn't even the *Ivoire* that she thought it was, but another old Dignity Vessel with the same name.

She knew next to nothing about the makeup of that model of Dignity Vessel. She didn't even know what its defensive (and offensive) capabilities were.

"Tiberius," she said to Kibbuku. "Put a team on *Ivoire* research. We need to know as much about this ship as we can. Duplicate Intxausti's work. Make sure you can confirm the identity of this ship."

"Already on it," Kibbuku said, in that dry flat way of his. Of course, he had already double-checked Intxausti's work. He double-checked everyone's work when it had an impact on his own.

"I want to know ship specs, if you can find them," Nyguta said. "Otherwise, I want the specs for that Dignity Vessel model. I also want to know if there was a mention of the *Ivoire* after its purported disappearance in any of the Fleet records we've confiscated. Any *Ivoire* sightings, any clue how it got here."

"So far nothing," Kibbuku said, in a way that let her know he was slightly offended she had even given that instruction. He was ahead of her on research. He always was. "I also have three different programs running to check the Scrapheaps we've encountered for any record of the *Ivoire*."

That was a case in point: He thought of a detail she hadn't. If the *Ivoire* had been stored in one of the Scrapheaps and then recovered, that information wouldn't be in standard Fleet record-keeping. It would be a part of the Scrapheap itself.

If the *Ivoire* had been stored in a Scrapheap, then she would know when and where it was recovered, and maybe even who commanded it now.

"Good, thank you," she said.

That took care of the *Ivoire*, at least for the moment. She would have a plan to deal with the *Ivoire* once she found it.

Right now, though, she had to find it.

By isolating the *Ivoire's* energy signature as well as the subtle variations in its *anacapa* drive's energy, she was able to find the path the *Ivoire* left.

She wasn't used to seeing a path that was so strong and so clearly marked. For a few moments, she hesitated, worried that she was seeing some kind of planted trail.

But no ship of the Fleet knew how to track in foldspace—at least, the Fleet hadn't known that centuries ago. Nothing in the Fleet's research files over the millennia led her to believe that the Fleet would develop tracking technology.

Sure, the Fleet had once had foldspace search vessels. The *BilatZailea* had been modified from one. But the Fleet's foldspace search methods were complicated and ineffective.

The Fleet was wasteful. It left ships all over the sectors it passed through. It would abandon its people in foldspace rather than search for them to the bitter end. It would leave entire communities behind at its sector bases, while leaving them little to survive and thrive on.

The Armada wasn't governed by a group of military leaders eager to get to the next sector. The Armada had been built by engineers. Finding and correcting errors was in the Armada's blood. And, in the beginning of their existence, they didn't have enough personnel to lose.

So anytime someone got trapped or injured or lost, the Armada searched for that person. Searched until the person was rescued or the body was recovered.

In its entire existence, the Armada had never abandoned anyone. The Armada rescued or recovered its people, and it recorded its history. It valued detail, because it was built by engineers, and it valued those who worked for it.

It also valued time. Searching, using the old Fleet method, was wasteful in time and personnel. Which was why the Legion of Engineers had learned how to track in foldspace. That way, ships didn't lose entire years searching for someone.

Instead, they tracked the lost ship. What got in the way of finding it wasn't the methodology. It was the time slips that happened with a malfunctioning *anacapa* drive.

Replicating those had once been almost impossible. But the Armada had found a way around that as well. It hadn't been able to take its people back along the same track as the injured ship, but it was able to answer questions about what became of that ship and its crew.

At some point, the Armada would learn how to handle the time slips. Only then would it feel like it had completely conquered foldspace.

Nyguta forced herself to concentrate on the *Ivoire*'s path. The *Ivoire* wasn't traveling the way she had expected it to.

There was a logic to foldspace, one that took a lot of study to understand. Her entire team understood it though.

If she had been required to predict where the *Ivoire* would travel, she would have predicted that it would have gone forward from Base 20, past Base 21 and into the areas beyond.

But, it looked like, the *Ivoire* was going backwards, toward Base 15 or maybe even farther back—in distance, anyway.

She had no idea what was back there. She hadn't traveled that far backwards, not even through foldspace.

Most of her trips had been sideways, making rescues that had gone awry, working within the sectors where the Armada currently existed, not the ones where it had existed before.

And there was something about Base 11 or maybe Base 12 that niggled her memory.

"Anastasia," she said to another of her researchers. Anastasia Telli was even quieter than Kibbuku, but she worked faster than any other researcher that Nyguta had.

"Captain." Telli lifted her head. Her slender face was pale and she had deep shadows under her eyes. She hadn't been sleeping again, but that usually wasn't a medical problem with her. It was often a research problem. She would find something she was interested in, and forget to sleep.

Nyguta set aside that thread of worry she always felt when she saw Telli look so pale and tired.

"Do you recall something odd about the bases around 11 or 12?"

Telli nodded and suddenly seemed animated. Information excited her. Imparting information excited her more.

"Yes, sir, I do recall," she said. "We didn't use the sector bases that the Fleet left behind for Base 12 and Base 13."

That was it. Those sector bases were among the few that the Armada hadn't coopted for their own.

"Do you recall why not?" Nyguta moved her holoscreens slightly, so she could observe Telli and keep an eye on the information that flowed across the screens.

"Yes, sir," Telli said. "One base, Base 12, was in hostile territory. We lost fighters in some kind of war, and the Jefatura decided that it wasn't worth our while to try to capture the sector base. It took us too deep into that hostile region."

Nyguta felt a tingle of nerves. She didn't like how this was going. And she hoped she was wrong.

"And Base 13?" she asked.

"The sector base we would have coopted was destroyed long before we ever got near it. Destroyed so thoroughly that there was no point in even trying to salvage it." Telli gave her an uncomfortable smile. "There are a few other bases we didn't use, but they're even farther back. I'd have to research which ones exactly. Base 7, maybe?"

"No need to research that at the moment," Nyguta said. "Thank you."

Her stomach had tightened. Whoever piloted that skip had been brilliant. The skip had arrived at the *Ivoire*, and the launch into foldspace had been nearly perfect. The journey seemed to be pretty consistent as well.

But not in the direction she expected. Backwards. Toward those older bases.

She hoped she had given Telli the correct instruction. She hoped the *Ivoire* wasn't going back as far as Base 7 or Base 6.

She had made long foldspace journeys before, but she had always prepared for them. And she had never taken the *BilatZailea* or this crew on a journey that long.

If it looked like the journey was going to be long, she was going to have to pursue the *Ivoire* in parts, which the Jefatura wouldn't like. But she wasn't going to risk her crew on a long foldspace journey that was unplanned.

She hoped that the *EhizTari* wouldn't do that either.

But she had a feeling that the *Ivoire* wasn't going all the way back to Bases 6 or 7. Most well-captained ships didn't make long journeys just to escape a bad situation.

Most well-captained ships fled to their own base.

And then she felt that tingle of nerves again. If the base was in territory the Fleet had traveled through millennia ago, and that the Armada had already passed beyond as well, then she wasn't chasing someone from the Fleet. She was chasing someone who was using a Fleet vessel.

Mixed with her nerves came a thread of disappointment. She wanted to be the captain to discover the Fleet.

But the direction the *Ivoire* was taking through foldspace led her to believe that she wasn't going after a Fleet vessel.

Unless whoever captained the *Ivoire* was a brilliant tactician, something she couldn't rule out. Not after what she had seen in that firefight.

The words "hostile territory" kept resounding in her brain.

If she were captaining a lone Dignity Vessel against ships with twice the firepower hers had, more ships than she could ever hope to fight, all she could do was outrun them.

But if she worried about being tracked—and why would a Fleet ship worry about being tracked? She set that question aside for a moment and tried again. If she were worried about being tracked, she would lead the ships that followed her into a trap of some kind.

Or maybe that hostile region was home.

It didn't matter either way. She had to be prepared.

She turned to her team.

"The moment we come out of foldspace, we have to have shields up and weapons at the ready," she said.

"You think a single ship will turn around and attack us?" Rockowitz sounded skeptical.

"I have no idea. But the *Ivoire* knew it was outgunned. It might have assumed ships were going to follow it through foldspace, like the *EhizTari* had. So the *Ivoire* might have gone somewhere it could defend."

Santiago Pereira shifted slightly, something he did when he wanted to speak, but didn't know if he should. He was thinner than most of her team, and shorter as well. But she relied on him, particularly for tactical information.

"Standard practice for the Fleet is—was—to launch into foldspace, and then return hours later, after the fighters cleared out," he said.

She had already thought of that. She wasn't going to argue with him over the words "standard practice." He had already covered the fact that they knew little about the current Fleet with the word "was."

"I wouldn't do that in this instance," she said. "Because of the base and the quick arrival of the other ships."

He nodded. "We can't entirely rule it out," he said. "But I might enact a feint."

"A feint as in go elsewhere, and then return," she said.

He nodded again.

"That presupposes they know we can track them through foldspace," she said.

The Fleet knew nothing about the Armada, but other cultures did. Which lead her to believe that the Jefatura was wrong about this. The *Ivoire* might once have been a Fleet vessel, but she doubted it was any longer.

"Even if I knew that my pursuers could track me through foldspace," Pereira said, "I wouldn't do anything elaborate. I would take those pursuers as far from my home base as possible, and then I would cross a bit of regular space, and open a new foldspace window, and head home."

"And hope you weren't tracked again?" Intxausti asked.

"Yes," Pereira said.

Nyguta thought about that for a moment. "I would do something similar," she said. "If nothing else, it would buy time. Whoever tracked the ship through foldspace would be looking for a base or other ships or something first, before trying to figure out what happened in regular space."

She let out a breath. She had to be prepared for anything. If the *Ivoire* was heading back to its home base, it would attack anything that came through foldspace. If the *Ivoire* wasn't heading back to its own base, then it would travel through regular space to get to either another launch point or a good attack position.

She wished she could contact the *EhizTari* now. They should have coordinated after all. But the *EhizTari's* enthusiasm and, perhaps, its captain's desire to impress the Jefatura, made that impossible.

The Jefatura would note where the two tracking vessels emerged from foldspace. Both had automated systems that contacted the Armada the moment the ships arrived in a real space location. The messages would be sent across real space, and through a foldspace system, using the communications *anacapa*.

The Armada would figure out, just like she did, that the *Ivoire* had gone backwards, not toward some other base.

"Changes ahead," Rockowitz said.

That was internal code for the fact that the energy pattern they were following was growing, the way that it should just before a ship used its *anacapa* to leave foldspace.

"All right," Nyguta said. "Shields, weapons. Battlestations."

She almost never got to say that. It made her nervous. But she was ready—and she hoped she was up to the task.

3

THE *IVOIRE'S* FOLDSPACE TRAIL ENDED ABRUPTLY, not far from the *BilatZailea's* position.

"This is it," Nyguta said, and braced herself again for the *BilatZailea* to exit foldspace.

Her crew was ready, and the ship was on alert. She had no idea what she would face.

As they vibrated their way out of foldspace, something caught her ear. Before she could ask, Rockowitz said, "We're getting a distress signal."

"Sent into foldspace?" Intxausti asked, echoing Nyguta's surprise. She'd had ships send messages through foldspace, but they usually weren't standard distress signals. They targeted the Armada, to keep anyone with foldspace capability away from their disabled ships.

"Yes," Rockowitz said.

Nyguta glanced at the telemetry in front of her. "The *Ivoire*," she said.

Had it been hit in that barrage of laser fire? She thought only the shields had been hit. Or maybe the skip had done some internal damage when it launched itself into the ship.

Why would the *Ivoire* come out of foldspace and ask for help? To bring in its own warships? Some kind of backup?

If so, she was ready.

The *BilatZailea* vibrated a moment longer, then emerged from fold-space right next to a gigantic starbase, long, tilted, damaged, and seemingly abandoned. If the *BilatZailea* had missed her entry coordinates by just a little, she would have ended up in the middle of that starbase.

Nyguta's heart was pounding. That captain of the *Ivoire* was as smart as she had assumed. That *Ivoire* captain had deliberately exited foldspace in this spot, knowing the starbase was here.

The starbase looked like it had been built by the Fleet, but she didn't have time to check it, because laser fire was streaking all around her. She used the sensors to see what was going on as the distress message continued blaring around her.

She shut off the message using one of her screens rather than ask someone else to do it. The bridge was suddenly blessedly silent. She moved her screens and brought up the wall screens—

Which showed the *EhizTari* in the middle of a ring of large ships of a type that Nyguta didn't recognize. The *EhizTari* was cratered on one side, and most of her lights were out. Her shields were down, and she was listing.

"Target those ships," Nyguta said to her crew, "and fire."

The laser canons fired almost before she completed the command, their pulses zooming toward the ships surrounding the *EhizTari*. Seven ships. Seven, all larger than the *EhizTari*, all of them armored and shielded.

The laser pulses dissipated along the edges of the larger ships' shields.

"These shields are odd," Pereira said. "They seem to rotate energy and power levels."

"In a predictable way," Rockowitz said.

"More than predictable," Nyguta said. "A known way."

She recognized one of the icons on her screens, although she had only seen that icon once before. The *BilatZailea's* computer recognized the pattern, recognized everything about those ships, and wanted to use a set program.

Normally, she would have investigated, but she didn't have time. She initiated the program, and immediately the pattern of laser fire from the *BilatZailea* changed.

"Hey!" Pereira said. "I just lost control of the weapons."

"I did that," Nyguta said. "It's all right. I've got this."

And she did. The laser pulses got through the shields on all seven ships, hitting their armored exterior. Each pulse seemed to punch through that exterior.

"Let me work with the program," Pereira said.

"Not yet," Nyguta said. "It seems to be working. I don't want to mess with it."

"I just want it to target propulsion," Pereira said. "That'll—"

But he didn't even have a chance to finish before the ship closest to the *BilatZailea* exploded. Then the next ship exploded, followed by another, lighting up the entire area.

The ships farthest from the *BilatZailea* spun, clearly about to leave the area. The fourth ship started to follow, but as it spun, a laser pulse caught its side, and the entire ship glowed for a moment before exploding.

The remaining three ships sped up, stuttered a bit, and then seemed to expand.

Nyguta recognized what was happening. Apparently those ships had a nanobit component, and those nanobits were unbonding. The ships were going to come apart.

And just as she had that thought, the ships *did* come apart, but not in a full explosion like the others. More like a slow-motion disassembly, as pieces fell off. The ships stopped moving.

Nyguta's breath caught. She knew what would happen next. She'd seen it before. The ships started coming apart and then the nanobits disassembled something crucial, and that something touched something else, and—

All three ships exploded.

Bits of ship shrapnel spun in all directions, some of it hitting the unprotected *EhizTari*, doing even more damage.

"Contact the *EhizTari*," Nyguta said. "We have to get them out of here. And figure out where here is."

"Already done," Telli said. "Here is something called the Enterran Empire, and that abandoned starbase was what the Fleet called Starbase Kappa."

"So this was where we would have had Base 12, if we decided to use the Fleet's sector base," Nyguta said. Right here, in hostile territory, just like her staff had mentioned.

Apparently the territory was still hostile.

"Base 11, actually," Telli said. "But yes, the Armada has history here."

"The Enterran Empire is a military culture," Intxausti said. "They don't accept defeat easily. They will be back."

None of them doubted that the ships had contacted colleagues before the explosions. How long it would take the messages to get through was anyone's guess. And once those messages arrived, there was no way to know how long it would take for more ships to arrive.

"Any sign of the *Ivoire*?" Nyguta asked.

"None," Rockowitz said. "I'm sure there's an energy signature—"

"But right now, there's too much going on for us to find it." Nyguta shook her head, trying to tamp down the admiration she felt for the *Ivoire's* captain.

She had figured the captain might attack. She had figured that the captain might enter a region and then leave it quickly. But she hadn't expected the captain to use ships from another culture as a diversion to prevent her—or the *EhizTari*—from following the *Ivoire* to its home base.

She would follow it, though. She would find that home base, and she would bring that captain of the *Ivoire*, the ship, and its crew back to the Armada.

But first, she had to deal with the *EhizTari*.

She had to get it out of here before the Enterran Empire ships returned.

Because she no longer had the element of surprise.

I value honest feedback, and would love to hear your opinion in a review, if you're so inclined, on your favorite book retailer's site.

Be the first to know!

Just sign up for the Kristine Kathryn Rusch newsletter, and keep up with the latest news, releases and so much more—even the occasional giveaway.

To sign up, go to kristinekathrynrusch.com.

But wait! There's more. Sign up for the WMG Publishing newsletter, too, and get the latest news and releases from all of the WMG authors and lines, including Kristine Grayson, Kris Nelscott, Dean Wesley Smith, *Pulphouse Fiction Magazine*, *Smith's Monthly*, and so much more.

Just go to wmgpublishing.com and click on Newsletter.

ABOUT THE AUTHOR

New York Times bestselling author Kristine Kathryn Rusch writes in almost every genre. Generally, she uses her real name (Rusch) for most of her writing. Under that name, she publishes bestselling science fiction and fantasy, award-winning mysteries, acclaimed mainstream fiction, controversial nonfiction, and the occasional romance. Her novels have made bestseller lists around the world and her short fiction has appeared in eighteen best of the year collections. She has won more than twenty-five awards for her fiction, including the Hugo, *Le Prix Imaginales*, the *Asimov's* Readers Choice award, and the *Ellery Queen Mystery Magazine* Readers Choice Award.

To keep up with everything she does, go to kriswrites.com and sign up for her newsletter. To track her many pen names and series, see their individual websites (krisnelscott.com, kristinegrayson.com, retrievalartist.com, divingintothewreck.com, fictionriver.com, pulphousemagazine.com).

The Diving Universe
(Reading Order)

CPSIA information can be obtained
at www.ICGtesting.com
Printed in the USA
LVHW030337080221
678681LV00001B/9

9 781561 463718